"It would be hard to imagine a more timely new book than *The Emblem*. With warmth and passion, Alisa Weis, transports readers to the early years of Roslyn, Washington, a coal mining town where tensions between white miners and Black laborers have reached a breaking point that alters the lives of many. Though the town quiets in following years, a spark is about to reach the powder keg when a young white woman falls in love with a Black man—decades before Loving vs Virginia and the widespread legalization of interracial marriage. As long as there are racial tensions in the world, this book is a must-read."

~DOUGLAS BOND, author of thirty books of
historical fiction and biography

"Alisa Weis has constructed a brilliantly written tale of the unfortunate division of classes by color in a small 1880s mining town, and the secrets they hold close. Never a writer to flinch from revealing the truth, Weis takes readers through the realities of hard labor in coal mines and the disputes between ownership and labor. But *The Emblem* knows about love too. Open to page one, and you'll be along to the finish."

~E. HANK BUCHMANN, author

"*The Emblem* is a powerful story, written with honesty, empathy, and pathos."

~D.L. FOWLER, author of *The Turn*

"Weis weaves in a delightfully accurate description of Roslyn (WA)—its peoples, homes, businesses, churches, and surroundings. Having lived in this area all my life, I found her descriptions of the area to be spot on! I found the many levels of her story compelling and believable and, in fact, impossible to put down until I'd read the last page."

~CHARLENE KAUZLARICH,
Northern Kittitas County Historical Society

"A delightful read full of nostalgic history from an area I personally love. Roslyn, Cle Elum, and the Cascade mountains are a perfect setting for the storyline Alisa crafts. She plunges us back in time to an area where relationships had more challenging class issues, race differences, and the obstacles to love were extremely pronounced. She artfully tells the depth of the characters' personal history and intrigue draws you in. Read and enjoy!"

~CHARITY RATTRAY, founder of United by Love

www.mrscharityrattray.com

"Weis has written an intriguing story that takes its inspiration from Roslyn's rich history."

~NICK HENDERSON, historian

former president of the Roslyn Historical Museum

The
Emblem

ALISA WEIS

INKBLOTS PRESS

ISBN: 978-1-945062-14-8

The Emblem is a work of fiction.
Names, characters, places, and incidents
either are the product of the author's
imagination or are used fictitiously.

Scripture from the New American Standard Bible
The spiritual "Deep River" is in the Public Domain

Cover Design by Nancy Archer
Photography by Nancy Archer
Interior Design by Elli Seifert

The Emblem is set in Electra LT Std

Electra was designed by William Addison Dwiggins
in 1935. It belongs to the modern family of type styles.
It is not based upon any traditional model, nor does it
attempt to revive or reconstruct any historic type.

First Edition
Printed in the U.S.A
Published by Inkblots Press, Olalla, WA

To my mom, KIM TRILLER.
Thank you for exemplifying strength and grace,
and for directing me to important history when I was young.

My respects to the ROSLYN BLACK PIONEERS,
with regards to THE CRAVEN FAMILY.

The Emblem

Chapter 1
MAY 1889

W HEN HE EMERGED from underground after hours of toil, David couldn't deny the protest of his back any longer. But two years over thirty, his body gave him pain that he didn't think he'd feel until he was an old man. He knew the men who worked below ground beside him felt the same. Very few tried to hide their cursing; others couldn't hide deep, throaty coughs that demanded the relief of the mountain air. He shook his head. David had long since realized that the opportunity to mine in the Pacific Northwest wasn't as promising as Mr. Simonson had said when they'd shaken hands months ago in Illinois.

He remembered listening along with hundreds of other colored men to the earnest labor recruiter. Mr. Simonson knew something of the grit and perseverance required of them—he was once a slave. David endured the rattling ride over the mountains in the cattle cars with other hopeful miners; it was their arrival in Montana that snuffed out his hopes. There he learned he wasn't a mere mining recruit—they intended to make him a strikebreaker. Pinkerton guards set foot in the cattle cars, and the laughter and the optimism shared by the men disappeared like a canary down the pit. And yet, what good was there in turning back to mediocre labor or sharecropping?

David winced at the memories of his reception to the region. The striking miners who chased their train to the outskirts of Roslyn, wielding their rifles even as the Pinkerton guards lent the colored men protection. Their first weeks spent in shanties instead of homes with running water or pot-bellied stoves. The day the strikers tied the mine superintendent to the train tracks and left him to die. The mercy of the brakeman attendant who untied the ropes at the last minute.

He blinked. The sun had long since slipped into its pocket in the evergreens, but there was nothing so void of light as the underground. He breathed the cool, cleansing mountain air again, and his thoughts turned to them: his beautiful Georgina, precious Liliana. He thought of the spark in the little girl's amber eyes whenever she said *Daddy* and wrapped her arms around his neck. He smiled, in spite of the ache that went deeper than anything he felt in his physical being. They weren't here yet, even though most of the other wives and children had touched Washington soil three months after their men. He'd been waiting for the reunion with his girls for so long that a pain welled in his throat when he thought of them. *After the snow is done falling and the warm weather returns,* Georgina had promised in her last letter. *We miss you and love you so much.*

David felt a large hand clasp the back of his shoulder. He braced himself, wondering why he'd stopped carrying a rifle before hearing a familiar voice.

"David Ward, my man. What do you say about heading over to Simonson's Club and ordering up a whiskey?"

He turned to see the form of a large man. Were it not for the low, brazen quality of his friend's voice, he wouldn't have recognized him at all. Gerald's work clothes were doused with a thick layer of dirt that several washes wouldn't render clean. Even his hat was dented, marred with dust. David imagined he looked the same. He tried to soften the aggression across his face, but his friend took a step back, seemingly realizing that he'd startled him. Gerald let out his breath.

"Let's go—the first drink's on me."

He smiled sadly and shook his head. "Not tonight." Sensing his friend's disappointment, he spoke again. "Maybe after tomorrow's shift . . . I want to finish a letter to my daughter, make sure it's sent out tomorrow. . . ."

Gerald nodded. "Tomorrow night, my friend. I'm holding you to it. You write that letter to your little girl. Lily, did you say her name was?"

David swallowed. "Liliana," he said, grateful that the darkening sky hid his eyes. He wiped his nose with the back of his sleeve. "But I call her Lily."

Gerald gave a nod to their right. "I was out walking behind the church the other day . . . couldn't believe some of the flowers out this early in the season. Lilies . . . thought about picking some for the kitchen, but I let them be. . . ."

David smiled. "See you tomorrow, Gerald." He set off in the dark toward home but changed courses as soon as he was out of sight. The ache rose again in his throat. He didn't take it as happenstance that Gerald had mentioned the unexpected lilies, and he meant to find them.

He turned on his headlamp as he reached the church meadow. He had forgotten the protest of his back. David scanned the still ground for the flower and found several of them near a fallen tree. He'd heard *lily* and expected to find them white and delicate, but they weren't. These flamed orange-red before him, beautiful in their boldness. He smiled in spite of himself and plucked a few. He'd press one into her letter, save the others for the next time he wrote her. And when he ran out of lilies, he'd draw the likeness of one. It would be something they shared until she next ran into his arms and gave him that white, gapped-tooth smile of hers.

He could almost hear her whisper *Daddy*, as he stood to his feet and righted the headlamp, heavy now above ground.

"It won't be long, Liliana," he said as he cupped the flowers, their slight presence a blooming promise in his hand.

Chapter 2

1932

C ALLIE SHOVED LOOSE strands of hair from her eyes as she watched a stock boy stencil a lily on the display window of the Company Store. The symbol belonged to Burke Enterprises, and all of Roslyn had come to know it well over the past eighteen months. Though she'd yet to meet the man, Edward Burke was rumored to be the cousin of Northern Pacific's president. He had license to run the interests of the Company Store while the mining company turned their attention to boosting coal sales during the downturn in the economy. She'd heard grumbling from some of the miners over this decision, as Burke wasn't a local and couldn't possibly relate with the workers. Even her father had grimaced about the notion that the Company Store wouldn't be run by a retired miner, but she was indifferent to its management. And if truth be told, she was keen to catch a glimpse of Burke, the elusive, yet reportedly dashing businessman, who'd recently built a second home this side of the mountains.

Lucy, who'd run before her to grab some sugar, burst back through the doors and reached for the back of Callie's elbow. "Come here," she said, hazel eyes alight with green. "There's something you need to see."

Callie let her friend escort her inside, hoping that Mr. Burke wasn't in front of the store counter, passing out apple cider to all the laborers. If she were to see him, she hoped it would be from afar so she could make her own assessment. But she soon saw Lucy hadn't brought her inside the Company Store for that purpose at all. Lucy stopped her directly in front of the bulletin board, where locals posted their skills in hopes of finding work or listed their wares, praying that someone would find need for something they could no longer afford.

Callie's eyes didn't register the obvious and Lucy waited for a young woman and her mother in matching navy coats to pass behind them into the store. She then pressed one painted-red nail to the board. She let Callie drink in the words on the paper:

Tutor wanted, Burke residence. Must have an easy rapport with school-aged children and have flexibility weekday afternoons. Please submit a letter of intent to the Company Store.

Her mind turning fast, Callie looked to Lucy. "How long has this been up?"

"It was just placed," Lucy said, her voice cresting. "The clerk at the counter told me the stock boy put it up before he got working on the window. It's only staying up for a day since Burke doesn't want too many inquiries. But, what do you think? Oh, who cares what you think! You must apply. You will apply, won't you?"

How little it took to awaken that tremor of excitement. Wings fluttered in her stomach, and she nodded. "Of course I'll apply. So will every other unmarried woman in this town, but it's nice to think that—"

Her words were interrupted by several off-duty miners making their way out the front doors, sturdy boots lending a possessive strike to the floorboards as they clutched the newest carbide lamp model.

Callie turned on her heel, thinking about the paperwork she needed to assemble immediately. She glanced over her shoulder to see Lucy adjusting the help wanted sign, moving it behind an ad for Ruthie's window washing service. Callie began to tell her to move it back but was interrupted when Mrs. Carlson, one of the regulars from the seamstress shop, materialized at the door and gave her an unavoidable smile. "Miss

Callie, I was so hoping I'd see you so I could compliment you on the work you did on those curtains. They're as good as new."

By the time that exchange ended, Callie had forgotten her friend's slight manipulation of the board and thought only of the hope still rising within her—the hope that with the right words and presentation, she would be considered for a position that she'd only just learned existed.

✧ ✧ ✧

Callie hummed a few bars of "Always" to calm her nerves. Though she felt like wringing her hands at the prospect of meeting Mr. Burke, turning to song had the ability to steady her as nothing else would. A long look in the mirror had let her know that she could play the part of a tutor: her dark hair was cast in curls, her blue eyes sparkled, and her cheeks warmed at the hope of what awaited her. The green dress she'd chosen still had all its buttons, her sensible black shoes were laced up tight. Mr. Burke had placed a call to her parents' house, requesting that she come to his home for an interview a mere two days after he'd placed his ad.

Her mother had almost dropped the receiver after the caller identified himself, and Callie had to explain the process she'd begun. After she'd submitted her letter to the Company Store, Callie hadn't expected him to take a second glance at it. But here she was, about to meet the respected businessman face-to-face.

She'd secretly made the trek out to the Burke's house the week before. Mrs. Starek, the seamstress whose shop she and her mother worked in several times a week, had told her of its beauty. Her husband, Nick, had a hand in the renovation of the old house. She knew that it was painted white, that its shutters were green, but her own envy had kept her away. She hadn't seen the purpose in looking, knowing she would be shut out by a sizable cast iron fence. But now that she'd been summoned for an interview, she thought of all the possibilities. Perhaps God was answering her prayers? Two years past twenty, she'd felt stunted, her dreams of singing blighted since her father's work-ending injury in the mines almost a year ago. Every once in a while Callie was reminded she had a gift—she need only think back to the applause from her performance of the national anthem at the Labor Day Parade a year before— but there weren't enough avenues around these parts for her to profit from her talent.

Help Wanted. Manna from heaven for anyone in that dust-covered town, even three years removed from the Crash. It was strange to think that she'd glimpsed this notice without a line of aspiring applicants behind her.

She watched her black oxfords, durable and worn, crunch over the gravel underfoot and felt a tightening in her throat. With each strike, she imagined she could leave behind the matters she didn't want to carry anymore—the depressive tone felt in her family's home now that her father was out of work, the frustration she'd felt with herself for not seeing her dreams come to fruition.

"Please help me, help my family," she said, an arrow prayer right before letting herself in past the Burke's gate. It struck her then, in this hastily made request to God, that she hadn't devoted much time to prayer lately. She could see plainly her gradual neglect during the weariness of all these events. But maybe it wasn't too late for prayers. Maybe she could find her second wind after all.

Chapter 3

B EFORE THE BURKES moved in, there was barely a house left on the premises. The structure was boarded up in places, the wood rotted, the floorboards dashed with debris and mud. Callie had heard it was a boarding house for black miners who were brought to the region to work some forty years prior. All but one small segment was knocked down. It once had a meager frame but had now become an enviable home in the woods. As she approached the front door for the first time, Callie's breath caught in her throat. There was nothing rusted and old about this place. The paint was fresh, the pink and purple chrysanthemums flourished in their boxes, the grass beneath her feet was a life-giving green.

Before she had time to gather her composure, Callie saw the front door open. She found herself standing face-to-face with a woman with dark hair swept back in a haphazard bun. There were circles beneath her dark eyes. While she wasn't unpleasant to look upon, she certainly wasn't what the townspeople described when they mentioned the beautiful Mrs. Burke. There was nothing remarkable about her faded yellow housedress. Other than a small, gold cross hanging from her neck, she wore no jewelry. Callie thought to herself that a woman with such reported affluence must have precious gems — rubies, sapphires, emeralds, diamonds — overflowing her jewelry box.

She was not the *Harper's Bazaar* model Callie had glimpsed walking up Pennsylvania Avenue from a distance. Perhaps she'd

worn an elegant hat to the Company Store the afternoon Callie
saw her, and that artifact alone had been enough to fool her
into thinking of the woman as untouchable, a Seattle socialite.

Callie spoke quickly so Mrs. Burke wouldn't notice she was
studying her. "Hello. My name is Callie Rushton. I'm here
for an interview with Mr. Burke."

The woman tilted her head to the side.

Callie clamped down on her tongue in mild frustration before speaking again. Was Mrs. Burke going to act as though she
didn't know they had requested a tutor? When Callie looked
down, she noted Mrs. Burke wore simple brown oxfords. They
were shoes that belonged on the feet of Bess Starek, on her
mother, on her.

"The position's already been filled, hasn't it?" Callie said.

The recognition that swept over the woman's features told
Callie that she knew about the ad.

"You're not Mrs. Burke, are you?" Callie shifted awkwardly
from foot to foot.

"Are you fooling me?" the woman asked, admonishment
filling her dark brown eyes. "That's the first time anyone's
mistaken me for her." She chortled, making an unflattering
sound. "Sorry, I was in the middle of dusting the sitting room,
and I wasn't expecting anyone to actually show for an interview.
But here you are."

Callie nodded, wishing the woman could at least open the
door and allow her past the entrance. Desperation finally
brought Callie's questions to the forefront.

"Are the Burkes still looking to hire since you are already
working here?" Callie asked, biting down on her bottom lip.
Perhaps that wasn't the best phrasing if she wanted the interview to happen as planned. She was supposed to make them
think they needed her.

"Margaret . . . Mrs. Burke mentioned wanting to hire an
afternoon tutor. She thought better of it the day after the ad
was posted and told her husband a tutor might not be needed,"
the woman said. "But I don't have time to tutor with all the

other tasks on my list." She quickly closed her mouth. Pursed her naturally red lips.

The sound of approaching footsteps caught their attention and the housekeeper's demeanor became more composed. She straightened her posture and pushed back her shoulders, reached up to tighten the pins in her loosened bun.

"Who's at the front door, Annie?" Callie heard a low baritone voice ask from behind her.

"There's a young woman saying she's here for an interview, Edward," the maid said, stepping aside and lifting her dust towel once again. "You must be expecting her." Callie found it peculiar that she'd called Mr. Burke by his first name, but was too busy composing herself to give it a second thought.

Annie let the door swing open, and Callie didn't know what to look at first, the master of the house or the stunning interior. The paintings on the walls, the silver chandelier above her, and the ornate cherry wood grandfather clock against the entrance wall—she tried to pretend that none of those items existed. Mr. Burke might never hire her if he saw how the furnishings mesmerized her, suspecting that it would only be a matter of time before silverware slipped into her pockets and small trinkets lined her stockings.

With some effort Callie focused on Mr. Burke. True to the grainy photograph that recently ran in the newspaper, his eyes were intensely dark against his prematurely silvering hair. She found him effortlessly handsome, though his charcoal-colored suit, the crisp white shirt he wore beneath it, and the gold watch glinting from his wrist helped to give him the presence of a debonair businessman. Mr. Burke didn't seem to be any older than her own father. He extended his hand and her own palms were clammy to the touch. She tried to shroud this first impression by wasting no time in introducing herself.

"Hello, I'm Callie Rushton," she said, wondering if this voice could even be hers, so distant and deep it seemed. "Thank you for calling me for an interview."

He offered a brief nod and ushered her in. Beyond the

landing, Callie saw a staircase that one might expect to see in an old Victorian. The walls were buttercream, untouched. She'd never stood in a home so poised and perfect. Her home had signs of wear and tear—children's shoes scattered at the entrance, dishes strewn across the counter, empty places where valuables had previously been. She tried to hide her amazement at a home so surreal to these parts.

"Why don't we go to my study?" Mr. Burke said, already leading her down the hall to the right of the house. He stopped at the third door and stepped aside to let her in.

All the doors save the one leading to his study, were closed on the bottom floor. There was no telling if Mrs. Burke was home. Callie couldn't hear anything but the ticking grandfather clock and the swift movements of Annie, presumably dusting the sitting room. It was still too early in the day for the children to be home from school. Mr. Burke gestured toward the oversize chairs facing a polished mahogany desk.

"Take a seat, why don't you."

Callie sank into one of the chairs and prayed the right words would find her. She folded her hands in her lap to prevent them from shaking. She hated that nerves were getting the best of her. She could stand before audiences and belt out the latest jazz ballad the radio played, but now she fought for composure. A quick glance revealed a neat study, sparse but for the expensive desk and chairs and a framed American flag behind him.

Within a moment Mr. Burke sat across from her and she felt his assessment begin. He clasped his hands over a neat pile of papers on his desk and gave her his undivided attention. "I'm looking for an afternoon tutor for my children. I have a nine-year-old son and an eleven-year-old daughter, and they're both academically capable. Given my wife's commitments to various charities and the church choir, it will help her to have someone here three afternoons a week . . . to occupy them, teach them some local history, perhaps." He pressed his lips together. "Does that sound like something you'd be interested in?"

She nodded quickly, trying not to smile too wide. "Yes, I'm interested," she said. "I'd love to. I'm self-taught . . . I'm well read and . . ." So much for uprooting desperation. She tried to regain control. "I'm also experienced with children. My little brothers, they're twins, and ten years old."

Mr. Burke returned her smile, and his eyes crinkled in the corners. He picked up a pen and tapped it to the desk several times before saying, "This sounds promising so far. It's clear you know this age group. I have a few more questions I'd like to ask you."

She nodded, hoping her voice wouldn't falter.

"How long have you lived in these parts?" he asked, curiosity sweeping his features. He tapped his pen on the desk again, anticipating.

"My entire life," she said, easily. "My grandparents came from England and Poland to work in the mines."

He nodded, offered her a slight smile. "So, I take it your family is fairly settled and involved in this community."

"Yes, although I have another brother away in the Army. But we're lifelong members of Mt. Pisgah Presbyterian, and my father is part of the Odd Fellows. "

"And what are your interests, now that you've been out of school?"

She felt her face flush, hoping her gift didn't strike him as pretentious. "I love to sing," she said, daring to meet his eye. "It's been awhile, but I've been asked to sing the national anthem at ballgames, and it's great fun to sing with a piano accompaniment."

"Why did you stop?" Mr. Burke asked with a sparkle in his brown eyes.

She looked down at her folded hands before glancing to him again. "I think because I've needed to be more practical, with these hard times pressing upon our community, sir," she said. "But now that you ask, I realize it's something I'd like to return to. That I need to return to."

As she spoke, Mr. Burke's expression transformed into one

of keen interest. "I'd like to hire you, Miss Rushton," he said suddenly, smoothing his fingers over imaginary stubble on his chin.

She struggled to believe her good fortune. "Thank you, Mr. Burke. You can call me Callie."

Mr. Burke put a hand up, as if wanting to stifle her excitement. "Callie, then. I'd like to hire you, but that's only if you understand your employment here is conditional."

He offered her a pointed look across the desk. "Since my family is of interest to the public, it's of utmost importance that you keep information you may learn of Burke Enterprises confidential. Do you understand?"

"Yes, of course, sir. I won't say anything about your family or your business . . . to the public." She smiled as if she'd just received rousing applause.

While his statement made sense for a prominent businessman, it made Callie curious about what would be of interest to the public. Were there secrets about the Burke home he wanted her to keep?

He pressed his elbows down on the desk, drew his hands together and gave her a nod. "I'm glad that's understood. You give up a portion of privacy when you work so much in the public eye, and I don't want to give up more than we have to. . . ." She noticed the oversize gold watch on his left wrist again and tried to look away from it as he asked, "When can you start?"

"Now," Callie answered in a rush, not even taking time to ask him what precise tasks he'd require of her as tutor to his children.

She wondered how much he would be willing to pay her, but such thoughts made her squirm in the plush, leather chair. Anything would be welcome. Anything would help her family.

"How about Monday afternoon?" he asked, glancing down to study a calendar on the desk. "It's already the end of this week, so why not start fresh after a restful week-end?"

Callie's mind caught on the word restful. Her week-end

wouldn't exude the slightest sense of that word. Her family's deferred payments were mounting at the Company Store, and it was even becoming difficult to fork over money for animal feed. She doubted Mr. Merrick would be willing to part with a sack of flour if they didn't make a dent in the bill they'd accumulated in passing months.

"Should I arrive about half an hour after school on Monday?" she asked, trying to hide any ounce of desperation from her voice.

Mr. Burke nodded and rose from his seat, though it seemed they'd only just begun their conversation. Callie knew she was to begin working for the Burkes on Monday afternoon, but she didn't know what tutoring his children would entail. What were their grade levels, their strengths, their weaknesses, their interests? Several questions sprang to mind as he led her from his study, but she couldn't trust her voice not to falter when asking them. It must not matter too much to him what curriculum the children needed or what methods she used to instruct them if he didn't have anything to say on the matter. Wasn't it odd that his wife wasn't present for the interview? Typically mothers—more so than fathers—were even more cautious about the ones who oversaw their children's instruction.

Before he opened the study door, Mr. Burke crossed his arms over his chest, and knitted his eyebrows as he looked down at her. "You listed the seamstress in town as one of your references. Do you know the Stareks well?"

"I lend a hand with stitching and sewing at Mrs. Starek's Seamstress Shop several days a week." she said, intrigued by his manner. "Didn't her husband work on the renovation of your house before you moved here?"

He gave a short nod, and nothing else was said of the matter. As Mr. Burke led her back to the front door, she resolved to talk to Mrs. Starek. She turned on her heel when they reached the entrance and sought out his dark eyes with one more question. "What would you like me to emphasize most . . . in the children's studies?"

Several moments passed before he answered her. "Oh, just reading, local history. Before the weather turns, you might take them outdoors on occasion, help them get their energy out. Especially Jamie."

"I know all about that. From my twin brothers. They can barely sit still."

Mr. Burke gave her a smile so genuine that his near-black eyes glinted. He could go from impassive to charming with the flick of a match. The spark in those dark eyes was enough to catch her by surprise, make her wonder if he did that for everyone.

A telephone rang in his office and he put up a hand to wave farewell. She quickly let herself out and smiled at the colors gleaming in the flower baskets—their royal purples, pink golds, their optimistic yellow.

As she rested on the last step of the porch, a young man caught her eye near a shed to the left of the property. He'd just lined some wood up and was about to bring down an axe. He wore a cap on his head, khaki-colored trousers, and a light blue work shirt that hugged his strong arms. The shirt's faded hue contrasted with his skin, brown with warm undertones. She'd never seen him before. Roslyn and its outlying regions weren't large and she was surprised that they hadn't crossed paths. The Burkes were fairly new to the area, however, and it was clear they hired quite a bit of outside help—the house, the grounds, and now the children as well.

She'd let her gaze linger on him for a moment too long and she tried to steer her vision to the wrought iron gate at the edge of the property. But she hadn't looked away in time. He shifted his focus and their eyes met, his deep amber with her deep blue. Even with the distance of the yard between them she felt his presence ignite some life within her. Her existence had felt mundane and routine for at least a year, but meeting his gaze gave her a surge of hope, and she couldn't account for it if she tried. He gave a brief nod, then returned his focus to the wood stack before him. Callie continued her walk to the gate, though she wanted to introduce herself. There was nothing about her sudden new position at the Burke's that called for such an interaction, however. But Callie noticed it took him a few extra seconds to lift the axe again. She might not know all the residents in the black community, but she'd have remembered him. He wiped his forehead again with the back of his hand and set his attention to his task.

Yes, she'd have remembered him.

Chapter 4

C ALLIE RAN MUCH of the way home, marveling over her incredible fortune. Why would a family like the Burkes hire her—a young, self-educated woman with no formal classroom experience? The wonder of it made her lift her head and express her thanks. After her father crushed his leg beneath a boulder in the mines the year before, she'd allowed room for bitterness in her heart. Why did a man as diligent, as hardworking as her father have to suffer in the midst of an already difficult time for the nation?

As she rounded the corner to her family's home, she stopped, hearing loud, boisterous laughter. She knew only one person in this town who could make her father laugh like that. Mr. Sam Jacobson had come to visit. The two men sat on the front porch, smoking cigarettes, and reminisced about days of old.

"And then there was the time Trip Evers was trying to lasso his cow. Slipped on the rope, and got dragged and carried around at the Ellensburg Rodeo? Remember that?" she could hear her father say through bursts of laughter.

Mr. Jacobson let out a hearty laugh and said, "I wouldn't be joking if our man suffered any injuries, but that was the funniest thing you ever did see."

Neither of them cared for Evers, Callie knew, a sly smirk etching its way on her face. They were having so much fun, she hated to break their light-hearted conversation. But she was already approaching the gate and well within their line of vision.

"And how's Miss Callie today?" Mr. Jacobson asked, flashing his straight white smile. He, unlike so many men in the mines, had kept all his teeth. Sam was the son of one of the first black miners to arrive in Washington. His father, Frank Jacobson, a miner in Virginia, arrived during the strike of 1888. Many of the black miners had since left the region, seeking other, less grueling work than toil in the mines, but the Jacobsons made a home for themselves in the midst of Roslyn, planting a church.

She looked to her father's friend, who still waited for her to answer his question. "I'm well," she said, not sure if she was ready yet to announce her new position at the Burke's. "How are you and Mrs. Jacobson?"

"No more of this Mr. and Mrs. Jacobson." He removed the cigarette from his mouth, watched the embers fall to the porch floorboards. "Makes me feel older than my years. I already face aging enough, limbs creaking, reminding me I'm not a young man every morning. Back protesting, saying no to endless hours in the mines. Saying I've done this one too many times. He shook his head. "But Tessa, she keeps me young, and so does our grand-boy. God's greatest blessing, I'll tell you that."

Callie smiled at his answer. Sam counted his God-given blessings. If only her father would learn to do that more. She watched the two men sitting shoulder to shoulder and prayed that some of the light that Sam Jacobson carried would spread over to her downtrodden father.

✧ ✧ ✧

It's all about to change, Callie thought while swallowing a spoonful of chili that night. She thought of the Burkes and what working for them would mean for her family. She'd been hesitant to announce she'd been offered the position—she had an inkling that her father wouldn't favor the arrangement. With skill she'd avoided her mother's questioning glances all evening, as Mrs. Rushton had answered the call from Edward Burke himself, and was fully aware of the interview. But the current temperature in the dining room was so bleak that she knew she must do something to change that. Even a spark of disbelief would lend something to the dinner table other than quiet, uncomfortable chewing. Her family used to listen to music in the background—a burst of classical piano, swing, sometimes even ragtime hits—but they'd since sold their record player. Her father's radio had too much static for the enjoyment of melodies.

Callie finally tossed her napkin down and let her gaze wander from her parents to her twin brothers.

"I was hired for a new position today," she said, an unbidden smile taking over her face.

Her mother started to look at her in question. Callie shook her head and said, "This won't affect my shifts at the seamstress shop. I'm going to work as a tutor for the Burkes three afternoons a week."

Once the words were out of her mouth, she felt as vulnerable as the first time she'd sung before an audience. But there was a relief in knowing that she'd said them, that she wouldn't have to sit with this secret welling in her chest.

Though she saw her mother's face light up, it was her brother Charlie who spoke up first. "Those kids? They're so strange."

He wrinkled his nose, and Stevie immediately chimed in.

"They dress differently than the rest of us . . . I think the girl, Julia, even has a fur coat."

"Of course she does," their father said. "Their father owns a shipping business and presides over the Company Store."

Instead of congratulating his daughter on her promising opportunity, he lifted his glass and took a long sip of water.

Callie didn't know the Burkes well enough to defend them, and yet she wanted to. So they were different and they had more means than anyone they knew. Did the fact that they stood apart mean they couldn't be trusted? A swell of indignation rising in her throat, Callie looked to her mother with a silent plea in her eyes. *Say something kind, say something hopeful.* Callie's mother took the cue. "This is encouraging news, Cal."

Her father threw his napkin down on the table and gave a

brief shake of his head. "Encouraging?" he asked, blue eyes narrowing in suspicion. "I'd hardly call it that, not when we hardly know the man, not when what we do know is that he's aloof with most in this town."

Callie bit down on her lip before speaking. "Expect a prominent businessman to carouse with the miners at the Brick?" She heard the exasperation in her voice and tried to soften her tone. "He's probably selective with who he gets close to."

Her father had more to say on the subject. "Some of the men I used to work with say that he chose an isolated site in the woods to take up residence since he . . . has something to hide. Something must have driven him from the Seattle region, made him want to settle here. I know there are questions about the man's moral character. He's married now, but some say he's been caught up with inappropriate women in the past and . . ."

"He hired me as a tutor to his children, not as a personal secretary," Callie said, her face starting to burn up. In thinking of her one sit-down exchange with Mr. Burke, she hadn't sensed that he had any ulterior motives for hiring her. He was pleasant, as was his fashion, but he hadn't let his eyes linger too long on her face or her form. He hadn't asked her any untoward questions. She didn't know why her father was crediting some rumored indiscretion attached to Edward Burke's name.

"You're an intelligent girl," her father went on, lifting a hand in explanation. "But one grows suspicious in hearing that he hired a young woman he just met and not a classroom teacher."

Callie pressed her hands together beneath the table, willing that she maintain her calm. She hated reminders that she hadn't gone on to music school, made a name for herself. She gauged her words before speaking.

"I took the opportunity to apply when I saw the sign for employment. Our family needs the income, and I couldn't care less what townspeople have to say about him."

The frown on her father's face only increased. He cleared his throat, making a sound like clothes being run over a washboard. Though frustrated that her promising news was met with disapproval, Callie tried not to let her heart harden toward her father. "I haven't even started working for them yet. Please," she said, an unintended plea in her voice, "can't we give the Burkes a chance before drawing hasty conclusions about them? If it's not a suitable place, I don't have to stay."

While she could see her father was unmoved, she watched him give a brusque nod, heard him tell her, "You might have an uneasy feeling about that family after a few days. You just make sure you listen to it instead of putting aside your intuition for the paycheck."

Callie lifted her glass and took a considerable drink before meeting her father's eyes. "I might not get any feeling about the family at all," she said with a crisp expression. "I wouldn't believe everything the mining men have to say. They're hardy and they know how to endure." She paused. "But they're not always right."

Chapter 5
1889

WHEN DAVID SAW the letter on Bella Johnson's kitchen counter, he sought the privacy hard to come by in the boarding house. Bella's husband, Gerald, offered him a bowl of soup, but he couldn't hide the fact that Georgina's words were to him more satiating than a hard-earned meal. He set the bowl down quickly, wincing at the spill he left on the counter. Bella picked up a rag and wiped it away without the slightest complaint. He murmured his thanks to her. His hands were shaking and he didn't want anyone to see how nervous he was about what she might say. Bella, Gerald, the boarders Charles and Willard—they had all stopped talking once he dove for the letter. Now with it in hand, he sought a place where he could drink in Georgina's words, and set off into the darkened hallway. Unseen by him, a fellow boarder edged up and tried to flick the letter from his waiting hands. "Back off, man," he said. The young man's questioning eyes peered back at him.

"I'm sorry, Robert," he said. "Got a letter from my wife here, and just between the two of us, I'm not sure what she's gonna say. Think you could give me a minute?"

In recent months he hadn't been able to tell her that his move west had left him with serious second thoughts. The Cascades were beautiful, this place where the Natives once gathered to hunt and fish and pick huckleberries. The endless blue sky stunned. The grass, when warm, showed its green splendor. But the living arrangements hadn't been as ideal as Mr. Simonson had said. He and the other men knew they'd bought a dressed-up lie. What could they do about it? Whatever remained for them in the east or the south held even less promise. Out west, they'd been told, blacks could make a name for themselves. They could be the men and women they'd been created to be, escape the confines of those still bent on oppression. If only it were that easy. He rubbed the spot below his eye and could feel the faint bruise there.

Robert nodded. Understanding washed over his face as soon as he heard David's request for solitude. He clapped a hand on his friend's shoulder and left him to the silence of the hall. David drew close to the flickering candle Mrs. Johnson had lit on a small table, noticed the irretrievable dirt embedded beneath his fingernails. Hadn't it always been there? He held his breath until he read her words:

> We'll be joining you in June, David. Please forgive me for not making our way to you sooner. I shouldn't have placed my performances here over a new life there with you. Liliana asks for you every night.

A dash of water struck the page before he even realized he was crying. David straightened up. He folded the letter back into the envelope, slipped it in his pocket. He looked up to find himself opposite the hall mirror. Only then did he notice the mottled swelling below his eye—an angry white miner had given it to him on his walk home two nights before with a glass bottle. The attack had been unprovoked. He'd never seen the man before in his life, though the hatred pouring forth from the miner's eyes was hard to forget. David could have laid the man out flat, but once he'd risen to his feet and saw the miner toss the bottle aside, he'd clenched his fists and told himself to breathe. By that time, Frank Jacobson had noticed something amiss. "There a problem over here?" he'd asked, approaching David, who had still been breathing through his nose.

"More than a hundred of us are leaving town since you've

tried to replace us," the miner had said before spitting on the ground. A sneer written on his face, he'd stormed off, kicking up plumes of dirt with his work boots.

Frank had started to take a step after him, but David had shaken his head and clutched Frank's forearm. "Let him go," he'd said, wincing from the pain of his wound. "We won't be working with him. The fool said he's leaving." He'd let out his breath, as Frank had given a nod.

Some of the white men were joining them in the mines already now that the strike was over. The ones who couldn't abide Northern Pacific's mandate—or working alongside colored men—planned a mass exodus.

David sighed again. He hadn't remembered a mirror there at the end of the hall. Wished Bella had put it elsewhere. He drew a hand up, as if covering his wound would diminish its significance. Georgina didn't know of his difficult reception to this place. If she gleaned anything of Roslyn from his letters, she still thought it was a treasure in the mountains—a retreat from the haphazard living they sometimes knew.

They could still make a life here, he knew, and if Georgina didn't favor the dusty roads or the back-breaking work, there was always Seattle to consider. He'd talked with enough of the other miners to know that black families were settling into the western Washington city and making a name for themselves now that they had the chance. He spent most of his extra hours looking for a place his wife and daughter could live. His pay, though higher than back east, wasn't substantial. He'd crossed a series of more desirable homes off his list. Forget indoor plumbing. Homes with two floors weren't feasible. Houses overlooking the plunging blue Lake Cle Elum came at too high a cost. Georgina knew she was moving to a mining town, but even so, he wasn't about to take her home to an old, decrepit shanty—its porch slanted, its foundation nonexistent, the rats scurrying at their feet and keeping them up at night with their incessant gnawing.

The mine boss, who admired his work ethic, mentioned

promoting David to a safety officer position on several occasions. But David wasn't one to count his dollars before the actual check was in hand. He put in a word for a cabin close to the No. 3 mine and tried not to bank his hopes on it.

✧ ✧ ✧

On a chilly May morning, David tagged in with a few other miners and placed his open flame cap on his head. He said a prayer, asking God to shield and protect him and the other miners as they descended below the earth, their pickaxes at the ready.

"What're you praying for?" Ian McLaughlin, a Scotch-Irish miner who'd recently been rehired asked. "If I'm being honest with you, that makes me more nervous 'bout this thankless job we do."

Robert laughed as they continued to descend.

"Nah, you're good. The prayer helps me. What's the alternative? Not acknowledging that we put our lives on the line every damn day?"

Ian wrinkled his nose as they descended to the cold, dank underground, the coal car coming to a rickety stop now that they'd arrived at their worksite. "Yes, sir. Let's try not acknowledging or mentioning it. We're only here to get a job done."

Robert whistled through his teeth.

"Alrighty then. Let's set our sights on that which we can't see but can imagine. Those lovely ladies that'll come out to dance tonight at Simonson's Club."

"That's what I'm talking about," Ian said, the open flame lighting his features, showing off his white smile, effortless and charming to the fairer sex. "There's this one, Janie, I think her name is, that I'd like to see again. Thinking of her will make the hours down here go faster."

David laughed at the single men's camaraderie. He'd been to several taverns, enjoyed the thrum of the banjo and the plinking of the piano, but most often made for the boarding house when his day's work was done. He grew weary of telling the women who came to speak with him, sidling up for the chance to dance, that he was already taken. Some of them didn't care that he had a wife and a daughter, and that's when going out with the miners at night was more trouble than it was worth.

Half an hour's toil passed with the miners turned to their respective places, working the seams to loose black diamond. Time and time again, David struck his pickaxe. As was his habit, David ventured away from the other men, preferring to work alone. His hands were large and fast, and the mine boss had on more than one occasion praised him for the great portion of rock he delivered. He was in tune with the slightest change in his environment in which he'd been placed. He listened to the strike of the other men's pickaxes almost as closely as he noted his own. The sound came suddenly—the start of crumbling rock above where Ian and Robert worked. It was as if the earth rumbled at them for their audacity to tamper with it. David threw down his tools and scrambled over to his friends, the open flame of his headlamp leading the way.

"Oh God, help!" Ian cried out before he could even reach him. He saw first the young miner's scrunched-up expression, as he lay on his back, sweat droplets beading his forehead. As the fallen rock settled, he realized that the man's leg was trapped beneath a boulder. Robert, who'd been working close by, let out a choking cough and said, "How bad is it? Oh Lord. We gotta get out of here. There could be more. The rock might not be done falling."

"We need to get him out of here first," David said, shielding his eyes from the dusty plumes.

Robert adjusted his miner's cap and said, "I'll have one of the foremen bring down support. We gotta go, Davie. Look how his leg in wedged in there real good." Robert knelt down near Ian and said, "We'll send help. I promise we will." Ian didn't respond, but he continued to whimper in response to the pain.

David was shaking his head, drawing his hand to the rock that trapped his friend's leg. "It's not overhead. We can move this, you and I." He locked eyes with Robert. He couldn't in good conscience leave Ian, knowing there was a good likelihood he could still pry him loose.

Before Robert could weigh in on the decision, David was leaning into the rock, pushing back with everything he had in him. His forearms strained and he shouted as he mustered his strength—the same strength that gave him impressive yields in the pit and saved injured miners. He'd tunneled back down the pit twice to hoist men over his shoulder in previous weeks. The dust and dirt spun, but still David leaned in to free his friend from death's jaws. He winced upon seeing the crush of Ian's lower leg, the blood spilling over the tops of his boots. Quickly he tore at his sleeve and tied the loosed fabric around the man's boot to quench the bleeding. He then hoisted him over his shoulder and nodded at Robert, who shook his head, astonished that his partner had pulled off such a feat. Sweat poured into David's eyes as he carried Ian, moaning and nearly unconscious.

All David could think of was a prayer that made it to his lips. "Lord Jesus, don't let me fall." He struggled under the dead weight. By the time he at last laid Ian's body down, he saw that his friend was barely moving. He propped him up, for the man was by this time a marionette who could be manipulated this way or that. "Save his life," he said, his voice tight.

"You did. You and the good Lord," Robert said, as they surfaced above ground together. He turned to the men from the safety crew, who were at the ready with a stretcher.

"Hurry. His leg is crushed, and he's still losing blood. Think he'll make it, though."

He turned back to David and shook his head at his friend's show of courage. "You're growing quite a name 'round these parts, putting your own life at risk to save your fellow man."

Putting your own life at risk. He could hear Georgina's voice. *Diligent as you are about your plans, you are reckless when it comes to the consideration of your own life above others.*

David grimaced and turned away. He felt no elation.

Chapter 6
1932

O N THE EARLY SEPTEMBER afternoon Callie was to start with the Burkes, rain fell in colorless sheets. She'd stood in front of the hallway mirror moments before, adjusting her curls, but Callie could feel the polished effect was undone after only a few minutes of walking. Sighing at the inconvenience of it all, she felt at least grateful for a halfway decent dress to wear that afternoon: navy blue and cinched at the waist with a small black belt.

More than twice she had to stop because of the mud puddles underfoot. She tried to steady herself, meanwhile balancing her other possessions—a small black purse, a dented apple, and an American history textbook. A door opened and her heart clenched as she saw Maura Merrick step out onto the porch of her blue house. Today of all days she would run into someone with the power to unravel her. She had thought she was beyond it all, and yet one chance encounter with this girl who had stolen her fiancé threatened to undo months of progress. The sight of Maura yanked her back to those sleepless nights after Paul's betrayal and his plans to call off their engagement. Those were the nights she'd woken to tear-stained pillows, to a heart she thought would burst from her chest.

Their engagement had been over for a year now, but it didn't take much to recall how shamed she'd felt every time someone looked at her with pity written in their features. Callie found herself studying Maura's gold-spun hair. Maura's dress would never be regarded as an ordinary housedress like her own. It was plain, yes, but the color of chardonnay, and so much more elegant than the one she wore. Maura's father was the head clerk of the Company Store, a job he'd retained under Mr. Burke's new management.

A lump lodged in Callie's throat when she thought about the Merrick's prosperity compounded with Maura's success in stealing her suitor. She tried to sidestep Maura's view by moving behind an age-old evergreen. But it was too late. Her rival had already seen her.

Maura offered her a smile. "Callie," she said, with condescension. "How are you?"

Callie pressed her fingernails into the palms of her hands, causing half-moons to appear.

"Wonderful," she said. Maura's eyebrows rose and Callie couldn't hide her smile. "I just got a position working for the Burkes as their new tutor." The words rolled off her tongue sweetly, making her want to taste them again.

In response, Maura raised her hand to adjust her hair, her modest engagement band clearly visible. "That should help your family out, shouldn't it?"

It didn't take long to hear anything in this town, and Callie had already heard about Paul's proposal to Maura two weekends before. She no longer loved him, but his deception still summoned a flattened feeling, like she'd stood in the way of a rolling barrel. Their broken engagement had set her back so much. She had stopped singing at events, she still lived under her father's roof.

Maura continued talking since Callie hadn't been quick to respond. "I mean, with your father done in the mines and all, your family could probably use the money."

Callie's tongue grazed the roof of her mouth. "Anything helps, but we're managing fine." She turned the apple over in her palm and bit back her words. She wouldn't give Maura the satisfaction of seeing her riled. Even so, Callie took another glance at the apple, tasting the urge to throw it. She could even picture Maura's expression as it spiraled through the air, but she stifled her compulsion.

"Have a lovely afternoon," Callie said, turning away from the Merrick's residence before Maura could prattle on about her engagement. Callie could feel her cheeks begin to flame as she walked on toward the Burke's home. Tears stung her eyes, and she was angry at their persistence. She willed them back as she soldiered through the rain to the first day of her new position.

Callie adjusted the hood of her coat several times since the rain wouldn't let up. She shook the droplets of water loose, even knowing it was no use. She'd envisioned looking more polished when she met the Burke children, but she had no say in the weather. Relief washed over her once she made it to the top of the hill. Her desire to be indoors crowded out any nervousness about making a favorable impression. Glancing at the spacious house, she could envision a rollicking fire in the sitting room. She couldn't wait to warm her cherry-tinted hands before settling in the study with the children.

Callie lifted the gate's lever and drew in her breath soon as she looked back up. The young man she'd seen the other day was once again stacking wood near a shed to the right of the house. He wore a tattered work shirt and dark blue pants, toiling hard despite the rainfall. He glanced up from the woodpile soon after she closed the gate behind her. He set the axe down, gathered a few logs to his chest, and turned toward the front porch. He gave her a polite nod. "Good afternoon," he said as she approached the stairs.

When she drew her eyes up to meet his, warm brown with a hint of amusement, she found herself unable to look away. That she felt anything at all caught her off guard. There were handsome men to be found in the region—the veil of dust and labor gear couldn't hide that—but she hadn't felt a spark with any of them since her engagement had ended. And now, her instantaneous draw to the young man before her left her feeling heady. Who was he? Had he possibly lived in the Upper

County for long without her knowing of it? She'd have remembered him, had she ever seen him on Pennsylvania Avenue. And yet, she knew she shouldn't feel anything at all, for society wouldn't deem it appropriate.

"You must be here to tutor the Burke children," he said, nodding just as she did. "Here, let me get the door for you." Though one arm was full of wood, he opened the door and let her walk before him. She smiled up at him to murmur her thanks. She was about to ask for his name when she saw Annie already at the entrance of the house, ready to usher her in. While Annie didn't offer a formal greeting, her dark eyes were earnest and expectant.

"I'll let Mrs. Burke know that you're here," Annie said, turning away from the new hire without a proper greeting. She gave a brief nod to the young man and said, "Perfect timing. We could use another log thrown on in the sitting room about now. It's miserable out there today."

"True," he said, his voice betraying a hint of tiredness. "But as soon as I throw this log on the fire, I need to head over to the west side."

"How long will you be this time?" Annie asked.

"Should be back Tuesday night," he said, sounding hopeful.

Left alone at the front door, Callie carefully removed her rain-dashed coat, her mud-laden galoshes, and tiptoed into the sitting room. She expected refined excellence, but nothing could prepare her for the vaulted ceilings, the plush blue sofas, the stuffed floral armchairs, the expensive side tables of mahogany, and the paintings capturing the staggering beauty of the Pacific Northwest gracing their walls. She'd have let her gaze linger longer over the furnishings, but there was someone already waiting for her. She'd also wanted another chance to say something more to the young worker resting the log on the fire, her name in exchange for his own, but he left the room as quickly as he'd entered.

Callie found herself alone with a girl, who walked over to her, curiosity written in her delicate features. The girl's eyes were impossibly blue and round. She wore a dusky rose dress with a black sash tied around the waist, hardly attire for a rainy afternoon in a coal-mining town.

"Hello." Callie stepped toward the young girl, extending her hand. "My name is Callie Rushton . . . well, Miss Rushton to you. You must be Julie."

"Julia Burke," the young girl said, correcting Callie without a moment's hesitation. The name was fitting for the girl. It denoted her status, her youthful sophistication, the wealth her father had accumulated. She squinted her eyes at Callie. "Is it true that you're going to be my new tutor?"

Callie found herself nodding, wondering how long it was going to take for Julia's mother to surface. She again noted the items she'd decided to bring with her today: the bruised apple, the tattered black purse, the American history book she'd found on the family bookshelf. She didn't know what she would have brought instead, but suddenly the three items she'd brought seemed inadequate. "Yes, I'm your new tutor. I'm Cal . . . Miss Rushton," she said, correcting herself.

Glancing around, Callie again noted the splendor of the sitting room. She hesitated to sit on one of the sofas or in an upholstered chair, noting how perfect they were in comparison to the threadbare furniture that remained at her parents' home.

"My younger brother is hiding," Julia told her new tutor, interrupting her thoughts about the disparity of class. "He doesn't want you here. He doesn't think we need a tutor."

This revelation took her aback. She hadn't expected opposition, figuring the Burke children were acclimated to having a new tutor.

"My mother is looking for him right now," Julia continued as she played with her loosened black sash. Callie was tempted to adjust it herself, but she looked up and noticed a slender figure appear, belonging to a woman who couldn't be anyone other than Mrs. Burke. Callie knew it wasn't polite to stare, but it was difficult to resist. Mrs. Burke belonged to the motion pictures, not to this unknown town. Callie noticed a simultaneous sadness with her beauty. Her black hair framed a lovely face—one that came with blue-violet eyes, a slightly upturned nose, and a full mouth. She wore a dress the color of champagne. The fabric, which looked light and breezy, grazed her still-trim figure and stopped right at her shapely calves. Her shoes were the color of night, and the elegant heels tapped with precision across the wood floors. She held an embroidered clutch that surely contained more of the rouge and lipstick that was painted on her face. Callie felt her stark difference and momentarily wished she'd spent more time working on her appearance. She drew the worn history volume to her chest. How un-befitting it was to this house.

"Hello," Mrs. Burke said, extending a hand to Callie. "I'm Margaret Burke. I assume you're here to tutor my children."

Callie nodded and gave her name. Mrs. Burke offered one of those smiles that didn't quite meet the eyes. She didn't have an abrasive air like her housemaid, but there was no joy written across her features. She pressed a hand to her temples as soon as she let Callie's hand go.

"You'll have to forgive me. I've had these headaches coming on sporadically, and I'm doing what I can to ignore them." She let out her breath. "I need a glass of water." She assessed Callie again and said, "It looks like you're wet through. Is it storming out there that much?"

Trying not to wince, Callie drew a hand to her damp hair and said, "It's about a ten-minute walk from my place to yours."

"You don't have someone to drive you?" Mrs. Burke asked, reaching for her ignition keys inside her clutch. "What a long walk for you in the coming winter months. Perhaps we'll have someone come to your house to pick you up as soon as the weather turns."

She placed her hands again on her temples. "My son Jamie is hiding in the closet of my bedroom," she continued, wincing. "I don't have the energy to reason with him today." She shook her head, and Callie could feel the woman's agitation simmer. "If you wouldn't mind walking in there and coaxing him, I know he'll come out. He only does this for attention."

Annie resurfaced with a rag in hand. Mrs. Burke turned toward her housemaid. "He played a similar game when you first came to live with us, didn't he?"

Annie nodded, the annoyance palpable on her face.

Mrs. Burke looked down at her clutch again before raising her troubled eyes back to Callie. "I'm going to town for various errands. I expect to be back by five-thirty or so."

"Is Mr. Burke home this afternoon?" Callie asked, curious as to whether he would be around while she attempted to extract his nine-year-old boy from the bedroom closet. There was nothing Callie would rather do less than this. In fact, she found it surprising that Mrs. Burke had even asked her to step into their bedroom the first time they'd ever met.

With a dismissive wave of her hand, Mrs. Burke gave her answer. "Edward is so rarely home. It's a wonder why he decided to move here." There was unquestionable strain in her voice, making it more than obvious that their first year in this place had not endeared her to the Upper County.

"Where is your bedroom?" Callie asked, reminding herself this was a natural question, considering the circumstances.

"Julia will show you, won't she?" Mrs. Burke said, bending down to give her daughter an airy kiss on the top of her head. While her hand rested on Julia's head, Callie glimpsed the glinting gold of her wedding ring, which was offset by a marquise diamond. Callie thought of her mother's ring and how diminutive it was in comparison.

Julia tugged on Callie's sleeve and said before her mother was gone from the property, "Come on. I'll show you where Jamie's hiding."

"It might take you a while to get him out of there," Annie warned as Julia led Callie down the spacious hall that extended past the sitting room.

"That's alright," Callie said, turning to acknowledge her, although Annie already returned to straightening the couch cushions. "I'll see if I can convince him to come out to meet me."

She saw Annie wore an expression that made her look like she'd bitten a tart cherry. Callie wondered what ailed her. It seemed Annie would not make an easy ally, so she concentrated her efforts on befriending the little boy.

"He's in here," Julia said, swinging open the door to the bedroom.

Callie couldn't stop from drawing in her breath as soon as she saw the size of the room and all it contained. Not only did the Burkes have a canopy bed, but all of their furniture was a rich mahogany: the side tables, the matching dressers, the vanity with its gilt mirror. And while it was better to appreciate them for their aesthetic quality alone, she mentally contemplated their worth. The furniture in this one room alone outshone anything in her parents' entire house.

She stopped at the sight of Margaret Burke's vanity table. Perfectly shaped roses bloomed on the gilt frame surrounding the mirror. While Mrs. Burke didn't clutter her vanity, there were cosmetic brushes and lipsticks and compacts resting on top of it—all prestige items that few women could afford. But it wasn't those things she cared to linger on. What she wanted to see were the framed photographs lining the bottom of the mirror. She wanted a glimpse into the life of the family. She stole a quick glance at a framed portrait of the Burkes on their wedding day, hoping Julia wouldn't notice. A glance was enough to show her that there was sunlight written across Margaret Burke's face as she stood facing outward, encircled in Edward's arms.

Callie pulled herself away from the pictures. "Does your brother do this often?" she asked Julia, turning her attention to the task at hand. This ploy of his—hiding in his father's closet—was something that the twins would have never got away with. Her father would have unbuckled his belt faster than either one of them could blink. She wondered what type of disciplinarians the Burkes were, since their son hadn't stopped hiding, even upon their requests for him to cease and desist.

"Jamie only does this to get attention," Julia said, pinpointing her brother's motive. "My father is gone so often—and now

Mama is, too. So he knows if he disappears, they have to stop and look for him."

Callie frowned. If this were true—that a little boy would feel his only method of acquiring his parents' attention was to vanish—it was one of the saddest truths she'd heard in a long time.

"I can hear you, you know," Jamie called, apparently not minding that he was giving himself up. "And they're not usually the ones that stop to find me," he pointed out.

"Gabe is too busy to find you," Julia called out, sounding bossy for her years. It might be just as difficult trying to wield control over her as it would be for her brother. Thus far, she was as calculating as a house cat sitting smug in a corner.

"Gabe?" Callie turned around to face Julia.

"Yes. He brought the firewood in after you," Julia said by way of explanation as she held open the door to her father's closet. "Mama doesn't approve of our spending too much time with him."

As soon as the closet door swung open, she saw Jamie wasn't hidden too well. Even though he'd chosen to slide behind a column of his father's suits, his large, dark eyes peered out over the tops of the hangers.

Keeping in mind that a certain look or tone could make this boy's mind up, Callie took the route she thought would work best. "I know you'd rather be outside playing with other children. But since you can't be right now, wouldn't you like to come out to meet me?"

Jamie frowned, unconvinced. "Not really. I wish we could play after school like other children. I think my father wants us ahead of our class so he can send us to a boarding school in a few years."

Callie realized she had a melodramatic child on her hands.

"I don't know what grade level you two are at yet, but I'm sure if we got to work, we could assess which skills you need to work on. You might even like the material," she said, motioning toward the volume of American history she still held.

Both children shook their heads at her simultaneously, and she wondered if they knew something that she didn't. Julia threaded her black sash through her fingers before lifting her chin to look at Callie with keen eyes. "We've already studied from that history book. Our last tutor in Seattle had it. We already know about immigration to Ellis Island. About the Missouri Compromise. The Gettysburg Address."

Callie pressed her short nails into her palms again. She doubted her brothers could recount such standout historical events as easily. She knew the Burke children were about to challenge her.

Not wanting to waste the afternoon in Mr. Burke's closet, Callie reached for Jamie's hand and said, "Come out and join us, please. If you've already read this book, that's fine. I'll find others. You can learn about real life cowboys. Not today, but sometime later we can look for articles and other books in the library. . . ." Seeing that she wasn't convincing him, she added, "And we don't have to stay indoors for all of it, either. Don't you think it'd be fun to learn local history too?"

Jamie hesitated. It was difficult to miss how much of his father was written on him. He'd inherited the same eyes,— nearly black as a raven's wing—and the same strong jaw. He furrowed his forehead, causing little lines to emerge, giving a hint of how he might appear in later years.

"Gabe doesn't think we need a tutor," Jamie burst out. "He says that we read more than any children he's ever met."

Callie looked at him critically. "I understand you like this Gabe. But are you sure you want to take your education advice from the gardener?"

Julia suppressed a giggle by covering her mouth.

"The gardener! He works for our father, and he's the best friend I have," Jamie answered in a matter-of-fact voice, as though Callie should already know this.

Julia narrowed her eyes at her younger brother as he made a move to leave the closet. "I wouldn't let Mama hear you say that," she heeded.

Now, fully intrigued, Callie hoped the children would continue divulging their family secrets. There was certainly tension in this exchange — one of them claimed that Gabe was his closest friend, while the other did not. Perhaps Jamie just looked up to the young man who worked for his father and wished they could be friends.

"Does Gabe work on the property often?" Callie asked as Julia led her from her father's closet and down the hall, back toward the front of the house. She knew it was risky to ask something of this nature when Annie was just down the hall, but if she hadn't, the question would have burned in her throat the entire afternoon.

The Burke children exchanged a look.

"Sometimes," Jamie said hastily.

Standing before the door to the children's study, Callie knew that now was not the time nor the place to press them with further questions on this subject. But it only meant she'd file it away for later. Her interest in the Burke family and the people who worked for them grew by the minute.

Chapter 7

THEY STEPPED INTO the study, where two wooden desks faced a spacious window. Callie saw a large map of the seven continents against the back wall, and near it, a table with a basket of sharpened pencils, erasers, crayons, and beside that, a tray of writing paper.

"Has this room always been here for you?" she asked, setting down the things she'd brought with her on the windowsill.

Julia nodded. "Yes, but we haven't used it much until now."

Callie cleared her throat. "Why don't you grab a pencil and a piece of paper? Jamie, you can wipe that look of dismay off your face. In a moment I'm going to have you both write down a few questions you might have about the Pacific Northwest."

She caught Julia wrinkling her nose at the implication that there'd be any questions at all. She leaned over the eleven-year-old girl's desk and summoned a smile. "Trust me on this, you're going to enjoy discovering more than you knew before."

Before long, the Burke children completed their several questions. While Julia took to the assignment, Jamie's gaze drifted toward the open window—no matter that the sky was dull and gray, and the trees scattered raindrops from the wind's sway. Callie observed him but said nothing.

"I already know what Jamie will write," Julia said, glancing up. "He's going to want to know about the mines and all the men that have come here from different places."

Jamie nodded, offered an impish expression that made his

dark eyes crinkle. He held up his list, hastily scrawled. Callie stepped closer, extracted it from his hands. His sister's read on him was accurate. On the page, he'd written:

1. *What happened during the first strike in Roslyn's mines?*

2. *What was life like for the black miners who came to live here?*

Callie hadn't expected them to narrow in on a little discussed element of the town's history. Her thoughts pulled her to his emphasis on Gabe, their father's young worker, and she wondered if the young man helped plant the seeds to this interest Jamie now had. Did Gabe have roots here, and if he did, how was it that she'd never seen him or his family before? But instead of mentioning his keen observations, Callie handed the boy's paper back and said, "One more question please."

Jamie chewed on his eraser at the end of his pencil. Callie shook her head at this absentminded gesture, and he removed the soggy eraser from his mouth. He shrugged. "Not sure I have another question. Those things . . . they're what I'm most interested in." He blinked. "S'pose I'd like to know where most of the black miners have gone. Cause there sure aren't as many left in Roslyn anymore."

Callie nodded as he picked up his pencil and turned her attention to Julia, who sat with her hands folded on top of her desk. When she gave the girl a nod, Julia studied her list and looked up at her tutor, "I'm more interested in fairy tales than history. But if I had to decide, I'd say it would be interesting to find out more about the town's first stores and social clubs. It's not nearly as engaging here, as it is in Seattle."

Callie bit down her smile at the girl's summation of the Upper County.

"You've both given me a lot to consider, and I think it will be enjoyable, exploring our town's origins," Callie said, collecting both their lists and folding them in half. "There's a lot I can tell you about Roslyn, since I've lived here all my life. I can tell you about the restaurants, the owners of the Roslyn Bakery or Carek's Meat Company. But what I can't tell you as much about is the first strike Roslyn ever had."

"I think the strike is the most interesting," Jamie interrupted. "Did you know this house used to be a boarding house for the first black miners?"

Julia threw him a disapproving look which shut him down. Callie didn't know her reason for doing so, but decided she would encourage his interest, not diminish it.

"If that's what you're interested in, we're in luck. I know a few of the grown children of the first black miners. We could ask them questions about what it was like to migrate to the west and face the surprise of an angry mob." Callie's mind turned automatically to the Jacobsons since she'd heard hints of their family's history over the passing years.

As the clock struck five, Callie had the Burke children set down their pencils.

"My stomach's rumbling," Jamie said suddenly. "Why don't we go get a snack?"

Callie glanced at her bruised apple sitting near the window-sill and felt sudden pangs of hunger. She'd grown so used to them. "What would you like to eat?"

Julia pressed down on her pencil to make it stay. "Let's go to the kitchen," she said.

It was near impossible for Callie not to think of her family back home and what they'd be eating for supper. They would probably split small potatoes, their only embellishments butter and salt. If they were lucky, they'd have a side of greens from the garden, but she doubted there'd be any meat.

Callie caught Jamie staring at her apple with fascination. "Why did you bring that?" he asked, completely unaware that this piece of fruit was all she had for the afternoon.

"In case I got hungry," Callie said, taking a large bite as they reached the bright, beautifully lit kitchen. The wooden floors were polished to a shine. The cabinet space, like everything else in this house, abounded, and the counter tops sparkled, not a crumb in sight. Their icebox was twice the size of the Rushton's and appeared brand new.

Jamie opened up the spacious cupboards, and sure enough, there was plenty to choose from. The shelves were stocked with canned goods, bags of rice, packaged soups. There were also boxes of crackers and packages of tea cookies, untouched. Callie pressed a hand to her stomach, remembering the abundance before times got hard.

As Jamie pulled out fresh bread from the bread box and a full jar of huckleberry jam from the icebox, Callie wondered how she might get him to cut a slice for her without revealing the extent of her hunger. The apple had done little to satiate her. Were it not for her sticky fingers, she would have doubted its existence.

"You should try this jam," Jamie said, offering a slab of bread to Callie before she could say anything.

"Oh, I shouldn't," Callie said, although her grumbling stomach suggested otherwise. How would it appear to the Burkes were they to hear that their tutor was taking her meals in their home without permission?

"Go right ahead," Annie said as she made her way into the kitchen. She tossed her cleaning bottles beneath the sink and washed her hands before opening up their cupboards to see what she could find for herself as well. "A little late for a snack, but we probably won't eat until about seven tonight." Then seeing that Callie didn't believe her, she smiled insistently. "Their kitchen is your kitchen. It's one of the benefits of working for the Burkes."

The children didn't disagree with their housemaid, but then they barely noted her arrival to the kitchen in the first place. It became as plain as the apron that swung around Annie's waist that the children were disinterested in her and, in turn, she with them.

Once the last of the crumbs were swept off the counter tops, Callie redirected the children to the study and quickly found a deck of cards for them to play with near the basket of supplies at the back of the room. They could tackle history next time. While Julia passed out cards, Callie glanced out the window of the study and let her gaze drift across the front lawn.

The afternoon's rain had finally fled. Still, beads of water glistened on the leaves of trees. But shifts in the weather were not what really interested her. From her window in the study, her gaze drifted down to a small angel statue that she hadn't noticed until now. The angel overlooked the last flowers of summer and was beautiful in form and face, although her eyes were vacant as any carved in stone must be.

Whether it was the glint of sun after the rain, Callie didn't know, but she suddenly noticed lettering below the statue's foot. It was indecipherable from where she stood, on the inside looking out. The stone angel was a memorial; that much she surmised. She noticed both children had stopped shuffling their cards and were watching her.

"Tell me about the statue," Callie said aloud, her curiosity getting the better of her. "I just noticed the lettering below it."

When she turned around, she saw Julia was searching for words. But it was Jamie who first spoke. "It's for the colored miners. We're close to the No. 3 mine, and since this house used to be where they lived, Father wanted to acknowledge it."

Callie's interest piqued at Burke's thoughtful gesture. All the same, she didn't understand why Edward Burke felt so inclined to pay tribute to people he'd never met, people whose lives undoubtedly involved grit and determination unlike any he'd ever encountered.

Chapter 8

JUST AS THE clock chimed 5:30, Callie glanced out of the window of the study and saw Mrs. Burke drive up in her sleek sedan. How peculiar it was to see a woman driving, and yet Mrs. Burke seemed undaunted at the task. Although the mistress of the house turned off the motor right away, her hands rested on the wheel as if she were deciding whether to come in.

"Quick," Julia said, abandoning her unspent cards. "Let's go outside and see if she needs help bringing anything in. She told me she was picking up some fruit from the Winslow's farm this afternoon."

From where she stood at the window in the children's study, Callie could see Annie walk outside, then wait at the driver's door. She greeted Margaret with an uncharacteristic wave, and soon enough, Margaret emerged from the vehicle with a black umbrella in hand. Moments later, Julia and Jamie charged in front of the housemaid to retrieve the crates of fruit they were expecting from the back seats of their mother's car.

Entranced with the goings-on outside the window, Callie shifted the children's assignments back and forth in her hands until she felt the edge of one of the papers nick her finger. She drew her finger to her mouth to still the drop of blood, and at that moment, both women turned to see her peering out the window at them. Her face flushed, but Callie offered the best recovery she could and raised her hand in a friendly wave.

Instead of returning the gesture, the women resumed their conversation and headed toward the front steps on the heels of the children, crates of apples filling their arms.

Callie moved forward to greet Mrs. Burke as she entered the house. Annie waited behind her. Determination knit her brow in place of the smile she'd seen several minutes ago.

"How did they do?" Mrs. Burke asked, feigning interest. Once Julia returned to her mother's side, Mrs. Burke peered down at her daughter and straightened the ribbon in her hair.

"Wonderfully," Callie said, without hesitation. "Your children are . . . quite bright." She didn't want to tell Mrs. Burke that they knew almost as much American history as she did.

Mrs. Burke merely nodded. "Wednesday afternoon, then. You are free to leave now."

Callie nodded. She sought eye contact with Julia, who chose not to look at her new tutor at all now that her mother had returned.

"Thank you for coming," Mrs. Burke murmured, turning to her daughter, who smiled sweetly once she had her mother's attention. Jamie had already fled into the deeper recesses of the house.

I'll have to watch out for this one, Callie noted. Although Julia's brother might be the child cited for his mischievous wiles, there was a wildfire that crackled in the young girl's eyes.

"Thank you for having me," Callie said hastily. "I'll see you Wednesday." Mrs. Burke nodded, expressionless.

As she turned toward the door, she brushed her hands over the worn black purse on her arm. Who was she fooling? Her dark blue dress had a tattered hem, and her shoes were worn. This family knew that she, like most of the Upper County, was swimming upstream just trying to make ends meet.

Callie quietly opened the front door and let herself out. She walked down the pathway at the center of the manicured grass, humming to herself, a bit of "How Deep is the Ocean," one of her recent favorites from the radio. She caught snatches of it sometimes at Mrs. Starek's Seamstress Shop.

As she lifted the gate's lever, Callie heard the door open behind her. She saw to her surprise, Jamie, the same boy who had hidden in the closet when she'd first arrived. *How swiftly he's changed his mind about me,* Callie thought, letting her fingers rest on the cold, metallic gate. Callie waited for him to reach her, wondering what it was he wanted to say.

"If I tell you about her," he said, motioning toward the stone statue with a brief nod of his head, "will you promise not to say anything to them?" He looked in direction of the house.

"Look, Jamie," Callie said, dropping her voice a few octaves in case there were eavesdropping trees surrounding them. "I don't want you to do anything to get yourself in trouble. Understand? The statue is a beautiful work of art. That's the only reason I was interested in it."

"That's not true," Jamie said, as though reading her intrigue with his family. He reached into his left pocket, carefully placing an envelope in her hand. "Here's something that will tell you more about that statue."

Callie shook her head, any natural curiosity dulled by her need to maintain a professional relationship with the Burkes. She started to hand the envelope back, treating it as a hot potato, when the front door opened suddenly. Such instantaneous fear flickered in Jamie's eyes when he glanced at the envelope that Callie made a swift decision to slip it into her purse. She then raised her head.

Annie stood on the patio. Her eyes cast across the front lawn, not stopping until they fell upon her and Jamie. The flowers around her rollicked, catching tailwinds, but she paid no heed to their pink, purple, and golden beauty.

"Bye, Miss Callie," Jamie whispered hoarsely before turning back to the front porch. "See you next time."

Though Callie couldn't hear just what Annie was telling him as she caught him by the sleeve, she watched his expression grow somber. He didn't argue with the maid, but found a way to extract himself from her draconian grip and entered the house. Although a strand of the sun glinted off the porch, it wasn't difficult for Callie to mistake the cold press of Annie's eyes on her once she was done speaking to the boy.

Since the tension felt thick as a winter fog, she thought she'd ask her a friendly question, anything to lessen the intensity Annie cast her way.

"I imagine you've traveled a fair amount, living with the Burkes. How do you like the Upper County?" She immediately felt awkward, but there was no taking the question back. She felt her toes curl in her shoes.

Annie immediately crossed her arms over her chest, and her dusky eyes flashed. "I'd like it more if there wasn't so much coal dust, but that's unlikely to change." She glanced to her right and left, as if assessing whether they were being listened to, but only the waving trees stood in attendance. "I've been with my brother's family for a long time," she said tightly, as if pressing down a secret.

Callie tried to conceal the surprise at this blood connection Annie revealed. There was an unmistakable likeness to their expressions, once pointed out. And a similar shade of darkness in their eyes. But she couldn't place the dissatisfaction spread across Annie's face. Or fathom the reason for it. There were countless women in Kittitas County who would love to stand in her brown oxfords, understated though they were.

Annie made her way down the front steps and the pathway to have more of a word with her. In her wariness, Callie all but forgot about the envelope Jamie had handed her, its contents still unknown to her as it rested in her purse.

"I'm well aware that people here talk about my brother's family . . . and I happen to be protective of them . . . very much so. While you're here, I ask that you simply tutor the children and go on your way without . . . without nosing around. Do you understand?"

Callie nodded. "Believe me," she said, without divulging her mounting fascination with her new employers. "The reason I'm here is so that I can help put food on my family's table. My father injured his leg in a mining accident, and our funds are dwindling. As soon as I was made aware of the opportunity—"

Annie put up her hand. Clearly, she'd heard all she wanted to. "Good, then. You understand the importance of protecting family."

Callie nodded again, starting to wonder what secrets Annie might be keeping for her brother's family.

"I'll see you on Wednesday," Callie told Annie, facing her while stepping backward and gently unlocking the gate. "It was nice to see you again." She summoned a smile, perhaps in hopes that both of them would believe those words.

When she reached the bottom of the hill, Callie remembered the envelope Jamie had given her. She could scarcely believe she'd made that instant decision to cover for him. The desperation in his eyes made her curious to know its contents now.

Careful to hide herself beneath the overarching pines, she grasped at the envelope greedily. The top of the envelope was open and she shook out the contents. Into the palm of her hand, a grainy photograph fell.

She squinted into the dark, beguiling eyes of a woman who appeared in her late thirties. Her lips were full and enviable, her skin tone hinted at nutmeg. Her hair was set in waves, and she wore a dreamy, silken dress befitting a socialite. She had never seen its likeness in these parts.

"Beautiful," she said aloud, though none could hear her.

The photographer, whoever he might be, had captured not only her beauty, but the strength of her presence. Her glimmering dark eyes suggested nights of big bands, swimming pool parties, and refilled glasses of champagne. And while the woman didn't smile at the camera, the expression she wore beckoned, invited attention.

"Who are you?" Callie whispered. She turned the picture over and read the faint cursive writing. *1925, Liliana.*

Why would a nine-year-old boy like Jamie Burke share her image with his brand-new tutor? Where had he found this photograph in the first place? And what connection could she possibly share with the black miners given tribute through Burke's small memorial?

"Liliana," Callie said aloud, not knowing the answer to any of the questions. "I wonder where you are and what's brought your picture to a coal-mining town like ours."

✧ ✧ ✧

Sitting cross-legged on her bed that night, Callie drew a finger to the picture, feeling that if she were to memorize the woman's features, she'd learn more about who she was to the Burkes. This Liliana appeared to be a city girl, one belonging to the likes of Chicago or Boston or New York. There was an undeniable sophistication to her. Not much would catch her eye on this side of the mountains. In that way, she seemed strangely similar to Margaret Burke. But Callie knew better than to think the two women had much in common. No matter how refined Liliana's tastes were, she wouldn't have the same privileges as Mrs. Burke. Even if some fine establishments did invite her in, there were still some that would close their doors to her because of her color.

Callie's door suddenly burst open, though she'd deliberately secured it. She was about to yell at one of her younger brothers when she saw Lucy standing before her instead. Callie hit her back on the wall as she hurriedly slipped the picture in its envelope.

"You scared me half to death, Lucy!" Callie exclaimed, rising from her bed and smoothing down the front of her dress. "I could have been changing."

Lucy closed the door calmly and gave a slight shrug. "And if you were? It's nothing I haven't seen before," she said. Her blond hair peaked out of an angled beret. She wore a deep purple cardigan, a white blouse, and a fitted gray skirt, always managing to incorporate pops of color in her wardrobe no matter the dwindling of her funds. "What do you have there?" Lucy asked her, nodding toward the envelope still clasped in Callie's hands.

Callie shook her head, knowing it was impossible to keep a secret from her best friend. "I haven't quite figured it out," Callie said, opening the envelope and letting the image of Liliana fall into her open palms. She saw her friend's eyes widen in fascination, and felt no surprise as Lucy took the photograph from her and dropped it in her own hands for analysis. "Jamie Burke gave it to me after I asked about the family's statue in the front yard. It's this monument to the colored miners. I mean, I know the Burkes live on property . . . where the first black miners came to live, but I don't know what their interest is in colored folk beyond that. And I don't know who this woman is, this Liliana."

"Curious," Lucy said, squinting down at the image, as if trying to place her. "She's stunning, I'll tell you that. But one would wonder what a young boy like Jamie Burke would be doing with her picture. Think she's related to any of the black miners that came here?" The green sparks in Lucy's hazel eyes outshone the brown.

Callie shook her head, dumbfounded.

Lucy dropped the fragile photograph back in Callie's hands and shrugged. "She must be related to one of those miners if that boy told you she had something to do with the memorial." She licked her lips. "It shouldn't come as too much of a surprise, really. A lot of the black miners didn't stay here. They found better work across the state, migrated to Seattle and Spokane. And who can blame them, really? How inspiring is it to stay in the pit when you could be above ground? Still doesn't explain how the Burkes got her photo, but darling, you have plenty of time to figure that out. Didn't you say today was your first day working there?"

Chapter 9

JUNE 1889

D AVID THOUGHT HE heard footsteps on the floorboards as he left the house, but couldn't be certain. He was the only one in the house on the early morning shift, so he'd thought little of it—only that someone needed to use the outhouse. He walked the short jaunt to the mine with his head down, hands shoved in his pockets, and his thoughts consumed with the wife and daughter he was soon to see.

David arrived at the mine and had yet to fasten his head-lamp when he heard someone's heavy breath. He turned to see Gerald, smiling at him with tired eyes. He reached out and took the headlamp from his hands before David knew what was happening. "I've already talked to the boss, brother. You ain't going down the pit today. Not on the day your wife and little girl come."

At this act of benevolence David shook his head, searching for words. "You didn't have to do that, man. Georgina and Lily, their train won't get here 'til about five o'clock tonight."

"That don't matter to me," Gerald said, placing the headlamp on his own head and adjusting the straps. "I know you wanted to get more done on that little place of yours before your girls arrived, and I thought it was the least I could do, take one shift for you when you've done it for me . . . and other guys."

David clapped Gerald on the shoulder, seeing his friend wouldn't be swayed. He let out his breath and said into his cupped hands, "It's barely more than a shanty, but at least it's

57

furnished. At least it's a place we can start. . . . Thank you for giving me the day."

Gerald set a firm hand on his friend's shoulder and said, "Think nothing of it, brother. I'm happy to cover for you. You think of us all and our families and now . . ." His eyes watered. "It's an honor to do something for you."

With a quick nod of his head, Gerald turned toward the worksite. He left David with his hands deep in his pockets, marveling at his kindness.

✧ ✧ ✧

David adjusted a curtain rod over the front window, his mind still steeped in thoughts of the reunion with his wife and daughter, but something told him to still his hands. He set his hammer on the cold, uncarpeted floor, and brushed his hands on the thighs of his pants. And he waited, and he listened. Hearing nothing, he told himself to take a deep breath. His heart took an unnatural drum roll in his chest, and he shook his head, certain that the anxiousness he now felt had everything to do with Georgina and Lily's impending arrival. What if Georgina decided not to come? He grimaced at his own absurdity. Georgina was unwavering and honest to a fault. She hadn't wanted him to board the train with the other black miners at Mr. Simonson's offer, but now that he was here, as her last letters to him expressed, she wasn't willing to live apart. He picked the hammer back up, bolted the frame against the wall, took the spare curtain Bella had given him up in his hands. *Please keep my girls safe*, he prayed. *Let them arrive to Roslyn in perfect health and with your hand upon them.*

Having spoken these words, though, he still felt uneasy and stepped down from the back of the worn-in blue sofa he'd been standing on. It wasn't his girls he ought to be worried about. His mind shifted. *Gerald.*

He threw the door open, careless to how it protested on its hinges. He didn't make time to close it. He needed to get to the mine. The siren pierced the mid-morning air just as he broke into a run. When he reached the entrance, his eyes took in the wild scene before him. Smoke billowed from the pit and the miners who'd made it out buried their faces in their sleeves, coughs deep, their eyes scrunched up from the dust.

David moved forward, past the shouts and strangled cries. He sought the safety crew and saw with fixed attention the stretcher pointed in the direction of the mine, the reluctant men who weren't able to make it down. Willard put a hand on his shoulder and Frank Jacobson said no one was going down yet. It was a suicide mission to even try, when the cave-in might not be finished. David pushed his way past his comrades. Though members of the safety crew tried to ward him off, he protested.

"I've had all the training you have!"

The men stood silent and unconvinced.

"I'll take the risk if I have the chance of helping even one man up. I'm going down," he said, turning back to Frank. "Gerald took my shift this morning, and I gotta get him out. Can't live with myself if I don't." He set foot in the cart. Such conviction swept over his features that he left Frank with little choice but to lower him down.

"You don't have to do this," Frank said, his eyes crazed. "We don't . . . none of us know what it looks like down there. There's at least three men down there. Gerald, he'd be a hard one to save. He's bigger than you. You know that, right?"

"Don't matter to me," David said, his dark eyes like steel. "Can't live with myself if he's trapped or injured and I didn't at least try to get him out. I gotta try to save him." His eyes stung. "I should be the one down that pit right now. Not him." He pushed himself forward in one of the cars, looked at Frank with all the intensity in the world. "Please let me do this. I'll come back up in five minutes, Frank. That's all the time I'll give it."

Still hesitant, but following the desperate request of his friend, Frank agreed to lower him down. "You know it takes that amount of time to get you down there, and if anything happens . . . "

"If anything happens, it's not your fault," David said pressing his eyes to his fellow miner's. "It's not your fault. This is God's business now. You hear?"

Frank nodded, as if willing himself to believe his friend's words. "Lord be with you."

He had his headlamp, a pocketknife, and a white sheet he'd snatched from the medical supply. As he descended, there was a metallic taste in his mouth, but he didn't regret his decision. He covered his fear with the words of the psalm his mama had whispered to him when he was a boy, barely older than his Lily:

. . . *In whose hand are the depths of the earth, the peaks of the mountains are His also.*

These words, he uttered again and again. They centered him, steadied him, kept his trepidation secondary to the work ahead.

He felt a hand clasp him at the shoulder soon after tunneling down. The miner had to ease his grasp in order to cough. It was then that David turned to him and saw the deep gash on the man's hand. David recognized right away the miner's injuries weren't fatal. He was covered with dust and dirt but was otherwise unscathed.

"Please," the man said, "The other two, I couldn't save them." His eyes pooled with tears. "One of them, he's my brother."

David assisted the miner—he thought his name was Lenny—closer to the entrance, though there was resistance in the man's limbs.

"The entire wall crumbled, and one of them isn't moving. The other is trapped, and I couldn't . . . lift him out."

He rubbed his eyes with the heels of his hands.

"I'm gonna call up and have one of the safety crew help you up now. I'll be up in a few minutes," David said, knowing that his agility and strength was greater than most. "I promise you that. I won't try to salvage . . . what isn't possible." He'd been around enough explosions to know that a man who wasn't moving might have passed out. That a man who was pinned beneath a wall might be able to separate from the rock. He wouldn't let the accident itself claim the finality it so wanted.

After giving Lenny a reassuring nod, David turned toward the dark. He edged further into the abyss, a desperate prayer on his lips. He'd been able to help at least one man arrive to safety. Now if he could only help the one he came here to rescue.

✧ ✧ ✧

Lily stepped from the train ahead of her mother, taking in the panoramic view of her new home — mountainous terrain decorated with the greenest trees and a vibrant show of purple wildflowers. She found herself wrinkling her nose, the little quirk that signaled she was overcome with emotion. Her daddy had pointed it out more than once, told her she had a cute little button nose. She'd shrugged at his remark, wanting to tell him it was better than fielding off tears of happiness, sadness, or what have you. She searched for his kind brown eyes, his chestnut skin so close to her own, his wide, endearing smile. Surely he'd be here at the train depot, awaiting the arrival of her and her mama. The family had never spent this long apart. Her mother clutched her hand so tightly that she could feel fingernails stab through her red mittens. She wished she was strong enough to help her mother with the luggage, but didn't want to break her attention from the platform where her daddy said he'd be waiting for her.

She couldn't wait to run into his strong arms and catch the musk and wood smoke of his jacket. For many months she'd buried her face in the collar of a shirt he'd left behind, unwashed, until her mother had plied it from her hands and said, "Darling, if you miss your daddy so much, why don't we write him another letter?"

Her mother didn't know at this very moment that she'd carried his letters — the lot of them — folded in the right pocket of her coat. Along with the several lilies he'd pressed and sent with them. The thought of seeing him again was making her eyes sting, not just causing her nose to wrinkle.

Though she'd fully expected him to be here ahead of time and was taken aback when she felt passengers' coats brush against her as they moved toward their loved ones, she had no inkling of what would come next. Didn't imagine for one moment that the woman who came forward, a Mrs. Johnson, might be there to give them shattering news. Or that when her mother sank to the cold platform on her knees and bloodied them, she was doing so because her father wouldn't be coming for them after all. She felt for her daddy's letters again, held them tightly, not realizing she was trying to hold on to something forever taken from her.

Chapter 10
1932

Gabe trudged up the stairs of the Burke's residence late Tuesday night after an exhausting, rain-soaked day at the Colman Dock in Seattle. His eyes struggled to adjust from the lacerating wind near the water, and his throat still felt hoarse from giving directives to other workers above the sounds of the elements. He could have taken lodging in downtown Seattle at a hotel he and Mr. Burke frequented when they were bound up in business dealings, but he'd craved the comfort and familiarity of his own bed. He'd spent several hours behind the wheel of his truck to reach the house at a late hour.

Just as he'd predicted, the Burke residence was still and calm at his arrival. He parked the truck near the two other vehicles to the right of the house. Grabbing his jacket and his bag, he walked toward the front patio. He was grateful that someone had left the lamp on for him, its honey glow emanating from a corner in the sitting room. He hadn't expected anyone to still be awake at this hour.

Gabe saw a single moth rise to the lamp's glow, still awed at the number of insects out here in the wooded brush. He rested a hand to the doorknob, found it was unlocked, and set foot inside. If anyone sat up in the sitting room, he suspected it was Margaret Burke. Annie often retired to her room soon after the dinner dishes were washed, preferring the blare of her radio over the voices of the people in the house. It was

Margaret, but she didn't rise to greet him. He would have been surprised if she had. Once he'd removed his work boots, he felt the last weight of the day fall from his being. He moved lightly as he paced up the staircase, caught the scent of candles edged against the drafty walls. No matter how many fires he helped start down in the grate, the high ceilings had their way of inviting coldness in.

Gabe smiled at the thought of throwing himself under a warm blanket, but his lightheartedness was cut short. Soon after he turned on the lamp in his room, he could tell that someone else had been here. His top drawer, the one containing his most prized possessions, was noticeably ajar. After rifling through it, he could see that he was missing something in particular.

How could someone invade his personal space? Though his mind entertained several possible culprits, he rushed down the stairs to talk to the one still awake in the sitting room. He no longer cared what unholy hour it was. He needed the comfort of leaving for a few days and knowing that his belongings would remain untouched.

"I just need to ask you a question," he'd said, his heartbeat audible as he stepped in the room to see Margaret. A look of surprise, followed by concern, swept over her features. She pressed a finger to her place in a gilt-edged book, drew her burgundy robe closer to her frame, and cast her serious blue eyes on him.

He rolled up his shirt sleeves, so he could cool down, and he told himself to watch the edge that might creep into his tone. "Do you know where my picture of Liliana is?"

"Do I know anything about what? A picture of Liliana?" Margaret asked, as if taken aback by the question.

"You heard me," Gabe said impatiently. "Do you know who took my only picture of her? And what someone was doing in my room in the first place?"

"No," Margaret answered coldly, "what would anyone want with your mother's photograph?"

"To dispose of it," Gabe continued, unperturbed. "You've

made it clear you don't want my mother's name spoken in this house."

"That's true," Margaret said. "But I don't set foot in your bedroom, Gabe. You should know that."

He swallowed. "I do know that, but I haven't been here, and I thought I'd ask someone who might know what's gone on since I left."

Margaret's expression hinted at a sudden contemplation. "Why don't you try asking Jamie? I've caught him hiding in your room on several occasions. He's borrowed your baseball bat, he's tampered with your record player. Who's to say he hasn't—but be kind to him, please."

Before she was finished speaking, Gabe turned his back to her. "I am every time, Margaret."

He didn't know why he hadn't approached the little daredevil first. Perhaps it was because he wanted Jamie's mother to do something about it. There was more than one person in this house he didn't trust.

"You don't have to confront him right now," Margaret called after him. "I'd rather you wait till the morning."

Gabe drew a hand to his close-cropped hair and turned to face her briefly. "I'll talk with him now. He's probably still awake, listening to this whole exchange." He sighed deeply, willing his heart to stop its drumming.

The words *I'm sorry* rested on the tip of his tongue, but he couldn't open his mouth to say them. He couldn't find it in himself to tread toward an actual apology to Edward's wife. Not after the way she disregarded and dismissed him, so often edging past him without so much as a hello.

✦ ✦ ✦

Jamie wasn't asleep when Gabe opened his bedroom door and flicked on the lamp near the boy's bedside table. His covers were a tangled mess, looking as though he'd been tossing and turning 'mid restless dreams about monsters. The boy immediately sprung up with his comforter drawn over his shoulders like a cape. As if seeing the intensity in Gabe's eyes he said, "I'll get it back from her, I promise."

"Her?" Gabe asked incredulously. He feared that his favorite possession might be in someone's hands within this household, but he hadn't figured that it had reached someone he didn't even know. "What are you talking about? Who did you give it to, James?"

Gabe seldom ever called him James. He saw the formality made the boy bristle. "My . . . my new tutor kept looking out the window at the statue out front, and I told her . . . told her about the inscription. I thought she was nice . . . and pretty, and I wanted to show her what was behind it all."

At this, Gabe released a deep sigh and dropped onto the edge of Jamie's bed, leaden as one of the dumbbells he kept in his room. This was worse than he thought. What would he have to do to get it back now? He thought of the bright-eyed young woman he'd recently met and couldn't imagine seeking her out to ask that she return something that rightly belonged to him.

"Listen to me, Jamie," Gabe said, deliberately softening his tone. From experience, he'd learned that he wouldn't make any strides with the young boy if he conveyed anger. "She's here to tutor you, not to learn everything about the past."

Jamie shook his head, making strands of his dark hair sweep over his eyes. "Well, actually, we are learning about Roslyn's past since Julia and I . . . we already know so much of American history."

Gabe shook his head firmly. "Learn about Roslyn then, but don't divulge so much of my history."

Jamie traced over the baseball pattern etched into the section of comforter near his fingertips and nodded, intuitive to grasp Gabe's meaning without having to ask further questions of him.

"What did you tell her about Liliana?" Gabe asked, after reminding himself he wouldn't raise his voice, regardless of the answer. Still, he dreaded the young boy's response.

"Nothing," Jamie said, desperation coating the word. "I told her not to show it to anyone. I asked her to return it to me when she comes back here on Wednesday."

"What did she say?" Gabe inquired, balling his hands, willing his aggression to simmer so Jamie would keep talking to him.

"She said she'd return it to me," Jamie said, sounding hopeful, "and I think she will."

"Don't you know what could happen with that picture in the wrong hands?" Gabe suspected his face had frustration written across it. "I know full well that the past catches up with you, no matter where you go. But I don't want him to suffer needlessly about things that ought to stay in this family."

"I'll get it back from Miss Callie on Wednesday. I promise you I will," Jamie said soberly, blankets cocooned around him reminding Gabe just how young he still was.

When he finally found his voice, Gabe said, "Sleep well, kid." Then he turned off the light and headed for the darkened hallway, back to his room where he'd hoped to find nothing more than sleep and rest.

Chapter 11

WALKING DOWN PENNSYLVANIA AVENUE, Callie noted the uncharacteristic busyness around all the places of commerce: The Brick, Cascade Telephone Company, The Cigar Shop, the Roslyn Cafe down toward the end of the street. There were a lot of people milling around for a Wednesday morning.

It didn't take her so very long to see Ruthie Sloane. The small black woman bent over her bucket, washing the front window at Cascade Telephone. As if aware that Callie wanted to speak with her, Ruthie paused her soaped-up rag and raised her eyebrows. Callie felt a familiar flutter in her stomach, wondering if she might just ask her about the photograph tucked away in her purse. If this Liliana had ever lived in the region, chances were high that Ruthie would have known her. She'd lived in the Upper County her entire life, the daughter of Mr. Lenny Rollins, one of the first black miners to arrive to the state. But Callie shook her head at the wayward thought. Hadn't Annie spoken to her yesterday about keeping confidence? So instead of pausing to question her, Callie just smiled and kept walking to the seamstress shop.

Bess Starek stood near the front window. The short, red-haired seamstress rushed toward her soon as she opened the door. "Oh good. I didn't want to close up shop, but I'm running out of chalk for my measurements. Would you mind running over to the Company Store to pick some up for me?"

Bess wandered over to the till and clicked it open so she could pour the loose coins into Callie's outstretched hands. "This should be enough," she said hopefully. "Chalk doesn't cost so much. One of the only things that doesn't have a hefty price tag nowadays."

Callie nodded her understanding and said, "I'll be back shortly." She turned toward the door.

In her hurry to make it down the street, Callie remembered that she'd left her handbag near the register. On any other day she wouldn't have thought twice, but she felt more protective of it with the photograph inside. She remembered that while Bess might have inclinations toward investigating other people's laundry, she wouldn't likely sift through her personal items. Still, over the last few years, the three seamstresses—Bess, Callie, and her mother—had uncovered some telling items from folk in this town: everything from poker chips to hastily scrawled telephone numbers to packaged rubbers. Every once in a while, Bess would toss her discoveries back into the pockets they'd come from and close her eyes. "I didn't need to know that," she'd say.

As she let herself inside the Company Store, she pushed her way toward the front counter so she could speak with one of the clerks. Mr. Merrick, the lead grocer, and also Maura's father, was deep in conversation with a young man and she'd have to wait.

Though the young man's back was turned toward her most of the time, she took increased notice of him as she walked toward the counter. He was undeniably strong, dressed in a pressed white shirt and trousers untouched by dust. His skin was the color of coffee with cream poured in, and unable to take her eyes from his profile, she took note of his features—his strong jaw, his perfect nose, his full lips. It was the young man from the Burke's house. She felt color rise to her cheeks.

Mr. Merrick nodded briefly upon seeing her but didn't stop his dealings with Gabe to ask her if he could help her find anything. He probably knew that whatever purchase she was about to make wouldn't amount to more than the price of a mop. Callie glanced over at the exchange taking place at the counter. Gabe tapped a pen on a product brochure, wanting to point out several features, but Mr. Merrick was already reaching into the box to see for himself.

"Those are the newest model," Gabe said, resigned. "They provide greater safety than the carbide lamps they've been using. I thought you'd like to see one. "

Mr. Merrick smoothed the ends of his mustache as he waited for the young man to empty more contents from his box onto the counter. The store clerk scanned the invoice laid out for him and looked up at the fellow nervously. "They're not getting any cheaper, are they?" He picked up one of the new electric headlamps. "Are you sure they're the model we signed for?" He thumbed the bracket at the front of the helmet, studied it with eyebrows narrowed, all his focus set upon it.

The young man lifted another of the headlamps and looked at it critically. He bent over the counter and drew a finger to the exact order on the page. "Yes, these are the new headlamps the mining company called for. They're less cumbersome than the carbide lamp, and they eliminate the need for an open flame."

Mr. Merrick touched the ends of his mustache again, mulling over the headlamps as if he were the one making the final decision and not Burke, or the mining company. "I'll take them," he said at last. "I would still like you to find a lamp that meets safety demands at a more agreeable price."

Callie looked at the sides of the boxes with their unmistakable emblem, a lily. The mark of Burke Enterprises. Just as she sensed she ought to feign interest in a product on their shelves, Mr. Burke's employee turned around. Callie bent down to pick up the first item her hands could find—a package of hardtack, anything to make her look busy. He hadn't turned back to the counter, so she glanced up to meet his eyes, knowing that it was unnatural to look at plain old hardtack for long. There was such unassuming kindness in his warm gaze; he didn't have to speak for her to see it. For another moment she met his eyes, and he gave her a steady smile. Just then the packet of hardtack slipped from her hands, and the wax paper packaging broke open, launching wafers across the floor. She stammered, staring at the mess she'd made on the ground.

"Oh, let me help you with that," he said, before Callie could tell him he didn't need to.

"I'm sorry," she said, feeling herself flush. "I'll pay for them," she looked up at Mr. Merrick, who was tapping his fingers nervously behind the counter. He was still studying the price sheet given to him by Mr. Burke's stockman. Gabe found a broom at the side of the counter and started sweeping the crumbs into a dustpan.

"I thought that you . . . .The other day when you were chopping wood . . ." she stammered.

"Thought what?" he asked, narrowing his eyes slightly before easing up. "I was the family's handyman? I can see how you'd think that, but no. I work for Burke Enterprises. I help with occasional upkeep on the grounds, but I'm a stockman for the company. The main stockman."

"The children said your name is . . . Gabe" The conversation she'd had with the children washed over her, especially Jamie Burke's description of his closest friend.

"Gabe Ward. Wonderful kids, aren't they?" His tone sounded forced. What was it about her starting with the Burkes that gave him pause, if anything? Perhaps he felt uncertain as to how to proceed in conversation with her, a white woman, in the presence of others.

Callie nodded at his question, although she didn't know if they were wonderful children or not. From what she could tell, Julia had a knack for positioning herself as the favorite, and Jamie was a wild card who used manipulation to get what he wanted."Jamie said you were his closest friend," Callie said, offering a small laugh at the absurdity of it, "so that must mean he likes you a lot."

Mr. Merrick cleared his throat a little too loudly. It sounded as though he'd caught an entire swarm of flies in his larynx, but it was evident that Gabe wasn't paying attention to the store clerk. He stilled the broom in his hands, his job with the hardtack nearly complete.

"Julia denied it, though, said Jamie likes to exaggerate."

"I've always thought that Jamie liked me a little more than his sister," Gabe said, his tone suddenly serious. He handed the broom and dustpan back to Mr. Merrick over the counter and turned to face her again. "What is your name?"

"Callie . . . Callie Rushton," she answered quietly.

Mr. Merrick cleared his throat again unnaturally. He seemed to be uncomfortable with her talking to a young colored man. Her father always said there was no difference between men, but she wasn't naive enough to think everyone upheld that belief.

"Something I can help you find?" Mr. Merrick asked her pointedly.

Callie was relieved when he paused there, not bothering to mention her father's lapse in work as of late or the tab her family had acquired during the months of not being able to afford their necessities.

"Mrs. Starek sent me here for chalk," Callie said without missing a beat, "for her measurements."

"Let me get that for you," Gabe said, since he was closer to the intended item than she. "How many do you need?"

"Only one bundle," she said, catching the edge of his cologne, evergreen and musk, as he pressed the chalk in her hands.

Callie wondered so much about him. But with Mr. Merrick hovering near them, Callie knew now was not the time to let her queries get the best of her.

Before she approached the front counter to pay for the chalk, she asked Gabe one last question that made her cheeks even rosier. "Will you be at the Burke's house soon?" There was no time to take the words back.

He'd nodded, then lowered his voice so that Mr. Merrick couldn't hear, "I live there when I'm not in Seattle."

Although Callie didn't mean for her emotions to show, her

face broke out in a smile. She tried to recover as she placed her chalk on the counter before the disgruntled looking Mr. Merrick. "It was nice meeting you, Gabe," she said, ensuring they met eyes once more before she left.

"And you as well, Miss Rushton."

Callie wanted to tell him right then and there that he could drop the "Miss," but it was probably for the benefit of Mr. Merrick, who would obviously prefer the barrier between them. Formalities sounded less dangerous than first names.

As soon as the paperwork was signed, Gabe clutched a leather-bound book at his side and said, "Thank you for your business, Mr. Merrick. I'll be back in two weeks. Please telephone me if you need anything."

"Thanks, Mr. Ward," Mr. Merrick said gruffly, raising his hand in a stiff wave.

It was difficult for Callie to tell whether he liked this young man from Burke Enterprises or not.

Gabe left quickly, without a glance over his shoulder, and Callie tried not to watch after him as he swung open the door and let it close behind him. Instead, she spilled out the coins that Bess had given her on the counter, hoping they would suffice.

"That Gabe, he's a nice lad and all, but he shouldn't be looking at you like that," Mr. Merrick murmured while opening the till. "I have a daughter your age and all, and working with 'em is one thing, but having them make a move on your little girl is another."

His remark made Callie's throat close. Gabe hadn't made a move on her. He might have given her his beaming smile when he'd first laid eyes upon her, but nothing had come out of his mouth that was even slightly suggestive. And if he had looked at her, who was this man to state his opinion?

"Oh, I don't think he was looking at me," Callie said, closing her fingers over the chalk she'd just purchased. "It's just that I work for his employer. He was probably interested in meeting another person who . . . who works there."

Mr. Merrick laughed. He didn't believe her. "You best watch your interactions with that colored man of Burke's." He shook his head. "Beats me why the man would hire one of them when there are so many other capable men out of work." He let out a humph, and Callie felt her blood start to boil. Callie bid him an abrupt good day and left the Company Store as quickly as she'd come.

Chapter 12

GABE LEFT THE store regretting the inevitable confrontation to come. He wished every conversation with the young tutor could be as pleasant as the one in the store. But he had little choice. He had to get that picture of Liliana back, and there was no way of knowing if she'd deliver it into Jamie's hands later that afternoon.

Edging up to one of the streetlamps, he took a deep breath, knowing it would only take a few minutes for Callie to emerge from the Company Store. Watch your tone, he told himself, just be direct and tell her you need her to hand over the photograph. That Jamie wasn't supposed to give it to anyone. And make it quick so all the townspeople don't think you're in an intimate exchange with a white woman.

When he saw her step outside the store, his need to grab her attention overrode his awareness of her large, startlingly blue eyes, her soft mouth, the dusting of freckles that powder couldn't conceal. He cast aside thoughts of the flattering fit of her floral dress, let his eyes press on her for other reasons. She saw he hadn't wandered far after bidding Mr. Merrick farewell, and she looked at him open-faced, expectantly, but soon glanced away. He imagined the serious expression he wore on his face was to blame.

"Miss Rushton," he started in, "I didn't think it proper to mention it in the store, but I learned that Jamie gave you an envelope the other day, an envelope that doesn't belong to him . . ." He watched her eyes widen and gradually settle into some sort of understanding. But before she could say a word, he plowed ahead. "I don't understand why you'd accept an envelope from a young child that . . ."

He saw defensiveness wash over her features but couldn't re-phrase his words fast enough to stop hers, even if he'd wanted to.

"No. You've misunderstood. I didn't ask Jamie to give me a picture of anyone. I don't even know who the woman in the photograph is. . . . He handed me the envelope as I was heading out and while I was trying to hand it back, we were interrupted by Annie. I sensed some tension and didn't . . . want him to get in trouble, so I put it in my pocket. I will return it right away."

Gabe chewed the inside of his cheek, berating himself for allowing his agitation to rise above the calm he'd wanted to show. He crossed his arms over his chest and nodded. A silent understanding was the least he could offer her. He knew that Annie wasn't the softest with the children. If she'd seen the photograph, she would have probably sentenced the boy to a host of chores.

"As luck would have it, I have your picture inside the seam-stress shop. In my purse. I was going to return it to Jamie later this afternoon, but . . ."

"If you wouldn't mind, I'd like to have it now," Gabe said, willing that she wouldn't ask him too many more questions, out here in broad daylight, when he was still trying not to be too upset with Jamie for placing him in an awkward predicament. "The picture is mine, you see."

When Callie nodded toward him again, he saw the questions in her eyes, and if he wasn't mistaken, the flood of color in her cheeks. "She's beautiful," she said nearly above a whisper, before she fled toward the seamstress' shop.

Gabe waited outside. He tried not to laugh. It seemed Callie had her own idea about who Liliana was.

Soon after emerging from the shop, she pressed the tattered envelope in his hands. "I trust you'll talk to Jamie . . . about not putting the new tutor in a tight spot again." Her lips upturned, perhaps her offer of civility. "And hopefully we can put this behind us."

He couldn't help but smile back at the new tutor. He noticed how a dark strand had broken from her set curls, how her eyes squinted against the sunlight, the blue of them sparkling like sapphire. He liked that she didn't apologize for the misunderstanding over the photograph.

He tucked the envelope in his back pocket and gave her a nod. "Thank you for understanding . . . Jamie never should have given it to you, but it's not your fault."

Callie nodded, beginning to work at a button on her black cardigan now that her hands were free. "I'm glad it's with its rightful owner."

This time when Gabe looked at her, the original warmth returned to his features. "Welcome to the Burkes, Miss Rushton. I trust I'll see you again." He gave her a friendly, though brief nod, and turned on his heel, his business with her done. There were more words on the tip of his tongue, words that sought out who she was and how long she'd lived in Roslyn, but they faded fast, as he was ever aware of their surroundings and the quickly averted gazes of white folk pretending not to care.

✧ ✧ ✧

"What was that all about?" Bess asked, when Callie finally dropped the chalk on the front counter. Her eyebrows were raised, and Callie knew she'd watched her entire exchange with the handsome young man from out the front window.

Callie sank into the closest chair she could find, a cherry wood rocker, and threaded her hands together as if she were in church. Knowing that Bess wasn't a woman who could be put off, she said, "I've only been with the Burkes for one day, and already their son, Jamie, gave me something I evidently wasn't supposed to have. Gabe, the one I was talking with, works for Burke Enterprises, and he asked for it back."

Bess threw her sewing project down on her lap and planted her feet on the floor, holding her rocker in place. Her painted-red lips opened slightly, but Callie merely wrung out her hands instead of saying anything further.

"There's more to the Burke's household than meets the eye," Bess said, taking on a pleasant smile. She arched an eyebrow at Callie.

Before Callie could begin to question the seamstress about her particular knowledge on the family, the door to the shop opened, and the women were distracted with the request of their next customer who needed her drapes mended. The door opened after that with such frequency that there was little time for conversation, but Callie couldn't put it out of her mind that Bess knew much more about the Burkes than she did.

✧ ✧ ✧

Gabe approached Slim's Place and was reaching for the front door when an old, rugged miner began to open it for him. He started to indicate his appreciation, but the man abruptly let the door go, almost clipping him in the face. The miner looked over his shoulder and offered a smirk, then a low, gravelly laugh. "You sure you wanna come in, boy?"

The man was Trip Evers, a miner with an unmistakable mean streak. He wasn't tall or of strong stature, but there was a scrappiness about the man that earned him deferential treatment. Miners either sided with him or they cleared his path, twiddling their thumbs and looking the other direction. Gabe hardened his jaw and set his eyes ahead. While he was used to certain townspeople waiting for him to step in the gutter so they could take the path, Evers outdid them: spit out his chew right before he passed, wrinkled his nose, and murmured things about *you people* or *your kind*. Gabe didn't want to deal with the hassle, but had told his fellow employee, Ben Livingston, he'd drop by.

"I'll get the door myself, thanks," Gabe said, daring to look Evers in the eye. The miner averted his attention to his boots.

It was a rousing hour for those workers who weren't in the mines that day. He heard loud banter, glasses set down harshly on scuffed tables, ice clinking as drinks jostled about in men's hands. He wasn't in the mood for such camaraderie and felt relief to see that Ben had a small table in the back corner. As he crossed the room, a dark-haired woman leaned over the bar, her purple dress molded to all the right places. She fixed her doe eyes on him.

"Is there something I can help you with, darling?" she said, her voice practiced, sultry.

He shook his head and cut his eyes from her, uninterested in the indulgences she might have to offer. He found Ben with his shock of red hair bent over his glass, tired eyes partially closed. The man hadn't had a day off in some time, Gabe knew. He ought to talk to Burke about giving the man a holiday. Livingston had a wife and several children he hadn't seen much lately.

Gabe clapped a hand on Ben's shoulder. He watched the man straighten himself and rake a hand through his unwashed hair.

"Gabe," he said, willing a vivaciousness to his voice that he clearly didn't feel, "want me to order you anything? I'm just finishing a quick drink," he said, gesturing toward a glass with mostly ice left in it.

He shook his head and sank into the wooden chair opposite Ben. "You look like you could sleep for a year."

Ben nodded glumly. "Showing that bad, is it?" He shook his head, and his red curls bobbed. "You know my younger son, Owen, has a sour stomach, don't you?"

Gabe nodded. He had heard Ben mention his son's illness more than once, but he wasn't aware that the situation hadn't improved.

Ben drummed his fingers to the crude wooden table and looked at his fellow employee, unable to hide his weariness. "His health is getting worse. He can hardly keep anything down, and we don't know why . . . the tests needed . . . they're beyond what I can afford. And it's not the fault of Burke Enterprises. Burke, he's given me several raises since I started." He cleared his throat, lifted his glass, and drank the remaining liquid.

Gabe was about to rest a hand on the man's shoulder again,

tell him that he was sorry for his family's struggles and that he could at least ask Burke if there was anything more they could do for young Owen when Ben shook his head abruptly and said, "Something wrong, Gabe? Seems you have something on your mind."

At this, Gabe pressed his elbows into the table. "I dropped off electric headlamps a few minutes ago, and Merrick thought we were overcharging for them. He second guesses a lot of materials we supply, whether they're boots, tools, lanterns . . ." He swallowed down the lump in his throat, well aware that this newest communication couldn't hold a spark to the distressing bit Ben just revealed about his young son.

"Have you told Burke about his questioning?" Ben asked, shaking his glass of ice before taking one last sip.

Gabe shook his head, scrunched up his face. "Not yet. Burke has enough to contend with. . . ."

Ben shook his head. "You need to remember that Merrick works for Burke now, not the mining company. If he runs his mouth about any of the supplies, it could get ugly. Fast."

The two men were interrupted by a loud shattering near the front of the building. They both turned their heads, and Gabe rose to his feet, adrenaline coursing through his veins. He then saw all that had broken was a glass. It was the sound of shouting that drew most of their attention.

"Hey! Out of here! Out of the establishment!" The voice roared from behind the bar. When neither of the fighters got up to leave, the bartender emerged from behind the counter, ready to lay into the feud himself.

"Keep your hands off me!" protested the man who'd thrown the glass. A few steps closer and Gabe could see that the aggressor was Evers. He had the other man down on the dirt-streaked floorboards, jerking him by the collar every time he tried to pry himself up. As Gabe stepped closer, he watched Evers spit his chew on the ground and say, "You stole that position from me. I've worked my ass off in the mines for twenty-seven years, and you think you can replace me . . ."

The miner on the ground had a red face and was straining to get up, but couldn't rightly speak until a few other men came over and tore Evers' hands from him. Evers spit on the ground again, his anger creating lines on his forehead that hadn't been there before.

"I moved one car too quickly, made one mistake, and I'm taken from my outside position and put back down the pit. You meant this to happen, Carl," Evers said, rubbing a spot of dirt on his cheek. "You probably loosened the cart when I wasn't looking."

"That mistake could have been deadly!" The miner gradually rose to his feet with the assistance of a few fellow workers. "And you know it. Think you're gonna get your job back by threatening me?" The man laughed and backhanded a smudge of blood from his lip. A quick burst of red replaced the one he'd tried to wipe away.

Three men detained Evers near the front of the establishment, perspiring at the effort. Evers was not to be underestimated—the man was strong and wiry. The bartender wiped his forehead, already fatigued. "Throw Evers outside. He doesn't come back for a week."

"Enjoy your time outside, Evers," Carl yelled, before sinking into one of the nearest seats and lifting a partially used napkin to stunt the blood now freely flowing from his lip. "Don't expect to keep your job when you put men's lives at risk."

Gabe turned to Ben, who had risen to stand behind him and said, "Evers will have hell to pay for that display. . . . But just goes to show you how bad the feuds over safety are getting."

Ben shook his head and closed his eyes. "Evers is a desperate man too. His wife is bedridden with illness, and he really needed the increase in pay. Doesn't mean he's a likable guy, but it makes me feel for him a bit more."

Gabe shook his head, decided to swallow his own words of his less than desirable experiences with the man. Instead, Gabe said, "How do you know all these things about Evers' situation?"

Ben shrugged. "You spend enough time in a tavern that still

serves up drinks and you come to know what's going on with folk. Their joys, their troubles." He lifted his near empty glass and winked. "Soda water, you know?"

✧ ✧ ✧

Callie's knock the second day on the job sounded nearly as hesitant as her first time at the Burkes. They'd welcomed her in as much they knew how, and still she saw herself as an outsider. Their way of life was foreign to her.

"Come on in, young lady," Annie said as soon as she threw the front door open. "Come on in. You must have done some magic last time you were here. They're waiting for you."

Callie moved on in, grateful that Mr. Burke's sister spoke to her, even if it was only a sentence here or there. It was a vast improvement over the first day they'd met.

Go ahead," Annie told her, sounding monotone. "I told the children to wait for you in their study. Their mother is meeting with the Women's Auxiliary and their father is, of course, away on business."

While walking to the children's study, Callie paused and studied several photographs hanging in the hallway she hadn't noticed before. There was so much she still didn't know of their family, and she sought further revelations. In one photograph, Margaret couldn't have been any older than Callie. Her hair was cut into a sleek bob which, instead of seeming boyish, brought out her femininity. Her face was like unblemished porcelain, her lips were reminiscent of rose petals. Her eyes shone in a way they no longer did. What was it about Mrs. Burke's present, entitled life that made her aloof and almost cold?

Before she could ponder any longer, Jamie pushed open the door of the study and welcomed her in. There were words on the tip of his tongue, but he couldn't ask them with his older sister so close on his heels, Callie surmised. "We've been waiting for you," he said, intensity brewing in his dark eyes.

"I'm glad to hear that. You weren't so sure about having a

tutor last time," Callie said, moving into the room, a number of articles about Northern Pacific clasped in her hands.

"I just so happened to see Gabe earlier today," Callie said before asking the children to settle down in their chairs. Jamie's eyes widened. He was on the verge of saying something but stammered. "There's no need to worry. I returned the envelope to him."

"We should probably start our lessons now, shouldn't we?" Julia asked, clearly uncomfortable with the direction of this discussion.

Trying not to blush at being put in her place by a child, Callie said, "Yes, we should." She directed the children to their blank sheets of papers, had them pick up their pencils, and start taking notes on the development of the railroad. While she told them of the Natives who made a home in the surrounding areas and the Chinese who worked the railroads relentlessly, it was almost possible to forget about Liliana's image burnished on the delicate paper. It was almost possible to forget that she'd met such a young man as Gabe. But her mind inevitably turned to him and wondered what goods he might be loading or unloading even now. Wondered if he was as struck by knowing her name as, she admitted to herself, she was in knowing his.

Chapter 13

MID-SEPTEMBER BROUGHT grey-blue skies, steadier rainfall, and an abiding chill. Since Mrs. Starek's work was backed up even with the help of her mother, Callie went to the shop more frequently during the week to lend a hand. At night, she sometimes invited Lucy over to talk about the fashions they couldn't afford and the travels they might never enjoy. They felt fortunate if they could rub enough pennies together to take the train to the windy town of Ellensburg to press their noses against the glass storefronts and admire from afar.

One night she and Lucy were resting on their stomachs on her mattress. They'd kicked their shoes off and relaxed in their stocking feet. Callie moved to the window to close the drapes, as her bedroom faced any oncoming traffic or lonely wanderers. When she turned back to Lucy, she saw her friend lift a bottle of red wine from a drawstring bag. Without a moment's hesitation, Lucy extended it to her, a gilded offering of sorts. Callie's laughter was stunned. Ever since the beginning of Prohibition, the two of them had developed a secret interest in wine, but they hadn't indulged together.

"Oh, don't look so amazed," her friend said, sounding brazen. "Pete is friends with the Foglios. A little Italian wine never hurt anyone."

Callie glanced at the curtains and made sure they weren't swaying, that no one could glimpse into the corners of her bedroom. "Is that the wine they've been taking orders for? If the inspector came to town . . ."

Lucy waved her hand carelessly. "The Foglios are clever enough to hide their wine in the pigpen when the inspector makes the rounds. Oh, don't look at me like that. It's been rinsed off." To demonstrate her conviction, she drew her lips to the bottle and planted a kiss on it. "Thankfully our local authorities know better than to knock on doors over every drop of alcohol."

She removed a corkscrew from her bag, popped the cork with expert precision, and extended the bottle to Callie. "Take a drink, why don't you? I think you'll like it."

Callie lifted the bottle and let the flavor of late-harvest grapes coat her throat. The taste was more bitter than sweet, but she'd already decided she was going to love it. It was a luxury she couldn't afford.

"You're not used to it," Lucy said, reading the decipherable map of Callie's face. "That's alright. Have another few sips. You might acquire a new taste."

Callie took only one more. After Lucy took another generous swallow, Callie caught her eye. "So when are you and Pete going to get married?" she asked, wondering about the young man Lucy had practically been betrothed to since grade-school days.

A loose strand of blond hair fell beside Lucy's mouth and she chewed on it. "I don't know. I kind of thought that we would have by now. . . ." She looked wistful, far from the girl whose hazel eyes danced with mischief a few minutes before. "He thinks he's going to strike it rich by uncovering gold in the near future, take me off to Teanaway Valley, and build me a home in the rolling hills." She laughed dryly. "He's always reading books about prospectors and thinks he has just as good a chance as anyone. And when his grandfather dies he'll get his gold claim."

"So he's just worried about the money."

"I guess," Lucy said, taking a long swig from the bottle. "But he needs to face the music and realize that that's not going to happen. I'll be patient a while longer and see if he comes to his senses." She took a long time to swallow. "What about you?" she asked. "Now that you are completely over Paul—the schmuck—is there another interest?"

"No," Callie began, an adamant shake of her head. Lucy's eyes pressed hers, and she began smiling in spite of her efforts to remain impassive. Since Lucy would never release her without an explanation, she sought fast words. "There is no other interest. I did just meet someone who was really nice, but it's impossible."

"Wait a minute," Lucy said, sitting up and swinging her legs over the side of the bed. "There really is someone on the horizon?"

"Do you . . .?" Callie began, hesitant even with her closest friend. Upon seeing her nod, Callie almost whispered. "Gabe is really nice. But I can't look at him like—"

"Oh, Callie, the stockman for Burke? He is unbelievable, but you can't . . ." Lucy grappled for the right word choice. "He's colored." She whistled through her teeth and her eyes popped, even though they were already as round as could be. She was quick to add, "Some in this town wouldn't have a problem with it, Callie, but your daddy would."

Callie wanted to put up a hand to hold her friend's insights back, but it was too late. "Why—why do you think my father would have a hard time? You know, never mind. It's silly to be talking this way. I've only just met him, so it shouldn't matter . . ."

"But you were taken with him," Lucy said pointedly, as she reached down to straighten the creases in her stockings. There was a small hole on the right knee that she tried to hide, but the pair was done for.

"Think of Mr. Jacobson and how close my father's been to him for all these years," Callie pointed out. "Not that I'm saying there's anything there. Like I said, I've only just met him."

But Lucy was shaking her head decidedly. "Major difference," she said, "is that Mr. Jacobson was your daddy's partner in the mines. There's no threat of stirring the waters there."

"I told you how intent he was on having that picture of Lili-ana—whoever she is or was—returned to him," Callie insisted, reaching again for the wine bottle and taking a more urgent sip this time.

Lucy gave her a disbelieving stare. "But we talked about this, Cal. The year—1925—is a dead giveaway. Liliana is more likely his mother than his lover. There's a great chance that a man kept as busy by Burke as he is, isn't tethered to a wife and children. Which is why you need to watch yourself and tell yourself *no* at the outset. It's not worth the heartache."

While everything in Callie wanted to argue with her, say it wasn't so, she knew that truth was on her friend's side. Roslyn might be different because black folk were given more oppor-tunities here than in many cities throughout the states, but that wasn't saying much. In this territory, blacks had the oppor-tunity to make as much as whites while they labored in the mines. And if they'd had enough with the ever-present danger of the underground and didn't want to mine anymore, they could take to the railroads or the lumber yards for their living. Here, the black children attended school with the Slavs, Croats, Italians, Poles, and Scotch-Irish. But all these rights didn't translate into being perceived as truly equal.

Some might claim that skin tone shouldn't determine one's worth. But many people raised eyebrows when colored folk stepped through the doors of their establishments; others let them know they weren't welcome at all. There was a marked difference in her father working alongside a man who was colored, and letting a colored man take her to the pictures.

But it wasn't as if those fault lines were going to be tested. Callie assured Lucy there was no need to worry, least of all for her sake. Gabe was her employer's right-hand man. That was all. But she'd defy any woman to be completely indifferent to him—not only because of the pull of his smile, but because of his kindness, the warmth in his voice. There wasn't anything more to it than that.

Chapter 14

JUNE 1889

LILY HEARD THE woman when she shared the news of her father's death to her mother on the train platform. Mrs. Bella Johnson had stepped forward in her poppy-red housedress, a light black jacket swinging like an impromptu cape over her shoulders. The woman reached out her hands to take her mother's in such a way that Lily knew, instinctively, that something was amiss.

"Oh, Georgina," Mrs. Johnson began, as if the two women were already on familiar terms, though Lily knew they'd never met before this early June evening. "I'm so sorry to tell you that he's gone. David's gone and my husband Gerald and a miner named Laurence Rollins. All three of them in the mines this morning."

Lily didn't care about the loss of the other miners with him. She heard her daddy's name, *David,* and the gravity of it made her heart drop. No one could hear it fall, but she'd never forget the moment those words were spoken. She turned away from the woman, pointed her simple black boots in the other direction, and let her hand fall on the letters that were nestled inside her coat pocket—the only thing that could keep her warm.

It wasn't long before the tear-streaked face of her mother hovered at her eye level, but she refused to look at her, trying her utmost not to break. Maybe they never should have come here. Maybe if they had remained in Chicago and kept to her mother's performance schedule, her father wouldn't have lost his life. These letters, the ones she crumbled in her hands even now, could have sustained her. Could have been enough. But no. Her mother had listened to her when she'd gone to her almost nightly in tears, begging, "We need to go to him. We need to live where he lives and be with him all the time."

"You heard, didn't you, Love?" Georgina asked her, placing her hands on her daughter's small shoulders.

When all Lily did was give a nod, Mrs. Johnson loomed before her and said, "I'm sorry, sorry. I wish it weren't so. Your daddy—he saved more than one man's life. And he went in trying to save others."

Lily blinked but hadn't any words to offer. Her internal landscape screamed and said this was all a terrible mistake, that it couldn't be real, that her daddy was stronger than anything the mines could throw at him. If she opened her mouth, she thought she might scream. And her brave father—he deserved more from those he left behind. This she knew as she hardened her jaw at age six. She wouldn't be a wilted flower. He was more than that, and she, with his blood coursing through her veins, was more than that, too.

✧ ✧ ✧

She didn't take to Roslyn as she might have if her father were alive. Once in a while she caught herself smiling out the window of Mrs. Johnson's sitting room as she thought of how her daddy would have set her on top of his shoulders and shown her around. How he would have bounced stones over the choppy blue waters of Lake Cle Elum, invited her to watch him play baseball with other miners at the Roslyn Ballpark, and treated her to a hot chocolate after. Sung to her, though his voice wasn't trained like her mother's.

The first days passed without distinction. She knew her father had been preparing a place for her mother and her, but neither of them asked to go there. It was still unfinished, she knew, from her daddy's correspondence with her mother, and they didn't want to set foot in a place that brought an even greater measure of pain. Mrs. Johnson near about cried her eyes out every night, her tears mixing with whatever she was cooking over the stove. But any time the other tenants tried to lend a hand, she pushed them away and said, "The good Lord gave me a purpose. If I wasn't here, cooking for y'all and darning your socks, where do you think that'd leave me?"

Sometimes at night Lily caught snatches of conversation shared between her mother and Mrs. Johnson.

"*There's no reason to stay here,*" she heard Bella say to Georgina. "*I'm thinking of giving Charlie, Robert, and Willard a few weeks and closing this joint. There's too much sadness here for us and not much to do without our men. And I'm thinking you should come with me to Seattle, you and your Lily.*"

An offer her mother paused upon but didn't overtly refuse.

"*Seattle has so much more to offer us, and especially you. We could get a place together if you'd like, and while I'd look for something as a cook or laundress, you, my friend—you could sing again.*"

"I don't know I have the heart for that anymore," she'd heard her mother say. "*Not when so much of my reason for singing is gone.*"

"*You still have Lily.*" A force overtook the usual wilt of Mrs. Johnson's words. "*She needs to see that her mama has resolve so she can find her own way.*"

"That much is true," she heard her mother say, though that wasn't the night she agreed they should go. Almost a month would pass before that decision was made.

Lily lost track of the days but kept herself centered with the reading and re-reading of her daddy's letters. She left more than one out on the mattress she shared with her mama. One afternoon when she looked up, she noticed a kind-faced man staring at her from beneath the door frame. He wore tattered dark clothes and was roughly the same shade as her daddy, but older. When he opened his mouth, she noted that he didn't have all his teeth. It didn't stop her from sensing a warmth about him, a light that persisted despite his world-weariness.

"She won't talk to you," Georgina said, materializing quickly at his shoulder, her own face scrubbed free of its habitual makeup, her hair cast beneath a cobalt blue scarf. She didn't look like her mama in this moment. But Lily wasn't like herself either.

Georgina moved into the quaint, undecorated room that David had lived in the months they were apart. The visitor remained beneath the door frame, not about to move one step closer without her say-so. There was nothing to it but a small, dimpled mattress, scuffed side table, a lamp, and a dented set of drawers. Her mother sank onto the mattress beside her. "I know you'll speak again, Lily. But I won't make you do so today. What I am asking you to do is look over at that man. His name is Mr. Rollins, and he was the last person your daddy saw alive." Georgina stopped, trying to keep the tears from her voice. "Do you know why that is?"

Lily slowly nodded, and several long-held tears swam down her face. She didn't backhand them away, sensing that if David were here, he'd tell her it was alright.

"Daddy went to save Mr. Rollin's brother," Lily said at last, breaking free from the five days she hadn't said a word to anyone.

Georgina clasped a hand around Lily's face and said, "That's right, my love. Your daddy went in to save him."

Mr. Rollins nodded, his own eyes pooling. He moved to the foot of the bed at Georgina's request. "I had to meet the daughter of the man who tried to save my brother's life, you see. Me and the other miners . . . we'll go on remembering him for all the rescues that he made. And there were many." He crossed his arms over his chest, as if uncertain as to what else to say when he happened to glance down to the mattress and catch a corner of one of her beloved letters. His eye paused on a pressed flower that matched her name. "*Lily,*" he said, those two syllables touching her heart again, giving her name new life.

Chapter 15
1932

OCTOBER SOON SWEPT over the Upper County with its crisp red and orange leaves, gusty wind, and creaking trees. Callie's threadbare cardigans weren't keeping her warm. She traded them out for wool sweaters and shawls, some of which she borrowed from her mother's thinning closet.

She hadn't seen Gabe in several weeks. They had no chance encounters at the house and none in town, despite her frequent glances out the window whenever she went to work for Mrs. Starek. Julia and Jamie scarcely brought his name into conversations, perhaps having learned a valuable lesson about betraying family confidences since that first afternoon they'd met. It was for the best. There was nowhere for prolonged interactions with Burke's stockman to go.

For all she knew, he could be engaged or even married to another woman. Like the beautiful woman in the picture. He might have swept the floor at the Company Store out of pity for her that afternoon and nothing more. Perhaps he offered every girl he met that brilliant smile of his and didn't think twice about its lingering effect. She wished that afternoon hadn't ended on a terse note—he had been very direct with her once he realized who she was and what she had that belonged to him.

Sometimes as she walked the steep incline to the Burke's, she tried to imagine how it must have felt to be a black miner finally let off the train in Ronald, left to begin a new life different than the one that was promised. What was it that made Mr. Burke so fascinated with those colored miners? Now that so many of them had fled town for other, better livelihoods, what made him pay homage to those who'd come here some forty years before?

In honor of the black miners who built our region.

Those were the words on the small gold place setting. What was it that prompted him to inscribe that message in front of his house to begin with at all?

✧ ✧ ✧

One October evening, Mrs. Burke arrived home earlier than usual. Callie watched her approach the house out of the study window. She was dressed like a film star on the front of *Photoplay*. The frock under her well-cut coat looked as though it had been dipped in pink lemonade, falling gracefully over her slight figure. She held tight to her hat with one hand, making it slant stylishly over the right side of her face. The aggressive wind could have easily thrown it to the ground. Despite the unpredictable weather, she wore an uncharacteristic smile.

As soon as Callie told them their mother was home, Julia and Jamie dropped their pencils and let them roll across their desks. They sprung from their seats and all but ran to the landing to meet her. Callie followed at their heels.

"How are my lovelies?" she asked, her voice so sweet that Jamie wrinkled his freckled nose. "Did you miss your mama?"

Instead of giving them ample time to answer, Mrs. Burke turned her attention to Callie. "Thank you for being here. My meeting with the Ladies Auxiliary was canceled. They double-booked the meeting hall, and a group of miners won out. Apparently, they need to discuss the terms of the United Mine Workers." She looked lovingly at her children. "I almost forgot," she laughed, letting her gaze rest on Callie. "It's time we paid you."

She found a chair in the sitting room and proceeded to reach into her purse for her ledger. While Mrs. Burke signed the check, Callie clenched and unclenched her hands, expectancy growing. How quickly could this check transfer into bread or even a turkey, drenched in fattening gravy? Not nearly fast enough.

As soon as Mrs. Burke tore the check from the ledger, Callie thanked her and folded it, so she wouldn't see the amount until later.

Julia quickly sought her mother's attention. "Miss Callie assigned so many discussion questions on the railroad company today, Mama. I'm not finished yet, and Jamie won't catch up any time so—"

Jamie crossed his arms over his chest and glowered.

Mrs. Burke pursed her lips. "You couldn't expect any less from a tutor your father hired, now could you?"

When Mrs. Burke noticed Callie was still standing there, waiting to be dismissed, she nodded at her and told her she could go. Callie tried not to break from the house too quickly. Once she'd latched the gate behind her, she set out on the unpaved terrain, trying her best not to land in mud puddles and further dirty her shoes.

When she was little more than halfway home, Callie paused behind a thick fir tree, and with trembling hands opened her purse, seeking the check. The anticipation of drinking in the number, almost like thirst-quenching water after a drought, made her eyes blur before registering the amount. And then her jaw came unhinged. She let out a laugh, unable to stop herself. Thank you, Lord in heaven! They'd given her close to thirty-five dollars for a month's work, and it was an effortless earning compared to her father's former work in the mines.

Before opening the front door, Callie decided that she must be careful about how she broke the news to her family. Her elation slipped down a notch, and she hid her smile. She had to consider how she could share these earnings without denting what remained of her father's pride.

As soon as her mother looked up from the kitchen counter, Callie could tell she was eager to ask if today was the day the Burkes paid. Mrs. Rushton kneaded the last of the bread dough and waited for her to speak. Her mother's wedding band flashed as she worked and Callie's heart swelled to see it. It was there, just as Callie hoped it would remain. She had heard her father hammering out in the shed when she'd come home—no doubt making dining tables and chairs—so she set the check on the counter and drew in her breath, waiting for her mother's response.

Mrs. Rushton lowered her chin and stared at the check for a number of seconds before laughing out loud. "Good heavens! Am I seeing this clearly?" She walked over and planted a kiss on her daughter's cheek. When she'd settled down a bit, she admitted, "I never dreamed they'd offer so much."

"Neither did I," Callie said quietly, folding the check and placing it back in her purse. "I'll cash it first thing tomorrow morning."

Her mother nodded happily. "Your father and I really appreciate your doing this for us, Callie. But we also want you to know that you should spend a little on yourself . . . buy a new dress, find a pair of earrings that you've wanted for a long time . . ." She noticed her daughter's expression turn to alarm.

"I'm not going to spend it on myself. Please don't tell him how much they gave me. . . . Please . . . I know that it would bother him when he always deserved much more than what the mines gave him."

Her mother sobered enough to nod her head and say, "I see what you mean, Callie. But you know how open your father and I are with each other. From now on, you just do what you can for . . . us," she said, making a sweeping gesture with her hand to indicate the household, "but don't show me your checks, and I'll have an easier time pretending ignorance about the amount that's given." She lowered her voice. "I mean it. Don't you feel guilty for one minute about buying yourself some items you need . . . or want. Callie, don't shake your head at me. I'm serious. You deserve to have a few nice things. Whatever way you look at it, the money is yours."

✧ ✧ ✧

Bess had begun to lose her spirit about the store when the weather turned. Instead of chattering cheerfully while stitching from her rocker or filling the air with the latest Big Band record as she was apt to do, she was noticeably different in her approach to her work. She was a lot more tight-lipped with customers, and Callie noticed her nervous tics. She often stood at the cash register, clasping a hand at the back of her neck. She frequently played with the black pins woven through her thick, auburn hair. She twisted her earrings and even broke one. For all the business they still had, the shop wasn't turning much of a profit, Callie knew. Bess had slashed her prices for struggling customers. And often they finished working on a garment only to have it sit there, uncollected since the customer couldn't pay.

"I might as well operate this store out of my home. I've had a man come in here, asking how much longer I intend to keep my doors open. He is looking for a site to open a shoe store."

On hearing this, Callie tried to will the worry from etching itself on her forehead. "Have you talked about closing up shop with your husband?" Callie asked, sewing a button onto a lady's winter coat. Still early in October, the cold was already wrapping itself around them, seeping into their bones whether they were ready for it or not. Callie shivered in spite of the coal burning in the wood stove.

"Oh, we've talked about it a little," Bess said dismissively. "He thinks it's only a matter of time before we should operate out of our home."

Any business owner would want a shop at the center of the town—but only so long as that store brought in revenue. It wouldn't mean so much to the Stareks if, come winter, they couldn't afford the coal required to heat the place. The walls weren't well insulated, and as layered as the seamstresses were with blankets and wool sweaters, they were catching cold and had runny noses to show for it. Callie and her mother spoke in hushed voices on their way home from the shop sometimes, wondering how many weeks they had left before Bess closed her shop forever.

Talk of closing the shop had dominated recent hours, so Bess surprised Callie with her next comment. "It's been awhile since you've talked about your work for the Burkes," she said. "Tell me, how do you find them?"

Callie prattled on about warming to the initially standoff-ish children, but she stopped mid-sentence when she noticed Bess staring at her with studied gray eyes. "Have you run into Edward's right-hand man again?" she asked, the light of interest transforming her features.

Callie shook her head slowly. How she wished she hadn't opened her mouth and told Bess that she'd met Gabe that afternoon at the Company Store. The mention of the photograph had sparked the seamstress' interest, and Bess looked as if she were on the brink of adding more to the conversation. But when the seamstress didn't indulge her curiosity, Callie answered. "No, I haven't seen him since he asked me to return that photograph . . ."

The front door opened, and with it came a customer and a gust of unkind wind. From that time until the close of the store, there wasn't an opportunity to return to that conversation, and Callie thought it just as well. She wanted to honor what Mr. Burke had asked her and keep family confidence, even if she didn't yet know which secrets she was keeping.

✧ ✧ ✧

Bess went out the back door to lock up the shop while her husband waited with his black Chrysler in the alley. Standing outside the front door, Callie returned the key to her purse and gave the door one last tug when she noticed a pair of work boots paused in front of her. She didn't have time to raise her head before the owner of the boots edged closer and gave a playful tug to her scarf. Her heart quickened as her blue eyes met the gaze of Paul Dightman. He'd taken so many shifts in the mines, undoubtedly saving up for his future with Maura, that she hadn't seen him much around these parts.

She noticed the people milling about Pennsylvania Avenue — loud voices emanated from the many establishments fronting as soda shops, townspeople emerged from the Company Store with arms full of goods, patrons who could afford a meal out bustled through the doors of the Roslyn Cafe. Even this many months later, Callie hoped the folk that her family knew — the Adams, the Garellis, the McLaughlins — wouldn't see her standing at the entrance of the store with the man who had broken her heart.

He wore a smile on his face, and even now, when he'd left her for another woman, she found herself caught between simultaneous desire and revulsion for him. She'd tried so hard to avoid him, and she fought off the urge to turn her frustration inward. Why had she forgotten to scan her surroundings tonight as she'd trained herself to do in the year since he'd broken their engagement? She'd mastered quick turnarounds, ducking out of a store or keeping to a certain aisle when he was there. But now it was all for naught. His fingers still touched the frayed edges of her deep blue scarf, and she wanted to throw it at his feet rather than wear something brushed by his hands.

"I thought I'd find you here, Callie." His endearing tenor bent around her name in just the right way. "I hear you found a second job."

Of course you heard, she thought.

"I best be on my way, Paul." There was a tightness in her throat already. She wished she hadn't allowed herself to say his name. All he had to do was press his eyes to hers, tilt his head to the side, take her in — and he brought her right back to the time she was his. When her heart sung at the sound of his voice, when her hand fit in his, large, calloused, and possessive. How hard it had always been to break away when he wanted more than she could give. How she struggled even now to escape when his presence was a temptation against reason.

"Congratulations on your position with the Burkes, Callie. Not just anyone could land a job with them, and I'm happy for you." Paul gave her an admiring look.

The words broke the spell, however, and Callie pulled her eyes from him.

"Thank you," she said, though she didn't want to thank him for anything. Not for asking her out after she'd praised him for his speed at a track event. Not for acting like she was the most beautiful girl he'd ever seen. Not for making her believe they'd spend the rest of their lives together. "The job came at the perfect time, and my family is blessed by it. Now, if you'll excuse me . . ."

She turned from him and prayed that a wall of emotions wouldn't hit her now—not before she was several blocks away. Her heart was still bruised, but she felt proud of herself for not lingering in Paul's presence, for waiting until she was around the corner to backhand the few angry tears that sprang to her eyes.

Chapter 16

B EFORE CALLIE HAD the chance to raise her fist to the Burke's door, Jamie appeared to welcome her in. His expression rivaled that of the pumpkin he'd carved only last week. He wore an impish grin with several missing teeth to complete the look.

"Think we could go on an adventure walk this afternoon?" The words rushed out of his mouth.

The siblings were captivated with the history in their own backyard, and Callie could understand, as her own interest grew in the Upper County's first pioneers. There weren't many landmarks she knew of to point out on the Burke's acreage, but she supposed it wouldn't hurt to walk with them and imagine what it was like for the mining families who'd forged a life without running water.

"I don't see why not," she said, keeping her coat on. "I'm glad to see you're so interested in our local history."

"Nah," Jamie said, affecting indifference as he stepped back to welcome her in. "But since we have to do more school on top of school, at least we're learning something that doesn't put us to sleep. Where do you think we'll go today?"

"We best not veer too far off the beaten path." She made her blue eyes large and credulous. "Wouldn't want to tamper with any ghosts from these parts."

Fully expecting Jamie to take her last statement and run with it, he surprised Callie by the sudden stillness in his expression.

This time of year especially ghost stories resounded off the school walls, and Jamie Burke was bound to have heard more than one about spirits supposedly haunting the large, drafty grade school.

As she edged past Jamie, the last thing she expected to see was Mr. Burke standing several feet back from the entrance. Realizing he'd heard her mention Roslyn's ghosts, Callie silently scolded herself. She did her best to maintain her composure.

But Mr. Burke didn't furrow his brow like she feared he might. In fact, he offered her a welcoming smile. "How are you, Miss Rushton?" He stepped closer and extended his right hand. Though often serious, he could be fully present, and Callie felt grateful for his kind notice.

"I'm well," she said, accepting his handshake. "And you, sir?"

He merely nodded. But then he straightened his navy-blue tie and glanced down at the wood floor, as if contemplating his next words. "James, please go meet your sister in the study while I speak with Miss Rushton."

Jamie raised his chin. "Yes, Father," he answered, as though speaking to a commanding officer. How quickly his lopsided grin fell from his face. Then he slunk down the hall, and Callie remained, standing near the front entrance before Mr. Burke.

Instead of leading her toward his office like he had the first time they'd met, Mr. Burke said, "We can talk here." He glanced around the spacious entrance, momentarily letting his eyes flit around and said, "Both my wife and my sister are out this afternoon."

Callie nodded without understanding why it mattered at all. Surely what he had to say to her wasn't going to be so confidential that neither one of the women could hear his words.

"I wanted to tell you, Callie," he said, now using her first name, "that I'm encouraged by your work with the children. They seem to like you. My children tell me they're learning not only of the diverse background of our miners, but of the Natives' presence here as well, their hunting and fishing at Salmon La Sac. I appreciate that you're wanting to give them a more complete look at the roots of our region, that you're going beyond what a single textbook will describe."

He paused.

"It's also come to my attention that you're getting acquainted with the folk who work for my company. Gabe tells me that you've met."

She tried to edge out any show of surprise over this line of questioning. She felt he was sniffing close to her interest, a bloodhound drawn to easy quarry. Her hand smoothed a loose tendril before she could stop herself and she spoke as naturally as she could muster. "Yes, we met at the Company Store. He was kind, and I thought he handled his exchange with Mr. Merrick well."

She instantly admonished herself for saying too much and pressed her lips together. She didn't know what he was looking for, but Mr. Burke's brown eyes flickered, as if pressing her for more. When she had nothing to add—for she wasn't about to divulge the incident of the photograph—he adjusted the band on his watch and slowly met her eyes again. "Yes, Gabe is a valued employee. Gets more done than a lot of my other men. This Merrick . . . was he giving him a hard time?"

"Yes," Callie said without hesitation. "He insisted that the cost of the electric headlamps was too high, but I'm sure Gabe relayed that information to you." She shifted uncomfortably, unable to discern what information her employer wanted.

Mr. Burke shook his head. "And they gripe that their equipment isn't up to par. . . ." His gave a frustrated laugh, and as if sensing her discomfort, let his easy smile return. "I won't keep you any longer. The children are anxious to see you, no doubt. If you go far up the hill at the back of our property, you'll have to watch your step carefully. There isn't a clear-cut path. I haven't spent much time up that way since we moved here. Too much to do."

Callie nodded her thanks and bid her employer good afternoon. "Enjoy yourselves, and watch your step on that hill," Burke called over his shoulder before heading back to the confines of his study. He sounded as if he'd much rather go with her and the children than devote time to incoming orders.

✧ ✧ ✧

As fascinated as Julia and Jamie were with the unfolding history of their new home, Callie knew their foremost reason for being outdoors was to experience more of what their classmates did after school hours. They undoubtedly longed for the outdoors, even with the air grown brisk. The Burke children weren't allowed to ride their bikes up and down Pennsylvania Avenue, or on the back roads near the train tracks. Their mother didn't want them climbing trees unattended, didn't want them visiting homes of people she didn't know, didn't want them playing with stray dogs. They were made to settle for adventure with their tutor.

As their feet struck the front porch, Callie noticed that the sky had intensified its tone and clouds were gathering, suggesting an approaching downpour. Perhaps they had an hour to spare? A dousing in rainwater was the worst that could happen, so she said nothing of the weather and led the children from the porch.

They walked for about ten minutes up behind the Burke's house. Gauging the children's uncertainty as they trooped alongside her, Callie sensed that neither Jamie nor Julia had ventured on the land much farther than the faded red barn. Even then, they didn't make it out this way often. Their chestnut horse, Clairmont, had quickly become their aunt Annie's charge. She was the only one who would muck out the stalls and feed her on a consistent basis.

The immediate land behind the Burke's house spread evenly, yet it didn't take long for it to edge up against a wooded trail. Though overgrown, it wasn't so hard to see where footsteps were intended to land beyond the waylaid branches, the first scattered leaves. Jamie made a sudden display of energy, and led the way into the brush. When the house disappeared from view, Callie calculated the distance they were traveling more closely, not wanting to become entangled in the woods when dusk fell upon them. Julia seemed to have lost her enthusiasm for the outdoors. She sighed heavily with nearly every step she took and complained of scratches from jagged branches on her arms. But Jamie seemed to love every minute of the unbridled adventure, relieved that he wasn't made to sit at a desk and hold a pencil any longer.

"How are we supposed to find our way home when everything looks the same out here?" Julia asked, pausing again while her blue eyes flitted from one tree to another, an aimless bird looking for a perch.

"It's not all the same," Jamie called from ahead. "The farther up we go, the more wildlife you'll see. There's a squirrel up ahead right now. He's looking right at me."

Julia bristled. "You won't ever catch him, Jamie. I want to go back home."

"Alright," Callie said. "Julia's right. Your odds of catching Mr. Squirrel aren't great."

"But I'm not done exploring," Jamie yelled, far ahead of them. He'd managed to leave her line of vision. She was forced to linger behind with Julia, who took measly steps and clung occasionally to the tree trunks, despite the fact that she'd traded her Mary Janes in for sturdy galoshes.

"You'll have to come back another time," Callie called out. "Come back right now, Jamie!" The farther she went, the more uphill the path became, demanding carefully plotted steps, lest the soil start to give. She'd have a hard time convincing Julia to go any farther.

But he didn't respond to her beckoning. Julia and Callie remained where they were, waiting to see his navy-blue jacket through the slots in the trees, but after another lengthy minute, Callie still didn't see him. She couldn't hear him snapping the twigs in half or crunching on the leaves anymore. She only heard the rustling branches ahead. It didn't take long for her blood to still. "You stay right here," Callie said, turning to face Julia. The young girl began to pout, but Callie didn't have the energy to tell her to lighten up. She had to ensure that Jamie hadn't wandered so far ahead that he didn't know his way back.

"Jamie!" Callie yelled, breaking into a run on the uncultivated dirt path. She no longer cared if she destroyed her dress in the process. She brushed aside stubborn branches and tried not to falter on the uneven ground. "Jamie, come back!"

Turning around another bend and praying that Jamie's dark blue jacket would appear before her, Callie fought to keep a sense of calm. Yet she felt her breathing take on an unnatural, jagged rhythm. Burke or not, there was nothing more she wanted to do than shake him as she reproached him for defying her. Where had he gone?

But before her eyes registered his jacket, she heard his voice reaching her. "Sorry, Miss Callie. I'm right over here." His tone was urgent, breathless as her own.

"James Burke, there is no excuse for running away—" Callie began, but stopped when she saw him standing near the top of the hill, face bent toward the sodden ground.

He was approximately twenty yards ahead of her, and she was afraid to step closer, thinking that he might have found an earthen-colored rattler, coiled and ready to strike. No nine-year-old boy's stance would still so much just to study a plant at his feet.

She dropped the formality. "Jamie, come back right now. Your sister is waiting for us, and we need to go back to the house before your mother starts to worry."

"She's across town," Jamie said disinterestedly. "She won't be back until nighttime since she's at another Ladies Auxiliary meeting."

"I need you to come back right now. I didn't realize how heavy the clouds were." Callie said, refusing to give in to Jamie's whims. The clouds had increased and darkened to the color of lead since she first noticed them. Jamie didn't move. Callie stepped closer to her charge, wanting to yank his arm, send him practically tumbling back down the trail with her. But as she was about to pat the arm of his jacket, he quickly turned to face her and pushed her back so that she had to hold her arms out to keep from falling.

"I'm sorry," he said quickly, "I had to . . . because you were about to step on the . . ."

But he didn't finish. Callie's eyes followed his gaze, and she inhaled sharply. Jamie stood mere inches away what had to be the markings of some graves. There were three distinct patterns of carefully placed stones in oval shapes, side by side. At the end of each oval lay a large brick, which Jamie had already uncovered. Each brick bore a date—1889. She trembled as the wind latticed through the mid-section of the trees. As soon as the next gust passed, she bent over to read the markings on the ground herself.

"Two of the names you can't read anymore," Jamie said. "But the third has a marker. '*Rollins: 1862–1889*', it says."

"Is that all?" Callie asked, forgetting to reprimand him for disobeying her. Instead of awaiting his answer, she peered as closely as she could at the oval stones and saw he told the truth. The names scrawled on the other headstones had tragically eroded, but Rollins' name was still distinguishable.

He nodded. "I wonder if anyone knows who he is. . . ."

Callie swallowed, thinking fast and hard. *Rollins*. There was a familiar ring to it, but she couldn't place it immediately.

"Why wouldn't they be buried in the Roslyn Cemetery with everyone else?" Jamie asked, his forehead scrunching in little lines.

"I don't know," Callie said, digging her fingernails into her palms, wishing she knew the answer. "Let's go. Your sister is waiting for us."

Jamie's mouth opened in question. "But what about . . .?" He motioned toward the gravesites, long since abandoned and overrun with fallen twigs, leaves, and debris, rubble wrought by the wind.

"Mr. Rollins will keep resting here whether we leave or not," Callie said, turning toward the direction from where they'd come. She glanced to the tumultuous sky, saw the clouds were starting to break as she feared. If they didn't head back to the house, they would be drenched to the bone in no time at all.

Yet she felt compelled to turn back around, to fix her eyes upon the graves below her feet. She obeyed the nudge and saw something she'd missed before—a faint etching at the center of the unmarked graves. It looked like a flower—a lily, to be exact, similar in shape to the ones that marked every box shipped through Burke Enterprises. Callie felt chills at the back of her neck, the wonder of this coincidence rushing through her. Jamie, without noticing the object of her focus, interrupted her spiraling thoughts.

"But don't you want to find out who Rollins was?" He asked, finally giving her his attention. "And the other two?"

"It'd be interesting," Callie admitted after turning, holding branches back so Jamie wouldn't scratch his face any more than he had already. "But I don't think that's going to happen here."

"Why not?" Jamie asked, relentless as they trudged down the hill, back toward the house.

"There is no description on his grave," Callie said. "It's barely a marker." She acted like she hadn't a second thought to spare on the newly-found burial site, but in truth, the discovery stunned her. Especially the lily. If she showed fascination though, she knew Jamie would want to get to the bottom of it. And when they returned he'd mention his discovery to everyone, replete with a description of how he'd run off and found it all on his own.

Callie sighed in relief to see Julia waiting exactly where she'd told her to, farther down the path. Once Callie reached for the girl's hand, she didn't look back. But Jamie was mesmerized with the knowledge that there were people buried in the back woods, and his crooked smile showed it.

"What did you find up there?" Julia asked, squirming.

Callie grimaced. Surely her inability to manage Jamie would get back to their mother, or worse, their father, before she had the chance to say anything. She wondered what Mr. Burke knew of the graves they'd found, if anything at all. Borrowing a little time, she gave no answer to Julia as they made their way down the hill.

The level ground at the back of the Burke's house hadn't seemed so lovely until Callie glimpsed it the second time. It was a relief to return. The trees governed this stretch with their thick trunks and russet-colored foliage, orange and red and golden splendor. She noticed a grey Ford truck parked to the right of the house that hadn't been there when they'd set out.

Callie told the children to pick up their stride, just as the first drops of rain pelted their faces. Julia continued to hold Callie's hand, while Jamie strode ahead of them, staying within eyesight this time.

"Do you know if Annie will be back in time to cook supper for you?" Callie asked, not certain who was taking the children off her hands that day. She debated telling one of the adults what they'd discovered on the upper reaches of the property. If she kept silent on the topic, she could only imagine what Jamie might do with this information—begin constructing his own investigation, visit the site again on his own, scare his sister with stories of unknown people buried in the back woods.

When they finally reached the house, Julia let go of Callie's hand, and dashed up the steps to walk in with her brother. Callie smoothed back her wayward tresses and swallowed, preparing the words she might say to whomever waited to greet them inside.

Chapter 17

CALLIE DIDN'T KNOW what she would say about Jamie's discovery in the wood, but she promised herself she wouldn't leave the Burke's home without mentioning it to someone. Before she had long to think through her words, she heard excitement pitch in the children's voices.

"Gabe!" Jamie's jack-o-lantern grin colored his exclamation. Callie's heart leapt.

"Hello, Gabe," Julia sang sweetly. She seemed to have forgotten her unwillingness to speak of him earlier.

Callie tried to smooth out her tangled hair, knowing it had been hours since she'd scanned her reflection. After weeks without seeing him, she hadn't expected Gabe to return from his travels today. As she stepped inside, she saw Gabe down on one knee on the landing. He smiled as he ruffled Jamie's tousled hair and patted Julia on the top of the head. "Hello there," he said to them, genuine affection in his voice.

Callie took inventory of him while he was caught up in their childish enthusiasm. He wore laborer's gear—the sleeves of his blue work shirt were rolled up, and there were splashes of dirt on his pants. His hair wasn't as short as the first time she'd seen him; he had loose, black curls falling over his eyes. When he turned to face her, he gave her a gradual smile. She hadn't been mistaken before—he was without a doubt, beautiful.

"What are you doing here?" Jamie asked. "Father said you weren't coming back for another week."

"Finished early," he said, momentary hesitation flickering in his eyes. "Wanted to come back so I could see you two. What were you doing outdoors right before a storm hits?" He turned to Callie, the question still present in his eyes. She opened her mouth and closed it, having no answer.

"Miss Rushton," he said, rising to his feet and extending his hand for the first time. As soon as her fingers rested against his palm, she felt her discomfort dissolve. She couldn't possibly be imagining it—the spark when they met eyes, the rush of energy that filled her. Knowing the children were their captive audience and fearing they would sense something between them, Callie glanced down toward a trail of dirt on the floor. Jamie hadn't taken his boots off fast enough.

"How are you?" Gabe asked, summoning her attention again. She looked up to find his eyes fixed on hers. She felt a nervous temptation to draw back her fingers and run them through her wind-strewn hair, but she kept her hand in his.

"I'm well," Callie said, even as she tried to search for something more profound. "You're right. It was a little windy for a walk, but it isn't raining too hard yet. How . . . how are you?"

Gabe released her hand before breaking his gaze. He was about to answer when Jamie interrupted him.

"You'll never guess what we found out there today." He didn't wait for Gabe to inquire. "We found an abandoned graveyard at the top of the hill. Only one grave was marked. It said 'Rollins: 1862–1889'."

Gabe looked at him, his expression calm but his eyebrows slightly furrowed. "I'm surprised you went out that far," he said.

Callie bristled, hoping there was no implied criticism in the remark. She doubted it, all the while reminding herself that he wasn't her employer.

"Does that mean you've seen them before?" Julia inquired, raising her marble-blue eyes to Gabe.

He nodded. "Yes, I've seen those graves before. There are probably a lot more on this acreage, but I haven't encountered others marked like that one."

"Do you know who 'Rollins' was?" Jamie asked, intent on getting to the bottom of this well. He was the very picture of a mischievous boy: ragamuffin's hair, fingernails that couldn't remain clean for a minute, freckles dusting his nose.

Gabe didn't answer.

Julia broke in, "I don't want to go back out there. It's creepy that there are people buried on our property."

"There are graves in many places," Callie told Julia, trying to convince her that there was nothing to fear in what they'd found. "If you traveled to Westminster Abbey, you'd be walking over hundreds of buried bodies. And that doesn't bother anyone."

"It doesn't?" Julia asked, wrinkling her nose in classic schoolgirl fashion.

"No," Gabe said, coming to Callie's aid, "and it's a historical site . . . just like this property. . . . But the history over there is much older than ours." He abruptly changed the subject. "Why don't you two go wash up for supper? Since your mother and Annie aren't here, I'll go ahead and fix some dinner."

His offer to handle the evening meal impressed her. He was so versatile, no wonder he worked so closely with Mr. Burke.

"What's Father doing?" Julia asked, glancing to the right wing of the house toward the study. From where they stood, Callie glimpsed a sliver of light beneath the door.

After a few seconds of silence, it was apparent to all that Mr. Burke was speaking to someone on the telephone. Every once in a while, his dress shoes made a creaking sound on the wooden floors, especially after what sounded like a decisive statement. Callie could not detect the words. But even so, she imagined his tie loosened around his neck, the precision in his words pulsing through the line. He was a man with such a steady demeanor, he didn't have to say much for his words to be felt.

Gabe raised his eyebrows in response to the intense business exchange. He said, "Never a dull moment in the business." Then he turned to Callie. "Would you like to stay for dinner tonight, Miss Rushton?"

Jamie instantly brightened, and Julia offered her uncharacteristic exuberance. "Oh, will you?" she exclaimed.

It was more than tempting for Callie to remain for dinner now that Gabe was there, but she shook her head.

"I really should get home before that storm breaks. Perhaps next time . . ."

"Do you really have to go?" Julia asked, pleading.

Until now, Callie hadn't seen how much the eleven-year-old girl was warming up to her. She smiled, though she felt the sting of having already refused. "I need to head home before my folks worry, but I'll say yes another time."

"I'll hold you to it," Gabe winked at Callie before turning his attention back to the children.

Callie smirked. She'd only seen him three times, only exchanged words twice, and it amused her how quickly she was drawn to him. "Just say when," she said before turning toward the front door. The words embarrassed her and she felt her face start to flush. *Just say when* . . . How desperate did that sound? Where was the sense of intrigue within those words? But since she had so rarely encountered him, was there really any damage in letting him know that she wouldn't mind another invitation?

She offered a friendly wave to Julia and Jamie, who didn't seem all too disappointed to see her go after all. Their corresponding waves were brief, their eyes fastened back on Gabe in no time at all.

"It was good to see you again, Miss . . .?" Gabe called after her.

"It's Callie," she said, turning to face him once more.

She met his gaze again. He wasn't looking away, and it was hard to stop her smile. "It was good to see you too, Gabe."

"It's windy out there. And raining, as you said." He hesitated, and she saw something catch in his eyes. "Would you like a ride home?"

Just as she was about to answer yes, she thought better of it. She'd seen the momentary hesitation flash in his eyes once the question was asked. She didn't know what Mr. Burke would say to him if he drove her home. She didn't know how her parents might respond either, and while she knew that shouldn't matter, she didn't want to field those questions so soon into her employment here. "Thank you. Maybe next time. . . . I'm fine to walk since it isn't too dark yet."

He nodded, accepting her answer, hands hovering near his pockets. Neither of the children noticed how long they lingered there on the landing. They were already in the kitchen, rummaging through the icebox for chicken. "Good evening, Miss—" He caught himself and smiled slightly. ". . . Callie." She said goodnight softly and turned the knob. Her stomach fluttered, and she shook her head, not knowing why she was so easily overtaken. Didn't she know enough not to trust these unreliable emotions? Where had they ever taken her but to disappointment's door? And yet, she couldn't admonish herself too deeply for this indication of life. It uncovered a light still inside her that Paul hadn't the power to blot out.

With the door closed behind her, Callie drew her winter coat closer to her frame and approached the wind and the rain. Instead of begrudging its relentlessness as she had earlier, she tilted her face upward and welcomed the wind's rush, reveling in the fact that her heart was alive. Now, if only she could discipline it, forbidding it to take her somewhere she was never meant to go.

Chapter 18

CALLIE LET HERSELF in the door just as the rain turned to hail, pelting the roof like small bullets. Gathering balls of ice ricocheted off the windows, and Callie shuddered, grateful to be home. She removed her rain-saturated coat and hooked it to the peg right inside the front door.

"I was starting to worry about you," Mrs. Rushton said, hurrying to her side. "It's an hour past the time you're done tutoring those children."

"It was longer today," Callie said, beginning to remove her boots. There was no need to divulge the rest of the details, the unmarked graves in the woods or Mr. Burke's highly appealing right-hand man. Hearing those truths would only add to the fine lines around her mother's eyes.

"You're becoming quite attached to them, aren't you?" her mother asked.

Her tone was so flat, Callie couldn't tell if she thought of this as positive or negative.

"I wouldn't say attached," Callie answered lightly, smoothing back her windblown tresses, "but I enjoy tutoring them more than when I started."

Her mother returned to the kitchen so she could stir the beef stew she had cooking in a large metal pot. There were more carrots and onions than meat. Despite handing over that first check to the family, her mother was in the habit of being frugal.

"Have you heard that Bess is closing her shop before winter?"

Mrs. Rushton asked, right as Callie was considering the family expenditures.

"W–what?" Callie asked right as Charlie swept into the kitchen to lift a spoonful of stew to his mouth. Mrs. Rushton swatted him on the behind and looked back to Callie.

"Her lease is up, and someone wants to put a shoe store in its place," her mother explained. "So it's done. She didn't seem too grieved about it." Mrs. Rushton took out five bowls and served up a portion in each of them, with a more generous helping for her husband. "She'll be resuming her tailoring services out of her home, and her customers will be loyal, you know . . . those that can still afford to come to her."

Callie tried to maintain an unruffled expression. The veteran seamstress would do this without either one of them—she knew it. Keeping Callie and her mother employed was an unneeded cost. Now that she was downsizing her location, Callie had a premonition Bess would work alone. Her mother smiled against the flickering candlelight in the kitchen, but the strain across her face was evident. "We still have the small payments from the mining company. I wish there was more I could do to contribute."

"You already do so much," Callie said. She thought no payment could compensate for the tending of her father's shifting moods and the attention to the home and those living within it, but she didn't dare speak these thoughts aloud. Charlie still lingered near the outskirts of the kitchen, concern writ large across his brow. Mrs. Rushton let the conversation fall and walked toward him. "Do me a favor and go tell your brother and father that supper's on the table." She ruffled her son's hair and the smile returned to her face.

✧ ✧ ✧

The wind continued to roar against the windows without letting up. Several hours into the storm, Callie's father called her to join the rest of the family in the lower level of the house. She crept with her pillow and blankets downstairs. Every once in a while, they heard a branch sever in half, and her father limped off the couch to make sure it wasn't tilted toward one of the windows. No one was keen on the idea of him endangering himself to inspect the situation, but they knew better than to try to stop him. His stubbornness could match that of a mule's.

When Callie finally closed her eyes and willed sleep to claim her, her thoughts found Gabe. She sighed heavily. She knew what was on the other side of soft-spoken words and looks of longing. But still, she thought of Gabe, and summoned those eyes that seemed as true, as certain as oak. Replayed how it felt when he shook her hand. Yet she felt she shouldn't be thinking of him—she should stop errant thoughts before they took root. The hallway light crackled and flickered off and broke up her thoughts without effort. The next moment a knock sounded upon the front door.

Stevie bolted upright and threw off his blankets first. Callie saw the outline of his deranged hair against the wall. Charlie followed suit but, was slower to emerge from his covers on the ground. He'd been nodding off to sleep, and it took him a moment to get his bearings. Both their parents were asleep, although her mother stirred when she heard the second knock. Callie's father continued to snore like a wolf. Mrs. Rushton tapped him on the shoulder and whispered, "Bill, someone's at the door."

The clock was upstairs, so it was impossible to know the time, though Callie guessed it was a hair past eleven. It was a peculiar hour for visitors, but the knock didn't necessarily warrant the attention her father gave it once he opened his eyes.

"Everyone stay down here," he said, his tone taking a harsh bent. He rose quickly to his feet. Stevie was about to climb the steep stairs, but Mr. Rushton waved him off and said, "Including you."

Her father reached for a lantern he'd brought downstairs and used it to guide his footsteps up to the to the front door.

"Be careful," her mother called after him. The knobby tree limbs rattled against the walls, and Callie could see that the sound increased her mother's wariness about the unknown visitor. It could be anyone: a drunken fool, a beggar, a working girl. *That lacerating wind could drive anyone to the nearest door*, Callie thought.

"Don't worry," her father said, without turning back to face any of them. Answering a knock on a blustery night was far less of a risk than the post he'd held for a number of years, after all.

It didn't take long for him to reach the top stair, even with the damage done to his right leg. The rest of the family waited, silent and still. Callie hoped that the voice of the visitor would be immediately recognizable, that she would catch a drift of it through the vents. But she could scarcely hear her father open the door at all. The swirl of the wind wrapped itself around the house, covering any traces of rusty hinges and spoken words. Each one waited anxiously until they heard footsteps over their heads and then the door to the downstairs open a crack.

"You'll never believe who's here, Renata," her father called, his voice cresting on a wave.

Her mother made her way to the top of the stairs by the dim light. "It's not . . . Will, is it?"

"Hi, Mother," Callie's brother Will said in answer, his familiar tenor filling the basement.

In the light of the lantern, Callie could make out the outline of her tall, younger brother as he appeared before the rest of the family. He was leaner than when he'd left, his chin was sharper, his clothes baggy as those lent to a scarecrow. Callie thought again of how sparse some of the meals had been lately and knew their mother would attempt to make them heartier for his sake.

"What are you doing here?" her mother asked, laughing aloud. "I didn't have anything on the calendar about you coming home until Christmas." She went to her son, and he bent down to hug her. "And in this outrageous weather!" she said, standing back to look at him. "How did you even get here?"

"It's called a surprise, Mother." Will laughed as he removed his rain-soaked jacket. "I have a few days leave from Ft. Lewis, so I took the train over the Pass. I didn't expect it to be storming like this."

"Don't tell me you walked here from the train station," their mother said, recoiling at the notion of hail beating down over his head, the darts pinging at his jacket. She reached up to touch the dampness on his cheek.

"I started to," Will said in stride, "but when the hail picked up, I ducked into Slim's. It's crazy how many people are out cavorting in this chaos. I half expected the billiard halls to be closed."

"You'd think," their mother said, put out with the prevalence of drinking—for she knew it was more than soda water keeping the miners out at all hours. "We would have driven into town to pick you up."

"I asked him why he didn't call ahead," her father said, playfully swatting Will on the back of the shoulder. "But the telephone lines have static. Helen must be having one heck of a time connecting the calls tonight."

Will smiled without showing his teeth. Callie knew that he wouldn't have called even if the phone lines were up. Their parents rarely fired up the old pickup. It sat before the house as a just-in-case vehicle, but was seldom driven anywhere.

"Hello, Charles and Stephen," Will said, affecting a stiff tone. He saluted them in the dark, and both boys rose a little higher as they went to bear hug their big brother.

The twins were thrilled he was home. After Will's departure some six months ago, the boys had been left on their lonesome outdoors, and it hadn't been the same without him. Everything they'd learned about constructing tree houses and forts they'd learned from Will. There was no one as thorough as their older brother when it came to building a home in the woods. He had everything mapped out—from the booby trap entrance for intruders, to the floor-plan in the kitchen, to the dimensions of the sleeping corridors. Both Charlie and Stevie were more than eager to pick up where they left off now that he'd returned—even if the weather didn't clear.

Will turned to offer his older sister a hug. "Ah, Callie, I've missed you," he said. When he stepped back to look at her, he narrowed his eyes and added, "But I've been dying to ask you about . . . this fellow I met at Slim's Place who apparently knows you."

Callie immediately stiffened, possibilities flashing through her mind. She wondered if Will had somehow met her employer, before reason reminded her that Mr. Burke was not someone who would carouse with miners in a lively establishment at all hours of the night. She noticed that her parents were waiting for one or both of them to further explain. But not knowing to whom her brother referred, Callie waited for him to tell her more.

"I've never seen these guys before," Will said by way of explanation. "One of 'em is young, colored. He was sitting with a redheaded man when I walked over and asked them if they knew someone who could give me a ride." Her brother paused. "This colored guy took a look at my uniform, asked my name, and said he'd heard of Rushton before. He stared at me for a long time and asked me if I was any relation to a girl named Callie. When I told him you were my older sister, he said he met you through his employer, Burke. He offered me a ride home even though it was only a few blocks."

Callie itched the side of her nose on hearing of this unexpected encounter. She was about to admit how surprised she was that Gabe left the house so soon after arriving back from Seattle, but caught her words. She couldn't afford to make it sound like she had any interest in his comings or goings.

Callie's father was quick to enter the conversation. "Wait a minute. How are you meeting Burke's stockmen when you're at home tutoring his children?"

"Sometimes they stop by the house," Callie was quick to answer, not wanting to mention that Gabe boarded there when he was in town. "Burke works from home sometimes, so his stockmen come to see him there," she added, hoping to offset their interrogation.

"So he drove Will here," Callie's mother said, resting a hand on her son's arm. "He must be respected in the company if he gets to drive one of their vehicles."

Will nodded. "It's not even a five-minute drive, but the hail really picked up again. I was grateful for the ride." He cleared his throat. "Strange, isn't it, how a man like Burke doesn't lack for anything? Meanwhile the rest of our country is waiting in bread lines and selling their valuables wherever they can." He gave a quick shake of his head before hunkering down with his family for the rest of the night, their only other companions the unsteady branches amidst the shattering rain.

Chapter 19

CALLIE WASN'T EXPECTED at the Starek's shop the following afternoon, but she had to speak with Bess. The veteran seamstress sat in her chair, her worn black shoes tapping the ground with each rock, her record player spinning a Big Band favorite. She greeted Callie with a nod and a smile. Gone was the agitation she'd expressed before making the decision about turning over the shop. While her dress was nondescript, she wore a pair of faux ruby clip-on earrings and lipstick that seemed a counterbalance to the successive grey days they'd been having.

"Lose track of your days?" Bess asked, arching an eyebrow. She stopped what she was doing long enough to take a sip of chamomile tea waiting for her on a side table.

"No," Callie said shortly. "I was restless at home and decided I'd rather be here." She reached for a nearby garment, sized it up quickly and saw the fabric had snagged near the shoulder. She quickly found a needle and some thread.

Bess became distracted with tailoring a pair of pants, though, and didn't have much to say as she yanked the stubborn threads away from the hemmed legs. "Absurd stitching," she mumbled beneath her breath.

When she couldn't hold up the charade after five minutes of mending the blouse, Callie paused her needle and thread. She set aside the garment she was working on. "My brother Will came home last night in the middle of the storm. He didn't realize it was so severe and stopped at Slim's Place to hitch a ride. You'll never guess who drove him home."

Bess paused her handiwork. Her earrings bobbled as she pondered. "I wouldn't imagine Edward Burke frequents establishments with your everyday man, but was he out and about?"

Callie shook her head and swallowed before answering. "No, it was his . . . stockman, Gabe."

Bess' eyes betrayed interest, and she offered a close-lipped smile. "Well, that was kind of him to give Will a ride. So Will must know the two of you have met?"

Callie nodded. "Yes, Gabe mentioned knowing me. As you can imagine, my parents had immediate questions, and I told them that sometimes the stockmen drop by the house. I didn't mention that Gabe actually stays there sometimes. Now I've raised suspicion, and my father is already worried that . . ."

Bess pressed her back against her rocking chair, and her lips upturned. "You're smitten with him already, aren't you, girl?"

Callie let out a startled laugh. "What?! I . . . I've only spoken with him twice, and he's nice, but . . . You can't be suggest—"

"I'm not suggesting anything," Bess said, picking up a pin and threading it through the pants she was working on. "Only observing. Your father's only looking after you, and you can't really blame him since he saw how much you suffered over Paul. He wants to insulate you from harm and . . ."

"The reason I'm at the Burke's is to help put food on the table," Callie said defensively. "It's not to befriend the workers, but it feels like I can't win. No matter what I do, my father doesn't want me working for the Burkes."

"He'll have to adjust," Bess said, her flow with the needle unbroken. "As do we all." She glanced up. "When all feels dull and drab, it can be tempting to find a light, Callie. And I see it in your eyes again, a little hint of hope. I think it's because of the fascination you've found with the Burkes, and it's understandable. But you might think of guarding your heart before you get any closer with a certain . . . young man. Don't shake your head. There's no fooling me, Callie."

She reached for her teacup on the side table and took another sip. "Now you're not going to hear me saying it's wrong or unlawful . . . to have interest in a colored man. But there are considerations, painful decisions you must make, and I ask you to pray about it before it's too late. That young man, he means a great deal to Mr. Burke, and he's not going anywhere—but you, if you aren't careful . . ."

Had Bess not seen her pacing these same floorboards after Paul's swift dismissal, hair askance and eyes red and swollen, she might have disregarded the older woman's words. But as it was, she knew the seamstress had her best interest at heart. "I'm not falling for Gabe," Callie said. "That's not something you need worry about." She busied her hands with her stitching, unwilling to meet the seamstress' eye, lest the older woman continue. She'd rushed into Mrs. Starek's shop seeking any advice the woman could give her on keeping her parents content. She hadn't expected to have the questioning turned on her.

✧ ✧ ✧

Callie drank in the aftermath of yesterday's storm as she walked along the tracks to the outskirts of Roslyn. Some branches had snapped off trees like decrepit limbs and lay strewn across the ground. Drops of water glistened from remaining branches and threatened to shake down on her with the next gust of wind. Despite the hint of sunlight peeking through the trees, the yellow beam wouldn't hold any promise for long.

Mrs. Burke answered the door. She offered a smile that reminded Callie of weak coffee. Strangely enough, she wasn't dressed for an outing. Her jewelry was minimal, her dress a muted grey, and she wasn't wearing shoes, only her stockinged feet. Mrs. Burke seemed to notice Callie studying her and reached for her wrist.

"Oh, come in, come in. It's still miserable out there. I don't know how you manage to walk."

I have no other option, Callie answered in her thoughts, but maintained her manners. Once she'd closed the door behind her and hung her winter coat near the door, Mrs. Burke looked at her with imploring eyes.

"Annie is gone for the afternoon, helping Mr. Burke with a shipment that came in. I think I'll take a nap since my head is pounding again." On cue, she raised a hand to her temples.

Callie nodded, wondering if Mrs. Burke had ever seen a doctor for her condition. It wasn't polite to ask, so she said simply, "I'll make sure to keep the children quiet. I plan to give them a little quiz and then thought we could spend some time outdoors . . . once we are bundled up."

Even if the weather had taken a dreary turn, today's relative calm meant they could still walk around the town. She thought it would be interesting to take them to see the effects of the fire of '28 in Ronald. Only four years prior, a still had caught on fire there. The flames spread, taking out numerous homes and business establishments, but fortunately no lives. Since then, the town of Ronald had dwindled, the residents leaving in favor of Roslyn and Cle Elum.

Mrs. Burke nodded at Callie's suggestion. "I wouldn't take the children too far in the back woods again. It hasn't been brushed up since the storm, and we haven't assessed what trees might need tending."

"I'll be sure not to wander too far from the house," Callie said reassuringly. She already knew how Julia felt about tiptoeing over gravesites. She hadn't mentioned their discovery of the gravesites to Mr. or Mrs. Burke but was certain the children would have told of such a finding.

Just then Jamie and Julia rushed to the top of the staircase and leaned over the polished wood banister at the same time, hearing their tutor's voice from their upstairs bedrooms.

"Hello, Miss Rushton," Jamie said, foregoing Callie's first name since his mother was within earshot.

"Hello, Jamie," Callie said pleasantly. "Hello, Julia. Why don't you both come downstairs so we can get started? We have a quick quiz and then we'll take a walk before it gets too dark." The children trundled down the stairs and stopped before her. Noticing Julia's wilted look, Callie sought her eyes in understanding. "We won't stay out there too long today. Remember, in little over a month, it will feel like midnight at barely past four o'clock, and we'll have snow. We should go outdoors while we still can."

Mrs. Burke's attention was waning. She pressed her fingers to her temples again. "You both listen to Miss Rushton. I need to go lie down for a while." The children didn't watch after her for long. They were accustomed to her headaches, Callie surmised. The children settled at their desks with their papers and pencils and quiz. But Jamie looked up at her instead of his paper. "Our boots—we'll need them for our walk. They're upstairs in our closets."

The first opportunity to see the upper floor of the Burke's home loomed before Callie. She tried to conceal her curiosity. "You keep working on your questions from today's passage, and I'll get the boots for you."

She expected protests, but to her surprise, both children turned their attention to the quizzes she'd written for them. "No talking amongst yourselves now," she said softly, knowing full well that Julia wouldn't be tempted.

When she closed the door of their study behind her, Callie sighed in relief, but a glance in the direction of the master bedroom reminded her that Mrs. Burke might hear her footsteps on the stairs. There was absolutely nothing she needed from the top floor of the house. She could have sent the children up to fetch their own boots, but curiosity got the best of her.

Callie heard nothing from the master bedroom—no brush being set down on the vanity, no ballads filling the air, no creak of a chair moving against the wood floors. The stillness was a mixed blessing. It was quiet enough for Callie to believe that Mrs. Burke was truly asleep, but it was also so soundless that the slightest misstep could cause the lady of the house to open her eyes. Taking hold of the banister, she moved slowly, checking the impulse to rush to the top as fast as she could. She was grateful for the consistency of the antiquated grandfather's clock, her only shield of protection. Its tick-tock helped cover her breath, hid her whispered steps as they rose on the stairs. She was in part intrigued by the placement of the rooms and the knowledge that Gabe lodged here too, but she'd hardly admit that truth to herself.

Callie pressed a hand against the cream-colored wall at the top of the staircase. Jamie had left his bedroom door ajar; from her vantage point at the top of the stairs she could see that his bed was still unmade and that baseball cards were strewn across the floor. No other doors were open, but she guessed Julia's room stood directly across the hall. Callie took a deep breath and made her way to Jamie's room. The boots were easy to find and soon in hand. She set them down in the hallway and looked at the doorknob across the hall. It wasn't the only other room and she couldn't be sure it was Julia's, but there was only one way to find out. She knitted her brow together and told herself that nothing else would interest her, save collecting the children's boots. Part of her regretted she'd already come this far in the name of curiosity. So quiet that only a sharp ear could tell she was singing, she began humming "Always" to offset her nerves. She grasped the doorknob.

Chapter 20

SOON AFTER SETTING foot in the room, she sensed she wasn't alone. The song died on her lips. What first gave the room's occupancy away, she couldn't place. There was no one in sight, but perhaps it was the unmade bed, the partially open door leading out to a balcony, or the several work shirts thrown over the base of the bed. Another second rolled over her, but she already knew there was no way this room belonged to Julia.

She immediately saw her family's livelihood disappear before her eyes—disgracefully let go due to trespassing, precisely what she'd been warned against in this household. Callie tried to quietly do an about-face, but the floorboards groaned as soon as she turned. It was too late for her to leave without notice. The curtains near the balcony fluttered, and she heard a quick male voice.

"Who's there?"

"I . . . I'm sorry," she choked out before she could even turn to see who it was surfacing on the balcony. Once she spun round—her only option now—she couldn't stop her look of astonishment. Gabe stood in the balcony doorway. She hadn't expected to find him here, home in the middle of the workday. Undoubtedly, this was his room. A framed baseball jersey hung on one wall, a photograph of Chicago nightlife on another, a record player sat close to his bed. It took Gabe a moment to lose the uncertain haze in his eyes. She must have been one of the last individuals he was expecting to find standing here in his bedroom.

"How . . . how do you know that song?" he asked, confused yet not unkind. He took one step closer to her, closing the door to the balcony behind him. The question caught her completely off guard. He didn't ask her to explain her presence, and she found herself minutely aware of his. Every little detail of his being—suspenders down at his waist, the white undershirt that offset the golden brown of his skin, the intent look that accompanied his question—deluged her thoughts. None of that should matter to her, yet she almost forgot she hadn't answered him.

He asked the question again. "How do you know that song?"

"I—I heard Mrs. Jacobson, the pastor's wife, singing it when she and my mother visited on the porch. I . . . I'm sorry to walk in like this. . . . I was looking for the children's boots so we could go on a walk, and I mistook your room for Julia's."

Gabe cocked his head to the side, looking to Callie as if he was trying to decide whether he would believe her. She'd held onto a photograph that didn't belong to her not so long ago. What reason would he have to believe she wasn't finishing the work that Jamie had begun, playing detective on him?

If Gabe was going to say anything on the topic, he decided against it and studied her, contemplation writ across his brow.

"What—why are you home in the middle of the day?" Callie asked before she had time to consider that she was the one who ought to be questioned. She felt herself begin to burn up and balled her hands. She wanted to turn and leave, but knew it would only make things more awkward.

Gabe looked to the ground, as if deciding what to tell her, before raising his eyes to meet hers again. "Burke sent me home for the day. I just about lost my cool with Merrick over at the Company Store this afternoon."

Callie shook her head, despite not knowing what had gone on between them. "He's insufferable," Callie said. Unable to resist her line of questioning now that she'd started, she continued. "He must be a nightmare to deal with. I only caught the tail end of that exchange about the lamps and . . ."

"It's not about the miners' headlamps," Gabe said, leveling with her now that he'd decided to confide his dealings with the man. "He doesn't like me for my color, and he lets me know at any given opportunity."

Callie frowned, thinking of the man's chastisement of her friendly exchange with Gabe the first time they'd officially met. She leaned against the heavy oak dresser behind her and said. "I'm sorry. And yet I'm not surprised. . . . What happened?"

Gabe studied the floor before looking back at her. "I brought in another order of headlamps, same as last time. Except today he was even more agitated and mumbled a lot about the cost. I decided to ignore that since I'm not the one who sets the numbers," He let out his breath. "I didn't really have time to stop for lunch, so I asked him for a peanut bar behind the counter and set down some change on the counter. He told me I couldn't have it." He glanced back toward the balcony. "Most days I'm used to taking it. But sometimes it just gets to be too much."

Callie shook her head, disbelieving. "He's ridiculous."

"I thought about taking the whole box of headlamps with me," Gabe said, "but Merrick would have raised an uproar, and Burke would never hear the end of it." He looked back at her, fury leaping into his eyes. "He still might not hear the end of it. I told Merrick he could keep his stale old bars and that I'd find lunch elsewhere." Gabe grimaced. "I don't know who all was there, but several shoppers heard me on my way out."

Callie threw her hands up. "What does he expect? Refusing to sell one of those cheap bars? Why doesn't Burke replace him with someone else?"

Gabe shook his head. "Burke might not like the man either, but he's grandfathered in by Burke's cousin and not likely to go anywhere." He shrugged. "Look. I don't want to burden you with things you can't change. . . . The man angers me, but I'm going to have to deal with him again. Just not today."

He looked up at her, his amber-brown eyes kind, if not a little weary. "I'm glad you're the one Burke found to tutor the little ruffians." He smiled. "I can hardly call them that . . . but really, it's good to have you here. Is there . . . is there anything I can help you with . . . other than directing you to Julia's bedroom? Help you find her boots?"

Callie shook her head, taking a step back, aware that she'd overstayed her welcome. "I best be getting back down to the children. I can find Julia's bedroom. . . . It's one door down from her brother's, isn't it?"

He nodded. There was a flicker of amusement in his eyes, and the slow smile he gave her made her heart quicken. She turned, lest he sense her attraction to him. She felt reduced to a schoolgirl in his presence and rebuked herself for it. Hadn't life shown her that no flurry of butterfly wings could be trusted? These were uncertain times, and she needed to snap back to reality. She was, until recently, nearly penniless, had a father battling darkness, and needed to cement her position here with the Burkes. Why, in the midst of these hardships, would she allow herself to develop illogical feelings for someone she could never have?

But she didn't know how to categorize their conversation as she left his room. Gabe could have posed more questions at her trespass—or at the least, her mistaken entrance—yet he'd shown her grace. Callie barely let herself breathe until she reopened the door to the children's study. They were so quiet as she entered that it was troubling, until she noticed their pencils sliding across the paper, heads bent over their papers in deep contemplation. *Imagine that,* Callie thought, *they didn't miss me in the slightest.* It was only then she discovered she hadn't come down the stairs with their boots in hand at all.

Chapter 21

OCTOBER CONTINUED TO show an abrasive side; the wind unleashed its sway over the Upper County. Mrs. Rushton reminded the family to wear the same clothes for as long as bearable. There was no way she would spend much time outside hanging dripping wet clothes on the line. Chances were, they would freeze into contorted shapes instead of righting themselves in the wind. The forbidding cold—just a shimmering indication of what was to come—normally sent her into a stupor of sorts, but Mrs. Rushton drew her scarf closer to her neck and said little of it. Callie knew the reason she wasn't as gloomy was due to her brother Will's surprise visit home. The few days he had with them that would linger like a sweet refrain. His return brought long-time friends and relatives out of the woodwork. Will smiled endlessly and made people cheerier after being in his presence. He was thoughtful enough to take a trip to the Roslyn Bakery and purchase a fresh lemon pound cake or two so their parents didn't bear the strain of hosting his guests.

Despite being warmed by the presence of her entire family in the same house, Callie's mind wandered back to Gabe and the last conversation she'd shared with him. She'd spent five minutes in his room at most, yet she felt like she was keeping an illicit secret. If she wasn't careful, the beginnings of a smile would play around her lips, and she feared her siblings would suspect something. Her brothers drew her back to the present moment. "Remember the time I convinced Stevie to be my pet turtle for the Harvest Festival?" Will laughed at the memory from happier times. "And Mother made his costume out of the lid from the garbage can?"

Stevie's expression soured. "How did you convince me to do something like that? And Ma, what were you thinking? A garbage can? To wear? Do you know how many of Dad's old overalls were thrown in there? How much chewing tobacco he and his mining friends spit into that bucket?" He'd wrinkled his nose. "I don't even want to think about what else could have touched that lid. Why didn't you take me to Mrs. Starek's to ask her for a costume instead?"

"Enough," their mother had giggled, drawing her scarf closer. "You survived, didn't you?"

"Yes," Stevie said, dramatically, "but you should have thought about all the threats before . . ."

By the time they'd finished recollecting standout moments from their childhoods, their mother was dabbing her eyes with a handkerchief, unable to contain her tears. Callie hadn't seen her like this since she could remember, and she couldn't force some selfish thoughts from her head—*what would it take for me to get such adoration on her face?* If I left for some training program and came back months later, would she beam when she saw me? Loathing her natural predisposition to compete with her siblings, Callie busied herself, helping straighten the sitting area, stirring the potatoes as they boiled, setting the table for dinner.

Her father's heaviness cast a shadow over the dinner table that evening. Mr. Rushton waited until his dinner plate was picked clean to fold his arms across his chest and broach an unsettling topic with Callie. As soon as he said her name, she set down her fork and swallowed her last bite of turkey without being able to taste it.

"One of our neighbors brought a recent altercation at the Company Store to my attention," he began, his tone somber. "Tom McLaughlin told me he overheard Burke's hired help getting upset with Merrick the other day." He scratched his forehead. "That young colored man told Merrick he didn't want to eat one of the stale bars behind the counter."

Callie thought of Gabe's distress that afternoon and knew she had to tread lightly here. She wanted so much to correct Mr. McLaughlin's mistaken observation. Yet if she did, she'd reveal the unexpected conversation she'd had with Gabe.

"Mr. Merrick is known to be difficult," she said, her voice tight. "I'd be careful before believing Tom's partial account."

"McLaughlin said Merrick called the colored boy a 'stupid coon' on his way out the door." Her father continued, "He thought the man was in the wrong for doing that."

Callie bristled at this part of the story. "And did he speak up, tell Merrick to take those words back?" She was indignant.

Her father shook his head but didn't stop to ponder. "Name calling never helps anything, but . . ."

Callie flinched. She saw Will studying her across the table, but she couldn't help herself. "There is no but," she glowered. "That's the end of it. You call someone a name like that, and all bets are off. Gabe owes the man nothing and shouldn't be made to deliver anything to that fool."

"What's a coon?" Charlie asked, his voice barely above a whisper.

Her mother took a weak sip of her water and set down the glass. "It's not a nice term," she told her son before he could ask any further questions.

Her father threaded his hands and rested them on the table. "Merrick's too rough, I'll give you that. But the mining company never should have contracted with Burke in the first place. He hasn't been down the pit a day in his life. Doesn't know a thing about the needs of our miners." He pressed his elbows into the table and leaned forward, as if vindicated by that declaration.

"Who thinks Merrick knows the needs of the miners anymore?" Callie asked. "He's never been down the pit a day in his life either."

Mr. Rushton laughed offhandedly. "Maybe not. But how did

you get to be so defensive of the Burkes? If I were you, I might reconsider . . ."

"I won't," Callie said, defensively, "This position is allowing me to put some bread on the table for all of us." She motioned toward the partially devoured meal on each person's plate and paused, not caring at this moment if her words stung.

Charlie nodded vigorously. "It is, even if you are tutoring Jamie Burke. He's one odd duck, don't you think? Constantly walking around with that notebook in hand, looking to record anything he can about the history of the school. . . ."

Callie didn't answer him since she watched her mother's mouth open, as if she wanted to stop her from wounding her father's pride. She could tell her mother wanted to correct her—it's *the sales of the dining room tables that are putting the bread on the table for this family*. But they all knew that was a lie.

"It's at least helping, isn't it?" Callie asked, the only amendment she was willing to make.

She watched her father remove his elbows from the table and lean back in his chair. He let his arms rest at his sides, and his face was as vacant as a statue's. He must have known that he couldn't argue with his daughter on this one. It was never her intention to set him in his place or make him feel defeated, but she didn't want to hear another word of criticism about working with the Burkes.

"Who is going to play Charades in the sitting room?" Will asked, standing up from his chair so fast that he caused his dinner plate to spin in orbit. Only Will could lift the dreary mood and inject some life into the Rushton household when no one else thought it possible. Had anyone else suggested this, Callie knew her father would have bowed out before the first round, opting to return to his shed to finish the polish on another table. She wouldn't have normally felt like shifting so seamlessly from direct interrogation to a family game, but Callie had to hand it to her little brother for saving them from another of their father's brooding moods.

✦ ✦ ✦

Once his bag was packed and he was ready to catch his train back to Ft. Lewis, Will good-naturedly kissed his mother on the cheek, shook his father's hand, and ruffled the twins playfully on their heads. His goodbye for Callie he reserved until last. He'd asked her, only her, to walk him part-way to the train station in Cle Elum to bid him farewell.

No sooner did he unlock the front gate than Will turned toward his older sister and said, "Tell me this. Are you seeing someone, Callie?"

There was no twinkle in his eye when he asked the question, no smile of amusement as he used to display when she went to the pictures with Paul. There was actual concern written across his face, and that's how she knew he suspected something was amiss.

"No," Callie answered too quickly, although she spoke the truth. She adjusted a button near the top of her winter coat and kept walking, knowing her younger brother had a train to catch.

Dissatisfied with her answer, Will reached for her wrist and forced her to look at him. "I'm only asking because I'm concerned about you, Callie. You seem overly protective of the Burkes, and it's clear you have your guard up." He shot her a wary look. "I hope you don't feel like you have to hide anything from the rest of us, especially from me."

"What would I have to hide?" Callie asked angrily, shoving her loose-fallen strands back from her eyes. "I think Merrick is wrong, and I can't say so without being questioned?' Once she'd said this, she tried to rein in her tone, remind herself that within an hour, her younger brother would be boarding a train for the west side of the state. She needn't berate him for asking a question or showing that he cared.

"You're not usually this defensive," he said, his head tilted to the side, measuring her up. "I was careful not to say anything around them," he motioned in the direction of their parents' house, "but there's something a little suspicious about your working for the Burkes. It seems like you're holding something back. . . ."

"Like what?" Callie asked, willing the lump in her throat to dissipate like the sand in an hourglass. The more defensive she acted, the more Will would wonder about her working arrangement.

"I thought it was strange how angry you got about the colored boy. . . . Seemed like you were protecting him, or at least Burke. . . ."

"It's not like we've never had this conversation before," Callie said, frustrated. "Sam's come out of the Company Store muttering under his breath before. Even told Father that Merrick deliberately messed his order up on more than one occasion."

Will nodded. "And yet, your reaction was so immediate. You act like the wrong's been done to you."

Callie bit down on her lip. "Shouldn't it matter to everyone if someone is being mistreated?"

He adjusted the pack on his shoulders and shifted gears. Instead of responding to her statement, he said, "Soon as Burke moved here, I heard women talk about how handsome he is, and I know you might be tempted by that form of . . ."

"Thanks for thinking so highly of me," Callie said, her tone flat-lining. "Just because I was engaged to a man who couldn't keep his eyes from wandering doesn't mean that I've lost all reason."

Will shifted his weight from one boot to the other. "Something seems off. Don't look at me like that, Callie. Maybe there's nothing to it, you just don't seem quite like yourself."

She was at a loss for words. She couldn't claim to be acting like her typical self when he could see that it clearly wasn't the case. "Times are still hard," Callie said, not wanting to part ways with her brother on less than amicable terms. "But it doesn't mean that I'd be willing to be of any service to Burke beyond what I'm doing right now . . . looking after his children. Truth is, he's never expressed an interest in me. Have you seen his wife? He lacks for nothing."

Will shrugged. "If not him, what about one of the guys I met at Slim's? Don't look at me like that. The colored one was quick to know your name." His eyes turned even more serious.

Callie was about to protest, but drawing attention to him, defending him, would raise a new brand of suspicion. She studied her scuffed boots, hating that his questions volleyed her into silence.

Will rubbed his hands together and blew into them to warm them from the cold. He bent forward and kissed her on the right cheek. "I'm not going to make you walk all that way," he said. "Take care of yourself, Callie." He stood back. "And don't involve yourself with someone that might not be good for you." He shook his head, sullen. She would have reproached him for making insinuations had she not felt as drawn to Gabe as she was.

"I'm your concerned little brother, is all," he said, lightening up. "Take care of yourself." He beamed at her and was on his way once he'd adjusted the strap on his Army pack.

Chapter 22

ALLIE WALKED UP to the Burke's porch for her next shift and sensed a quiet around the house. The curtains weren't drawn, yet there was no hint of movement from anyone inside. The only thing that stirred were the flowers quietly shedding their petals before winter, the silvered wind chimes tinkling above her head. As soon as Annie opened the door, Callie marked the knitted lines of her forehead, the uncertain flicker in her dark eyes.

"He's out of sorts today, Edward is," Annie whispered in a low register, throwing a wary glance over her shoulder at the children. "We're all tiptoeing around here . . . lest we ruffle his feathers."

Callie didn't even bother to remove her coat. She motioned toward the children who'd made it to the front entrance, bent her head close to theirs, and asked them to hurry, grab their boots. They would take to the outdoors. She caught Julia's expression—the wilting flower—and clutched her by the shoulder. "What if I told you that I'll fix you some hot chocolate when we get back?"

"Oh, come on," Jamie said, not concerned with his sister's reluctance. "It doesn't take long to walk down to the abandoned miners' houses."

"I would lower my voice now if I were you," Callie told Jamie in a hushed tone. "We don't want to disturb your father." Her eyes darted down the hallway.

"His problems at the Company Store shouldn't have to get to us all," Annie said, shaking her head so hard, a pin from her hair fell to the ground. "If you ask me, he needs to override his cousin and let that Merrick go."

Callie nodded, couldn't stop herself from saying, "I know that he didn't treat Gabe well last time he was in."

Annie tilted her head to the side and more dark tendrils escaped from their haphazard arrangement. "He told you, did he? I scarcely want to walk down Pennsylvania Avenue right now." She blew a wayward strand out of her face. "Mrs. Burke already made her escape for the afternoon, said she needed to find a new pair of winter boots. I thought you could leave with the children, too. Edward doesn't often raise his voice, but he tends to pace when he's upset. And he's upset a great deal right now. Merrick started sending a petition around town, hoping enough people will sign it to have Gabe barred from entering the Company Store."

Callie felt the blood rush to her ears. How dare that man treat Gabe so disdainfully and cast blame on him when he was the one in the wrong? If she so much as saw anyone of her father's friends sign that cursed petition, she would scarcely be able to contain herself.

"Callie," Annie said, brushing a hand over her shoulder. "They'll stop the petition."

She shook her head, pursed her lips. "How can you be so certain? How do you know that?"

"Because I know my brother," Annie said, resolute. "Now, put these distressing thoughts from your mind and focus on these two children before they drive me to an early death."

"We'll be on our way shortly," Callie said, forcing back her fury. She threw direct looks at the Burke children and motioned them back up the stairs to collect their belongings for the outdoors.

✧ ✧ ✧

Once outside Julia looked at Callie critically and said, "There aren't many other places you can take us, Miss Callie. A lot of the stores, the churches, and boarding houses are no longer here."

Callie drew her coat closer before responding to the perceptive girl. "You're right. We've seen a lot of the beauty that Ronald has to offer. We can walk the train tracks to Roslyn this afternoon. Visit a few of the churches. It's not a long walk, and it aligns with our lessons. The black miners didn't stay in Ronald all that long, you know. But long enough to allow one of their churches to be used for a community school, a gracious act on their part. A few years after the strike they settled into Roslyn. Built several churches there, homes, went to the Company Store for their goods."

She needed to get off this track, lest she start thinking of Merrick's dealings with Gabe at the Company Store again.

Jamie brushed up near her right shoulder. "But we didn't finish learning about the unmarked graves." His eyes snapped in their earnestness. "We know only that one of them belongs to a man named Rollins, but nothing else."

Callie bit down on her lip. "Heading back up the hill won't answer anything more for you, Jamie," she said, adjusting her scarf. She'd known the boy was interested in the graves on the back of the property, but not to this extent.

She started walking, leading them from their spacious abode for humbler places in the neighboring town. Jamie scurried to keep up with her while Julia kept to her own stubborn pace.

"We don't have to head back there, but what if we went to talk with someone who might know? The librarian might know who lived here in the 1890s, and if not her, maybe a church would have a list . . .?"

Callie reached for Jamie's mitten and said, "I like how you think. We can certainly try, Jamie. But since there are several other unmarked graves, it's highly unlikely we'd run into someone who knows about them."

Julia narrowed her eyes and said, "Gabe knows a lot more than he'll say. I've overheard him mention the graves to Father, but Mother sent us upstairs right when the conversation was getting started. Said what they were discussing was of no importance to us."

She thought of what she'd been tasked with, teaching the children the history of this region and couldn't comprehend how evading the identity of those buried in their own backyard would help them any. It wasn't as if they were evacuating the bodies from the ground, they were simply seeking the identity of the people laid to rest.

"Instead of visiting one of the churches today, we'll go to the Roslyn Library, and we'll ask the librarian if she can tell us anything about the graveyards." Callie said. "It's not as if we're going hundreds of years back. We're only talking forty to fifty years, at most."

Less than half an hour later, the three of them stood at the desk and approached the woman who kept the books. Jamie came right out and questioned the young woman. "What can you tell us about the unmarked graves near the No. 3 mine in Ronald?"

That caught the librarian's attention. Her pensive expression gave way to a puzzled smile, and she all but dropped the pencil she'd been holding. "Well, that's quite a question, young man. I can't say I know anything about people buried in Ronald, though it doesn't surprise me. I've heard the first miners were so angered by the strike that there was threat of bloodshed here. And even with the guards, there were probably a few early deaths."

Julia, clearly frustrated with the length of time their trek had taken them, leaned over the counter and said, "We've been learning of the first strike our town ever had, about how the black miners were brought here, not knowing they were recruited to be strikebreakers. Maybe you could tell us when the black miners cemetery was established, and that would give us more of a start."

The librarian raised her eyebrows at Callie and said, "I'm fairly new to the area, but this place gets more interesting by the day." She quietly excused herself so she could look up the dates they were requesting, and when she returned, fascination lit her features. "While I can't tell you anything about the unidentified graves you mention, I can tell you that the Black Miners Cemetery wasn't established for several years after the colored miners arrived. That leads to the question—where were the dead laid to rest? Because even if not many passed away in the first years, we all know what it means to live in a mining town."

"Would you happen to know of a family named Rollins? One of the graves we found is marked, and that's the name given."

The librarian adjusted her glasses, and a look of contemplation swept over her face. "I don't know the answer off the top of my head. But we do have a record of a lot of the first people who came here to mine. Give me a few minutes, and I'll see what I can find."

After scanning several lengthy lists, the librarian looked to the expectant children's faces and then back to Callie. "There were brothers who arrived from Virginia back in '88, Leonard and Laurence Rollins. Those names don't ring a bell, do they?"

Despite living in the region her entire life, Callie slowly shook her head. She'd never heard of the Rollins brothers. But that wasn't too surprising—once the strike was over, many of the black families who'd come out west quickly departed for opportunities throughout the state. They started businesses, ran bed and breakfasts, worked as chauffeurs, and took to the shipyards—more than ready to leave their prior calling to coal behind.

It was probable that the descendants of the Rollins family had moved on from Roslyn long ago. Still, Callie took mental inventory of their names, knowing it wasn't impossible to locate the living brother. Forty years wasn't too long in the past. Someone in the Upper County must know where Leonard Rollins had gone.

Chapter 23

THE NEXT TIME Callie saw Gabe, he was walking out of Slim's Place just before dusk fell. Balancing the box of groceries in one arm, she raised a hand in greeting, not bothering about who might be observing them. Though he gave her a brief nod, she noticed his hesitation as he scanned the street before them. Burke had sent him to Seattle for over a week, and his absence was something she'd felt. Against her better judgment, she crossed the street to greet him and stopped when she found herself staring into his dark eyes. He stood back from her, his hands hovering over the pockets of his trousers, collared shirt light blue, his jacket an affront to the brisk autumn wind. She saw that he was taking her in too, though quickly.

"Miss Callie," he said, giving her a slow, but sure smile. Then, remembering what she'd requested, he corrected himself. "Callie, I mean. How are you?"

She raised a hand to her hair, but stopped herself, "I'm fine. It's been a while since . . ." Not even a minute in his presence, and her heart stirred.

"Just arrived back in town about an hour ago and stopped by Slim's to see what I've been missing." Callie glanced toward the locale he'd just mentioned and saw it was brimming with people. A tall man with reddish hair burst from the tavern door and swooped over to bid goodnight to Gabe. "Thanks for stopping by," he said, placing a hand on Gabe's shoulder.

The man nodded in her direction and didn't betray a hint of reservation. Callie saw him around town before but couldn't place him.

"Callie, this is Ben. Ben, Callie," Gabe said. "Burke's new tutor for the children."

Ben tipped his hat at her and offered a warm handshake. "A pleasure. Welcome to the Burkes. Couldn't find a better man to work for," he said, before wishing them both a good · evening. Gabe watched after his friend as he blended in with other bustling passersby.

Observing people spilling downstairs, throwing open doors, greeting their friends and associates as they passed, Callie rushed on with her words for Gabe.

"How've you been?" Tired of repositioning the box of groceries, she set it on the ground near her feet.

It was but two minutes since she'd seen him, and the initial thrill of being in his presence was forced back by a new reality. As residents passed by, a few, if not more, watched after them with studied eyes. She couldn't stay out here, speaking with him under the lamplight's glow for long. Gabe seemed to sense the entirety of her unease, but replied calmly. "I've been well. Busy at the rainy ports, getting a lot of work done before winter. How are you?"

Before she could answer, her mother's friend, Mrs. Adams stepped in front of her and clasped her wrist. "Oh, I was hoping to catch you before the shop closed tonight. I have a question about mending a skirt . . ."

Doubting the existence of the skirt, Callie was forced to turn her attention to Mrs. Adams entirely. She didn't miss the questions springing from the woman's concerned blue eyes, nor the straining of her forehead as she angled her body in front of Gabe's. *What are you doing, talking with this colored man?* Callie felt the question in her strategic positioning.

Hoping that Gabe wouldn't give her a short nod and set out for the night, Callie raised her eyes over the shorter woman and gave him a look that conveyed regret. Once Mrs. Adams finally walked off, her arrangements to bring in the skirt settled, Callie turned her attention back to Gabe. "It's nice to see you," she said, knowing she had no words to waste. She'd already kept him too long.

"And you," he said. His next question flew in the face of the uncomfortable situation. "You're having trouble managing those groceries. Would you . . . like me to help you carry them home, at least to the gate?"

She recalled that Gabe had been to her family's home once before, when he'd given her brother Will a ride, so he knew the positioning of the gate and how it might be a more comfortable stopping point for them both. "Yes," she said, before reason could play further interference. "I should have had them delivered," she said, watching him lift the box of purchased goods in his arms, "but thank you for helping me."

It didn't take them long to leave Pennsylvania Avenue for the quieter residential streets. Even away from the pedestrians, she could hear the loud chatter, the carefree laughter the night afforded them. If Gabe felt nervous about walking with her, he hid it well. It only helped that his footsteps fell behind her and that he carried her groceries.

"So how have the rascals been doing for you?" he asked, an attempt at lightheartedness in spite of however he might be feeling.

She laughed. "Well, they keep me busy. They're bright kids. Inquisitive as ever."

"You have to hold your ground with them sometimes." There was a smile in his voice. A hint of exasperation too.

Her stomach twisted, and she tried not to care what anyone might think who passed them by. In spite of the guise they'd used to protect themselves, what would either of them say if a miner or his wife rounded the corner and saw them walking this close? Their words quieted the closer they got to her parents' house.

"Good night, Callie," Gabe finally said, as they came to First and Utah.

"Thank you for walking me," she said softly.

He nodded, but she saw the strain in his throat as his eyes fixed on the lit shed, where her father was working.

"You're welcome," he said, before turning and slipping into the anonymity of night.

"Callie, is that you?" she heard her mother call, opening the door before she made it to the front porch. "It's cold and dark. Please, come on in."

Chapter 24

HOW COULD CALLIE have possibly known that her first trouble at the Burkes was about to occur? Except for Mrs. Burke, everyone was home that particular afternoon. Annie was preparing dinner and told her when she came in that Edward and Gabe were both home after a long trip at the Seattle port. Callie knew this from her small interlude with Gabe, when he carried her groceries home a few nights before. Edward was now in his study fielding several phone calls, Annie told her, and Gabe had gone in to help him with the books.

Callie settled in with the children, working steadily with them on maps of Kittitas County before Jamie set his pencil down and announced that he needed to use the restroom.

"I'm not feeling too well," he added, and his unseemly expression convinced her that his break might be longer than most.

She didn't think to check on him for ten minutes, certain that his stomach was bothering him. She found the restroom doors open and the interior empty, including the one upstairs. Then she walked toward his bedroom, thinking perhaps he'd gone to lie down.

She threw open his door but sensed right away he wasn't inside. His bed was nicely made, undoubtedly by Annie. His baseball cards were in a neater than usual pile, but his closet door was left open. Her gut told her to look for one item—his boots. When she saw they were not there, her throat tensed.

Her heart sank, and her next footsteps felt leaden. She nearly jumped when she heard the springs on the door give way, but she breathed relief when she saw it was Gabe who had followed her in. She'd feared that Jamie was sicker than she'd realized, but she hadn't thought until now that he might be lying. Was it possible they'd just missed each other, and he'd gone back down to the study?

"Julia told me that Jamie was acting strange when I dropped in to say hi," Gabe said. "What is it? Did he run away from you?" He shook his head, frustration transcending his features. "If he did, this wouldn't be the first time."

She winced. "I'm afraid so. Let me run back downstairs and rule out the possibility that we just missed each other."

When she tore back into the study, Julia glanced up and stilled her pencil. "So he's missing then? Jamie . . . he was acting peculiar. He's been carrying around his notebook, writing down anything that might lead him to discovering the identity of those abandoned graves."

Callie's stomach tightened like a vise. "What—what has he discovered since we went to the library?" On the brink of those words was the pointed question—and why didn't you tell me anything about this? But she held her tongue.

Julia shook her head. "He didn't say much, only that he needed to visit the gravesite again . . . since he didn't write down the years Rollins lived the first time we went up there."

Callie tried to maintain her calm, but already the taste in her mouth was metallic. She shook her head and said quietly, "But we've said this a number of times, the year on the marker was 1889, the year of the first strike in Roslyn. Remember?" Callie dug her fingernails in her palms. "You stay here and keep working on your map. I'll be right back."

She dared not mention that she had reason to suspect that Julia's little brother was no longer on the premises, but clearly the girl was perceptive enough to know. When she bounded back up the stairs, she saw that Gabe had searched the entire upstairs. He'd thrown open all the doors, rummaged through the closets, and was shaking his head at the lack of his findings. It struck her then that he cared as much about Jamie's whereabouts as she did, though he wasn't the one responsible for him.

"Julia thinks he may have gone up to the graves on the hill. Ever since I took him up that way, he's been fascinated with them. I wouldn't let him or Julia go back up there since we had that storm and didn't know what trees needed tending." She shook her head. "What should I do?"

Gabe's hand grasped the burnished rail, and he glanced down the stairs before looking back to her. "Let's tell Annie what we suspect. I don't think we need to involve Burke at this point. Would you go with me to see if we can find him?"

✧ ✧ ✧

"You best go now," Annie said, her eyes thundering at Jamie's disappearance. "It will be dark in less than an hour."

Gabe nodded quietly. He didn't want to draw Burke's attention to the boy's ploy, not when he and Callie might have him back in the study before dark. One time he'd found him visiting the Ronald Elementary School after hours, trying to break in through a window. Another time he'd found Jamie near the No. 3 mine, examining leftover piles of slate for kernels of undiscovered gold.

If Annie had any reservations about Gabe taking Callie to find Jamie, she didn't show it. She adjusted her apron strings and said, "I'll let Julia know she can lend a hand in the kitchen. Go on ahead."

Gabe felt the pressure settle in his temples, but it wouldn't help to fume at the kid for his careless antics. Still, he wished he'd been the one to tell Jamie everything he knew about the unmarked graves. He'd seen the boy walk around with that notebook where he wrote down all the interesting anecdotes that caught his attention. For Gabe those unmarked graves were more than an unexplored history lesson. When Jamie expressed interest in them only a few weeks ago, he'd felt the sacredness of them something too dear to surrender.

He and Callie were over halfway up the hill before he realized he hadn't said a word to her. He'd pushed the wayward brush and branches aside for them both but was too lost in his thoughts to carry on a conversation.

It was Callie who spoke first. "I just don't know what he's trying to prove."

Gabe chewed on the inside of his cheek and shook his head. "He's genuinely interested in history, I'll give him that. Inherited that from his father. Jamie is someone who likes to know."

When they finally reached the graves some fifteen minutes after leaving the house, Gabe was dumbfounded. He'd remembered the remote location where the bodies lay, but he could not believe that Jamie wasn't here or anywhere else on the path. He'd been more than sure that this was where Jamie would be, waiting for the others to surround him so they too could stand back, amazed that two of the three graves' markers were weather worn, without discernible imprints. The site was well-kept, considering he hadn't been up this way since they'd first moved here. A small bundle of purple wildflowers bound by brown string occupied the midst of the graves. He felt a little spasm of guilt and wondered who'd set it there.

Gabe crouched close to the ground to catch his breath and pay homage to the dead. He brushed a hand over the dirt at his feet, closed a hand over a portion of it and let the earth sift between his fingers. His eye fell upon the mark of the lily. He still had to blink at the oddity of finding it here that first time. It was uncanny seeing it again.

He was soon back on his feet, scanning between tree limbs for any sign of young Jamie. There were no muddy footprints in the earth save for his and Callie's.

In a futile effort, he shouted Jamie's name once, and then again and again. He called so much that his throat began to burn as if sandpaper had scratched it. His frustration with Jamie only intensified the difficulty he had in swallowing. He watched as Callie raked her hands through her hair, but he had little to say to console her.

"He can't expect us to be mind readers," he said instead.

Ready to turn back down the hill, Gabe looked toward the unidentified graves once more and saw Callie pick up something. Near Rollins' faded grave lay a folded piece of paper. When Callie opened it and held it out for him to see, he could tell it had only been there for several days at most. Although rain had eroded some of the words, he instantly recognized Jamie's hurried scrawl:

Laurence Rollins: brother of Leonard Rollins, uncle to Ruthie Sloane.

"This is a game to him," Gabe said, accepting the paper that Callie extended. He quickly tucked the piece of paper in his pocket and looked at her, trying not to let frustration take the upper hand.

"I don't know if I'd say a game," Callie interjected. "Ever since we found the graves, he's wanted to know more about the people buried here. I . . . I took the children to the library to see what we could learn about Rollins. He thought that could be the start—"

Gabe felt his throat tighten. "I could have told him who Rollins is. But that's only one person. There are, no doubt, more than these three people buried up on this hill." He smoothed a hand over his chin. He felt low-grade irritation at Callie for trying to uncover the truth of the unmarked graves, though he didn't want to feel this way. Not with her.

He wiped the rest of the dirt on his pants and tried again.

"Black people weren't permitted burial at the Roslyn Cemetery in the beginning," he explained. "While I don't have a count on how many died, you can imagine there were more than three. Especially with that strike that brought them here. You ask around a little, and you start to hear the stories." He shook his head. "There were mining accidents. There was a report of a black miner shot to death because he sang too loud at a tavern. There must have been other deaths too."

He saw her take in his words, seriousness flickering in those blue eyes. Gabe pointed toward the paper Callie had found.

"At least Jamie was kind enough to let us know where we need to check next."

"Ruthie's?"

Gabe nodded.

When they returned to the house, Burke stood at the door with his arms across his chest, his expression thoughtful and shrewd. Gabe had hoped they could leave for Ruthie's without delay, but it looked like explanations would have to be made. Callie stepped in, breathless behind him. He felt her come to an abrupt halt at his shoulder upon seeing Burke, but she didn't attempt to smooth anything over. There were greater things at stake than explaining to Edward Burke how the two of them were on such familiar terms.

"He wasn't at the back of the property?" Burke asked.

Gabe heard Annie and Julia making a clamor in the kitchen, their voices intense. "No," he said, letting out the breath he'd been holding, "but he left a crumpled-up note. Identifying Ruthie Sloane's uncle. Callie and I . . . we're heading to Ruthie's house next to see if he dropped by."

Edward shook his head. "You'd think the boy would learn. If he wanted to know, he could have asked one of us." He adjusted the clasp of his gold watch and let out a heavy sigh when he looked back at Gabe. "If that's a trail he left you, it's probably where he went." He turned toward the kitchen. "Annie," he said, after which she surfaced quickly, apron swinging over her ample hips. "Could you phone the operator and place a call to Ruthie Sloane's home? That's where they think Jamie may have gone."

She knitted her brow, but merely nodded, presumably aware that now wasn't the time to ask questions. But after several attempts to get through to the Sloane residence, Annie put the phone back in its cradle and rushed back to the entrance, where they waited for her.

"The lines are tied up and static. I'll keep trying, but it might be best for Gabe to head on over. Callie can wait here with us."

Before she could think it through, Callie resisted Annie's redirection and said, "I'll go with Gabe. We're already in the search this far, and I want to help bring him home."

Edward narrowed his eyes momentarily, then turned his attention back to Gabe without a word on that end. "Come back if he's not there right away. You will, won't you? I know Jamie's done this before, but we can't have him out there after the sun goes down."

Gabe nodded, an ache forming in his throat. "Yes, sir," he said. "We'll come back quickly whether he's with us or not."

Much as he respected Burke, it was difficult to address him with such formal language. Still he remembered to do so in the presence of others. His position as Burke's right-hand man already gave people pause. He knew—he saw the speculative looks across their faces—that some vendors wondered why Burke hired a black man for such a coveted position. He grew weary appeasing everyone, proving that he belonged.

Edward's smile was tight. Gabe feared he might have added to the man's tension by revealing his familiarity with Callie. As yet, he hadn't mentioned his growing friendship with the new tutor, but this incident showed they weren't strangers.

But more pressing matters were before them. "Thank you," Edward said. "I'm going to look out back, though I don't think I'll find him there."

Gabe shook his head. "Not likely. Jamie hasn't shown much interest in learning to ride that horse."

✧ ✧ ✧

As Callie climbed into the passenger seat, Gabe reached for a cigarette from his back pocket. He lit it and inhaled deeply. Once he let out a breath, she saw all the tension he'd been holding while in Mr. Burke's presence fall from his shoulders. He climbed in the truck and swung them out on the road.

"I gotta say," he started in, "this is a very creative runaway idea, even for Jamie. He managed to hike that hill again on someone's watch a day or two ago and left that note, hoping we'd find it." He shook his head and drew the cigarette to his lips again.

Callie sighed. "He's a little daredevil. He knew we'd come looking for him in the place we told him he couldn't visit again."

As they drove closer to Roslyn, Callie had a hunch that Gabe, like herself, was trying to think of what they'd say once they climbed from the truck and began heading toward the residence of Ruthie Sloane and her father. He parked the vehicle near Minto's.

"They must live either on Washington or Nevada—I've seen Ruthie walk home in that direction. We're gonna have to ask a few people to tell us which house is theirs so we don't waste any more time."

"Let's ask some of the men here," she said, nodding toward the entrance of the small billiard house, where off-shift miners corralled at the entrance. Half-filled, unidentifiable drinks occupied their hands, their laughter filled the brisk October air. She knew that Ruthie had washed the windows for this establishment in the past and thought perhaps the owner would know where she lived if they wove in between all these miners to ask him.

It took a minute for Callie to realize that the laughter among the men died down as soon as she approached the establishment with Gabe. She saw the narrowing of her neighbor, Mr. Garrison's, eyes, the twitch of his mustache as she neared him, and didn't know why he didn't say hello at first. She saw a few miners she didn't know by name frown at their arrival together, murmuring in low, undistinguished tones. They hadn't even reached the entrance yet. She steered her eyes ahead and pushed the front door open, no time to concern herself with the immediate judgment cast in their direction. She didn't turn to look back at Gabe, knowing full well he didn't have time for this nonsense either. Burke's nine-year-old boy was missing.

Trying her best to focus on finding the owner, Callie still couldn't miss the disdainful stares and the exaggerated coughs some of the miners gave as she and Gabe moved across the wooden floorboards.

"I'll be damned," she heard one of the men she didn't know say. "What're ya thinking, Little Miss, being seen with one of them? Does no one any good. It just ain't right."

"You watch your tongue!" Callie said. Her chastisement did nothing to lessen the miner's sneer. She heard Gabe say tightly at her back, "I can head back out if . . ."

"No," she. "No. Please stay here with me."

The owner, Mr. Wilkins, showed no such distress at seeing the two of them together, and leaned in closer to hear her question—did he know where Ms. Ruthie Sloane resided? He scratched at his thinning hair, trying to generate an address, but one of his young waiters gave an immediate nod and said she lived at the top of the hill on Nevada. The small house was a faded green, the porch tilted, its boards needed repair.

As soon as he said the words, Gabe and Callie gave their simultaneous thanks and sought the front door. Though neither heard another word of protest for their arrival together then, Callie wished the hostility of a few disheveled miners was easier to shake.

Chapter 25

ALLIE HAD ONCE heard that Ruthie's husband, Mr. Anthony Sloane, perished when a pile of timber fell from a barge on the Columbia River and toppled over him. The only child they'd had, a little boy, died after suffering a bout of pneumonia when he was five. Ruthie had no one left, save her father, but not many in the town considered her tribulations. They were too immersed in their own sorrows to realize that in many respects, their lives were still more intact than Ruthie's. They faced diminishing jobs, crumbling roofs, bread and butter they could scarcely afford. But they hadn't known the devastation of so much loss, the way it bruised the heart and drove a soul to see everything in life as impermanent.

Callie knew when they looked at Ruthie the townspeople most likely saw her threadbare dresses, her raw, soap-sudded hands, her monotonous work, her color. They didn't see a spirit on the mend, doing whatever it took to become alive again.

When she and Gabe emerged from the truck and walked quietly toward the green house, it was difficult for Callie to refrain from speaking, taken by the fact that this place was still standing.

There was no foundation, and the dwelling—one couldn't exactly call it a house—tilted to the left. Some of the wood structure looked so worn it seemed another storm could render it obsolete. The shutters were faded and barely serviceable. A ladder leaned against the side of the house as though someone had climbed up to investigate, but little work had been done to mend the roof. Would the shingles survive another winter?

When they climbed the stairs to the porch, Callie could see that despite the shelter's constraints, someone had tried to introduce glimpses of beauty where they could. There were flower boxes sitting outside the window ledges, orange and rust-colored marigolds nodding off to sleep before the months of hibernation to come. There was a woven straw mat at their feet, inviting visitors to go ahead and knock, and a spiral of smoke escaped the chimney.

Before he knocked, Gabe pointed out what he had seen first: Jamie's boots laid on their sides, the laces flung outside them in abandon. Feeling such instant relief, in addition to the tremors of anger she imagined mothers felt when finding their runaway children, Callie shook her head. "He has a lot of nerve, that boy."

Gabe swallowed, his Adams apple jolting.

"I feel like wringing his neck first," Callie surprised herself by saying. "But I won't. I'll just tell him that the search is over, and it's time for him to come home."

Gabe nodded and raised a fist to the door. There was scarcely time for them to plot their first words before they heard someone tinkering around with the bolt, beginning to unlock it from within. A few seconds later, Ruthie stood before them.

In place of her typical tattered dress, she wore dark-colored trousers and a man's white work shirt. Several sizes too big, it engulfed her, but there was still something undeniably feminine about the way she wore it. Perhaps it was the top few buttons left open, exposing her collarbone. She wore a green band in her hair, and small gold hoops dangled from her ears.

Uncertainty flashed in her deep eyes, and it was evident that visitors seldom came to call. At least, not unexpected ones

Ruthie drank in Callie's features, nodding as she recognized the young woman who'd worked in Mrs. Starek's Seamstress Shop. A laugh suddenly played around her lips as she saw who was standing behind her. Ruthie shook her head in surprise and opened the door wider.

"Miss Ruthie!" Gabe said, warmth filling his voice despite the circumstances.

If Jamie Burke hadn't just been missing, Callie would have wondered more at their familiarity. Gabe didn't know precisely where she lived until minutes before, so they couldn't be all too close.

"May I help you?" Ruthie asked politely, as if restraining the rest of the words that wanted to come out. Her eyes fled to the boots Jamie had removed. They were undoubtedly here to collect the boy.

Callie nodded, knowing that as soon as she started to speak, Jamie would hear her and either come running toward the front door, pleased that they had found him, or else he'd retreat into the nearest closet he could find.

"I'm sorry to trouble you, Miss Ruthie," Gabe started in, "but I can see Jamie made his way here, though without permission. If we could talk with him—"

Ruthie opened the door even wider to them. "Yes, come on in. He is a curious young man," she said. "I asked him if anyone knew he was here, and my understanding was they did." She shook her head and frowned. "Almost sent him on his way, but it's awful cold outside. Wanted to let him warm himself by the fire first."

Gabe motioned for Callie to go before him. Once indoors, he rested a hand on Ruthie's shoulder. "You'd have no way of knowing, Miss Ruthie."

"Come on in—let me put some tea on for you, if you'd like. It's so cold you can see your breath spiral."

"Oh, no thank you, Miss Ruthie," Gabe said, refusing her offer of tea as kind as he knew how. "We're not able to stay. Perhaps another time."

She nodded, her understanding unspoken, and ushered them further into the sitting room. As soon as they moved past the entrance, Callie saw Jamie sitting on the edge of a faded, wine-colored sofa across from Mr. Rollins, whose back was pressed into a plush chair. The nine-year-old's chin was bent in the direction of the crude wood floor. When he wouldn't look up to greet them, Gabe stepped forward to acknowledge Ruthie's father.

"Good evening, Mr. Rollins." Consideration filled his voice in spite of the circumstances. He clapped the older man on the shoulder and watched Mr. Rollins' expression brighten after he turned his neck to see who was greeting him. "Gabriel Ward!" he said, clearing his throat. "You must have been busy lately, son. Haven't seen you at church too many Sundays, but then again, I've been a little laid up with my aches and pains." He smiled so that his eyes crinkled like paper in the corners. "Old, though I hate to admit it."

Gabe met the old man's greeting. "Ah, you have a young heart, Mr. Rollins. We'd love to have you back at church." He fixed his attention on Jamie and tried to keep his voice steady. "I'm here for this young man. . . ." He turned toward the little troublemaker. "You had us all worried, Jamie. Did you know that? We best be getting on home. . . ."

Beginning to stammer over what he'd done, Jamie looked to the floor and said, "I wanted to find out more about the people buried on our property and knew that no one would bring me here to ask any questions." Callie did everything in her power not to physically extract him from his seat as he tried to make this excuse.

She was unable to take her eyes from Jamie. Instead of the self-assured child she'd always thought him to be, he now looked fragile in his tongue-tied condition.

As if sensing the boy's overall unease, Mr. Rollins clasped his weathered hands together and said, "I didn't realize that Jamie here would come over without asking permission. Even so, we had a pleasant conversation, and you, young man," he said, looking up at Gabe. "If you want to know more about the three graves on the Burke property, you can come speak with me anytime."

Gabe cleared his throat, clearly uncomfortable at this turn in the conversation. Callie's heart went out to him, but Mr. Rollins didn't seem to sense the young man's discomfort in the slightest.

"I buried all three of them," Mr. Rollins said, his voice thick at his own disclosure. "Gerald Johnson on the left, my brother Laurence in the middle and . . ." he paused a good, long time. "David Ward on the right."

He shot Gabe a knowing expression. She watched how Gabe sighed, releasing the strain he'd been carrying as the third man's name was spoken aloud. Questions were already being answered in her mind.

"I could only afford a suitable marker for my older brother, Laurence, you know. . . ." Mr. Rollins drew his hands over his mouth to smother a cough before continuing. "I always regretted that, but I couldn't afford more at the time . . . still can't," he croaked out.

"I buried them after an explosion in the mines out at the No. 3 in Ronald. It was before the cemetery was ever an option." His eyes had a fogginess to them. "Before there was ever a house for the Burkes, there was a small boarding house for black miners. It belonged to Gerald Johnson and his family. Once Gerry was killed, his wife up and moved a few weeks later. I believe she settled somewhere near Seattle, where she could find work as a laundress. Never will forget that woman. She made grits for all the men, did the wash, gave a lot of lone boys a pillow to rest their heads on, even though she didn't have much. She about came undone when Gerry passed. Disheartening to see a strong, capable woman like that collapse in mourning. She begged me to bury all three of them. Mrs. Johnson, she was one of the only ones who knew where the bodies were buried, you see. I didn't want to tell anyone else. Didn't want the land meddled with. Didn't trust no one to pay their respects to the dead."

Ruthie settled a mug of steaming tea in her father's hands, and he lifted it to his parched lips. He patted the side of the cup, nodding his thanks to his daughter before giving them his attention once more. "The third man, David, he talked about his beautiful wife and his little daughter and how he couldn't wait to see them again. He would talk about them while the soot covered his clothes, and he had scarcely anything left to wear. They were what made him not mind the nature of the work, you see." He turned toward Gabe and said, "You come and see me again, young man."

Gabe shifted his weight from one boot to the other. Callie watched him from the corner of her eye, digging his hands in the pockets of his pants. While Gabe clearly attended Sunday service with Mr. Rollins and his daughter, it was increasingly evident he hadn't opened himself up for such vulnerable discussions with them about the past. He hadn't looked at Callie since the elderly man began to speak.

Mr. Rollins continued, "My brother and I both came over as miners, but I hated going down the pit and took to homesteading after Laurence died. The only reason I lived was because David . . . he came down the pit to save us. He wasn't even on shift that morning, but he had a premonition something was wrong and insisted on trying to save us. He helped lift me out before he went in for the others," he said, a sad smile finding its way on his wrinkled, yet kindly face. "He'd already developed a reputation by then for saving men's lives before that final act."

Gabe nodded, his hands still wrestling inside his pockets. His jaw tightened, and Callie saw he was working hard not to say anything further in the presence of others in the room. "I'll come see you soon, Mr. Rollins. We best bring this boy back home. The Burkes are expecting him."

"Thank you, Mr. Rollins," Callie echoed, moved at the stories the old man had shared with them. "Jamie, please go outside and put on your boots."

Jamie nodded and took a step toward Mr. Rollins, extending his hand to the man who'd answered at least some of what he'd wanted to know. "Thank you for telling me about the identities of the graves. It's more than Gabe—" He turned around and looked up at his father's trusted worker. "It's more than Gabe wanted to tell me." He gave the notebook he'd been toting an extra pat before turning toward the door and reaching for his discarded boots.

Callie saw Ruthie smoothing her hands over the front of her pants, her lips pressed together in a line of uncertainty, perhaps over what her father had revealed. But as Jamie walked before her, she seemed to let that thought pass.

"You come back here anytime, young man," she said peering down at Jamie, smiling again, perhaps at the cowlick in his dark hair or the traces of dirt smudged on his cheeks. "Anytime your Ma or Pa says it's alright, you hear?"

On his way out, Gabe shook Ruthie's hand, and she held him there for a moment. "You come back too, at least to our Sunday services. We miss you when you travel."

Gabe smiled at her and said, "I will, Miss Ruthie. I'll be there this coming week. Ran into Preacher Jacobson in town and got to talking to him about the church. Thought he could use a hand since he's been down in the mines so much and I'm helping a few days this week on the property, clearing out branches and raking leaves. I'll be there Sunday as well, now that I'm back in town."

Ruthie's smile beat on. "Thank you for doing that, Gabe. It's good to have you home."

Jamie gave Mr. Rollins and Ruthie a farewell wave, then slunk into the back of the truck for the jolting ride back up to his house. As she climbed into the passenger's seat, Callie mulled over the unexpected revelations. Gabe had integral ties to this region. He had ties she may never have known, had Jamie Burke not gone looking for them. There were so many things she wanted to turn and ask Gabe. Had he put in a request for work in Roslyn because of those ties? How many in this town knew that he was a descendant to one of the first black miners to set foot on Washington soil? Had he ever visited his relatives here before? These things she wanted to ask him, one after the other, but she'd seen vulnerability wash over his features at Mr. Rollins' account and knew that now wasn't the place or the time.

Chapter 26

1908

H ER MOTHER HAD raised her to be demure and composed, yet Lily could hardly stifle her curiosity as her
train clattered over Snoqualmie Pass. White-capped
mountains came into view, and endless Douglas firs surrounded her. Open window or closed, she all but inhaled the clear
mountain air just by coveting its cleansing. Tears pricked her
eyes. She was finally doing this, making this trek to the place
her father had lived and died. It had only taken her nineteen
years to return. She smiled to herself, at the sweetness of the
six-year-old girl who'd remained with her still. She needed a
retreat from the life she'd been living: the preparation, her
nights of performing, the revolving door of silk gowns, the
straightening of her hair, her insufferable, yet well-meaning
mother, the man she'd almost married, but hadn't. All these
things and people she needed a reprieve from, and yet she'd
tucked more than one show-stopping dress at the bottom of her
luggage, thinking it might be fun to perform in a small place
where no one knew her name. Where someone—one person,
even—might remember David Ward's instead.

Lily hadn't remained in Roslyn long enough after his passing
to hear people speak of his courage, but she felt the substance
of who he was in her bones. His early departure from her
life—and so many others—made her sometimes tremble, as
if a breeze had swept into her bedroom, though there were no
windows open and the curtains didn't even rustle. As a little

girl, she told herself that she'd return to the coal-mining town someday to honor her daddy's memory.

"There's no reason for that," Georgina would say, though not unkindly. "Your daddy didn't live there very long, and even if they admired him there, so much time has passed. Lily, look at me. Your daddy . . . he's with you wherever you go."

Lily stopped mentioning Roslyn after that, but she didn't abandon thoughts of returning there. Even if it were only to walk the same main streets her father had walked, to nod at a few of the miners who may have met him and conversed with him, or to visit the church where he once worshipped. But life got in the way, and she was for too long occupied with her studies and piano lessons to entertain thoughts of a little place at the center of the Cascade Mountains.

She and her mother had found the inner resolve to plant themselves in Seattle, to not only bloom, but flourish there. Yet her father's death in the mines was something she carried with her always, like one of the pressed lilies tucked away in the recesses of her purse, locked inside a letter he'd sent her. The years passed. She lost her cherubic cheeks, growing more and more into the female form of her father. She had her mother's voice, but everything else she'd taken from David Ward—the round, doe eyes, their almond warmth, the high cheekbones, her plentiful lips. Her laugh mimicked his, or so she was told. It gave her mother pause more than once, just as likely to make Georgina tear up as to bring her to laughter. And heaven knew, laughter was what she needed.

Georgina had no trouble finding work in music halls and clubs in Seattle once she, Bella, and Lily settled in. They found an apartment in the Central District and Georgina hurriedly made a home of their quaint, two-bedroom quarters. Bella's hands might be chapped and worn from all the sheets she folded for a living, but on her own time, the artist in her emerged. She knew just where to place bowls of dried rose petals. She found silk gardenias and set them in a vase near the window. To offset the endless sheets of rain, she livened up the place with lamps lit on the nights they were home. Lily had come to know Miss Bella well over the years. She spent more evenings in that woman's company than her own mother's. It was Miss Bella who prepared most of her meals, who took a seat with her at their small dining room table. Once in a while Lily looked up and saw her smiling fondly at her, longing rising over her face.

"Sometimes I wish Gerald and I'd had a child," she said, only once. "The good Lord gave us ten years together, but He didn't fill our arms. Not in that way, though He did in so many others."

Lily wanted to ask her what other ways He'd filled them. Seemed to her He'd taken a lot away. Miss Bella didn't have any blood relatives in these parts—she had only her makeshift family, her emerging laundering business, and the African Methodist Episcopal Church on Sundays. But that was enough to give Miss Bella an inner peace that made others wonder and even envy her happiness. Her mama took her to church Sunday mornings when she'd had enough rest and often said prayers over her on nights she was home. But it was Miss Bella's faith— her strong ship atop rough waters—-that Lily marveled at over the years as she passed through grade school with straight A's, as she joined the church choir and was told she had the gift of song. Her mother trained her to sing classically, but Lily wanted to depart from the operatic style and looked for every opportunity to sing lively ditties that left audiences charmed.

"If your father could only see you now," Georgina had said, quickly brushing her lips over her daughter's cheek, an unceasing sparkle in her eyes as she stood back and held her firmly at the shoulders. And while she accepted her mother's glowing praise, Lily wished she could turn the mirror toward her mother and allow Georgina to catch even a glimpse of what others experienced in her presence. The intangible beauty. The allure that set off her amber colored eyes. The perfect poise and command she exuded on the stage. While Lily could more than hold her own, she didn't aspire to be as ethereal.

She was inclined to shimmy with a liquored-up guest, laugh in the midst of a song if she flubbed a few of the words before coming back in strong, to drop her reservations as easily as the fur shrug her mother had tossed from her shoulders.

Lily searched now through her disorganized handbag for the name and address of the woman she'd be staying with for the next three days, though she didn't need to review that information again. There was something about lifting it out from the tangle of artifacts that comforted her, made her decision to come here more concrete. It had been almost a month since Lenny Rollins had written her back, telling her that he had just the place for her. She was welcome to take residence with him and his wife, of course. But he had a young, recently married daughter in Cle Elum whose company she might relate with even more. Her name was Ruthie, and she would gladly show her all the hidden gems to be found in the small, unassuming coal town. Feeling nervous stirrings as she approached the train depot, Lily shook them off with a laugh at the memory of the form-fitting gowns she'd needlessly packed.

Chapter 27

1932

JAMIE TRUDGED UP the stairs to his house, each footstep made more leaden by his boots. Callie and Gabe followed a few feet behind him, still quiet from the unexpected adventure they'd taken together. As soon as Jamie opened the front door, Julia surfaced at the landing with her arms over her chest. "Father is not happy with you," she said.

"Jamie, come to my study." Mr. Burke entered the room behind Julia. He quickly nodded his thanks to Gabe and Callie and ushered his young son down the hall so they could talk behind closed doors.

Julia pressed her hands together, as if satisfied to find her younger brother would be met with some form of punishment, even if she didn't yet know what it entailed. She turned right in time to see Annie burst into the room. She looked more disheveled than usual, her dark hair fallen loose from her bun. One glimpse of the girl's smile and Annie shook her head. "Be frustrated with your brother all you want, but smiling at his consequences won't help you any. If Jamie's tied up it just makes you a little more tied up too."

Julia frowned and pulled at the loose sash around her dress. In an uncharacteristic move, Annie bent to clasp the girl's chin in her hand. "I understand your frustration. Just make sure you check yourself, Julia. Do that for me, will you? A bitter heart won't help you."

Julia gave a reluctant nod before turning toward the stairs.

She spun around and met Callie's gaze. "Maybe it's best we stop learning about the history in this town. It makes him too curious, and now it's got him in trouble. What good does it do any of us to learn about a bunch of long-gone miners anyway?"

She was gone before Callie could begin to phrase an answer to that question. Hadn't she been doing what her employer had asked her? How was it possible that a reprimand from an eleven-year-old had the power to make her stammer, inwardly questioning every lesson she'd developed since they'd begun?

✧ ✧ ✧

Gabe and Callie scarcely had time to debrief with Annie in the sitting room before they heard the crunch of tires over gravel. Sure enough, a glimpse out the spacious front window confirmed that Mrs. Burke was home.

"What an answered prayer that she missed the entirety of that episode," Annie said, before making way for the kitchen, where Callie could smell garlic chicken roasting in the oven and freshly baked bread.

Callie thought about leaving Gabe to tell Mrs. Burke about her son's disappearance, but at any moment, Jamie could come bounding out of his father's study. She wanted to be on hand to answer any further questions that Mr. Burke might have for her. So Callie let Mrs. Burke find her and Gabe standing quietly in the sitting room, though she was playing with the seams in her navy-blue skirt, and Gabe was walking over to the hearth, about to stoke the flames of a growing fire.

When Mrs. Burke saw the two of them in the room together, she let her eyes deliberately settle on one, then she took in the other. Her black heels paused at the periphery of the room. Callie thought the mistress of the house looked more than ever like a paper doll than a living, breathing woman. She wore a fitted, belted gray jacket, an elegantly matched skirt and a blush-colored blouse. It was an ensemble Callie might have admired more on a different occasion.

As if sensing Mrs. Burke's hesitation, Gabe broke in. "Jamie ran away and had us looking across town for him this evening."

She shook her head, not attempting to hide her frustration with her son. "Why? Where did he go this time?" She drew a hand to her string of pearls and waited.

Gabe started in before Callie could speak. "He's grown interested in the unmarked graves on the property. He noticed that the only marked one had the surname 'Rollins' and walked all the way to the house of the only known Rollins to ask him some questions."

Mrs. Burke absentmindedly placed her pearls in her mouth. "That boy needs to find a better pastime." She shook her head. "There's nothing to be gained in trying to identify men long buried in the ground."

Callie saw thunder brewing in Gabe's eyes and the considerable restraint required for him not to say anything. She spoke so Gabe wouldn't have to. "Jamie's back now. He's in the study with his father. We brought him home."

She and Gabe weren't met with immediate gratitude for finding her wayward son, but with a wan smile, like a patron's response to an underwhelming performance. "Whatever would that boy have to find at Ruthie's house? Isn't she that colored window washer?"

Callie didn't miss Gabe's withering look at her dismissive words. He said only, "It was really Ruthie's father he wanted to see. . . . He figured Mr. Rollins knew some of Roslyn's early years and wanted to ask him some questions, thinking that none of us would take him to do so."

Mrs. Burke gave a brittle laugh. "He was right to think that. Why would we go to an old nobody . . . ?"

"He's not a nobody," Gabe broke in. "Jamie learned that Mr. Rollins came to Roslyn some forty years ago and he wanted to ask him questions about his family's history. . . ."

Mrs. Burke looked none too happy to be corrected in her own home. She shook her head, perhaps a more appropriate show at frustration.

"Let's stick to the history books from now on. Jamie's curiosity takes us all places we don't need to be. Now, where's my daughter? This must have upset her greatly."

✧ ✧ ✧

Once Mrs. Burke fled for the upstairs, Callie smoothed the imaginary wrinkles in her skirt once more. "I should clean the study and be on my way," she said, more quietly than intended. She kept her eye contact with Gabe short, trying to maintain her calm after Mrs. Burke's reprimand. Hadn't she done what Mr. Burke asked—taught them what she knew about the settling of the Washington territory, brought them to the library, encouraged them to create their own maps, and taken them on nature walks? How could she be held responsible for the unmarked graves on their own property and the fascination of her nine-year-old charge?

She made her way to the children's study, began to pick up pencils and slide chairs in place. The door opened and partially shut, almost causing her to jump. Gabe had followed her. He fastened his eyes on hers. "Thank you for helping me find Jamie tonight. . . . Having you there at Ruthie's kept me from saying . . . a lot of things that ran through my mind."

She smiled, not knowing what to say.

"I can take those for you," Gabe said, glancing at the maps she held. They were clenched in her hands so tightly, it was surprising she hadn't torn them. She gave him the marked-up papers, her stomach stirring at the touch of his hand. Once he set them on the back table, he turned toward her again. "You didn't do anything wrong. In fact, I love that you're going beyond textbooks—but I'd stick to what keeps Mrs. Burke happy. At least, for a while." His voice was droll.

When Callie didn't offer anything to those words, he pressed on. "You know, we were so hellbent on getting Jamie home that we didn't think how our appearance in public would look," He placed his hands near his pockets. She nearly interrupted him, but there was a pull in his throat—she became conscious of the cost in these words. "Callie, I would like to know you more, but I can't. Please—when we see each other, let's be civil, but go on our separate ways." There was an earnestness in his voice that she couldn't disregard. "I'll go on thinking highly of you from a distance, knowing it's for the best."

"Do you want me to pretend that we're strangers?" Callie asked, surprised by how her throat began to close on her. She couldn't understand herself, but was glad she was able to regain her composure without too much trouble. What he said made perfect sense. When a minor crisis had drawn them together, they were still treated with derision from those who saw them side by side. She hadn't missed the look on Mrs. Burke's face when she came upon them in the living room.

Gabe began to shake his head, but then thought better of it. "Doesn't matter what I want, Callie,' he said, smiling toward the ground. "What matters is that we do what's best, and even being here with you now isn't fitting. I think highly of you, and I wish . . . it doesn't matter what I wish."

"Yes, it does," Callie broke in before he could walk away. "It matters to me."

Her words didn't keep him for long. He looked down before reaching for the door. "I like hearing that, Callie . . . but it doesn't change anything. I'll see you around, alright?"

Chapter 28

CALLIE HAD A HARD TIME accepting Gabe's parting words. She'd ridden next to him in the truck only three days prior, united with him in their need to locate Jamie Burke, and felt the warmth of standing close to his shoulder. Those exchanges seemed more real than a closing plea to go on greeting each other with an intentional distance. She was gathering items in her arms from the Company Store when the reality of that decision swept over her like a melancholic tune. She had no time to taste the sadness of it or even ask herself why her feelings were so severe—a man's familiar voice at the counter caught her ear.

"Mind if I take a look at one of those new headlamps you've ordered in?"

She analyzed the items in her possession—a loaf of bread, a jar of honey, a pound of flour—and wondered how discreetly she might place them on a shelf and hightail it out of the store.

"Hello there, Callie Rushton," Paul Dightman said. Mischief was alight in his blue eyes, corrupting any sincerity in his smile. His effortless good looks didn't entirely escape her, although she knew what they were worth. Something had shifted since last she saw him: she could notice his charm and yet insulate herself from it. She knew him better now. Knew how shallow his predictable smirk and flattery were. He wordlessly handed the headlamp back to the store clerk and walked toward her.

"You're looking well," he said, his eyes scanning her form.

She wore only the same belted, floral housedress of weekdays and wished her face wouldn't start to flame. There was something about his recognition that used to make her bloom. Now she only felt the stain of embarrassment. She didn't thank him for his compliment this time. Instead, she mustered a response and said, "I best be going now." She tried to evade him. There was enough room in the aisle for them both to pass, but he took it upon himself to place a heavy hand on her shoulder and speak close to her ear. "I miss talking with you."

She drew back, forcing his hand off her shoulder. "I don't think you should tell me that," she said.

He gave a wistful smile that made her ache, though she wished she felt nothing.

"I'm human after all," he said by way of explanation. He shook his head, but she had no presentiment of what came next. "Word is that you're seeing a colored boy, Callie." He drew a hand to her scarf and tugged on it lightly, enough to irritate. "Taking chances now that we're done?"

She flinched under his touch and moved away, then looked up into his unbelieving eyes. She didn't want to waste time wondering which crude miner had gossiped to Paul, as if her choices affected him in any capacity at all. "Someone has their sources wrong," she said, her teeth ground together. "I'm not seeing anyone at all. . . . Not that you have a right to know."

Paul persisted. "I didn't know you were taken with colored men. Why didn't you say so, Callie? That you could fall for the likes of Burke's stockman?"

She narrowed her eyes. He'd gone too far. "You know, perhaps I should consider being his girl. As it stands, I'm not, but he's kind to me. And in the short amount of time I've known him, he's proven a much greater man than you." Seeing the revulsion start to fill Paul's eyes, she pressed on. "He doesn't disappoint me."

She could feel his hot breath on the back of her neck as she moved away from him, far enough that he'd have to make a scene to converse with her again. But she was visibly shaking by the time she plunked her groceries on the shop counter, as she searched for the change needed to cover the cost. The store clerk had deeply compassionate eyes behind thick spectacles, and Callie was grateful he didn't ask her if she was alright when she clearly wasn't. Back out on Pennsylvania Avenue, she felt thankful for the safety of the few pedestrians around her. But Paul didn't follow her out, perhaps grown wiser after seeing he'd stirred up a hornet's nest within her.

✧ ✧ ✧

Callie set the box of groceries on the kitchen counter knowing she still needed to clear her head. Before her mother could ask questions, she buttoned her black winter coat back up again, drew her burgundy scarf around her neck, and took for the back roads in Roslyn. She needed to get away from this movement, away from the scattering of people making their last run to the stores or their first appearance at the confectioneries for the night. Her footsteps took her toward the Church of Christ, and she tried to pretend there was nothing out of the ordinary in coming this way. Her father's good friend was the preacher there, and if on the off chance she caught sight of him wrapping up his sermon notes, he'd greet her with a friendly wave, perhaps start talking of the next time he'd drop over for a smoke with her father. But her true motive, her hope against reason, made her ribs ache and her heart hammer in its cage. She clenched and unclenched her hands. She knew in all probability that Mr. Jacobson wasn't preparing sermon notes at this time. He was undoubtedly making his trek home from the mines.

Lights flickered from the windows of the faded grey church, and it was difficult for her not to wonder what any churchgoers would think if they burst from the front doors and saw her, a young white woman standing there. After years of working alongside Sam Jacobson, it wasn't as though her father had traded a Sunday morning service at Mt. Pisgah Presbyterian for one of the livelier mornings at Church of Christ.

A Chevy truck sat close to the entrance. It belonged to none other than Mr. Sam Jacobson himself. She suddenly remembered Mrs. Jacobson might be there, fulfilling the duties of a good pastor's wife. She was just that type of woman: give her a task, and she'd do it with a smile that was genuine, even with the small grandson she tended grasping at her apron strings.

Before Callie had time to fret about Mrs. Jacobson seeing her on the church property, she glimpsed a figure coming from the side of the church hidden from the road. He carried gardening shears and was wiping the perspiration from his brow. It was Gabe. She had hoped to see him, but hated her own desperation that defied his request to keep their distance from each other. She wrung out her hands, suddenly feeling foolish for coming there.

Before he could set down the shears, he saw her. His eyes narrowed in question and he stilled the shears in his hands without coming closer. She knew that she'd done the wrong thing, but it was too late to turn back.

"Callie," he said tentatively, "what are you doing out here?" Then, as if realizing he sounded accusatory, he added, "Is there anything I can help you with?"

Even if he'd softened his line of questioning, she sensed his immediate disappointment in her and remained rooted to the ground. Her face flamed despite the chill, but she couldn't hide her shame. She shook her head and said, "Please forgive me. . . . I . . . I shouldn't have come."

She turned from him and prayed that her eyes wouldn't flood. Embarrassment stung her worse than the pretense of being strangers, that consciousness that she'd disregarded his request. She took several steps away from the church before she felt his hand at the back of her elbow.

She paused. His right to be upset with her overrode any discomfort she might feel. Mercifully, the water threatening to spill from her eyes stood still when she turned back around. She raised her chin to meet his disapproval.

"You're right," he said, a beat of anger still present in his eyes. "You shouldn't have . . . not after I told you that people wouldn't understand." He wiped his forehead with the back of his sleeve and paused.

"I'm sorry," she said once again. She moved her weight from one foot to the other. Not knowing what else to say, she steered her attention to the church. It was grey, small and beautiful, against a landscape of russet autumn. The overhanging light sparked at the entrance. The wind played tug of war, reminding her that come winter the light bulbs would likely snuff out and require the replacement of candlesticks. Her eyes rested on the parked truck again.

Noticing her wariness, Gabe felt his remaining irritation dissipate. He spoke quickly. "It's alright, Callie—it's alright. I'm just trying to do what's best for you. I wish things could be different. . . . Look, I was just finishing up. Have you ever been here before?" He nodded over his shoulder. "No? . . . Before you go . . . do you want to wait a minute? I'm gonna tell Mrs. Jacobson I'm wrapping up."

She glanced around, hoping that the pastor's wife wouldn't come outdoors to see her standing on the church property.

"I left my truck at home," Gabe said, as if reading her mind. "Took the tracks down this way, as you so often do. You want to wait for a minute?"

She nodded wordlessly and felt hope rattle around in her heart in spite of everything. As much as he might seem reconciled to her presence right now, he'd respectfully asked her to refrain from what she'd done. And yet when he emerged from the church and bounded down the steps, he greeted her with a smile and she chose to forget the unheeded words.

"Here, come this way," he said, gesturing before them. They strode behind the church. After a few minutes, she could see only the roof behind them. There was something forlorn about the tall, unshorn grass. Yet, the deep blue expanse of sky sought to set the tone, told them they were welcome here.

Gabe slowed his steps to match her own. How refreshingly different he was from some of the mining boys she'd grown up with, boys who might hold open doors, but sometimes forgot not to spit out their chew or share a crass joke in her presence. The little time she'd spent with Gabe she could tell he wasn't a small-town boy. His eyes were open to more of the world than the ebb and flow of Roslyn. She wanted to ask him about his upbringing, but Paul's accusing words about her seeing a colored man barged into her thoughts and made her silently angry and defensive again.

Callie played with a button on her coat, trained her thoughts on other things. "I didn't even know this was out here," she said when they were standing in the midst of untamed grass interspersed with the last of the wildflowers and shrouded by evergreens.

"We come out here sometimes after church in the summer to have picnics. Sometimes the kids come out to play hide and seek." He moved near an impressive apple tree and rested a hand on the trunk. He nodded toward the generous branches, "You want a lift?"

Her sparkling eyes must have told him the answer, for he reached out his arms, placed them around her waist, and helped hoist her up to the branch. She did her best to maintain her composure, hide the thoughts swirling through her mind.

He kept his eyes on her, and the question she feared came her way. "Please tell me . . . why did you want to come here today, Callie?"

The slight rosiness in her cheeks gave way to a warm berry shade. "Isn't that obvious?" she asked, wondering why she didn't retreat while she had the chance. "I feel like I was just getting to know you. I like spending time with you . . . well . . . " she laughed. "Maybe not in the context of searching for a missing boy, but I like talking with you, and I don't want that to stop."

He broke in. "I didn't want to ask for distance between us, but I saw how those miners were looking when we stopped at Minto's—"

"I don't care about the miners we saw at Minto's. If they

want to make snap judgments, there's not much we can do." .

His expression was sober. "Callie, it's not only the opinion of one place we'd have to worry about. People wouldn't like us hanging around each other here in Roslyn, but they'd hate it more everywhere else. I don't think you know how much."

Callie shielded her eyes from the glare of afternoon sun. "I wouldn't know, Gabe . . . I won't pretend that I do." When he said nothing to that Callie changed the subject. She didn't want to spend their only time together talking about the disdain people felt at seeing her fair skin next to his golden-brown hue. "I thought I knew every inch of this place, having lived here my whole life."

He tilted his head to the side, analyzing her. "Have you? Lived here your whole life?"

She nodded, and he said, "I feel like I've lived here longer than I have. It's only been a year and a half."

She found a willing leaf from the branches overhead, plied it between her fingers and asked, "Why does it feel longer? Is that because you don't like it here?"

He shook his head quickly. "I like it here, most of the time. No, I think it feels longer since I have roots here." The words were out, and he kept going. "I didn't want Mr. Rollins to keep talking about the graves the other day. I knew you'd realize the third one buried up on that hill is my grandfather. Soon as you heard his name, I knew you'd have questions for me, and I . . . I wasn't in a place to talk about it when we needed to bring Jamie back to the house." He bit the inside of his cheek.

Callie let out her breath, reached for a branch to steady herself. Her mind's eye flashed back to the small lily imprint she'd spied on that grave, and she tried to hold back the flood of questions that had accumulated since that night. She didn't know how to start asking them, feeling that Gabe didn't owe her any explanation.

"I wasn't expecting to hear you had ties here," she said, finally. "Did you . . . did Mr. Burke know about your grandfather's burial site when you moved into the house?"

He shook his head quickly. "No. But then again, I didn't either. I knew that my grandfather traveled over with the largest number of black miners to Washington state. I knew that he was a hardworking, strong man known for his kindness. But I didn't know that he was buried up on the hill until I saw the lily imprint and did some more asking around. The strikes of '88 and '89 weren't too terribly long ago. He only lived a year or so after he arrived, but there are some folk who remember him. I obviously don't. My mother, she was only six years old when he passed."

Finding she wasn't balancing herself too well on the branch, Callie hopped down and said, "That woman in the picture Jamie gave me is your mother, right? Liliana?" When he nodded, she pressed on. "I thought she might be—oh never mind. She looks too young to be your mother, but the picture was dated 1925. I think I was too taken with her beauty to—"

Gabe laughed, amusement dancing in his dark eyes. "You thought she was—?" He cleared his throat. "That's my mother. Lily. It's the name her father gave her."

Callie swallowed her discomfort. "What—what happened to Lily and her mother after they learned that he was gone? They didn't stay here, did they?"

Gabe shook his head quickly. "No, they didn't stay. Neither did the woman who ran the boarding house, Bella Johnson. Wasn't anything left for them, and as much as my grandfather was respected by the black miners, he apparently wasn't honored enough to have a proper burial." He shook his head, stared at the ground in a show of frustration. When he spoke again, she noticed he'd willed optimism back in his tone. "They all moved to Seattle, since there were more opportunities for them there, especially in the Central District. My grandmother, she found work as a music teacher and performed as a classical singer. My mother followed in her footsteps. She learned how to play the piano and accompanied my grandmother. When she was old enough, she took to the stage on her own. But she didn't love opera as much as her mother."

"So, you were born in Seattle?" Callie asked, smiling at the mention of the rain-washed city that welcomed artists and poets and musicians.

He nodded. "I didn't know my father, growing up. I lived with my mother there until I was fourteen, and then I took a position with Burke." Before she could slide in more questions, he turned the inquiry on her.

"So, you've lived here your entire life? Your grandfather was a miner too, wasn't he?"

She nodded. "And my father after him. The tradition died with him, though. As much as my father respects mining, he didn't want his three sons to work with a pickaxe."

"I can't imagine being a miner," Gabe said, shaking his head at the absurdity of that thought. "My hands still get pretty torn up out at the docks, but it's not the same as being underground."

"Do you like working for Mr. Burke?" Callie asked. She regretted the question once it was out, but he answered her without hesitation.

"For the meantime," he said. "And until I'm prepared to leave it for something else." Instead of allowing her to insert more questions in the quiet, he touched her on the arm and said, "It's getting dark, Callie. I don't want to keep you, have you accidentally miss dinner."

She wanted to protest, tell him the sky wasn't bleeding itself of blue as fast as it appeared, but she knew he was right. As if reading her reluctance to leave, he surprised her by offering her his hand. She tried to hide the extent of her smile and let her hand settle in his as she moved with him through the field to the church. She felt a stab of disappointment when he dropped his hold of her as they came into the open. The Jacobson's truck was gone and no other vehicles were in sight, and still she felt his hesitation. He stepped back from her and said, "I'll be here working the next few days. If . . . you want to stop by, say close to four o'clock, we could talk again. If only for a few more minutes. And if not, then I'm still glad you came here today, Callie. Even if you shouldn't have."

She pushed her dark hair back, away from her eyes and said, "I'll come back again."

He smiled and she waved her goodbye. Every added minute out in the parking lot added to the probability of their being seen. Callie could only imagine the look on her father's face if he were to know that she was standing here—and so close to Gabe. Her mother would tell her that societal rules told them not to intermingle. Right or wrong, she must follow constructs, the oft unspoken expectation of the majority. Her family was cordial with the Jacobsons, but Callie wouldn't fool herself into believing there weren't limits within that relationship as well. Those barriers hadn't been pushed, but that didn't render them invisible.

While running home, she tried to shroud the elation of her stolen minutes with Gabe. What he'd told her—those were things he wouldn't tell just anyone. If they could see through her, any one of them, there wouldn't be any chance to meet him in the meadow again. There wouldn't be an opportunity to see Gabe again at all.

Chapter 29

MRS. STAREK'S SEAMSTRESS SHOP wouldn't become a shoe store until the end of October, but regular customers found the seamstress on the street corner, at the grocery store, even at her own home, requesting that she mend their garments. Knowing what a chore it was to disassemble the entire store, Callie went in to help sweep the cobwebs that had settled behind boxes, pronged between beams, and scattered in darkened corners. There was a surprising amount of dust hiding beneath the lone couch and the various chairs. Both she and Bess walked around with handkerchiefs close to their faces, so they could bat at their tearing eyes and keep on working.

As Callie came in after carrying a round of boxes to Mr. Starek's truck, Bess stopped her with a pointed observation. "I've heard you're spending time with that young man, Gabe."

Before Callie could respond, Bess came out with it. "Mrs. Adams said as much when she dropped off a skirt for me to mend. She mentioned seeing you talking with him right out here on the street one evening. Also how some of the miners saw you outside Minto's the day you were looking for Jamie."

Callie braced herself. "There were a lot of eyes on us when we went to Minto's, I'm coming to realize," she said, propping the broom in the corner. "I had no idea that people would jump to conclusions so easily. We were so focused on finding Jamie, that it didn't really factor in — what people might think."

But even as she spoke those words, Callie thought of Annie's reluctance to send her out with Gabe as part of the search. Bess pressed a finger to a water stain on the front counter. When she looked back up, she said, "Doesn't surprise me any. I've lived in this town my entire life. I know that people will look for something, even if there's nothing there. But if there is something there . . ." She blew a loose strand of auburn hair from her face, and looked at Callie, her grey eyes penetrating. Then, after Callie's silence said, "This is no passing fancy, is it?"

Bess' observation caught her off guard. She tried to understand her tone, but couldn't decipher if it was one of warning, alarm, or even amusement. Instead of answering the older woman's question, she watched the seamstress' earrings jangle, caught the silver tint of them against the late afternoon sunlight peering through the window.

"Perhaps you should untangle yourself before you get stuck." The concern in her eyes was all too apparent. "I'm sure he's a sweet young man. He's certainly handsome. It's that the world at large isn't ready or kind enough to . . ."

"Before I get stuck?" Callie asked. She hadn't maintained a level voice, so she couldn't begin to argue with the older woman even if she'd wanted. She glanced down to the remnants of spiderwebs on the wood floor, and she wondered if that was the reason Bess selected those particular words.

"I see how you react at the sound of his name," Bess said, refusing to let her suspicions rest.

"We were working together to find Jamie, is all. That's the reason I went with him to Minto's. We were trying to figure out the boy's whereabouts. It really had nothing to—"

"That might be the narrative you wish to tell your parents," Bess said, unconvinced. "And I understand it, I do. Heightened emotions often bring people closer together, but Callie . . . tell me if I'm wrong in thinking you might have feelings for him." Bess wiped at the stubborn stain some more. "My heart goes out to you if you do. . . . I wish our country was more accepting, but we're not there yet, child. We have a long way to go."

Callie shook her head. She so agreed with Bess' understanding. A man and woman didn't need to belong to a certain fraternal organization, a singular ethnicity, to be bound to each other. But she wasn't prepared to reveal the stirrings of her heart, not when she was already operating on borrowed time with Gabe. "There's nothing for anyone to be concerned with, but he's someone I could have feelings for . . . if I was allowed."

The seamstress narrowed her lips. "If only it worked that way, Callie. It's alright. You can tell me anything, when you're ready. You won't find hard words from me. There's enough of that in the world, and it only leads to division and oppression." She wiped a hand over her mouth, and her lipstick smudged. Before Callie could politely point to it, the seamstress traced a finger to the stain on the counter and tried to blot it out.

✧ ✧ ✧

Against her better judgment, Callie set out for the Church of Christ the following afternoon. Even though Gabe had eventually accepted her presence the first time and even hinted that he wouldn't mind her coming back, Bess' words were still fresh. But she was already bundled up in a coat over her favorite wine-colored dress and determined to bring Gabe a few gingerbread cookies she'd just baked. She could feel their warmth permeate the napkin and hoped they wouldn't melt or crumble in her palm before she reached him. It was well before the dinner hour, so she didn't cause too much speculation as she left, letting her mother believe she was meeting Lucy after her shift at the attorney's office.

Leaves tumbled loose from their branches, leaving their golden, red, and orange tones in the path of her feet. How effortlessly the trees seemed to let them go, despite the beauty they begged the world to see. Callie marveled over them. As she looked up from the leaves, she suddenly saw her best friend moving toward her, wheat-colored hair loosening from its clasp. She felt a prick of annoyance at being caught like this. Lucy reached for Callie's free hand and squeezed it in her own.

"What are you doing out and about?" Her eyes dropped to the gingerbread cookies. Callie was reluctant to answer and dodged Lucy's question.

"What are *you* doing out and about?" she said.

"I finished early tonight." Lucy looked at Callie's face again as if trying to read the riddle there. "So what are you up to?"

She couldn't lie to Lucy. Callie took a deep breath. "You know Gabe . . . who works for Mr. Burke? I'm meeting him at the Jacobson's church. He's doing some gardening there, and I made some cookies. It's getting so cold, and I thought he might appreciate . . ."

She didn't manage to get the rest of her words out before her best friend's eyes widened incredulously. Lucy wasn't as by-the-book as her other friends, but she braced herself for a lecture.

"Oh Callie." There was marked concern across her features that Callie refused to contemplate, not when she was determined to meet him before he left.

"I know," Callie said quietly. She held the cookies out like an offering, so they wouldn't crush in the palm of her hand. Familiar faces passed them, but Callie didn't want to get sidelined in a conversation. Lucy focused back on her, berry painted lips compressed in a straight line.

"I understand that you're drawn to him," Lucy said, her voice low. "But you'll have hell to pay if you make anything of this. Not everyone is so welcoming of little colored babies . . . even if they don't look—"

"Stop!" Callie said. "You're getting ahead of yourself." On the heels of Bess' lecture about untangling herself, Callie didn't want to hear her best friend's cautionary words.

Sensing her seriousness, Lucy changed tack. She rested a hand on Callie's shoulder. "You best go before it gets dark, then. We'll talk later, alright?" Her hazel eyes betrayed restlessness. Callie knew they'd have quite the conversation next time they met, but still she headed in the direction of the Church of Christ.

Today, unlike the first afternoon they met, no lights flickered inside the church. The windows were darkened. Callie peered over her right shoulder and saw a faded gray pickup truck in the church parking lot. While surprised that he'd driven instead of venturing on foot, Callie checked her own worries. His parked truck wouldn't signal a thing to a passerby; it was her presence here that would.

She stood on the sidewalk, hesitating. She had yet to cross over to the church property. She felt a few crumbs leave the napkin, and inwardly regretted bringing cookies for him at all. Gingerbread? Maybe he hated the flavor! But even as these doubts dented her armor, she remained there, knowing she wouldn't feel any better if she tossed the cookies to the ground and ran back to Lucy.

So lost was she in her thoughts that Gabe startled her on his way to return the tools to the church's shed. "You came back," he called out.

It took her a moment to collect herself. There was no going back now, so she gave a faint smile and walked over to meet him. She held out the cookies. They didn't look nearly as appetizing as when they first left the oven. She felt herself blush and finally said, "You don't have to eat them, but I thought . . . you might be hungry."

He nodded, taking them from her. He tore off a piece of one before she could protest. He swallowed it and he smiled his approval. "How did you know how much I missed gingerbread?"

Callie shrugged, glad that she'd decided to bake on a whim. The church was far enough away from the main street that they escaped the scrutiny of most passersby, and still Callie was mindful of where she stood, ensuring that she was behind one or more of the trees.

"I'm finished here after today," Gabe said, nodding over his shoulder at the church and its lot, "which is good since I have a lot to do for Burke in the next couple weeks." He hesitated. "You want to walk out to the meadow with me? If it's getting too late, you don't . . ."

"I'd love to," Callie said, her smile effortless. She couldn't eclipse all worry at the prospect of being found with him, but the fact that it was his last afternoon here brought that which mattered to the forefront of her mind—stealing moments with him when she could.

He picked up her hand in his own, and she was conscious of how it melded with his. Once at the meadow, he let her hand go with a final squeeze. "You need to invest in some mittens, Callie. Your fingers are cold."

"And some new winter boots too," she said before she could think better of it. He glanced at her scuffed, down-at-the-heels pair, and it was obvious that they weren't adequate in his eyes either.

Gabe folded his arms across his chest. She saw then that he was polished, even though he wore work clothes: khaki-colored pants, a white undershirt, and a newsboy hat that shielded his eyes from the last of the sun. "I might be overstepping myself a bit, but I'm figuring that everything you earn from tutoring you hand over to your folks."

Although he spoke the truth, Callie pursed her lips and protested. "They deserve it all . . . every penny. . . . I still live with them since I can't afford to be out on my own, and it's the least I can do."

He didn't argue, but said, "You need to buy yourself a new pair of boots. You've lived here long enough to know that we're only a month away from the weather turning on us. That pair won't last you through winter."

"Look," she said, defensiveness rising within her, "it's not as if I'm the only one going without. Take a look around this town, and you'll see plenty of hardworking people who are struggling to make ends meet." He hadn't asked for this, but she kept going. "Freddy Murphy knocks on doors to see if he can earn a dime for fixing appliances that most can't afford to even use. Ruthie Sloane is still trying to wash windows, even though the season is closing in on her. Bess Starek is going to keep mending clothes out of her own house, even though she can't afford to keep her store."

Undeterred, Gabe said quietly, "You think of your family's needs above your own." He gave her a knowing look as he led her back to the meadow.

Callie nodded. She directed her attention to the green expanse before them, the astounding fall glory. She watched as tugs of wind played interference with the trees, spun the colored leaves, and disposed of them near their feet.

When he paused just before her and turned, they were close enough to touch. "That's one thing that makes you beautiful, thinking of others." His breath was close and warm on her face, and she wished he'd step even closer. His eyes danced as he looked at her, and there was no one to bear witness or make them break away. But he stepped back.

"Tell me about yourself, Callie," he said, crouching down to pluck a tall piece of grass from the ground. He moved it through his fingers and rose again to his feet, waiting for her to respond.

What did he want to know? She rolled her thoughts, not knowing what to say first. That while she'd lived in Roslyn her entire life, she sometimes thought of leaving? That singing soothed her soul like nothing else would, and she didn't do it every day anymore? That she'd been in love once, and it had broken her heart? Where to begin?

As if noting her dilemma, he tried again. "What would you do if you didn't have to ask anyone else's permission?"

"Be here with you," she said, her laughter genuine. She surprised herself, that she admitted as much aloud. She kept talking in efforts not to feel the stripped-down quality of those words. "I'd like to sing, but my passion . . . it doesn't pay the bills. We sold our record player, and the radio's old and doesn't get good reception. We use it mostly for economic forecasts." Her voice was dry.

Gabe looked toward her, a thoughtfulness etched in his brows. "What if you didn't worry about paying for the bills for once and started singing, since it brings you joy?" Perhaps seeing the incredulity flash in her eyes, he leaned closer to her and reached for her wrist. "I'm serious, Callie. A lot of the places around here would love an evening's reprieve from coal dust. They'd love to hear you sing. You do something for them and keep your own dream alive."

She shrugged but didn't try to tug free from his hold. "I'm not so sure, Gabe. I don't visit many of those places," she said. "Even if many of them don't serve liquor these days, there are unwritten assumptions about young women who frequent—"

He shook his head and tightened his hold on her wrist before releasing his fingers. "Not at all of them. . . . Approach one that's known for their live music and tell them you'd like to sing a few songs . . ."

"You think I should do this now?" she asked, laughter bubbling up in her throat.

He nodded vigorously. "Within a week you should have a gig," he told her. "Time doesn't wait for any of us, and you'll knock the socks off them all."

"How do you know?" she said, taking a step back. A slight smile hovering, she looked to him and said, "You've never really heard me sing. I might be terrible for all you know."

He shook his head. "You couldn't be terrible. . . . Even from that little bit I overheard when you showed up at my room . . ."

She laughed, uncomfortable at the memory. She raised a fingernail to her mouth, thinking of the venues she might try. But, afraid of lingering too long on herself, she turned the questions around.

"How about you? What would you do if you didn't have to ask anyone's permission?"

"Well, I like being with you too . . . I wish we could keep coming here." He tore at the blades of grass and let the bits of green hit the ground. When he looked up, he spoke again. "I don't mind working for Burke. I'm fortunate to have that position, but if I had more time . . . I'd play more baseball, maybe even join a team. For work? Somewhere down the road, I'd like to venture off and help colored people buy homes and establish their own businesses."

"Is Roslyn . . . a place you want to end up?"

Gabe tilted his head to the side, his contemplation growing. "It has its charm, but I'm already thinking of returning to Seattle, for the opportunities to work with more people." He shrugged and Callie felt an unreasonable pang.

Before she could question it, he turned the question back to her. "Is Roslyn a place you want to stay?"

She chewed the inside of her cheek before raising her eyes to him and shook her head. "Not necessarily. A little over a year ago . . . I was engaged to my high school sweetheart. A miner named Paul. I thought he loved me, but I found out he was seeing someone else at the same time. And while I do everything I can to avoid him, Roslyn is such a small town." There was a small hitch in her voice, and she saw a shadow cross Gabe's face.

"He's a fool, and he doesn't deserve you, Callie."

Before she could utter a word, he rose to his feet, moved behind her and encircled her in his arms. She could feel his heart beating, the steady pulse of it, and also the warmth of him surrounding her, taking her in. She closed her eyes, not realizing the extent to which she'd wanted to be held by him until now. He whispered close to her ear, "Do you have feelings for him still?"

Her answer came readily.

"Resentment, anger . . . but not love." She let out a sigh and listened to the frolic of the wind, leaned back in Gabe's arms.

"I don't know how we're going keep seeing each other, you and me." She could hear the longing in his voice. "I keep thinking maybe it's best I move to Seattle now, but you wouldn't be there, Callie. And you don't know how much I'd miss you."

✧ ✧ ✧

How much time had passed since she and Gabe had set out for the secluded meadow? It was Gabe brushing her shoulder and saying, "Look there, Callie," that finally caused her to consider the hour. Though the sky wasn't entirely dissolved of its cloudless blue, the sun was quickly sinking below the tree line. She turned and saw that someone was moving through the green toward them. She took in the considerable swiftness of the woman's steps and the child she'd scooped up in her strong arms before recognizing Mrs. Jacobson making her way across the field. As the newcomer waded through the overly-tall grass with her grandson, Sammy Jr, propped up in her arms, Callie pressed her tongue to the roof of her mouth, suddenly aware of the situation. Tessa must have come tending church business shortly after she and Gabe departed for the meadow. Gabe's truck still sat parked nearby and she'd likely been unable to find him anywhere.

The pastor's wife wore a black cardigan over a threadbare rose-colored dress—one that had been mended repeatedly. Callie could tell that this would be the last season she'd be able to squeeze out its worth. The once lustrous pink was fading. But it wasn't her clothes that really interested her. She read the transparency in Mrs. Jacobson's expression. Concern, frustration, and awareness were written into her features.

"Mrs. Jacobson," Callie said as soon as the woman was within earshot. "How are you?" When there came no answer, Callie awkwardly prattled on. "Gabe and I . . . we both work for the Burkes. We were catching up and were about to head for home."

She didn't listen to what Callie was saying. Mrs. Jacobson merely shifted her grandson in her arms and looked levelly at Callie, as if she were reading her mind. She offered a glossed-over smile that didn't quite reach the eyes. Though Gabe had loosed his arms from Callie's shoulders as soon as they saw the pastor's wife, there was no denying the attraction felt between the two of them. Callie knew her explanation was meaningless. Their meeting here, alone and unattended, gave Mrs. Jacobson all the information she needed.

"Hello, Gabe. . . .Callie." the pastor's wife said, a hint of wariness in her voice.

Callie thought she caught Mrs. Jacobson looking at Gabe critically, but she couldn't be sure. Then Mrs. Jacobson turned back to her and said, "I'm surprised to see you here. Not too many know about our scenic little meadow. It's a gem, isn't it?" She shifted her grandson on her generous hip once more.

"You remember that I work for Mr. Burke?" Callie asked, hoping that this fact might override a hint of the speculation she saw on the woman's face now.

But telling her this did nothing to eradicate the uneasiness flickering in Mrs. Jacobson's eyes. She nodded slowly and said, "I s'pose I do remember Sam mentioning that. Seems I remember my husband mentioning something about you tutoring the children. But I fail to see what you might be tutoring Gabe in, Miss Rushton. Or perhaps it is Gabe who is teaching the lesson in this scenario?"

"Oh, that's not how things are, Mrs. Jacobson," Gabe started in, making attempts to smooth things over. "I'm sorry if it seems . . ."

Callie took a step away from them, not seeing how she could lighten the exchange. She rubbed her cherry-tinted hands together to ward off the sting of the cold and said, "I should really get home. They're probably waiting for me at the table. I'm sorry—I didn't realize how late it was." With barely a nod over her shoulder, she said thank you to Gabe. "Nice to see you, Mrs. Jacobson."

Regrettably, there was nothing more she could say in front of Mrs. Jacobson without betraying her emotions. She couldn't turn back to him, hoping for another tryst at another location. She wanted him to name another hour so she could be near him again. It might be weeks, months even, before she saw him again if he was traveling for business. This reality made her throat start to burn, and there was no hiding it, not even if Mrs. Jacobson had tapped her on the shoulder right then and there and spun her around to ask another question. Water stood at the back of her eyes.

"Good evening, Miss Rushton," Gabe called, giving her reason to turn around and offer a wave, if nothing else.

Even without assurance that they'd meet again for quite some time, Callie regarded his farewell as a bit of hope, knowing he didn't regret meeting with her. Even if it cost him something.

"Give my regards to your folks," Mrs. Jacobson said, no etch of frustration left in her voice. She lingered behind in the meadow with her grandson, finishing her visit with Gabe.

She'd nodded her assent, Mrs. Jacobson undoubtedly knowing that she'd be doing no such thing. To admit that she'd seen Mrs. Jacobson would open the conversation to all the specifics she couldn't afford to share—the when's and where's. As the sun finally dropped behind the mighty trees, Callie shook her head at her carelessness and how she would have still chosen it. She played with a button near the top of her winter coat, admitting to herself that she would meet Gabe Ward again if he asked her. Even if it defied reason for them both.

Chapter 30

CALLIE KNEW THAT word would get back to her folks about being seen with Gabe, but hadn't anticipated the continued outrage from some of the miners who'd seen them together that day at Minto's. She was sitting in the dining room with her family, swallowing the last of her potato soup after returning from the meadow with Gabe, when they heard a loud shatter of glass in the sitting room. The shards of glass had barely spilled over the wine-colored rug before her father was out of his seat, nostrils flaring. An object had been flung at their window. He reached for his rifle, stowed at the top of the coat rack.

"No, Bill. It's not worth it," said Mrs. Rushton.

He ignored his wife's words. "Go to your bedrooms," he said hoarsely, moving toward the front door to see who could have targeted them and why.

The twins looked, one to the other, with wide blue eyes. Stevie leaned toward Charlie and said, "We should build a booby trap out there, so if anyone trespasses on our property . . ."

Their mother shook her head and said, "To your bedroom, boys. Now isn't the time for that discussion."

Charlie narrowed his eyes. "How dare someone break our front window!"

Mrs. Rushton motioned toward their bedroom at the back of the house. "Do as you're told. We can discuss the rest later."

Callie remained at the table, still as a deer. There wasn't any reason to move to her bedroom, as one of her windows faced the street. The person who'd struck the sitting room window could just as easily throw rocks at hers. Less than a minute after being outdoors, her father returned with a hastily drawn note shaking in his hands. He replaced the rifle on the shelf above the coats and moved toward his chair at the dining room table, his eyes still taking in the words left for them on the porch.

"They left a note?" Callie's mother asked, moving toward her husband's shoulder and attempting to read it for herself.

But instinctively, he shielded her from it until he'd read the inscription for himself. He knit his eyebrows together and absorbed the words as if they were a bitter draught. Finally, he held the notice out and turned toward his daughter. "What— what is the meaning of this? It says here that our family better watch ourselves—our daughter's taken up with a colored man."

He raked a hand through his greying hair, and when he glanced up, looked at her with disbelieving eyes. Her mother sank into her own chair, her hands kept in her lap, her mouth parting slightly in question.

"What is the meaning of this?" He pressed Callie, jabbing a finger to the slanted words on the page.

Her throat was dry as parchment, but she found enough of a voice. "I only went to Minto's with Gabe to ask for an address since we couldn't find Jamie Burke," Callie said, regretting her qualifiers and her attempts to get her father from asking more questions.

"You don't have to get defensive, Callie," her father said, crossing his arms over his chest. "I asked you a question, that's all." In the dim light, she noticed the stubble on his face and felt like telling him he should shave. His negligence with the razor made him look older than his years.

"Appearances mean something," her father said, rising to his feet and waving the note someone had hastily written. "You show up with him at an establishment, and anyone will draw the same conclusion. That the two of you are together."

"I haven't even known Gabe for long," Callie said, feeling

unable to stop defending herself. "He is helpful and considerate, and I was grateful that day he stopped what he was doing to track down Jamie Burke."

"Why would you go with him to find Jamie instead of another worker?" her father asked, his nostrils flaring. "Don't tell me that Burke doesn't have other employees who could have helped you out. I've seen that housemaid of his out and about town. She doesn't seem too concerned with appearances, stopping by more than once at establishments most women wouldn't think—"

Callie shook her head, upset that he wanted her to admit that being associated with Gabe under any circumstance—even the disappearance of a child—was incomprehensible.

"That afternoon, Gabe was the one who helped me, and if tobacco chewing miners want to spend their time taking great offense to it, there's not much I can do. I'd go back there with him again, if that meant bringing Jamie Burke home safely. Or if Mr. Burke needed assistance with anything else. Gabe's a hard worker, and he's kind." She didn't mention that she'd go back there with him again if it just meant that she could spend more time with him.

"You're protective of this Gabe," her father said, his eyebrows furrowing as he looked over at her mother. "I'm glad that he's a kind person, Callie. That's all well and good. But you have to be smarter than this. No one wants to see a white woman with a black—"

She cut him off, having heard enough. "I'm sorry, Father, but I'm not willing to take moral cues from miners standing around in establishments with nothing more—"

As if angered by their apparent gridlock, her unwillingness to meet him halfway on this topic—he threw his hands up. "It's not only miners, and I think you've the wits to know that, Callie Elizabeth! In fact, most people don't even discuss the subject because it's known. . . ."

"Long-held beliefs aren't always right," Callie said, rising from the table and backing away from her father and his aggression.

"You're the one who's taught me that." She fought the pressure in her throat, remembering in the midst of her defense that Gabe's work at the Church of Christ had ended and there was no reason for him to seek her out again.

When she finished speaking, neither of her parents could find it within themselves to say anything further. Her father swallowed so that his Adam's apple bobbed in his throat, and she knew there was more there, but he couldn't find the words.

Here, he and Sam Jacobson had worked side by side in the mines for years as equals, and he'd said countless times that the shade of one's skin had no bearing on the quality of man. He'd told his family not once, but numerous times, that the plight of black folk—the sentence of slavery put upon them—was the gravest tragedy of an otherwise glorious nation. He stood at attention whenever Sam Jacobson spoke of his ancestors and took keen interest in his friend's heritage, sometimes humming the Negro spirituals that Sam had sung when working deep underground. But he seemed to be struggling with the suggestion that his daughter could fall for a man who looked like his friend. Sam he knew in isolation, and that partnership had fooled him into believing he was above prejudice. But here he was, twitchy at the thought of his daughter taking up with a black man.

"It's best for you not to lead him on, Callie. He inhabits a different world than yours."

She fought back the urge to give a retort because she knew her father was, at least in part, looking out for her as he'd looked out for her when her relationship with Paul came to a head. Only a year before her father witnessed her fiancé flirting with another girl outside the Roslyn Bakery. Paul had looked confused at seeing her father standing there, but he'd shrugged it off with a goofy grin before turning back to Maura Merrick. Her father had grabbed Paul's collar and slammed him against the sandstone building.

Try as she might to erase a painful recollection such as this, she knew her father didn't want to see her heart broken all over again. Yet there was more behind it than the condition of her heart in his refusal of Gabe. She bit her tongue, knowing this situation was entirely different. Paul Dightman had gotten a fair chance, Gabe Ward wouldn't. Their minds were made up. She couldn't talk with Gabe even in passing the way she could speak with another man.

Callie reached for her winter coat on its peg near the front door and threw it over her shoulders. She needed to contemplate her father's position, that she should end her friendship with Gabe before something really began. Even unspoken rules were for them written in intractable ink.

Chapter 31

BESS STAREK WAS taken aback to see Callie so soon — that much was evident when she swung open her front door and tilted her head. The seamstress wore her hair in a messier bun than usual, but Callie could see she'd taken the time to paint her lips and clip on emerald-like, teardrop earrings.

"Callie," she said, looking as though she didn't know whether to start smiling or let her face settle into seriousness. "What a pleasant surprise. Why don't you come in?"

She released her grip on the door, and from behind her Callie could see where she'd set up her new sewing station. It was quiet in her home and Callie hadn't seen a sign out front declaring business was open. One glance around the cluttered entrance revealed that Bess wasn't hurting for work, however. Beside her rocking chair, lay piles of clothes: suit jackets, dresses, and winter coats that awaited mending. There were half-filled baskets of thread, needles, and yarn scattered about, with no discernible semblance of order to Callie's eye. Yet she knew the seamstress had a structure behind the apparent chaos; she'd been surpassing her customers' expectations for years.

"I know it's sudden . . . me stopping in like this, but I wanted to ask your advice on something that's come up." She offered a smile, trying not to distract herself with the pile of clothes that spilled over the side of the rocker and filled most of the sofa.

"Come in, come in," Bess said, her teeth starting to chatter from the cold. "Advice," she said, while closing the door behind them. "Let me guess . . . this has something to do with your employment at the Burkes."

Callie nodded, miserable. She hadn't planned on telling the seamstress more, not when she was already flustered over Bess' concern about her growing interest in Gabe. But things had quickly changed, now that someone had targeted her parents' home and broken out their front windows. As she told the seamstress about the vandalism and the angry notice that accompanied it, Bess found herself a seat. She kept quiet, but her empathetic eyes took everything in.

"What my parents don't know is that Gabe and I have already met twice outside that time we looked for Jamie," Callie admitted, prepared for whatever Bess' response might entail. "The first time I went to the Church of Christ, I didn't know I'd see him, but I hoped I would. The second time, I went there knowing I'd see him. Mrs. Jacobson came upon us talking in the meadow . . . earlier tonight."

Bess raised an eyebrow. "Was there more than just talking involved?"

Feeling her cheeks take a sudden flame, Callie quickly shook her head and said, "It seems like there might as well have been, considering the response she gave us."

"So, let me guess," Bess said, rubbing her hands together and moving to heat them over the coals that lent warmth to the fireplace. "You're concerned that Sam's wife will say something and that you'll have more to answer for than being seen with him that afternoon Jamie went missing."

"Yes." Callie stammered. "I think she might say something."

Bess crouched near the fire and continued warming her hands. "She won't. Friends of your folks or not, if she was concerned about the two of you together, she'd go to her husband. She wouldn't risk the reputation of a young black man in her community."

Callie swallowed, admitting to herself that the seamstress

had a valid point. She still had another question to ask. "Is it foolish or selfish of me to want to keep talking with him?"

Bess lifted a ball of cobalt blue yarn from a basket nearby. She tossed it from hand to hand and thought on it. "If you were meeting him out of fascination or for a fleeting kiss, then yes, I'd say it's selfish. But if you genuinely care for him . . . I can see that you do." She turned away from the smoldering coals. "If he feels the same way about you, darling, you both need to brace yourselves for some difficulties on the road ahead. It is a brutal world out there. A shattered window is only the beginning of it."

"Just because there's attraction there," Callie said, choosing her words cautiously, "doesn't mean that we'd ever be anything more than . . ."

"True," Bess said, smoothing out her skirt before reclaiming her seat, "but you'll have to consider the possibilities of what falling in love will mean, hon. Would you like a cup of warm apple cider before I get started again? I've heated the tea kettle over that burner there."

"Yes, please," Callie said, almost tasting the pressed apples before their sweetness coated her throat. "But please don't get up. I'll pour some for myself."

She hesitated slightly, but spoke on, sensing Bess was someone she could trust. "He told me . . . he told me that his grandfather, one of the first black miners to the area, was buried in an unmarked grave at the back of the Burke's property, if you can believe it." She shook her head.

When the seamstress didn't answer her, Callie tightened her lips, lest her frustration manifest itself in words she'd later regret. Why wouldn't Bess disclose more of what she knew of the Burkes?

Callie began to search for a teacup in the kitchen just as the seamstress said her name. She paused and turned to see Bess set down the ball of yarn. She noticed how the seamstress spun her wedding band before raising her head.

"Alright," she said at last, "I haven't said all I know for a reason. My family has direct ties to the first black miners to arrive in Roslyn. . . . My daddy was one of the labor recruiters for Northern Pacific, you see. He had a hand in deceiving the black miners who came over. There was a colored businessman named Mr. Simonson, who convinced the men to board the trains, but my father helped orchestrate the entire affair . . . and it's difficult to admit as much aloud. He knew David Ward quite well. My father was called to the scene when the walls of the mine collapsed on him and the other men who lost their lives."

Callie stopped searching for a teacup at this revelation and turned toward Mrs. Starek, her back pressed into the kitchen counter.

"David's wife Georgina fought to have her husband buried in the cemetery, but no black miners were permitted there at the time. . . . I'm ashamed to say that my daddy didn't help the effort. So David Ward was buried on a forgotten hill near the No. 3 in Ronald by one of his friends. No ceremony, no marker to honor him. Unless you consider the lily embedded on his grave a marker. That lily . . . it's come to mean a lot to me. . . . You want to know why?"

Callie nodded, wishing that the seamstress wouldn't pause when she was already riveted.

"David's wife and daughter dropped into a store on Pennsylvania Avenue one day before they left for Seattle." She tugged at an earring. "I knew who they were since everyone was talking about how sad and stunning it was to lose a man like David. Especially with his wife and daughter just come to town." She dropped her head, willing herself to remember. "I wished at that moment that I could sink through the floor, feeling responsible for my father's coercion of the colored miners. I hadn't those words for it then, but I knew it was wrong. If he hadn't played a part in it, maybe David wouldn't have ever come to Roslyn. Maybe he'd still be alive. I crouched down to pretend I was interested in something on a shelf, and when I glanced up, I saw these warm amber eyes looking at me. That little girl, David Ward's daughter, was motioning toward something that had fallen on the ground near me. It took me a moment to see that it was a dried flower from her pocket. A lily. Her lip trembled, and she asked if she could have it back. She didn't mean to drop it, she said. It was from her father, and she wanted to save it.

When I handed it over, carefully, so that no petals would break free, she beamed. Said I could find more of their like behind the church in Ronald and that they just might cheer me up since it looked like I needed it. When her mother came around the corner and saw us engaged in conversation, she hesitated, but she let it be. Though her eyes were sad, she kissed the top of her daughter's head and said, 'You sweet girl.'

It was only later that I found out what that flower meant to her. David Ward's name was one I never forgot. Many folk out here remembered not only his ability in the mines, but the way in which he brought men to safety. Men whose lives would be over if he hadn't exerted his strength. So it unsettled me when I heard that he wouldn't have a place to rest in the Roslyn Cemetery. That no one seemed bothered that he was left without a marker. It was one afternoon, years and years later, that I ran into Ruthie and happened to get in a conversation about seeing David's little girl at the store one day. Her eyes lit up, and she told me she knew Lily. Not only the little girl Lily, but the grown Lily too. She said they were friends and asked if I ever wanted to meet her if she came back to Roslyn. When I mentioned how sad it made me that her father wasn't buried in Roslyn's Cemetery, she told me that her father had buried him and that she sometimes visited his resting place and left bundles of wildflowers for him and the other two men."

Callie was watching Bess so intently, she bumped against a canister of sugar on the counter, causing it to spill over. While she turned to scoop the granules up in her palm, Bess picked the blue yarn back up, oblivious to Callie's blunder.

"Turns out Edward Burke had no idea about the makeshift graves and was surprised when the men working on his house told him they existed. . . . My husband was one of them, remember? Burke knew that his house was a black miners' boarding house in years past, but not much more, you see." Her eyes took on a glow that promised more. "Did you notice that the imprint on the unmarked grave and on the boxes for Burke Enterprises are nearly one and the same?"

Callie nodded slowly but could only frown once she'd considered the question. She had no explanation for this finding, other than to think that lilies were commonly admired. But the way in which Bess phrased the question, the urgency flickering in her pupils, gave Callie pause. The question might be worth returning to.

Bess hesitated, as if weighing how much she ought to admit of her familiarity with David and Lily aloud.

"Did you ever meet Lily when she was all grown up?" Callie asked, her mind fleeing to the picture of her she'd held in her possession for one day.

Bess shook her head. "No, I didn't meet her. I thought about it, since she was such friends with Ruthie and all, but what would I say? I met you once when you were all of six years old and grieving your father's death?" She shook her head. "I didn't meet her, but I did hear her sing once at the Masonic Hall. And that was enough to leave an indelible impression on me to this day. She sounded better, clearer than any record you could hope to spin."

The conversation between the women came to a halt as Mr. Starek burst indoors with a triumphant smile across his face. Before he even set down his hunting rifle, it was obvious that he'd caught something out there today. His boots were muddied, and his untied laces were damp from swamp water. Even Rooster, their golden Border Collie, looked invigorated from his master's success.

"Not another step," Bess said, rising from before the fireplace to lay down a mat at her husband's feet. "Why don't you have Rooster go back outside?"

"Oh, Bess," Nick said, in mock disappointment, although he

opened the door to let the dog out at her request. "He wanted to let you know that we caught an elk out there today."

Bess let out a mirthful sound and tiptoed over to her husband, gave him a loud smack on the cheek. "Good," she said, sounding relieved that he'd had success.

It was then that Mr. Starek noticed his wife's young seamstress standing in the kitchen. "Hello, Callie," he said, smiling pleasantly. "Come here to work?" He made a face of mock distress while sweeping his eyes over the litter of clothing items around the front room, but a chuckle broke up the facade.

Callie shrugged and said, "I don't mind working on a few garments while I'm here."

The laughter died down, and seriousness gripped him as a new thought occurred. "Say, are you still working for the Burkes?"

Callie nodded, "I've only been with them for a month and a half, but the job's the best thing to happen to me in a while." When she noticed he was looking at her critically, she said, "Why do you ask?"

Mr. Starek found his comfortable chair and took a seat before answering. When he started speaking, he leaned forward and clasped his hands together. "I was curious about whether you'd heard anything about that tussle at the Company Store with Burke's colored man."

Bess shot her husband a sharp look, but he missed it.

"Some men I know were in the store and overheard a dispute between Merrick and Burke's man. Said that Merrick was grumbling over prices of the headlamps and was already pretty testy before refusing to give the colored man something behind the counter."

"His name is Gabe," Callie said despite her efforts not to betray her emotions. "And he asked for a bar to tide him over because he hadn't had lunch. Merrick wouldn't sell it to him."

Mr. Starek widened his eyes and scratched the stubble at his chin. He didn't ask Callie how she knew such intimate details.

"Can't say that man's ever been the thoughtful sort," he said instead. "But he's pretty put out by the whole exchange and calling for Burke to let the colored . . . Gabe . . . go. He's started a petition and asked other witnesses sign it—trying to force Burke to get someone else to make the deliveries to the store."

Callie blanched at this news. She looked at her cup of apple cider and took a sip, buying time before she'd have to formulate a response.

Bess beat her to it. "Oh, that's just nonsense, that bit about Merrick calling on Burke to let Gabe go." She'd set her sewing project down and looked at him, as if trying to wake him up from his delusion. "It wouldn't be easy to pick up the pieces after a silly shuffle like that, but Burke won't be letting his favorite worker leave."

Mr. Starek smoothed his hands over his chin before folding them at his knees once more. He nodded at Bess, letting her words go unchallenged.

"Imagine being refused something you ask for at the counter," Bess said, wearied by the idea. "And not because you couldn't afford it or had your pay stub 'snaked' either. But because of the color of your skin. The way God himself had made you."

Chapter 32

A WEEK INTO NOVEMBER, and there was not much for her father to fear. Callie hadn't seen Gabe since their last encounter at the meadow. She hadn't run into any others who might have questions—Paul with his incredulity or Mrs. Jacobson with her matriarchal concern. Though she tried against reason to retain her stolen moments with Gabe, the blunt reality of most days made her conversations with him recede. His name still summoned longing within her, but she hadn't heard him spoken of. He undoubtedly had a girl on the other side of the mountains.

She rehearsed this exact script as she left the Burkes the first Friday of the month, feeling loneliness cling to her like a well-worn sweater. She didn't want to walk into her darkened home, knowing that her father would be in the sitting room kept company by the static radio, so she walked instead to the heart of town. Just off Pennsylvania Ave, she absorbed the swell of voices, the ensuing laughter, the clashing musical styles emanating from the different billiard halls. She didn't partake in Roslyn's week-end revelries enough, and she never set foot in the confectioneries. It was unspoken knowledge that most young women wanting to protect their reputations avoided such unsavory locales. She secretly longed to see for herself if some of the establishments were serving up white mules, but she didn't want to risk the wolf whistles of bawdy miners. If there was a restaurant offering live music tonight, however, she might wander in, snatching a little life from the musicians practicing their art. How long it had been since she'd sung her heart out in front of an audience?

She tried to locate the sounds of a reverberating piano, finally ducking into the Roslyn Cafe. As she opened the door she heard the familiar plink of a piano's keys, and decided to waltz right in—if not to order from the menu, then at least to listen to the songs being sung. A few chords in, and she recognized "All of Me" by Louis Armstrong. Eyes pressed on the up and coming musician. He was a young miner, as Callie could see from his overalls and the dirt on his hands. The music held her in its sway and she stayed near the entrance, not caring that she had no intention to dine here tonight. She began to reach into the recesses of her purse, searching for coins she might throw in the musician's small tin, when she heard someone call her name.

"Callie. Miss Callie," he said urgently, from the back of the cafe. The caller struck her as familiar immediately, though she still turned all the way around to see who it was that sought her attention. Sure enough, it was Gabe, his kindly eyes crinkling at the corners, and his slightly perplexed partner—Ben, she thought—sitting across from him. As if forgetting where they were, Gabe motioned to her, and without a hint of reservation she sidled up to their back table, where steaming plates of marinara chicken and sautéed vegetables waited before them.

"How are you?" Gabe asked, once she was within earshot.

She nodded just as the redheaded man motioned toward an empty chair and said, "Join us for dinner, why don't you? We sat down a few minutes ago. The food comes faster than you'd expect."

Callie paused momentarily, considering the cost of the meal more than the cost of taking a seat with these two men, one of them married and the other black. Before either man could say another word, she took a seat and looked from one to the other. *Don't betray your attraction to Gabe in front of this man who works with him,* she told herself. *You don't want to compromise your position or his.* Even with this internal lecture, Callie couldn't help but notice how appealing Gabe looked. He wore a light brown jacket and a button-down blue shirt tucked into light-colored pants, and was about as far from a miner as one could imagine. "What brings you out and about tonight?" he asked.

She realized she hadn't answered his first question.

"I didn't want a quiet Friday night and thought I'd find out where the music was playing," she said, now that she'd taken a seat.

Gabe offered her a polite smile at first, but it grew wider when he noticed the black gloves she'd recently acquired. "You took my advice and got some new gloves. Attagirl."

Suddenly she heard Ben clear his throat, and half expecting to see him wearing a frown, she was relieved when he motioned toward his plate instead, saying "What can we order for you? We'd like to consider ourselves gentlemen. We don't want to eat all this savory goodness if you don't have a serving yourself."

As if frustrated that he hadn't caught that, Gabe slid his plate toward Callie and said, "Yes to everything Benny just said. It's all on the company. I'll order up another one."

Callie nodded her thanks and picked up her fork, surprised by the state of her hunger. She wasn't starving, but she'd long been accustomed to taking small portions of whatever soup she or her mother cooked over the stove-top. Two bites of the tender chicken, and she set her fork down. "I could have at least waited until yours . . ." She started in, but Gabe shook his head and motioned for her to keep eating.

Even as he waved that notion off, she recognized seriousness flicker in his eyes. Several minutes had passed, and she'd had the luxury to forget what he could not: patrons of this restaurant might already be taking issue with their shared meal, whether Ben sat with them or not. She shivered in spite of the warmth generated from her dinner plate, from the overhead chandeliers. The ceilings were high, and the wind found its way in.

She thought of the shattered glass on her parents' floor as

she pulled her coat closer. She decided then that she wouldn't tell him what happened. How could she and hope they'd ever share another moment like this?

She felt the press of stares on them from the nearest table. Or was it only her imagination toying with her, convincing her that the wife was tapping her husband's hand and narrowing her eyes in their direction? She was certain the previously laughing patrons were now speaking in low, grim tones and eyeing them with disdain. Should she glance up and meet her onlookers straight on, or would that tension undercut the rest of their evening together?

When she looked back to Gabe, she could see she wasn't conjuring up the hostile scenarios. The couple nearby favored them with a cold stare and whispered in discernible tones. "*Can you believe? . . . How shameful. An utter disgrace.*"

Ben, seemingly oblivious to the discomfort of the other diners, was distracted by someone or something at the front window. "You've got to be kidding me!" he almost shouted, rising to his feet and throwing his napkin down on the table. Before Gabe or Callie could ask him what was so unsettling, he said, "That son of a gun, Perry Winters, is going to the Brick when he still owes me!"

He made his way to the front of the cafe before Gabe could ask him a question or urge him to wait. He left his warm meal simmering in its place. Gabe took a measured sip of water before looking to her and saying. "Ben, he's a generous guy. Generous to a fault. But he can't afford to lend right now, not when his son needs medical care."

Callie reached for her own glass of water and delayed taking a sip. "That man outside ought to be ashamed of himself then, spending Ben's money on whiskey or whatever it is that sounds good at the moment." By the time she set the glass down, she drew in her breath, realizing what Ben's departure meant for her and Gabe. Whereas it may have struck other patrons as unseemly that she'd joined a table across color lines at all, she was now without the white man who helped neutralize her and Gabe's visit. She felt the condemning stares from the couple closest to them only deepen now that she and Gabe were alone. "Callie," Gabe nearly whispered, "you don't have to stay here with me." She began to shake her head when they both noticed their waitress returning with a hot plate in hand.

Gabe nodded appreciatively at the waitress with the auburn tresses, as she set the fresh plate before him. Questions rose in her green eyes about the missing patron across from them. "He had to settle up a debt with someone on his way to the Brick," Gabe said, before she could ask any questions. "I expect he'll be back soon enough."

The waitress nodded and leaned closer to Gabe and Callie. "That couple behind me—I'm sorry that they're worked up. They probably think I'm telling you that you shouldn't come back, but that's not the case. My boss would say that everyone is welcome here and mean it. Please don't feel you need to leave."

"Thank you," Gabe said, staring back down at his plate. He hadn't picked his fork up since Ben left them. Looking flustered, as if maybe she shouldn't have said anything in the first place, the waitress retreated to the kitchen and left Gabe and Callie to their uncomfortable silence.

"I'm not going to leave," Callie said quietly, her deep blue eyes leveling with his, amber brown. "I'd like to stay here and finish having dinner with you."

Gabe swallowed a long drink of water and set the cup down, fastening his gaze on her. "I'm glad you do, but that might make us fools. Especially me." His somber expression gave way to a tentative smile. "I don't think we can do this again, but it is nice to see you, Callie."

Several other patrons—those who were sitting at their tables and those just coming in—paused in their conversations and let their eyes wander back to Gabe and Callie as well.

Gabe glanced at Callie and said, "This . . . it just comes with the territory."

"I don't know what to say," Callie whispered.

He shrugged. "Callie, I deal with this almost all the time.

More often than not, and at least several times a day in some form. I see people try to categorize me, defer to Burke with questions I could answer, offer him service when I've waited longer. I mean, look what just happened with Merrick. You know he's trying to file a petition to let me go?" She didn't answer that, and he searched for words. "I've always had to act like second rate treatment was enough, and if you keep hanging around me, you'll experience it too. I don't want that for you." He spun his glass around and had to right it to keep from toppling over.

Callie set her napkin down on the table, not wanting him to see how hard she was swallowing. She wished it wasn't true, that five minutes into their first dinner they weren't already plagued with the perceptions of people saw nothing good in their connection. She was about to open her mouth, tell him that she'd take their judgment if it meant being with him, but she could see he didn't want to discuss it now.

Instead, Gabe leaned toward her and said softly, "So tell me . . . have you thought any more about scheduling your next gig?"

It took concerted effort for her to allow him to change the topic when there was still so much to say. She gave a half smile and shook her head. "Not yet. With no means . . . it makes dreams harder to come by."

He leaned toward her. "The Depression doesn't get the final say, Callie. Artists might have their challenges, but they find a way to create again. It's impossible for them not to."

Callie couldn't summon a smile. "These things don't always materialize, Gabe. Not from nothing. I'm in no position to sing for a living, and we both know it."

He didn't lose his spark. "Perhaps not now, Callie. But stranger things have happened than making a living as a musician."

"Maybe so," she said, wistful. "My parents sold their piano a few years back. We used to gather 'round it and sing the most upbeat songs. The Boswell Sisters. Duke Ellington. Louis Armstrong," she said, feeling herself start to blush.

"Perhaps we have more in common than we thought," he said offhandedly. "I can sing a little and play a few songs on the piano, but the musician's life didn't pull me in. I was a boy who wanted to run outside, explore the wilderness more than I wanted anything else. But, Callie," he said, drawing the conversation back to her, "it's not too late to sing. You should take every opportunity. If you don't find enough gigs to pay the bills, do it because you love it."

She leaned into his words, into the warmth and solace they offered her. Her heart was stirring again because his presence made her feel alive. There was an ease and intelligence to him that drew her in. There was still so much they hadn't uncovered about the other, yet she felt that he could so effortlessly gauge her thoughts and emotions, and that she could discern his.

A few bites into his meal, she asked him about his interest in real estate.

"It's something that galled me growing up in Seattle—seeing that blacks were denied many opportunities to lease and own properties. If I can start challenging and pushing against some of these regulations, maybe I can at least lay a foundation for change."

Their plates were almost picked clean when Ben resurfaced at their table, his hair disheveled and his shirt untucked. Before they could ask him what words he and Percy had shared, he sat down heavily and said, "He wanted to spend what little he had on a shot of whiskey . . . and I told him to go for it. He can repay me next check. I could see he needed that shot more than I do."

Gabe gave him a look of regret and said, "I'm sorry, Ben. That's rough. What was he needing it for anyway? He couldn't have needed the funds any more than . . ."

Ben stared at his fork, hadn't picked it back up. "I don't remember, truth be told. We'd both had a few too many one night at the Brick a few weeks back, and before I knew it, I was reaching into my wallet, handing him a few dollar bills." Ben shook his head. "Just goes to show that neither of us should be drinking as much as we do."

Once they left the cafe, Ben ducked out quickly, again oblivious to any scrutiny he might bring upon Gabe, too preoccupied with his own worries and tribulations. He left his friend standing under the lamplight with a white woman, as if there were no considerations to be made.

"I'll walk you to your front gate if you'd like," Gabe offered. She nodded, trying to let the fear crawling up her back dissipate. If those mean-spirited miners had thought it was a lot to see her enter an establishment with a colored man, what would they think if they saw her now?

Thinking several steps ahead of her, Gabe dodged into the nearest alley beside the restaurant and returned a moment later with a discarded box in his arms. "I'll walk just behind you, and they'll think I'm carrying your groceries," he said.

"Alright." She began to lead the way home, hating that they had to put up any pretense at all. Once they were away from Pennsylvania Avenue, Gabe held the empty box at his side. He stepped forward and reached for Callie's hand, entwined his fingers within her own. They walked closely together, their heads bowed toward the ground.

"Why aren't you already with someone, Gabe?" she asked when they were out of earshot of any passersby. "I'd think that a guy like you would be spoken for."

She leaned into the discomfort of her question, wanting to learn at least as much about him as he knew about her.

He smiled. "I was with someone . . . a waitress near the dock in Seattle . . . but it didn't work out. We parted ways a year ago. I had too many demands on my time and I think she got tired of waiting."

He shrugged his shoulders. "Can't say I blame her."

Callie dared to ask him what was really on her mind. "Did you . . . love her?"

Gabe turned his suddenly serious eyes toward her and said, "No. Not the waitress. I've loved one girl before, Marie. We were high school sweethearts, but she moved to upstate New York soon after graduation. We corresponded with letters and phone calls for a few months, but I could feel her grow distant from me over time. I knew she'd met someone else before she found the words to tell me." He cast his eyes to the ground, perhaps so that she couldn't show him any pity. "It hurt a lot, losing her. But I wish her well. I hear she married the other bloke and that she's a mother now."

Callie didn't press him with more questions, sensing that he didn't want her comfort. He'd moved on from the blow of losing his first love and was no longer the boy he'd been six years before.

He was the one who released her hand first, and she was happy that she wouldn't have to break away. Though the curtains of her family's sitting room were closed, she expected that someone was watching them—one of the twins, perhaps—that there'd be someone to answer to, as there had been at every turn since she'd met Gabe.

"Would you . . . would you want to go to church with me on Sunday?" he whispered, turning to face her. "I understand if . . ."

She found herself nodding, not caring that she'd have to answer to her father for accepting this unexpected invitation. Townspeople had smashed the window after seeing her with him in a confectionery. They wouldn't dare if they went to a house of God, would they?

When she finally stood facing him, he opened his arms and drew her toward him quickly. She wanted nothing more than to feel his arms slide around her waist, but reason stilled the impulse. She knew it wasn't wise to surrender to anything, not even a simple embrace under a sky pooled into darkness.

He caught the start in her breath and released her, took a step back. He brushed a hand over the crude wooden gate and lifted the latch. "Good night, Callie. I'll pick you up on Sunday morning unless . . ."

She nodded. "Good night, Gabe." She could sense a new

melody playing within her, one that hadn't awoken in her time with Paul, though she'd genuinely loved him. She'd thought she was wounded beyond repair when Paul asked for his ring back, but her heart was beating again, strong. The sweetness of her realization overpowered any discomfort she felt over knowing people wouldn't take kindly to her seeing Gabe. She let herself inside thinking how she couldn't wait to see him again, how the knowledge that she would overrode anything else that might stand in their way.

Chapter 33

BEFORE GABE COULD grasp the keys near the entrance of the house on Sunday morning, Mr. Burke stopped him with a touch at his arm. "Gabriel, why don't you come down to Mass with us this morning?"

Hope was woven into Mr. Burke's voice. Gabe suppressed a sigh, knowing that his answer wouldn't be what the man wanted. He could hear the clamoring of Julia and Jamie in the kitchen. He assumed they were helping themselves to warm, crumbly coffee cake that Annie was in the habit of making every Sunday morning.

Gabe turned toward Burke, wishing his words would come faster. He'd been down to Immaculate Conception on more than one occasion, but the atmosphere was not breath and life to him like the Church of Christ. Not to mention, he was the only colored person in attendance. The Church of Christ was a place where the music stirred his soul and the heartening sermons spoke to the sweat and sacrifices of the black families who had made their home here against so many odds.

Gabe adjusted the buttons of his work shirt before he looked Burke in the eye. He shook his head. "Thanks, but I'm . . . I'm actually picking Callie up this morning. . . . I ran into her last night when I was dining with Ben and invited her to church."

His mention of Callie was deliberate. He didn't need to utter a word about her in order to kindly refuse Burke's invitation. He watched Burke's face transform from lightness to somber reckoning. The emotion he betrayed wasn't necessarily surprise, but Gabe knew such news wasn't about to make the man's carefree spirit return.

"She's a lovely girl," he said, finally. "I thought so when I hired her. You know the challenges that you'll face in stepping out with her. . . . So many like to think the struggle's over, but it's written into our tapestry now. Prejudice will rear its ugly head in some of the same old ways it always has. You'll see that if you start going with her, even here. I don't want that for either one of you. Please, Gabriel, before you instill false hope in her, consider the cost."

Gabe nodded, not that he needed convincing. The truth Burke spoke of was something he felt in his being more than his employer could ever imagine. Over the past ten years, Gabe had grown accustomed to dining at fine establishments, wearing expensive suits on occasion, having doors opened to him as a prominent leader in the business. But unlike other men in his position, he was expected to act so darn grateful at every turn—nodding his head when the occasional businessman told him how fortunate he was as a colored man to be living the American dream, or said something glib instead of understanding the rights he should have been afforded in the first place. Gabe knew that some thought they were on the right side of justice simply because they opened their restaurants to people of color, bought a record by a black musician, or acknowledged someone with a darker shade of skin on the sidewalk.

As he stood before this man who was accustomed to events tilting in his favor, it was hard for Gabe to refrain from speaking of his experience. He bit the inside of his cheek so he wouldn't say something he regretted, so he wouldn't be tempted to mention his mother and everything she'd endured for swimming against the stream. But knowing the extent that Burke cared for him, he swallowed any sharp words and said only, "It's not just a whim, or I never would have asked her. I know it's a lot to take on . . . for her and for me." He tossed the keys from one hand to the other.

Edward pressed his lips together, his eyes creased at the corners. "I understand, Gabe. But most won't. They'll come against you passively and directly. You have to know that—"

"I do know that," Gabe said, an edge taking over his voice. "Which is why it's important that you don't take opposition like the others. You of anyone would know that popular opinion doesn't equal truth."

Gabe murmured his good day and set off down the porch steps before Mr. Burke could add another word. His decision to pursue Callie defied ease and logic, but he'd told her he would be there.

While he waited for the engine to warm, Gabe decided he'd go to the Rushton's front door this time. He would knock, wish whomever answered a good morning, and wait for Callie to come to the door. If he was honest with himself, he feared these critical moments the most. Her father might slam the door in his face, after telling him politely it wasn't proper for her to go with him. Or Callie might tell him herself, with a forlorn look in her eye, that it wasn't wise or worth it to step out.

He shook off these imaginings. Even if picking her up for church wasn't seamless, a backlash was worth it if he could see her in the open. Once she was at his side at the Church of Christ, they would let their voices reach the rafters and hear Preacher Jacobson's life-giving words.

But the longer it took for the truck to warm, the more the frost of the morning reached his lungs and pulled him back to reality. The Rushtons wouldn't likely overlook the barriers he was asking their daughter to cross over. For all the hardiness Callie had learned as a coal miner's daughter, she didn't know the first thing about being shunned for simply existing. She didn't know the first thing about being treated like a second-class citizen for the color of her skin. The reproach they'd experienced at the cafe was but a slight sprinkling in comparison with the storm they'd face if they continued.

He thought of his mother sitting at her dressing table, her dark eyes meeting his own in the mirror the last time he'd seen her. *I want you to know all the things you can have, Gabriel. Not how another man will limit you or hold you down. You're worth as much as that man. You're worth every bit as much and more. Keep your head up and don't let anyone talk you down.*

He wondered how his mother's words might change were she here to find him inviting an almost impossible situation into his life, opening his arms to someone he was told he shouldn't. He also knew that she'd relent, having herself fallen for a man she was told she couldn't have a long time ago. He pressed on, driving the meandering, winding roads back down to Roslyn. His heart led him there. He would arrive at her front doorstep at 10 o'clock as he'd promised.

While preparing to extend a hand to Callie's father, tip his hat, and say, "Good morning, sir," Callie let herself out on the porch before he had that chance. She closed the door so quickly, his words caught in his throat.

Gabe looked back at the closed door. "Shouldn't I . . ."

"Next time," Callie said. She drew her hunter-green scarf closer to her neck and bounded down the stairs ahead of him, her long, black winter coat nearly covering the grey-blue dress that skimmed the top of her ankles. Her low black heels tapped down the stairs before he could ask her another question.

Gabe opened the passenger door to her and closed it before leaping up to his own seat. It would take more than a single week-end to convince her parents that he was a good suitor for their daughter. He had more rivers to cross than others. Didn't his own father once teach him that obstacles brought on perseverance followed by greater character?

As they left the Rushton's property, he caught some movement in his rear view mirror. Callie's father stepped out on the porch, the lines in his forehead pronounced, arms crossed over his chest as he braced himself in the mid-morning cold. His tattered blue flannel waved at the wind's command. He narrowed his eyes at the truck as they drove away, but Gabe didn't make mention of it to Callie. Instead, he reached over and took her hand.

Before they even opened the church's doors, a robust chorus of voices urged them inwards. Callie glanced over at Gabe, as if to ask if they were late. He shook his head, told her the choir arrived early every week. They were just getting started. So full, rich, and vibrant were the voices singing.

> *Oh, don't you want to go to that gospel feast,*
> *That promised land where all is peace?*
> *Oh, deep river, Lord,*
> *I want to cross over into campground!*
> *Deep river, my home is over Jordan,*
> *Deep river, Lord,*
> *I want to cross over into campground!*

He nodded in appreciation when an usher welcomed them in. As they made their way to an open pew, he dropped his worries along with his winter coat at the back of the pew. He looked upon the triumphant faces of the churchgoers as they sang on, swaying to a song that instilled hope and perseverance across the generations. The men, women, and children had traded in their work attire for the Sunday best which he so admired. Some of the older women wore large tilted hats in jewel tones, setting the standard for celebration. Many of the congregants noticed his visitor, but Gabe was met with claps on the back, firm handshakes.

"Good to see you, Brother."

While Callie kept her eyes steered straight ahead for the most part, Gabe didn't miss a few of the younger women leaning over to whisper in each other's ear. He knew it must be because of his guest.

Mr. Rollins, accompanied by his daughter Ruthie, turned around in the row before them. Leaning over his cane, he said, "Lord's blessings. It's good to see you again, Gabriel."

Ruthie drew Callie into an unexpected hug and whispered, "Welcome," before turning back to listen to the choir.

Following a few more Spirit-filled songs, Pastor Jacobson took the pulpit and spoke on God's sovereignty through life's sufferings. He spoke on the need to acquire an internal strength despite any upheaval with the Union, not that they shouldn't speak their thoughts, but that any opposition should be considered before being voiced aloud. Gabe kept his eyes trained to the pulpit, except for the several times he stole a side glance at Callie, who listened intently. He knew she must be keenly aware that the congregants wondered at her attendance. He knew that she must feel for once, the one displaced.

When he looked back to the preacher, he noticed lovely Mrs. Jacobson turning back to look at them from three rows ahead to the right. Her eyes traveled quickly over him, over Callie, and while she didn't frown, there wasn't a smile to spare either. There was an honesty about Mrs. Jacobson that Gabe couldn't fault. He knew that even though she'd spent the majority of her years here, in this town which afforded them more equality than many others, she wasn't going to pretend that color didn't classify people and try to tell them where they belonged.

✧ ✧ ✧

"Thank you for going with me." Gabe said, before he dropped Callie off at home. He'd driven up to the gate, let the engine idle, and contemplated whether he ought to escort her to the door. But he knew the answer to that, having seen Callie's father looking distressed as they drove away, his shirt billowing in the wind.

"I want to go with you again," Callie said without hesitation. "I hope this isn't the only time." Her focus was stayed on him and not on her family home, her father who was outside feeding their cow, her twin brothers, taking turns swinging on the old, faded tire swing. She didn't seem to notice the simultaneous pause at their arrival like he did or the less-than-joyous expression on her father's face.

"Are you sure, Callie?" Gabe asked, his question the most urgent one for her yet. "Because I won't tiptoe around with you or hope for the next time we accidentally run into each other. If you want to be my girl, we can't only meet for church on Sundays. Are you sure . . . that's what you want?"

"Yes, I'm sure," she said, conviction threaded into her voice.

Gabe nodded. "I'm sure too," he said, before reaching for the car door. "What would you say about going to dinner with me tomorrow night? Say I pick you up around seven? Yes? Are you alright with me picking you up again?"

Once around the car and at her side, he saw a fleeting shadow pass over her features. "I think it's best I meet you there," she said. They were about to begin an emotional tug-of-war and he felt responsible for the upheaval she was bound to face.

If he'd only asked Burke for more time at the Seattle port. If he'd only been more resistant when she'd found him working at the church the first time. If he'd only stood to his feet and joined Ben in his pursuit to get back the money instead of lingering with her at the back of the Roslyn Cafe. If only. But she'd ignited something in him the first time he saw her. It was undeniable the day they'd spoken at the Company Store. He didn't know if his response came from the need in her wounded blue eyes, her quiet stubbornness, or the smile that played around her lips so often.

Though he didn't reach for Callie's hand in front of her father, they made enough of a statement walking together to the gate, the bottom of his shoulder nearly brushing the top of hers. While he thought it might not be suitable to wear a smile, he wanted to catch her father with at least a nod. He removed his hat and waited to see what Mr. Rushton would do. He expected Callie's father to call her name and turn his back, no acknowledgement on his lips.

Yet the rugged, retired miner walked toward them instead. Gabe swallowed. There was no trace of warmth on the man's face, but there was no discernible anger either. Mr. Rushton lifted the lever of the gate when they were upon it. Callie's father was at least two inches shorter than Gabe, but his lesser height did nothing to diminish his presence. He was hardy, strong, and earnest. Gabe felt this within several seconds. He quickly cleared his throat and said, "Mr. Rushton, I trust you're having a good Sunday morning. I'm glad Callie could join me today. Our . . . my church service lasts longer than most."

Mr. Rushton's features were drawn tight until he began speaking. "I know the preacher. I'd expect a long sermon from Sam. Heartfelt as he is." As if remembering they weren't here to find commonality, the upturn of his lips left and he stood inches away from his daughter and her beau, the wariness returning to his face.

Gabe held out his hand. "I haven't introduced myself yet. I'm Gabe Ward."

Callie's father extended his hand in turn and gave a swift nod as they shook hands. "Bill Rushton." Hesitation flickered in his dark blue eyes, like Callie's own. But it didn't prevent him from saying, "I know who you are. Burke's right hand man."

Gabe smiled at that. "I s'pose that fits. I've been with the company for ten years now."

He heard his voice thin at the end of the sentence and wished he knew how to hold his own for longer. He'd met a few other fathers at front doors and at gates, but not once had the father been white, and there was only so far he could go, trying to eradicate the obvious barriers built long before he was born.

As he tried to think of what to say next, Mr. Rushton turned his attention to his daughter and said, "Callie, why don't you come in now?" He pressed a hand on her shoulder and steered her toward him, signaling that the conversation was over. Sure enough, he offered a hasty nod and said, "Thank you for bringing her home, Gabe." No thank you for taking her to church. No thank you for taking good care of her. No nice to meet you, even. Yet, what had he expected? Not even a handshake, if truth be told.

"Thank you, Gabe," Callie said, craning her neck to look back at him. "I'll see you soon, alright?" There was restraint in her voice, and yet there had to be. She'd said nothing about their dinner date. Not in front of her father.

Chapter 34

TRY AS SHE MIGHT to maintain her joy in being Gabe Ward's girl, Callie's heart often sank when she came in from an evening of being with him. Gabe traveled regularly to Seattle to work at the ports, but when he was home he took her back to church, to the Roslyn Bakery, and even to pictures at the Rose Theater once the feature started playing.

She knew she was giving her father an original source of distress. With no solutions for him—save calling it off with Gabe—she did what she could not to mention Gabe for a time. Some people talked about them when they glimpsed them speaking on the sidewalks, even when they weren't holding hands. In the beginning, Callie naively thought disapproval from near strangers wouldn't infiltrate her heart. But then she noticed Mrs. Adams shake her head one afternoon after they'd stopped at the Roslyn Bakery together. Gabe had offered Callie a bite of apple pie on the end of his fork. She felt the ire written in that woman's stare and even asked her, "Have you never sampled someone's dessert before?"

Gabe's eyes had widened incredulously at her, as if to ask how she could bother to engage the woman. Callie felt herself start to burn up.

"Yes, but it was my husband's fork. This young man is not your husband, or I should at least hope not." Mrs. Adams righted her hat at the perceived indiscretion. The distressed woman gathered her shopping bags and hustled out of the bakery before Callie could press into her with a single cutting look or defensive word. Callie simmered and couldn't calm, even after Gabe laid a hand on the back of her arm and said, "You have to let it go."

There were other remarks—*Roslyn's a forgiving town. . . . Couples like you wouldn't stand a chance in most places. . . . You sure you know what you're doing?* Some townspeople met them with friendly enough nods. But they must have wondered how they'd fare if they caught a train to another state where black folk had their own dining establishments and were made to use their own washrooms. Were Gabe and Callie unaware of the ramifications? Callie still couldn't bring herself to tell Gabe about the window shattered at her home or the words that accompanied the act.

Callie tossed and turned many a night concerning her decision to see him. Her father's displeasure couldn't be any clearer, although he refrained from spelling it out more than he already had. Callie noticed as he retreated from her that he no longer joked with her or asked her questions about her time with the Burke children. He scarcely asked her anything at all. Her stomach grew leaden when she observed that she wasn't the only person her father avoided these days. He hadn't sought Sam Jacobson out in over a month. Callie suspected it was beginning to eat at him, just not enough to do anything about it yet. He couldn't invite the man in, talk about the rising tensions in the Union, and avoid all reference to the young man his daughter was seeing. He knew full well Callie had visited Sam's church, savored his sermon, and shaken his hand as Gabe's guest. If he spoke on the subject, Callie suspected the words would catch in his throat. Unhappiness would trace itself into the lines on his forehead. And if he didn't speak on it at all, it was much the same thing.

One evening she overheard her mother in the kitchen.

"*It's been a while since we've had the Jacobsons over for a meal. I'm starting to miss Tessa. Do you think we should invite her over?*"

"*Ask me that question again, Renata, and you'll see where the trouble starts sweeping in.*"

"*So you're having a hard time accepting that your daughter is seeing a colored man. I understand that. It's not what I would have hoped for her either. . . . He seems like a kind young man, but that is beside the point. Sam is going to understand our reservations, those fears of how they'll be treated. You might not talk about it with him on a daily basis, but I don't think he's forgotten what it's like to be a black man in this country.*"

She heard an exasperated sigh.

"*You're not getting it, Renata. My concern isn't over how they'll be treated. I've come to expect Gabe will be categorized a certain way. My concern . . . it's all for her.*"

There was a pause.

"*I can go on, thinking that I'm glad I don't have the same misfortunes as . . . Sam . . . and I'll even start to feel for him, but when it comes down to it, my defenses . . . they're up not because of what he weathers. They're about what happens to her.*"

Callie's mother broke in again.

"*Your prayers might need to change, Bill. In the meantime, think about telephoning Sam. It won't do you any good to keep him at a distance. That man's been a friend to you since you were boys. What a shame it'd be to let that one slip through the cracks.*"

A shame indeed, Callie thought, inwardly applauding her mother for speaking the truth. She hoped her father would consider just what he stood to lose.

✧ ✧ ✧

"You just let me know if there's anything we can get for you and your crew," the lead waiter told Callie, his blue eyes as serious as the part on the right side of his head. She had to restrain an impulse to laugh. This young lad, with his pressed white shirt, black pants, and all the pomade he could muster, wasn't a natural fit for this town. But he was earnest and helpful, and she couldn't fault him for trying.

It wasn't difficult to book a venue for a Friday night. Callie knew enough of the musicians in Roslyn to find accompaniment for her performance. Her voice wasn't as sultry as some of the jazz artists she'd heard on the radio, but her translation of the lyrics was always heartfelt. Aching, even. She knew that she captivated some of the least likely whenever she rose to sing. Before her performance, she gave herself a pep talk, reminding herself that she could still do this. It didn't matter if she didn't have anything glamorous to wear. She'd take the makeshift stage in a black dress she'd worn countless times before and ask to borrow one of her mother's necklaces, perhaps one with the burnt orange beads.

"Guess what," she said next time she saw Gabe on the way to the Burke's study, "I'm performing this Friday night in the billiard hall across from Hawthorne House, and I'd like you to come. If you're . . . if you're in town. It starts right at seven o'clock."

Realizing that she was speaking in a loud, excitable voice, Callie clapped a hand over her mouth just in time to see Gabe tip his cap to her and offer a wink. "I'll be there," he said.

When the evening came, she glanced around the humble surroundings of the corner establishment. There wasn't a trace of elegance, only roughly fashioned wooden tables and chairs, well-thumbed decks of cards, a floor that hadn't seen a broom in untold weeks. To think she'd spent many a night suffering from a twinge of jealousy as she watched townspeople go in. But she still felt her stomach clench, a dampness under her arms, and hastened breathing that made her feel like an imposter. She'd told Gabe the place and time, but he was nowhere to be seen, and that further intensified her mood. He was undoubtedly working late for Burke.

Marty Wakefield, the piano player, handed her a cool glass of water and told her to drink up. She obeyed and took it as her cue to gain her composure. *I can do all things through Him, who gives me strength*, she told herself, all the while aware she wasn't about to sing from a hymnbook. It didn't matter. God could give her a confidence here in a miners' establishment, as much as He could were she kneeling in a pew.

Feeling the press of eyes reach her as she approached the piano, she gave a quick nod of appreciation to Marty and the bass player, Ned Jurich. She stepped to the front of the room, refusing to take inventory of the thirty or so people within, lest she feel the blow at not finding Gabe among them. She summoned a wide smile and let herself be pulled into Marty's sparkling intro at the keys. She poured herself into the hit show tune, "My Baby Just Cares for Me," swaying to and fro all the while.

Once the song had ended and she'd gained attention and applause from the slight audience, she nodded her appreciation and dared to assess the company. It wasn't segregated, but a lingering look across the room told her Gabe wasn't one of the faces. There weren't any colored people sitting at the tables, standing near the bar, leaning over the pool tables. Callie was keenly aware, even in the midst of performing, that this wasn't an observation she would have had were she not looking for a particular person. She bit back disappointment, telling herself that something must have come up as she launched into "Blue Skies."

Several lines into the song she saw him materialize near the entrance. He wore his trademark cap, similar to so many of the men, but she noted his arrival right away. He stood behind a wooden beam, and she couldn't catch his eye. Perhaps that was a saving grace. Already she heard a lilt in her voice, the quickening of her heart as she saw the side of his face, the gestures of his hands as he leaned in to speak with someone at the door—the young waiter who'd been so friendly to her. She wanted the song to end so she could truly let her eyes meet Gabe's, express her elation and relief that he'd come.

She began the last chorus. He hadn't made his way closer to her, eager to catch the last notes of her song. Somehow, in the moment she'd looked to the piano player, she'd lost sight of him. He was gone from the doorway and there was no reasonable explanation for him to leave in the middle of her second song.

She withheld her suspicions until it ended, thinking perhaps Gabe had gone back outside to bring someone in with him before finding a table. Feeling her throat close, Callie drew her focus back to the door, and sure enough, she saw the earnest waiter standing before the entrance with his arms crossed over his chest, shaking his head. Then he'd thrown his hands up, incredulous. There was forced laughter. She couldn't hear what the other men were saying, but she understood edgy banter when she heard it, couldn't miss the ridicule written across their brows.

Instead of murmuring anything about their set to her band-mates, Callie let her eyes flit to the nearest window, where she caught Gabe walking away, his hands thrust as far as they would go in either pocket. There was no mistaking it now; he'd been asked to leave the premises.

"Give me a moment," she said, turning to both Marty and Ned. Both were entirely oblivious to what was happening, and ill-equipped to argue with her when she was already walking toward the door.

She wasted no words with the waiter who'd tried to win her over. "Step aside," she said when she reached the door.

"I think you're mistaken, ma'am," he said, his voice pitching. "Everything is calm now and can go back to normal. I told the colored man who came in that he might try Slim's instead. That's where more of his kind . . ."

"I asked you to step aside," Callie repeated, her voice tight. "Now that I know which type of establishment this is, I won't be coming back." She glanced over her shoulder once, mouthed an apology to her fellow musicians and motioned for them to carry on without her.

"What happened?" she heard a miner say to his friend.

"Maybe she noticed where most of the eyes were looking. . ."

She pushed the door open now that the small-minded waiter had relented and moved aside. "Fine, Miss," he said, wiping his brow with the back of his sleeve. "Your band is playing on without you."

Callie hadn't the time to process his barb or anyone else's as she ran across the street to reach Gabe. She called for him, but it took several times for him to turn around. Soon after he did, he caught her by the wrist and said, "What are you doing, Callie? You should be up there singing right now. You sounded swell . . . the little bit I heard, and the two of them can't make up the difference." He'd willed hope into his voice, but she could see the angry currents brewing in his eyes.

She shook her head, knowing her face had soured with disgust. "No. I saw how the waiter treated you, and I don't need to sing for them if they turn away my guests." She bit down on her lip. Hard. "What did he say to you?"

She knew it was the wrong question when Gabe dropped her wrist as fast as he'd picked it up and folded his arms across his chest.

"That he doesn't serve the coloreds. That I can shoo down the street and beg at someone else's table." His nostrils flared in spite of his best efforts to keep composure. "I shouldn't even be bothered by it since he's so puny. I mean . . . he couldn't last a day out at the docks. . . ."

"Shouldn't be bothered by it!" Callie threw her hands up and welcomed the wind's stirrings now that she wasn't perspiring before an audience. "That's impossible. As spineless as he is, he just called the shots in front of a bunch of men who didn't disagree. That's maddening."

Gabe swallowed, and his eyes took on a watery sheen she hadn't expected. It wasn't so much sadness as defiance she saw there. "Maddening, yes. But it doesn't surprise me anymore. Stick around me a while longer, and it won't surprise you so much." He straightened his cap and glanced around, nervously, took a step away from her. . . .

"You know, if Burke hears about this . . ."

"Burke is influential in many spheres, Cal, but don't forget that there are a lot of people who ridicule him. And his employing me," he said, closing in on his truck. He paused, glancing up and down Pennsylvania. "The heck with it. People have already seen us walking this far. Climb on up here, Callie. I'm gonna take you home. Not a chance I'd have you walking."

Chapter 35

S HE HAD SEEN GABE for less than two months outside of
her father's wishes. Callie knew she couldn't continue to
live under his roof much longer. Her father's frustration
was mounting, her mother was tense as a closed fist, and the
twins wished aloud she would stop seeing him. Every time she
prepared to go out with Gabe, her father stiffened. "Where
do you expect this to lead?" he would say under his breath.
Gabe had never once been greeted at the front door the times
he'd come to pick her up. No hand was extended to him, he
wasn't invited in for a cup of warm tea or asked how he was
doing. Not once.

Aside from the fun she experienced with her family—sleigh
rides with friends through winter's white, listening to crackling
Christmas carols over the radio, seeing lights strung around the
lampposts on Pennsylvania Avenue—a prevailing uneasiness
veiled even their happier times together.

One snowy night before Christmas, Gabe sat in the darkened
Rose Theater with Callie. The credits started rolling, and he
held her hand firmly as the people filed out after the show.
When he didn't rise from his seat, Callie looked over to him
and waited for him to speak. She could see the struggle setting
in his jaw. "I can't do this to you anymore . . . continue to see
you without your father's blessing. He doesn't want me on
the front porch, let alone in the house, and I don't see him
changing his mind." He looked toward her. "This is wearing

on your relationship with them. They want what's best for you. So do I, Callie. Don't look at me like that."

Her heart caught in her throat. She didn't know how to argue with the undisputed truth. "How do you know they want what's best for me? I can't say they do if they're not willing to give you a chance."

Gabe squeezed her hand before they rose to greet the cool winter air. Callie walked beside him in silence, her eyes welling from the shock of frost and sadness all at once. "The only other girls I've seen have been colored too," he said. "I knew at an early age that girls like you were out of the question, that their fathers wouldn't accept me, and neither would society. I don't know what I'm thinking to . . ." His voice drifted, and he let out a spiral of breath.

"What if we talked with my father together?" Callie asked, feeling it'd be a futile effort before it began, but not wanting to admit it. "He might be rigid at first, but he'll get to know you more and see—"

Gabe stared straight ahead. His eyes trained on the flickering lamplights down the main street. "I can't fault your father for wanting to protect you, Cal. I don't think speaking with him would ease his mind. He knows it's brutal out there, that in most parts of the country people can't go outside their own. Heck, some people tell me how lucky I am that I can sit at their tables or use the indoor washroom instead of the one out back." He shook his head, forced a laugh.

Callie turned to him, ignoring the squeals of children as they sledded down the hill behind them, sending sparks of white in the air. "I know he wants to protect me, but I fault him for letting fear dictate every decision he makes."

Afraid that he'd repeat those words he'd said in the theater— that he couldn't continue to see her outside her father's blessing—Callie looked up at Gabe and tried to read his thoughts. They moved toward the passenger side of his truck where it walled them off from the occasional person traipsing through the snow. Instead of stiffening, he reached out his arms to her and gathered her so close she could hear his heartbeat, faint, but steady within his winter coat. She rested her head against his chest, relieved that he wasn't turning her away, no matter what his words said.

"I'll talk to him," Gabe said, his breath warm against her hair. "If he's willing to speak with me."

Callie closed her eyes, taking in the scent of pine against his collar. "Here," he said softly, "let's get you out of this cold. Let me warm the truck up." He rifled through his coat pocket for his keys and opened the car door for her. A few passersby crossed before the truck, watching the placement of their own steps, laughing as they held out their arms like a snowman's and tried not to fall.

Once he set the key in the ignition, she turned toward him and pressed a hand to his cheek, feeling the start of stubble. He was surprisingly warm to the touch. Wordlessly, she moved in closer, her entire being begging to be drawn closer. She drew her face toward his, her hands now gripping his shoulders, pulling him close. "Callie," he began, his voice deep, aching. "Callie . . . I . . ." She brought her lips up to his, and if he was taken aback, he didn't show it. He pulled her into his arms and returned what she'd begun with a kiss that was at once possessive and tender. She was sure he could feel her heart drum against his chest. Another moment, and reason edged out their emotions.

He drew back and said, "Oh, we shouldn't . . ."

"I'm sorry," Callie said, stunned that she'd been the one to initiate their first kiss. She'd kissed Paul countless times and sometimes tasted the memory of him when she didn't want to, but she hadn't expected to be the one who turned this page with Gabe. His kiss felt right. She wanted to savor it again, but knew she couldn't. They were practically putting their hands to the grate. She glanced around their surroundings now; the street was lit, but most townspeople were bundled up, home in front of their toasty fires.

"Don't be sorry," he said, smiling in spite of the immense

difficulty they'd brought upon themselves. "We just can't . . . let that happen again. . . . Not until your father agrees to let us see each other. . . . And even then . . ." He looked away. "Best get you home, Callie. We have enough trouble without inviting more."

✧ ✧ ✧

Before Christmas, Callie's father was busy building a new bunk bed out in the shed for the twins. He scarcely looked up from his task except to wipe the sweat on his sleeve. Will, who'd been sent home for the holiday, helped him steady the boards, and even though their work was completed mostly in synchronized silence, Callie knew her father had informed Will all about the young man she was seeing.

She felt Will's posture toward her shift. Her only response was to avoid him, as nothing she could possibly say to explain her circumstances would appease him. Her every step was calculated—she didn't rise to rinse her dinner plate until one of the twins was out of his seat first, she didn't turn down the hall toward her bedroom until another family member headed in for the night, too, and she didn't ask Will many questions about his training at Ft. Lewis even when she wanted to know how he was faring.

While there was nothing for her to hide, Callie didn't want an interrogation so close to the conversation Gabe planned to have with her father. But Will was determined to speak with her. She knew this in the way he assessed her out of the corner of his eye. She saw long shadows fall upon his face when he studied her across the table. His ready humor with her had dissipated. He wasn't corralling her near the static radio in the sitting room to sing along with the latest jazz songs. He wasn't reminiscing with her about summers spent at Frog Pond. He wasn't sharing anything with her at all. The swift extraction of his presence made her shiver as if standing in cruel cold, though she drew warmth from the same fireplace.

Against her wishes, he caught her in the hallway after she

had finished brushing her teeth one night. "Callie, you didn't tell me the truth," he said, shaking his head at her.

Defensiveness rose in her like the spark of a just-lit flame. "I did. There was nothing between Gabe and me when you came home that night of the storm."

"How could there be now?" He winced. "Please don't bring condemnation upon this house, Sister. You're not meant to look at him like that. He's not . . . he's not one of us." He turned his back toward her before she could conjure up a response to meet his scornful words.

✧ ✧ ✧

Callie knocked on the Burke's front door with little time to spare before the Christmas Eve service at Mt. Pisgah Presbyterian. She'd brought small gifts for the children: a red hair bow for Julia and a hardbound notebook for Jamie with a map of Washington state stenciled on the cover. The children marveled over their gifts, and Jamie offered to run into the kitchen to serve her up some hot cocoa. While her face remained calm and steadfast, she clenched her hands more than once. Buried in the satchel at her side was a dark blue cap she'd knitted for Gabe, and she didn't know how she could possibly give it to him, though she had seen the lamplight flickering from his upstairs window. Carrying it while the minutes stole away gave her a quiet desperation, made it seem heavy as a lump of coal although it was nearly weightless. As soon as Jamie pressed a mug of piping hot cocoa in her hands, Julia walked over to the radio and shuffled through a few stations to find Christmas music. "It Came Upon A Midnight Clear" filled the air, and while it should have warmed her heart, Callie's eyes flitted toward the staircase.

"I really should be going," she said after taking a measured sip of the cocoa. She didn't have time to finish it.

"Come to Mass with us," Julia said suddenly, reaching for her hand. "We all light candles at the end and sing 'Silent Night.' It's my favorite part."

Callie let out a breath. "Oh, I wish I could, but my family is counting on me to go to Christmas service with them. Thank you for inviting me." She hugged Julia to her side, straightened the red ribbon the girl had instantly put in her hair.

When she looked up, she saw that Gabe was already beneath the door frame and walking toward her. He nodded, an unrestrained smile sweeping across his face. "Callie," he said softly, making her flush.

Better watch it, she told herself, *or even the children will notice you can't control yourself.*

He looked at Julia, then settled on Jamie. "Why don't you two get a bite to eat before you head out for Mass? Annie's baked some pies, and it looks like someone's already started in on the cherry."

It didn't take much convincing to send them scurrying. The two of them were left in the sitting room for a somewhat stolen moment. Gabe had alluded to Mr. Burke's knowledge of their attachment, but he'd never mentioned Margaret. She didn't know what had been disclosed or left unspoken.

Gabe moved closer to her and reached for her hand, opened her palm. She glanced down just as he placed a small, delicate, gold locket there. "Oh Gabe, it's beautiful," she said, barely above a whisper, meeting his eyes, which creased in the corners as he smiled.

"I thought it looked like you," he said. "I was coming home from a long shift on the docks, and it caught my eye in a store window. Would you . . . would you like me to help you put it on?"

She nodded, felt his warm fingers graze the nape of her neck as he searched for the clasp. It didn't take long for him to secure it, though she wished there was reason to linger. "I love it. Thank you."

They'd barely moved apart when Callie glanced up to see Mrs. Rushton standing at the periphery of the room. She may have missed the gifting of the locket, but there was a firm cognizance written in her cold blue eyes.

"Where are the children?" she asked in a sharper tone than necessary. She moved into the room, and Callie became engrossed in the beauty of her fitted, blue velvet dress, the unblemished pearls at her throat, the white fur stole draped over her shoulders.

"I encouraged them to help themselves to a small helping of pie," Gabe said, attempting to soften her barbed demand. "I thought it would help offset any hunger before Mass since they ate a while ago."

"I just wanted to wish your family a merry Christmas," Callie said. Her voice felt strained and frail. "I dropped by to give the children small gifts, but best be on my way. My family . . . we have a service to attend ourselves."

Mrs. Burke opened her mouth but seemed to think better of her words and merely nodded. "Merry Christmas. Thank you for stopping by."

Gabe turned toward her and said, "I'd like to walk you home. Unless you're in a hurry. Then I can drive. . . ."

"It isn't snowing. We can walk," Callie said, surprising herself by her own boldness. Though it seemed neither choice was one the lady of the house would approve, walking her home was the lengthier option, and it removed any lingering doubt Mrs. Burke might have about their closeness.

She turned over her shoulder to bid her good night and couldn't miss the distress written across the woman's features. She caught her slight head-shake at Gabe as she said, "Please don't delay. Edward will want you back here."

Rather than argue with her, Gabe nodded his understanding and stepped toward the entrance to reach for his black wool coat, Callie closely at his heels. "See you shortly," he called out, though no one lingered to see them go.

They were long past the wrought iron gate when they finally spoke to each other. Callie shook her heard. "Gabe, I don't know that we should have walked. She looks dismayed at seeing us together. It wouldn't surprise me . . . if she lets us both go."

Gabe didn't yet look at her. He kept walking, hands thrust

in his coat pockets. "I'd talk to Burke long before that ever happens. I'm not so worried about me, but about you. I'm sorry for adding to your anxiety. You don't need this, not the night before Christmas when all you wanted was to come over with gifts for the children."

She laughed aloud. "As much as I've taken to Julia and Jamie, they're not the only ones I was hoping to see." She thought of the knitted blue cap, which she still hadn't given him and stopped long enough to remove it from her purse and thrust it in his hands. "It's just something simple I made for you." Her cheeks warmed as she watched him study it, turn it over. It seemed so inadequate now that he possessed it, but she caught his eyes and could see how the amber warmed in them.

He turned to her after settling it on his head and said, "I'd like to speak with your father right after Christmas."

Callie stopped walking, heard her boots stutter on the snow. "Oh, Gabe, he hasn't warmed to the idea of us, and I don't want to hear what he has to say."

Gabe extended his hand to help her step over the snowy embankment. "I don't expect him to change his stance, but he deserves to know where I stand." They walked on in quiet while Callie thought of her next words.

"You're not afraid of what he might tell you?" Callie asked, wishing for an optimism that rivaled the light pouring into the season, the children's laughter, beautiful angels, and joyous carols. She felt dual tension—joy that Gabe would set aside his own discomfort to insist on pursuing her and dread at the leaden words her father would deliver.

He shook his head and stared at her boldly. "No. I should have started coming to the door from the beginning."

They were approaching her parents' home. Her mind fled to the shattered glass that had littered the floor of her sitting room, and she clutched the locket at her throat. She knew the words on the edge of her tongue would cost her, and yet it was cruel to keep the truth from him. "Other people make that impossible, Gabe," she said, feeling small snowflakes fall on her cheeks. "I don't know who it was, but someone smashed our front window a while ago and left an awful message about us. I didn't want to tell you since . . ."

He let out a spiral of breath, and his eyes fled to the front window, since replaced. "Why didn't you tell me this, Callie? Someone could be watching us now, and that could put you in danger."

"I didn't want to let someone else's bigotry ruin our time . . . or us," she said, an ache in her voice.

Gabe shut his eyes. "It's a wonder your father hasn't already come outside to evict me from the premises. I can . . . I can at least pay for the . . ."

Callie shook her head and tried to swallow the ache. She wiped her nose with the back of her hand. "It's already paid for. He found some used glass from a friend, and it didn't amount to . . . Gabe, please tell me this doesn't change your mind about us. I didn't want to tell you, but I had to."

He didn't answer, but he also didn't turn to go. They were staring too long at the wreath at her front door. Its shiny red bow seemed to taunt them. Gabe tapped her on the shoulder. "It might not make sense, but I'll still speak with your father. I hate that this happened, and it bothers me that we don't know who. . . ."

"It could have been any of those miners we saw the night we were looking for Jamie," Callie said, downtrodden.

"True," Gabe said, shaking his head. "I'm sorry that I followed you in. But I don't want you thinking of that tonight." He let out a long-held breath. "Merry Christmas, Cal," he said, glancing about, then daring to draw her close and press his lips to her forehead before he turned back toward the road.

✧ ✧ ✧

Callie set her mittens on an empty chair near the entrance and immediately sensed a relative quiet in the house. She stepped into the sitting room to find her mother reposing before the Christmas tree in the wing-back chair, her twin brothers in a rare moment of silence at the dining room table as they focused their attention to the scripture they were to read from the Gospel of Luke at service that night.

Instead of questioning her whereabouts, her mother studied the grandfather clock and looked toward her with understanding written across her still-beautiful features. "Did you give him that cap you've been making?"

Callie deliberated, not knowing what she'd find in her mother's answer, but eventually nodded. "How did you know it was for him?" she whispered.

"Do you think a mother's intuition fades once her girl is grown?" She shook her head. "You didn't take it out often, but I caught glimpses of it and knew it wasn't for your father. Or one of your brothers." She turned her attention to the old grandfather clock in the corner. "Will you please go out to the shed, tell your father we should head to service?"

She wanted to ask why he was working on Christmas Eve of all days, but knew better. As she watched her father set down the tools in his hands and look to her, she caught his attention.

"Daddy," she said, surprised to hear this term of endearment come out. "It's time for us to go to service."

At that moment, Will rose from his place on the other side of the bunk bed they were polishing. He cast a disbelieving expression in her direction. "What? You're not attending service at the black church with that colored boy you're seeing?" It angered her that he could be so callous, but she chose to ignore his behavior.

Her father coughed deeply into his hands. "No, Will. She's going with us. And that isn't necessary."

Will shot her a pained expression before lifting the hammer back in his hands and driving the nails into the boards. But she chose to ignore him once more, lest he vocalize his reservations. She could tell there was more than one opinion waiting on the edge of his tongue, but couldn't bear to hear any more. He watched her from out the corner of his eye and frowned when he saw the locket hanging from her neck.

"We best head over to the church" she said quietly, drawing a hand to her necklace unconsciously.

"I know you were out with him just now," Will said hotly, setting his hammer down. "We've had our front windows destroyed and the reason spelled out and still you persist." He shook his head. "You know it really surprises me that this Gabe dares to see you knowing what damage he's caused."

"He didn't cause it," Callie said before she had time to contemplate her next words. "The bigot who threw the rock did."

Callie's father put a hand up. "Please . . . please stop, you two. Leave it for after Christmas. We have service in a little while, and your mother will not be happy if you're at each other's throats."

Will wiped a bead of sweat from his forehead. "Alright. I'm still surprised that this guy has the nerve to see you, knowing our house has been vandalized, but I'll save it. No promises for the future, though."

She let her fingers fall from her locket, words rising in her. But she forced them down, let herself out of the shed, and gave the door a decisive tug.

Chapter 36

Two days after christmas, Callie grabbed a pen and began to compose questions for the Burke children about Washington, known for its evergreens and apples and snow-capped mountains. Callie lost herself in the material as she lay on her side atop her bed and didn't stop jotting down her questions and observations, even though her fingers were smeared in ink. So engrossed was she in the preparation that she barely heard her bedroom door open, barely sensed how Lucy had quietly entered the room, waiting for her to finally glance up.

Callie still didn't break from her concentration. She merely fastened her pen to the lined page and continued writing the lessons needed for the following week. It wasn't until one of the pages floated to the ground that she saw a hand go before hers to lift the paper from the ground. She'd recognize those painted-red nails anywhere.

"Lucy," she said, straightening herself and propping herself against the pillows. "What are you doing here?"

Her best friend planted herself at the foot of the bed and straightened imaginary wrinkles from her black fitted skirt before meeting Callie's gaze.

"I know I haven't said anything about your seeing Gabe until now, but I can't hold back anymore. Will told me that Gabe's written your father and arranged a meeting with him for later this afternoon. Both of us are worried for you."

Callie felt her ribcage tighten. She wished Will would go back to his regiment at Ft. Lewis. His idle time was making him meddle with her life, and she resented it.

"I can understand you and Will being concerned, but Gabe speaking with my father should make you feel relieved. He cares enough to address him, even though he hasn't once been greeted at the door."

Lucy brushed back a wisp of blond hair. "What makes you think your father would accept him? He can't, Callie. You know this. I love you . . . but you need to stop being so stubborn and realize what you're up against." She shook her head, indignant.

"I know what we're up against," Callie said, defiance sparking in her deep blue eyes. "If everyone rejects him without giving him the slightest chance, don't you see how that is ten times worse to me than strangers judging us out in the streets?"

"You know as well as I that your family doesn't place value on color," Lucy said, a nod toward their long-time friendship with the Jacobsons. "But there are anti-miscegenation laws holding in almost every state. Mixing is hardly advised anywhere. I can't believe I even need to bring this conversation up." She dropped her voice to a mere whisper and added, "Will knows a colored boy in the Army who went to prison for sleeping with a white girl. Did he mention that? . . . No? Well, they didn't even ask if the girl said yes. The colored boy was locked up for rape, and his life will never be the same. Is that what you want . . .?"

There was nothing fictitious in her words, and she listened as Lucy relayed more grim examples, persisting as if Callie had never considered them herself.

Lucy stepped closer. "Have you considered what's best for Gabe? Or how he might feel when his marriage proposal gets a refusal from your father?"

Callie looked at her best friend disbelievingly and leaned forward. "Who said anything about him asking for my hand in marriage?" But even as she asked this, she felt chills descend over her being. They had only known each other a few months, yet she knew that she belonged with him, that theirs wasn't a season's distraction. He wasn't about to ask her father that question yet. But could she imagine a future without him in it? She didn't want to.

"It's more likely that he'll start with asking my father if we can have a better arrangement for seeing each other. Like perhaps he could come to the door."

But Lucy shook her head, as if assured she knew otherwise. "He might start with those questions for now, Callie. But he wouldn't put himself in such a vulnerable spot if he didn't intend to ask for more." Lucy's eyes shone like sea glass. "The two of you were seen kissing out in front of the Rose Theater. It's safe to say, your relationship with Gabe has already begun."

Callie's hand rose to the locket at her neck. Quiet as the street was that snowy night, it seemed unsurprising that the wrong pair of eyes had fallen upon them. "Word travels quickly. Who told you that?"

Lucy shook her head. "It's not important. It only goes to show you that people are talking. And that you're not thinking about the consequences."

Callie reached for her friend's wrist. "Tell me, Luce. I want to know who told you. Someone already shattered the windows in the sitting room. I need to know who's against us." She didn't plan to release her grip on Lucy's wrist until she got an answer.

"I don't see how it matters, but it was Maura Merrick. . . . She and Paul were planning to catch the next feature. She told Becca Adams, and Becca told me yesterday at the Company Store. Word travels fast when you're going against the grain."

Callie covered her mouth, stifling incredulous laughter. Both of the individuals who'd hurt her had seen her and Gabe. What were the odds of that happening?

Lucy leaned forward and laid a hand on Callie's shoulder. She took a deep breath. "I don't see why you're laughing, Callie. If you really love Gabe, you'll think through your decisions and do what's best for him and for you."

"Oh, Lucy, I don't know what to do." Tears stood at the back of her eyes. "He's about to come over, and I'm not about to deny him this conversation with my father."

Lucy let any suggestion of righteous indignation drop from her. The intensity beating from her eyes faded to flickers of compassion. "I wish it wasn't this way. Don't deny him the conversation then, but know it won't end how you want, Callie. Just think of your family's windows. That's only the beginning."

Chapter 37

CALLIE HOPED FOR a chance to brief Gabe before the meeting with her father began. As the minutes melted away, she threw aside her lessons for the Burkes and opened her curtains to catch Gabe's attention. Perhaps she could motion him toward her window. But she spied her father's boots on the edge of the porch and knew he was smoking a cigarette, waiting for her caller to arrive. The only mercy was that her brother, Will, was nowhere to be seen.

Soon enough, Gabe's truck emerged from around the bend and she drew in a breath. He stepped from the vehicle, hands resting near his pockets and his newsboy cap partially shielding his eyes. He took it off and held it in his hand. *He's doing this for you*, Callie told herself. *That's all you need to know about this meeting. It will be fine.* Willing herself to believe this, she murmured a prayer that her father's heart would soften and relent. She let the curtains fall from her fingertips; they caught the air like a veil, whispering on their way to the ground.

Callie heard, with some satisfaction, both men move from the porch into the house. She hadn't formally asked her father to invite Gabe into the house, but hoped he wouldn't end their meeting on the wintry porch, the cold wind lashing their faces. There was only so long Callie could remain in the confines of her bedroom. She reordered the discussion questions and knew that if she stared at them any harder, she'd be delirious. Inwardly pleading that her father hadn't given Gabe three lines and asked him to leave the premises, Callie tiptoed out to the hall and pressed her ear against the wall.

As she silenced her breath, it was Gabe's voice she heard first.

"You're right, sir. I haven't known your daughter long, but I'm in love with her and I have reason to believe she feels the same toward me."

Stunned and wondering if she heard him right, Callie bit her lip to keep from letting out a sound. It was her father this time.

"To be honest, I was hoping your relationship hadn't reached that point yet."

Her father coughed heavily, but Callie could tell he was muffling the sound with his sleeve.

"Do you realize what you'd be asking her to sacrifice for you?"

Without missing a beat, he continued.

"There are many states the two of you could never visit together, there are places you could never go. You know all this yet insist on acting against her best interest."

Callie squirmed, but she knew it was best not to make her presence known. She might not want her father to put harsh realities into words, but she knew that Gabe had thought of every one of these contentions and would rather confront them than feign denial.

"Yes, sir. I know that people can be ruthless, and that Callie will deal with this no matter how much I wish she didn't have to. But I love her and believe that she loves me. The disapproval of strangers won't mean as much if we have the support of those who matter. . . ."

She missed the next few words spoken by her father, but then heard him clearly again.

"What would you do if either one of you became a target of a crime? That does happen, you know. Some folk won't ever regard yours as a union if you continue down this road. You've read the Jim Crow . . ."

"Of course, I have. I'll do everything I can to protect her."

As if those eight words were enough for her father. They were everything to Callie. She clung to them—and to the fact he'd said he loved her—so much that she nearly missed her father's closing words.

"My daughter's a stubborn young woman. She'll make her own decision apart from what her mother and I want for her. As nice a young man as you are, there are barriers in front of you both, barriers which I imagine will always be there."

He cleared his throat, and in this small fragment of time, Callie felt like clawing her way through the wall.

"All your best intentions won't make her life easy. If you're wise, if you truly love her, you won't want this for her."

Her throat tightening, Callie glanced to her right and caught sight of her mother emerging from her bedroom. She couldn't bring herself to glance up and meet her eyes—a look would tell her that she'd been listening to her father and Gabe talk.

"It's not easy for me to dissuade you from pursuing my daughter, but I believe it's for her best . . . for yours as well."

"You've given me more to think on, sir. But I don't know that I can say goodbye to Callie so suddenly. I . . . I'd hoped that you'd get to know me and reconsider our relationship in spite of the difficulties."

Gabe's words were met by nothing more than the ticking hands of the old grandfather clock, one of the only remaining fixtures her family held onto. Callie let her hand drop from the wall, and she made a move toward the sitting room. Her mother stepped before her, attempting to prevent her intrusion into the conversation. Callie shrugged her off and didn't stop until she stood on the outskirts of the front room where the two men sat across from each other, her father in the wine-colored chair, and Gabe on the worn family sofa of faded rose floral. Their eyes flickered up to take in her form. They'd been studying the rug at their feet, the same one recently littered with large shards of glass. Their distance was palpable.

"How long have you heard us talking, Callie?" her father asked, clasping his calloused hands together.

She hadn't expected to feel anything for her father when she saw him, least of all empathy, but she acknowledged through her mounting frustration that he was trying to protect her from the sharp edges of the world. But when she looked away from him and saw the crestfallen look on Gabe's face, she wanted to cry. The question went unanswered.

"Please consider my words, Mr. Rushton. I wouldn't be here if I wasn't serious about your daughter." Gabe rose promptly to his feet and barely glanced in Callie's direction. "Happy New Year to your family."

When he didn't ask her to follow him out, Callie forewent her father's repeated calls of her name, slid into some shoes left near the door, and shadowed Gabe down the rickety stairs at the front of the house. She landed in snow that came up to the ankles. "Gabe," she said, with a tremor in her voice, "please, please wait."

When he turned around, she could see the pain brewing in his dark eyes. He tried to prevent her from following him by putting out a hand. "Don't take another step. It's freezing out here, and you don't have your coat."

She listened to half of his instructions. She didn't take another step, but she refused to turn back to the house.

"I love you, Gabe," she said into the stillness.

She watched his face soften.

"You listened to the whole conversation, didn't you?" His tone was deflated, air running out of a tire.

Callie nodded, finding it difficult to maintain her distance from him.

"Listen," he said, trying to hide his disappointment, "we'll talk about this later, Callie. I just need time to think this through."

"I can't live here anymore," Callie said resolutely, wishing she'd thought to gather her possessions ahead of time. "I appreciate all my parents have done for me, but I can't answer to them for the decisions I make. Especially not the decisions about you."

Gabe shifted uncomfortably, his boots crunching over the packed snow. Callie sensed his unease and knew there was nothing he wanted more than to leave the premises. But he'd said he loved her.

Her throat tightened. If she didn't wrap her arms around him and press her face into his shoulder, she'd break. She forgot his request that she freeze in place, or turn back to the house to catch some warmth. She stepped closer and closer to him and entered the comfort of his arms. Gabe sighed against her hair, placed a hand in her tangled tresses. "His concerns aren't unfounded, Cal. You have to know that. Soon I'm returning back to the west side and it will give you some time. It will . . . please hear me out. It will give you some time to think about what's best for you. I love you, no matter what happens. I hope you know that." He swept his lips over the top of her forehead, tipped his cap to her, and left her with a smile that almost made her forget the cold air entering her lungs.

Chapter 38

"**G**O TO YOUR BEDROOM, boys," Mr. Rushton said as Callie stepped back in the house. Young as the twins were, she knew they understood the nature of this fight. Charlie made a disgruntled sound, and Stevie shot her an aggravated look.

Mr. Rushton rose from his chair. He threw his hands up. "This just isn't done," he said. "You should know better than to ask that young man here only to have me turn him away, tell him things you already knew."

"Then why agree to meet him at all?" Callie asked, feeling tears sting her eyes. She couldn't stop there. "Telling me that it can't happen means you're siding with the people that draw those lines."

"Don't you put this on me," he said. The lamplight from the side table washed over his melancholic features. "You've been sheltered your whole life, living here. The world's not as kind out there, and you'll have to find that out on your own. It's a real shame."

He shook his head as if she were a disgrace, and at that moment, it mattered little to her if the world was abrasive and cold. It mattered only that he wouldn't look at her.

"I agreed to meet with him since he deserves my response. Now he knows exactly where I stand, and so do you."

Callie took one look at him and shook her head, fighting back those tears. Once one escaped, nothing could stop their flight from her eyes. "I wonder how Mr. Jacobson would feel if he were to hear—"

"You leave Sam out of this," her father said, his eyes snapping in anger. "He has nothing to do with—"

"Doesn't he?" Callie challenged him, unwilling to clamp her tongue. "He's such a close friend of yours, why don't you share how you feel about your daughter being with a man who looks kind of like—"

"Enough!" her father yelled, the veins in his neck clenched tight as he came within inches of her face. "Don't you speak to me like this in my own house. Who do you think you are?"

"Your daughter," Callie murmured under her breath. With a tight smile she turned away before he could say another word. In this moment Mrs. Rushton softly entered the room. "Callie . . . I know you're angry right now, but please listen to your father's heart in all this," her mother pleaded, moving toward her husband's shoulder. Her tone was weary, a stripped birch after a fire.

It took considerable self-restraint for Callie not to lash out at her mother. The angriest person in the room was not herself; it was her father in all his pacing, his jagged breathing, the anger that flared in his eyes and vanquished any kindness.

"It's time for you to find another place to stay," he said in terse words, as if grit was lodged in his mouth. Callie heard her mother's sudden inhale, watched her attempted hand of appeasement on her husband's shoulder. Noticed his instant flinching away. "Your mother and I—we've done our best by you—and if you decide not to listen, there's very little we can do for you."

"This doesn't mean we need to send her out in the cold right—"

"She has plenty of connections," her father said, unrelenting. He refused to look at either his wife or his daughter. "I want her out from under my roof until she's come to her senses."

Her mother turned to her. "Everyone needs the chance to calm down. Maybe if you went to Lucy's for a few hours . . ."

Instead of speaking to her mother, Callie went down the hall and began to snatch cardigans and skirts from hangers and toss them into a suitcase that rested in a dark corner of her closet. She threw in her second pair of shoes and opened her linen drawer. She was aware that her mother had followed her and stood on the outskirts of her bedroom, intently watching her. "Please don't make this more difficult for me, Mama. I'm not trying to go against your wishes, but you won't give me your blessing since my father won't. I'm not willing to walk away from Gabe. I can't do that. . . ."

She tossed in enough clothes to fill her suitcase and let the top fall to the ground, leaden anchor that it was. She knew she wasn't returning any time soon. It might take months—years even—for them to come to terms with her decision. "I love you, Mama, but I need to go," she said, the pain rising in her chest. She turned her head away before her mother could see the tears spill down her cheeks.

✧ ✧ ✧

"So Gabe doesn't know you've left your parents' house?" Bess ushered Callie in with her suitcase and an invitation to stay with them awhile. The seamstress pointed toward an open seat on the sofa and had her sit down. Her husband, having heard someone at the door, moved toward the front room and then took a seat himself.

Callie shook her head. "He doesn't know where I am yet. My father told me to leave after he tried to dissuade Gabe from seeing me."

"So you're willing to leave your parents' house in order to be with him," Mr. Starek said, steepling his hands as if in prayer. Callie could tell he wasn't convinced that she should take this path of greater resistance.

Bess sent her husband a direct look across the sitting room. "Let's take this one moment at a time please, Nick."

Callie cleared her throat. "He told my father that he loves me. . . . My father's only response was to tell him we shouldn't be together. My father . . . he's been bruised by the world, and I don't want to cause him more distress. . . ."

The seamstress chewed on that thought for a minute and replied. "He doesn't want you to hurt. . . . We only have one son. . . . Michael. . . . But we think about him all the time." She smiled without showing her teeth. Callie had overheard her parents' late-night discussions about Michael Starek's involvement with bootlegging across state lines and his inability to sober up, but she wasn't about to let on that she'd heard a word.

Bess spoke on. "Your father's right in admitting that you and Gabe won't have an easy time of it."

"It wouldn't be any easier for me to say goodbye," Callie said, blanching at that thought. Gabe might have only entered her life months before, but the time didn't matter. Her heart would ache if she continued to tutor Jamie and Julia and never saw him. She couldn't imagine helping the children collect their belongings without wondering if he was home. She wouldn't be able to look at Mr. Burke without considering the man who worked closest to him.

"It might be tough for a while, but I believe your father will come around no matter what you decide," Mr. Starek said, suddenly rising from his chair and reaching for a spare blanket on the sofa to drop over Callie's shoulders. It was the benediction she needed. "He's a good man, that father of yours. He wants what's best for you."

"That might be true, but he'd opt for comfort over taking any stance against society." Her anger toward her father hadn't abated yet.

"If it makes you feel any better, your father . . . he refused to sign that petition circling through town to have Gabe banned from the Company Store."

"H-how do you know?" Callie asked. Her father didn't leave his property all too often these days.

"We were at the barber at the same time, and that paper was making the rounds," Nick said, weaving a hand through his recently shorn hair.

Callie pursed her lips. "It's well and good that he didn't sign it," she said, "but that doesn't mean he's treating Gabe as an equal."

The Stareks glanced for a moment at one another. "If you want peace about leaving things this way with your parents, write them a letter," Bess said, offering a small smile. "It won't mend everything quickly, but it's a start. Written words, they can cut through the riled emotions and lock in what we really want to say."

"That might be true," Callie said, careful not to negate the seamstress' advice. "And yet, I think it will take more than words to change my father's stance. And my brother, Will . . . it looks like he might be a lost cause."

"No one's ever a lost cause." Mrs. Starek had the last word.

Chapter 39

"I'M LEARNING THAT it all gets better," Ben said, his green eyes displaying an uncommon sheen. "I have great hopes for the future of this business and my son's health. I told you . . . didn't I? . . . Good ol' Eddy sat me down and offered to pay my son's medical bills straight up?" He looked at Gabe. "No?" He beamed. "That makes me respect the man all the more. He won't sing his own praises, but I will."

Ben Livingston and Gabe sat at a table at Slim's. So many of their daylight hours were spent maintaining patience and professionalism that it came as a relief to them both when they could find a table near the back on a Friday and let the pack of worries fall from their shoulders. They'd been in the place for two hours now, elbows pressed on the tables, voices low and urgent as they discussed everything from Merrick's petition, to changes in mining equipment, to the condition of Ben's son, Owen.

Ben leaned forward, downed the second shot of brown-gold liquid and turned to greet Doug Winslow, who emerged near their table, waiting to say hello. While many in Roslyn tended their own small farms, Winslow's provided apples and produce that wasn't as easy to come by. It didn't hurt that the man had a gregarious nature and knew just the right questions to draw a person out.

Gabe had no time to warn Ben that Burke wouldn't want his good deeds publicized. Once past their initial greetings,

Ben laid out his palm and sought to make himself heard above the strumming guitar.

"Life's real good these days. Wasn't expecting it, but I shoulda known that Burke would come through."

Doug was still out of earshot, so Ben rose from his seat and came within inches of the man's face. A guitar and banjo began a raucous bluegrass tune that had people tapping their feet, and he had to raise his voice to be heard above it.

"Burke is covering my boy's medical expenses," he said, relief flooding his voice. "Most doctors we know wouldn't take pay installments, but Burke, he's offered to cover it all." Ben smoothed a red curl away from his eyes. As if noticing Gabe for the first time, he slung an arm over his friend's shoulder and said, "I couldn't ask to work for a better father-son duo than Edward and Gabe."

As soon as the words were out, Gabe sought to reel them in. He shook his head abruptly at Ben, but it was too late. He'd worked long to keep this confidence, and yet all the while it felt like a tenuous walk near a cliff. One slight slip and there was no unknowing, no unseeing the truth.

If Ben caught his blunder, perhaps they could generate a quick recovery or at least put an abrupt stop to any more words. Perhaps the music was just loud enough for Doug to raise a hand to his ear and ask Ben to repeat what he'd said. But Livingston wasn't reading any of Gabe's cues, and in fact, he continued as a few additional dirt-covered miners edged up to their table.

"They might be take-charge and serious when you first meet them, but underneath it all they have hearts of gold . . . Edward and his son." He clapped a hand on Gabe's shoulder.

Several pairs of eyes surveyed Gabe, as if just comprehending the connection. Edward and Gabe were similar in height, in the amusement that crept into their dark eyes after they'd found commonality with a person, in the manner in which they tapped pens to the table when waiting on a decision.

Gabe had known all these things for years, but his skin color was a barrier that kept such comparisons to a minimum. At least, until exposed to the bare-bones truth. Gabe felt like he'd taken a surprise hit on a baseball field. He winced in spite of his efforts to remain impassive. But Ben finally caught up with his words. He clapped a hand over his face, flooded with immediate remorse. "Oh no. Gabe, no. I'm so sorry. I didn't mean . . ." But Gabe didn't have it within him to speak words of admonishment or to aggravate the man's conscience. His friend had merely made a mistake. This was no betrayal. Yet the effect was almost the same. All his life he'd had to shrink himself within the confines of the majority. Now even his true identity was offered up, against his wishes, for virtual strangers to explore as they wanted.

"It makes sense," Doug finally said, his wad of chewing tobacco plain to see as he took in the news. "I wasn't looking for it before, but the resemblance is striking." He grinned. "And you both like those same Snow apples at my stands." The words fell flat, no one cracked a smile.

While Ben sank back into his chair, Gabe gave an unfaltering look to the three or four men surrounding them. "That's knowledge we keep in the company, gentlemen. I trust it'll stay that way?" he said, all the while knowing that any hope for silence was a lost balloon plied free from his hands.

✦ ✦ ✦

Callie left the Company Store one evening in early January, eyes pressed to the snow-topped sidewalk, when a pair of work boots in her line of sight startled her. Caught unawares, a few groceries dropped from the box onto the snowy sidewalk. She uttered an apology and reached down to pick up the items she'd let escape—a loaf of bread, a box of rice, a pound of sugar needed to make a cake for Bess' birthday.

She swept back up to see Paul's incisive blue eyes studying her. Callie started, but quickly regained her composure, gathering the items to her chest. She tried to dart around him but he blocked her way onto the street. Why hadn't she noticed his controlling demeanor when they'd been together in high school and beyond? Was it simply because she saw in him what she wanted to all those years? Her mouth went dry. She looked for another chance to slip out among the pedestrians, but he was too quick for her. He leaned in close to her ear. "It's surprising to learn things about people that you thought you knew."

Callie narrowed her eyes at him, used her groceries as a shield over her chest. She had no interest in standing here with him in the tug of the night winds.

"I saw you in that colored boy's arms," Paul said, beginning to laugh incredulously. "In plain sight. I know that our . . . parting was difficult for you, but it's strange that you'd leave my arms for a Negro's. What'd he do to convince you to—"

"Nothing," Callie said bluntly, staring up at Paul with heat behind her eyes. "He did nothing to convince me to do anything. He has a name, whether you want to know it or not. He's not some *Negro*."

Paul rifled his hand through his disheveled blond hair. He was in his laborer's clothes, and a layer of dirt clung to him, doused his cheeks. At one time she had felt for him, his hard life in the mines, but her sympathies had simmered down. There was no possibility for this conversation to end well. She turned, willing to take the longer route back to the Starek's home, if only to escape him. He reached for her arm as if he still had a claim on her. "Wait, Callie."

She turned around angrily, but still she stopped.

"Why should I, Paul? What is it you need to say? What I do and who I see . . . that doesn't involve you anymore."

His laughter died down, but a ruthless smile still played around his lips, making his dimple on the right side all the more striking. How he could look so handsome in all his arrogance, she'd never know, but it didn't move her anymore.

"What might surprise you, Callie," he said, "is that I may know more about him than you do. I know who he is and how he relates to Roslyn. . . ."

"I know his grandfather came here with the black miners back in '88," Callie said, unable to stop herself. She hoped to shut him down so she could walk away, letting his words scatter.

Paul tilted his head to the right. "Curious observation," he said. "Did Gabe also let you in on the fact that he's Burke's bastard son?"

Callie blinked, first at the harshness of his words, then at the truth as the waves of possibility swilled and subsided. She might have seen such a simple conclusion on her own, had looked beyond the choppy surface. She steadied herself against the nearest lamppost and inhaled deeply as she thought of those subtle signs she'd overlooked. The way both men greeted people with an affirming nod before they said hello. How they shared square jaws and broad shoulders, though Edward was a clip taller. How beholden Gabe was to Burke. How Gabe dared to interact with his wife. His closeness with Burke's children, as if they shared an unspoken bond. She'd written off those telltale signs, believing they were alike because of the time they shared with one another.

"It wasn't so hard to come by this truth," Paul continued, though she wasn't ready for him to speak. "That employee of Burke's — Ben, I think — was liquored-up real good one night at Slim's, and his tongue got running. Told one of the miners that Gabe and his old man Burke had the same business savvy. Said it must have trickled down the bloodline or something."

Part of her wanted to ask Paul to speak on, tell her all he knew about the father-son pair, but she didn't want to hear this news from him. A key had turned in a door long locked and she stood on the border of the truth, waiting for someone worthy to guide her in.

Paul leaned in closer and whispered. "Ah, he didn't tell you his little secret, did he?" He shook his head. "Must not trust you completely yet. It makes sense, it really does. Not wanting to let the people of Roslyn know that his daddy is the owner of the shipping company that supplies so many of our goods. Should anyone learn that Burke had relations with a colored woman, they might demand another supplier." He raised his eyebrows. "Someone with more integrity."

"Stop," Callie said, absorbing enough in her stunned state to tell her former fiancé he'd gone too far. "You don't need to put words to what you don't know."

"What more do I need to know?" Paul asked, throwing his hands up. "His colored son is the proof. . . ."

Callie shook her head. She wouldn't let him cheapen something so significant with his demeaning words. She wouldn't let him see that this disclosure of Gabe's parentage affected her. Why hadn't he told her? He'd risked her father's wrath and his own safety to see her. He'd held her in his arms so close, and yet he'd left this important thing unsaid. Why hadn't he felt he could trust her? She felt the cold of the night invade her. The chill lashed her cheeks, bled through her mittens, pierced her lungs.

Paul stepped even closer to her, closer than she felt comfortable with. But since there was no malice in his eyes or incredulity, even, she let him speak.

"Look. I'm sorry if this news hurts you, Callie. I know I didn't do a good job protecting you, but you deserve so much more than this facade."

"Good night, Paul. I don't want to discuss this anymore." She was several steps in the right direction, away from him, when he called out to her.

"Think better of it, Callie. Don't sell yourself short, falling for him. Even if he stands to inherit. . . ."

"I told you to stop," she said turning around, her anger rising in a violent swell. "For all you think you know, Paul, there's so much that you never will." She pressed her groceries to her chest and only let out her breath when he was far behind her, a harmless shadow straining to be seen against a darkening sidewalk.

Chapter 40

"**Y**ou alright, Callie? Seems like something's bothering you." She sat beside him in the truck—the first time she'd seen him since the encounter with Paul, the encounter that made her feel like she was running against a flow of water. She'd felt angry, believing that he couldn't possibly love her if he withheld such an integral part of himself. However, it was dangerous to assume his reasons. Several brief phone calls had transpired between them but she hadn't been able to confront him over the phone.

Now she nearly laughed aloud, not knowing how to train the words on the tip of her tongue. She played with a button on her cardigan, felt it come loose from its thread.

"I ran into Paul outside the store the other night, Gabe."

"Yeah? What'd he want?" He kept his vision on the icy road.

"He . . . he told me that you're Edward's son, and I can't believe I didn't know . . . that you didn't tell me . . ."

She hadn't expected her voice to sound so accusatory. She watched a shadow move across Gabe's face as he took this in, saw his jaw tense and release. "Callie couldn't this wait? It's not something I want to talk about while I'm driving."

"When would you want to talk about it?" Callie asked, holding the loose button in her palm. Unbidden, her mind fled to the photograph of his mother, Lily. How blind she'd been. Though Gabe's skin was dark, he didn't have the hint of mahogany that Lily's photograph suggested. Why hadn't she thought in all of her imaginings that his biological father wasn't merely light-skinned, but in fact white? There was so much before her all along, so much that she hadn't seen.

"I would have told you," Gabe insisted, pulling his truck over to the right side of the road and turning to her, his brown eyes beseeching her to believe him. "It was only a matter of time before I did. You have to understand." He fiddled with his watch before looking back to her. "Burke . . . my father . . . has enough stacked against him without the entire town knowing that he has an illegitimate son, a colored one no less." He laughed, though nothing was funny.

Callie turned toward him. "I understand this, Gabe, not telling me at first. But to keep it from me for so long . . ." She shrugged. She wanted to ask him how he could work for a man who didn't acknowledge the truth of who he was, who was content to have others think he was the hired help.

He shook his head. "It's not about you, Callie. Have you considered that?" He studied his watch, though it was hard to see where the hands fell in the dark.

"I have my mother's surname, always have, and that made it easier to keep the truth from most. It was my decision, has been all these years. My father . . . he'd rather lose contracts than go along pretending . . ."

"But he does pretend," Callie insisted, hoping she wasn't being unkind. "He allows everyone to think you're his right hand man and nothing else."

"It's easier that way," Gabe said, tapping his hands on the steering wheel, as if to distract himself from any tug of emotion. "It's easier not to address each other as father and son so we don't have to know just how many businesses wouldn't want us . . . serving them. It was my decision, and yes, you could say he's at fault for going along with it. Ben — he doesn't think it's right and neither does Annie, but his wife certainly favors the arrangement. She's told the children not to ever admit I'm their older half-brother to anyone. . . ."

Callie pictured the walls of the Burke's home. There were

no photographs of Gabe displayed on any of them. Julia and Jamie loved him as the older brother he was, and they couldn't admit as much aloud. Her heart hurt, even though so many would look at his life as one of opportunity and privilege. She knew that this arrangement that he had with his father was not enough, could never be enough.

"He loved her once, my mother," Gabe said. "Met her in a dance hall when he was in his early twenties, and fell for her fast. They weren't together long. Her family didn't approve. His family certainly didn't. But in some ways I don't think he ever got over her. . . ." Callie saw the water swim in his eyes, but before she could say a word, he broke her gaze and looked out the window, at the imaginary passersby on the left side. It was, for whatever reason, a quieter night in the Upper County than most.

Gabe turned back to her and gave her a wry look. "You're stunned, Callie."

Callie shook her head. "If I'm stunned, it's because I didn't see it, and the truth was right in front of me all this time."

Her mind, integrating this new information, fell on the tell-tale emblem Edward had chosen for his boxes. She let out a laugh at her realization.

Gabe arched an eyebrow. "What is it, Callie? What's funny?"

She shook her head. "It's not that it's funny. I just realized that . . ." she looked at him with round blue eyes. "It was no accident, your father selecting a lily as his imprint, was it?"

Gabe looked back at his hands resting on the steering wheel and said, "No. It was no accident. He chose that symbol early on and kept it . . . even when they parted ways, a long, long time ago." He suddenly grew tight-lipped.

Callie couldn't hold back her indignation.

"It's me you're talking to, Gabe—not all of Roslyn, not some-one you can't trust. Me."

"We haven't been seeing each other long. What makes you think I wouldn't have told you?"

She turned toward him. "I never said you wouldn't someday

tell me," she said, tightly. "But you've held back on me . . . and I haven't held back on you."

He shook his head, put his truck back in drive and kept his eyes trained on the road. "There might not be so much for you to hold back, Callie. Have you ever considered that?"

She made no reply, so he filled the silence. "I might have some white in me, Callie. But I'm a black man. It's how the world sees me, it's how I see myself. Edward is my father, and I love him. But he'll never understand what it's like to be colored. And neither will you."

Callie nodded. He wasn't waiting for her words. He merely needed to speak his own.

"Sometimes I feel like my father came here to pay some kind of penance. I mean, I know he was taken with the place years ago, but it's a little unreal . . . renovating the very house my grandfather once boarded in." He shook his head. "Going back to my roots . . . it doesn't help much when I'm resistant to telling people who I am."

"Who else knows that Burke is your father?" Callie asked, surprised it had taken this long for word to reach her.

"Some folks in the black community. . . . Ruthie Sloane and her father. The Jacobsons, they know. Several others."

"The Jacobsons?" Callie asked, feeling the chills rise over her arms. "Why, they've never said anything. Mr. Jacobson, he's friends with my father, and he never mentioned a word. . . ."

Gabe shook his head. "Why would he? Knowing wouldn't have changed anything, and he's a minister, Callie. He knows how to keep confidentiality." He raised a hand to his recently cut hair and said, "I don't expect you to understand."

"Will you please stop doing this?" Callie leaned forward in her seat, almost banging her head on the dashboard when he turned a corner.

"Doing what?" Gabe asked, frowning at her. Defensiveness etched its way into his voice, swept over his features.

She wished she'd kept quiet, but couldn't so easily hold the words back now. "Acting as if I can't remotely understand anything about what you've gone through when . . . when you didn't even give me a chance to hear your story."

Gabe shook his head, incredulous. "You wouldn't understand, Callie. I never said it was your fault. I only said that you wouldn't understand what it's like to grow up caught between two worlds, sometimes feeling that if you show loyalty or interest, even, to one color, you are denying the other." He pressed the heel of one hand to his forehead. "Look, I know that this . . . revelation . . . caught you off guard."

She wanted to touch his shoulder at least or reach for his hand, but refrained when she read his defensiveness. "What does your mother . . . what does she think of you coming out here, working for your father?"

He closed his eyes briefly. "It doesn't matter what my mother thinks. She passed away from a terrible case of influenza when I was fourteen," he said. "Soon after I went to live with my father." He winced, and it looked like regret. "My grandmother would have taken me in, but I wasn't too interested in being that close to the music world as a teen. Thought the shipping industry sounded more adventurous."

"Oh Gabe, I'm sorry. . . ." Callie started in.

He smiled in acknowledgement but it faded fast. "It's hard to believe she's been gone ten years. I miss her every day. . . ."

He paused. "When I said it doesn't really matter what she thinks, it wasn't true. She's not be here in the flesh, but I think about what she would tell me all the time."

"What do you think she'd say about you working for your father?"

"I think she'd be in favor as long as I was," he said. "Things might not have ended with them how they should have, but she bore no ill will toward him. She was more gracious than she needed to be." He cleared his throat, "Callie, I'm going to drive you back to Bess' house . . . unless you'd like me to take you home."

Her throat burned, but she held her tongue for a moment. She had ventured into parts of him that he protected—what should she expect? But she couldn't abide the not-knowing, she turned to him again. "This shouldn't have to change us, Gabe. It won't, will it?"

He took his focus off the road for a moment, long enough for her to see there was sadness brimming in his eyes. At long last he said, "Look, Callie. I don't want it to. I really don't. But I mean what I say. I need to be alone for a little while. If your former beau is running his mouth on who I am, I can guarantee it'll affect Burke Enterprises all the more. He's hand-in-glove with Merrick over at the Company Store."

"I haven't forgotten," Callie said. "I don't trust the lot of them."

"Neither do I."

Chapter 41

1908

LILY DIDN'T INSTANTLY fall in love with Roslyn like she expected. Springtime didn't boast the showy seasons she'd heard of for so long. The wintry snowbanks that sealed people in their homes. Star-blanketed summer skies that invited folks to forget the hour. Her mother told her there wasn't much to see — just a main strip that boasted more taverns than churches — but Lily still wanted to know for herself.

Truth be told, she felt relieved she'd only planned a three day stay when her feet first touched the train platform. But then she glanced up and met the smiling eyes of the young woman she knew was Ruthie. She instantly let out the breath she hadn't known she'd been holding.

"Lily Ward?" Ruthie said, beaming so that her generous smile shone white against her dark skin.

Lily nodded and before she could help it, burst out laughing. As if there were any other colored women arriving at this small haunt in the mountains. In fact, the only other colored traveler was small, stout black man sitting near the back of the train when she'd first boarded. She'd sat two rows ahead of him. He'd given her a measured nod before turning his attention to the newspaper in his lap.

While there were no signs designating where she could or couldn't sit, she followed the unspoken mandates. Lily wasn't keen to invite any hushed intensity by sitting near the front of the car. The biting indignity of her "place" was something she'd learned to swallow down, though she was as worthy as any other person on that train.

Ruthie wore a simple blue dress, scuffed black boots, a red scarf over hair that hadn't been relaxed in some time. There was a simple beauty to her, but not of the kind Lily was apt to notice. Had Lily crossed Ruthie on the street in Seattle, she probably wouldn't have looked at her twice. Lily's hands brushed ivory keys. Ruthie's were given to scrubbing dishes and hammering nails into boards. And yet, their differences aside, the two bonded quickly.

On this occasion, Ruthie held the keys to the castle. Lily had banked all manner of questions about where her father had come to live, and Ruthie was the one who could give her the answers. The location of the No. 3 mine where he'd saved more than one life. The fledgling boarding house where he'd lived. The hill where he'd been buried along with the two other miners who lost their lives in the same tragedy.

Within a few hours Lily had gone to all the places her daddy's boots might have taken him. She'd wrapped a scarf around the hollow of her throat, but couldn't escape the cruelty of the spring afternoon. The wind flayed her cheeks, steered her gaze toward the earthen floor as she and Ruthie climbed the hill.

"You sure the graves are this far up?" Lily asked, calling ahead to Ruthie, who forged on ahead. Her new friend had confessed to only traveling this way once before.

Ruthie turned to her and nodded. "Yes. We're almost there." She slowed her pace and waited for Lily to catch her, then placed a steady hand on Lily's shoulder as she pointed to the place on the ground where three bodies rested.

Lily strained her eyes and felt a chill pass through her as she saw the small lily etched over his resting place, just as her mother had said. Her throat threatened to close on her. She was struck with a blend of anger and sorrow—sorrow that he'd been taken from her when she was so young, anger that he had no marker but the one Mr. Rollins had given him.

"My daddy saved white men's lives and look what they gave

him." She backhanded a first tear and then others. It was too cold to even feel them on her skin.

"I know," Ruthie said, her tone sober. "My father tells me that they all praised David for his work in the mines. His courage when it came to saving lives. Don't know why they couldn't have seen that he had a proper place to rest."

Lily tasted bitterness on her tongue. "It would have meant disrupting the unspoken order of the world." She swallowed her anger down, not wanting to think of those who failed to honor him. She thought instead of the man who did, whose daughter stood before her now. She crouched down before David's grave and pressed a finger to the lily inscribed by Lenny Rollins. After a moment she rose to her feet and took Ruthie's hand.

"He's not here anymore. I mean he is, but this isn't where I feel him . . . close to me. I'm grateful that I take him with me wherever I go." She looked at Ruthie, at Ruthie's compassionate eyes. She wiped her nose with the back of her hand and started leading her new friend back down the hill. "Thank you for showing me this place. It makes me sad, but I like knowing where he rests."

✧ ✧ ✧

A few hours later, Lily's tone had changed. As the women prepared a chicken and rice dinner, she turned to Ruthie. "Come out with me tonight. Put on a pretty dress, and let's find a music hall. Heck, I might even sing if I have a willing audience."

Ruthie looked at her, incredulity filling her eyes. "We don't have a shortage of taverns, Lily, if that's what you're asking for . . . but women like us, ladies, rarely go. Besides, I don't have anything to wear. I have dresses for church, but not . . ."

Once Lily felt determination, it encircled her and wouldn't let go. "Your Anthony can come with us . . . if he wants. There must be somewhere we could go."

Ruthie mulled their options over in her mind. "We could go to the Masonic Hall. They have dancing. Colored people go there too, and it's not strictly a drinking establishment."

Her tone was filled with more appeasement than eagerness to go. "Anthony will insist on coming with us. That is, if I can convince him to go."

Lily placed her hand on the shorter woman's shoulder and said, "It won't have to be for long, just long enough to make our presence felt. And you can borrow one of my dresses. We're roughly the same size." She let an appraising gaze fall over Ruthie's partially hidden form and said, "That man of yours will thank me, just you see."

An hour later Lily turned to Ruthie and Anthony and asked them if they were ready to go. The unhesitating smile Ruthie had given her when they'd first met was replaced with slight trepidation. Lily noted for the first time tiny lines written into Ruthie's brow that hadn't been there before. Fortunately, it took just a little persuading to change Ruthie's mind and cover her in smiles of amusement as they tried on Lily's elegant gowns.

The floor-length, midnight dress Lily loaned her did wonders. It had a low, lace bodice and a beaded silk skirt that made Ruthie float over the floorboards. As she'd expected, Ruthie's husband stopped his work to let his eyes follow her soon as she stepped in their sitting room.

"Ruthie," he said, brown eyes glowing like the fireplace embers. "You look as pretty as the day we married."

Lily smiled wide. "You both need to go out dancing more often. Take a break from the daily routine."

✧ ✧ ✧

Now that they stood outside the dance hall, Lily could see there was no discernible sophistication to the place. Hardy workers stepped inside, some of them with nicks on their chins from last minute shaves, decked out in slightly nicer clothes than the ones worn during daylight hours. The few women who went on ahead of them wore the best dresses they had beneath winter coats, but none of them were dressed remotely like she and Ruthie. For Lily, that was part of the allure—waltzing into the unsuspecting hall and taking center stage. Ruthie and

Anthony, their arms linked, led the way, and Lily followed far enough behind to assess the room. Ruthie turned over her shoulder and beamed.

Once the warmth of the indoors struck their faces, Lily traded her giddiness in for a cool reserve. She let her black fur cape fall from her shoulders and felt the press of stares as they glided across the room. She suspected Ruthie was beginning to realize a hint of the feminine power she possessed. Lily wore a floor-length, black gown embroidered with sequins that rippled against her like water when she moved. Anthony nodded toward a small, empty table, and she and Ruthie claimed it. They had barely sat down when an effortless smile took over her face. Lily recognized the tune clinking from the piano keys. She flagged a waiter and whispered into his ear before ordering a drink. Ruthie and Anthony looked at her questioningly, but she avoided their eyes and watched as the waiter crossed to the pianist, a slight white man. Listening keenly to the waiter's message, he pulled his eyes from the keys. The pianist studied Lily for a moment, then motioned her with a nod of his head, as if he sensed the musicality in her blood as only other artists could.

She grinned at Ruthie, then rose and crossed over to the piano. Lily seated herself on the bench next to the pianist and played a little impromptu solo above him. Then she stole over to the stage and let her sultry alto fill the room like slow, addicting honey.

She felt the collective hush of the room and knew she had them all, just as she had the city dwellers when she performed in Seattle. Their faces smiled at her or tilted in wonder, so rapt was her own face in song. Lost to the melody, she started to close her eyes when saw a young man leaning against a post, tall and handsome. He was dressed in a grey suit, it's white shirt unblemished. His eyes, dark and expressive, pressed upon her, taking her in. Once their eyes met, a slow, unassuming smile rose over his mouth.

Lily looked down at her shoes, grounding herself in the

present, but she was smiling too. His attention almost lost her a lyric, but she maintained her place and her composure. Why had he made her heart stutter so suddenly? He was hardly the first man to notice her. Hardly the first white man to notice her. She was grateful that the warmth of her skin couldn't betray her like it did other girls.

"Ladies and gentlemen, put your hands together for—" the piano player paused, waiting for Lily to fill in her name.

"Liliana Ward," she said, giving them all her full name.

"Encore, encore!" her audience cried after she closed out the crowd favorite, but she shook her head sweetly, having come here to do what she needed to do. Lily looked forward to gliding back to her seat across from Ruthie and enjoying her drink. Perhaps when she and Ruthie got home to that two-room cabin, they'd toast their feet over the coals of the fireplace and reminisce about their evening out.

But as she lifted the bottom of her gown—a feeble attempt to spare it from spilled drinks—she felt someone brush against her shoulder. When she looked up she saw that it was the handsome young man who'd been watching her. She grinned at him before she could help herself. Where was her icy remove? Her indifferent regard?

He started in. "Your voice, it's so beautiful." He shook his head in amazement, and Lily wondered at him, that he didn't seem to worry about the press of eyes soon to fall upon them. He had to be someone important. Men didn't walk around this coal town dressed so impeccably if they were loggers, farmers, miners. Yet if he was someone important, wouldn't he know that he'd already done too much, said too much? She knew without turning her head that Anthony's face would be solemn.

Instead, she smirked down at her toes, then lifted her chin to meet his warm eyes with her own amber ones. As they joined she heard her name, snagging her out of the moment's enchantment. "Lily!" It was Ruthie looking out for her, guarding her from the onslaught of unworthy men and their untoward advances. She ignored her for the moment.

"You know my name," she said. "Now, what is yours?"

"Edward Burke," he said. The amusement momentarily left his face at the interruption. "My friends call me Eddy. Sounds like your friends call you Lily. At least that's what she's calling you right now."

She couldn't hide her laughter. "That she is." Ruthie was clearly concerned about her, as she should be. She motioned to her that she'd be over in a minute.

"What brings you to Roslyn? I can tell . . ." he said, searching for words, "that you're not from this part of the state."

"Really? What gives it away?" she laughed and shifted her weight, the black sequins on her dress glittering madly. Before he could prevent it, his eyes traveled down the length of her gown and his color deepened before he could answer.

Sensing his disadvantage, she satisfied him with an answer. "I'm from Seattle—well originally Chicago—but I've been in Seattle most of my life. And you? You don't look like you belong to these parts either."

He smiled. "I don't strike you as a strong, strapping miner?"

Lily laughed, though she knew tongues would wag if she carried on her conversation with this white man any longer.

"I'm from Seattle too, but my father sent me here on business for a few weeks," he said. Eddy gave her a close-lipped smile, something she found endearing, and then he whispered close to her ear. "I don't want to disrespect your friends and intrude on your night, but I'd like to see you again. Would that be alright?"

It was hard to extract the sound of her mother's voice from her head, the voice telling her that nothing good could come from flirtatious banter or stolen glances across a crowded room. But she silenced Georgina, if only for one night. She was a grown woman and had lived long enough to have her heart broken once before. She could make her own decisions and needn't judge this young man harshly.

"Perhaps." She smiled coyly. "What type of business are you here for?"

He didn't mistake her meaning. "My father owns a shipping company. But I might have some business here of my own."

"Oh? That sounds intriguing."

"Tell me where to find you, and you might hear more of it," he said, his tone hinting at determination despite the calm demeanor he seemed to show the world.

She thought fast, knowing she was on borrowed time. She could see Anthony across the way, his arms crossed over his chest. "Frog Pond, noon tomorrow." It was a less densely populated area than many of the others Ruthie had shown her. "I'm here for only two more days, maybe a little longer." She tried to hide her own surprise at bending her itinerary. She'd said nothing to Ruthie about the thought of delaying her visit, and now, because of a chance encounter with a man she was undeniably drawn to, she was making decisions that just might change her life.

✧ ✧ ✧

The first time he reached for her hand and she felt an electrical current course through her, she knew there was no going back. Discretion was the name of their game, and it only intensified the hunger. She welcomed his stolen kisses on scenic walkways overlooking plunging blue waters, at the edge of street corners, in rooms where he'd find her long after she'd checked in under a fictitious name. Her heart hadn't been her first consideration when she'd met him that first night, but it caught up with her. She suspected he'd already fallen for her—in fact, knew he had. Whenever they met—in Roslyn or in Seattle—a goodbye stood on the cusp of her lips. But then it was too late.

Her gowns were soon enough tightening at the middle, and she'd had to tell him their days of laughing in the face of propriety were dead and gone. She was certain Eddy would try to do right by her, but he didn't come to her with an instant proposal. Lily watched him press his hands to his eyes at the initial news. Heard him apologize. "We'll figure this out, Lily," he said, his voice stripped of its persistent hope.

But he got to pacing the small, nondescript room where they sometimes met instead of turning toward her. When he finally circled around, she saw tears stinging his eyes. His father had caught word of them, she knew. A friend had seen them brawling in an alleyway. He hinted that the purplish tint on his forehead was from a barroom fight, but she watched Eddy wince at the mention of his father's name and suspected otherwise.

She swallowed down her disappointment and her tears and drew a ready conclusion before he could sort his feelings out. She wouldn't watch him writhe like a fly on a thread. She wouldn't entertain a marriage proposal that none in his family would acknowledge. She wouldn't accept, even if he did offer up the question. True love was sustaining, yes, but it sometimes meant having enough strength to let go.

Chapter 42

1932

G ABE KEPT HIS distance from Callie for the next few days. There was more that he couldn't bring himself to tell her just yet. While Gabe and the Burkes attended their respective Sunday services, an unknown person stole onto their property and shot out all the windows at the front of the house. Mrs. Burke instantly declared it was some disgruntled miner chomping at the bit to blame them for cost inflation. Gabe had a sickening feeling that it had more to do with him and Callie. He didn't voice his suspicions, but when he found his father crouched over a hastily scrawled letter, he knew what it involved. Edward crumpled the letter quickly in his fist, but Gabe reached out a hand. "Let me see it."

Edward shook his head. The light left his coal-dark eyes.

"It about Callie and me, isn't it?" he pressed.

Edward relented with a nod. "You don't need to read their message. I'm going inside to call the police."

Annie moved toward him and placed a firm hand on his shoulder. There was an uncaged wildness in her brown eyes. "Nothing they could possibly say about this family warrants violence. Don't waste your time reading filth."

Gabe reached for the balled-up letter in spite of his father's wishes and straightened it enough to discern the slant:

Keep that n—son of yours away from our women.

He'd expected as much, but there was something about seeing

the hatred in written form that made his heart sink. He found a porch step free of glass and sat down in silence until Edward returned.

"I shouldn't have let you see it," Edward said, trying to extract the note from Gabe's hands. "I should have tried harder to—"

"To what? Hide the truth and leave me unaware as to how people see me?" He laughed, but it made his throat ache.

"What is the meaning of this?" Margaret asked, rounding the bend and seeing there might be evidence held in her stepson's hand. "What was the motive for doing this to our home?" She'd lost her pallor. "There's glass everywhere. All over the bushes and the patio."

Edward hesitated, looking uncertain before telling his wife the sordid truth. "Someone's angry about Gabe and Callie seeing each other, but won't name themselves."

Margaret let out an exasperated sigh. "I told you something like this would happen, Edward! I knew as soon as I saw them in the sitting room after finding Jamie that trouble would follow us. I refuse to remain silent about it any longer. If the two of them want to go together, she can no longer work for us." The children caught up to them as she was saying those words, and immediately, Julia began to cry. "No, Mama, she's a great tutor for us. I want her to stay."

"Marg—" Gabe started in, a plea in his voice. He was still grappling with what he'd read but shifted to Callie's defense. "Please reconsider. She hasn't done anything wrong. We've gone on a few walks together and shared a dinner, but that can end. She loves the kids, and they love her. She doesn't need to lose her position."

"It's too late for that," Margaret nearly spit out. "You didn't give much thought to her position once your eye fell on her. If you care anything about her at all, you'll avoid even the appearance of—"

"Margaret, please," Edward interrupted, his brow furrowed as he opened the door and motioned her in. "You're forgetting that Gabe isn't the one at fault here."

Appraising the shattered glass all around them, she shook her head at her husband. "He didn't shoot out our windows, but his dalliance with that girl's made us a target. He hasn't left us with much of a choice, Edward. We need to let her go. And Gabe needs to end this if he wants to keep living under this roof."

Gabe's eyes burned as he faced his father's wife. It took considerable restraint for him not to let her have it, tell her that he'd seldom met someone with less compassion. But he couldn't lose his footing with her when she determined Callie's future. "She doesn't need to go, Margaret. I will end it with her, and I'll spend most of my time in Seattle. Don't do this to her—you know as well as I that she needs this position. If you don't have any regard for me, at least have some for her." Seeing her unmoved, Gabe walked closer to her and laid out his palms. "Consider, please, how your own father fared during the Crash and how if it wasn't for this business, he wouldn't have been able to afford medical bills—"

Her lips twitched, but she wouldn't allow for any further emotion. "You won't change my mind, Gabriel. This circumstance is different, and we both know it."

✧ ✧ ✧

Gabe tried to keep his distance from Ben Livingston, but the two still worked alongside each other. They took lunch the next day at Slim's, courtesy of Burke Enterprises. Gabe watched unsmilingly as Ben ordered himself a whiskey on his own dime. Words came out of his mouth before he could stop them. "Maybe if you'd lay off the drink, you'd have more funds for your son. And you wouldn't say things we have to smooth over for you."

Ben looked astounded. "What do you mean? It was only one night that I got to talking, and only a few guys heard. I told you I was sorry about it then, and I'm sorry 'bout it now. . . ."

Even as he turned from Ben, refusing to listen to the man's apology, Gabe wished he'd kept silent. He was used to keeping his emotions below the surface, but now his low-grade anger bubbled over, and he was losing his tolerance for things he usually let pass. He was accustomed to holding doors open for men who worked in the underbellies of the mines and hadn't sat down for a business meeting a day in their lives, but he was weary of his typecast role. Tired of being at his father's beck and call. Done with calling men his age "sir" and being called "boy" in return. Upset that he'd have to tell Callie there was nowhere for their love to go.

Their sandwiches arrived and Gabe stared fixedly at his plate, refusing to look at Ben. The two men ate their meal in tense silence. He knew that if he told his father that Ben couldn't be trusted, Burke would send the man packing in a day. But that wouldn't give Gabe comfort. As imperfect as their partnership might be, Ben wasn't so easily replaceable. There was a warmth and a genuine quality to the man. Still, he kept his distance from his friend, not knowing how to bridge their divide.

✧ ✧ ✧

After several days of avoiding Ben, speaking to him in clipped tones or not at all, Gabe couldn't keep on. He'd let a few calls from Callie go unanswered and knew he couldn't continue ignoring her either. But first Gabe reached for the phone and asked the operator to put him through to Ben. A few minutes later, they were set to meet at the Roslyn Cafe for dinner. He was relieved when Ben so quickly said yes. There was so much he needed to say.

Gabe set out for the Cafe still immersed in his thoughts. Ben and his good nature. His stepmother's reproach. Coming clean with Callie. Putting an end to their relationship. But as he walked down an alley he began to feel the press of eyes on his back. He tried to shake the feeling. He tried to tell himself that he was more wary since his connection to Burke had begun to spread throughout town. Not to mention the petition. Who knew how many men had signed?

There it was again. There was no mistaking the crunch of

boots this time. As the footsteps narrowed in behind him, he turned to acknowledge the stranger.

"There he is, that n—that thinks he's special."

Before there was even time to process these words a man in a dark coat rushed at him, pushed him into the nearby alley, and punched the side of his face. He felt a simultaneous blend of pain and fury as he sunk to his knees on the snowy gravel.

"You think you're something else," the man sneered now that Gabe was down on the ground. He tore something from his pocket, and it took a moment for Gabe to identify through blurry eyes the petition and signatures. It looked like it had wormed its way through town, collecting approval from folk aligned with Merrick's prejudice. "We'll set this here petition aside for a moment, though it won't be hard to get more miners to sign." He licked his lips. "What I really wanna know is . . . how you think you can get away with touching a white woman." Though his head throbbed, Gabe had enough clarity to discern that voice. He'd heard it before. It was the same one who'd sneered at him under his breath, who was given to barroom brawls. Why hadn't he anticipated he'd have a run in with the old, weathered Trip Evers one day?

"We've all seen you holding hands with Bill Rushton's daughter, and we don't like it," the man continued, grit in his voice. "We don't like it one bit."

Adrenaline coursed through Gabe and he rose to his feet. He saw Evers' fist rise from his peripheral vision, and he couldn't think of later repercussions. There was only the instinct to defend himself in the present. He swung back at Evers, felt his fist connect with bone, and was vindicated when his attacker fell back on the gravel—even more so when he saw the petition fall from Evers' hand.

But a second man emerged at Evers' shoulder, one who delivered a second, powerful blow close to where he'd been struck the first time. Gabe fell on his side, his hands warding off the painful clip of his chin against the sidewalk. He was too late to prevent the impact. He raised a hand to his face, pressed it, and saw blood streaming through his fingers.

"That'll teach you not to take the froth from the top of the bottle," the second man sneered. "Thinking that you're better than us, you working with your white father and now having your white woman." He breathed close to Gabe's face, not caring that sparks of spittle were flying from his mouth. "Wanna know something? She was mine first. She tell you that? No?"

Even in his pain, Gabe knew who the second attacker was. They'd barely exchanged a word, but he'd always felt uneasy around the guy. There was a darkness to him that didn't require words, that overrode all his sham acknowledgement at the Company Store in the past. And now he knew this was the man who had betrayed Callie.

Just as Gabe gathered the strength needed to raise his head, Evers took another blow at him. Gabe rested his head on the ground while the blood continued to flow near his ear over the snowy sidewalk. The imprint it left was reminiscent of crushed berries. He did his best to stunt the flow but had only his hand.

"We gotta get out of here," Paul said to Trip, urgency on the tip of his tongue. "Look, that fool who works for him is coming up. . . ."

As the pain started to overtake him, Gabe floated in and out of consciousness. He thought he heard Ben first run over to his side, then try to catch up with his attackers, who had already hightailed it to the dimly lit side roads.

"I saw those two men leave the Roslyn Cafe together, looking like they were up to nothing good. I know who they are," another, unidentified man said, running up.

"Wha—what happened?"

Ben tore his eyes away only long enough to lock eyes with the eyewitness. "Go call the police. There's a man down on the ground. Gabe Ward." As others surrounded him, Ben crouched down to his knees and rolled Gabe over on his back. "You're gonna be alright," he whispered intently, close to his friend's ear. "We're gonna get those bastards who did this to you behind bars. Just hold on, hold on."

Chapter 43

H E WOKE UP, heart pounding outside his chest. *Am I in custody?* He'd been locked up once before, as a teenager, after a middle-aged white woman had called the authorities as soon as he'd left her cafe. She'd smiled into his face. His offense was handing her a ten-dollar bill. *Did you steal it? Your kind don't rightly come by these numbers.* It was something you didn't forget. The humiliation and inner rage of being falsely accused came back with the memory. Sometimes he still saw the smirk on the warden's face, heard his power-hungry footsteps. He had only stayed an hour in that Seattle jail and the reason wasn't lost on him. He had telephoned Edward, and Edward's money had got him out. What if his father hadn't been a white man? He could almost sense the metal of the shackles he'd endured and felt that the walls surrounding him were cold and hard like they'd been for too many of his ancestors.

Last night he'd swung at a white man, knocked him to the ground. Bloodied him. How could he avoid paying for that, Burke's right-hand man or not? Before any title, he was a black man, and the authorities would make certain to remind him of it. His breath came out short and hollow and he thrashed, throwing the sheets to the side. He had the full use of his hands and realized he wasn't in the Ellensburg Jail at all. Voices rose around him, and he felt a strong hand press against his back. Gabe slowly opened his eyes and saw Callie looking down at him in a small, stark hospital room in Cle Elum. Water stood in her eyes. The gold locket he'd given her dangled over him, nearly brushed his cheek with its metallic weight. He wondered how much time had passed since he'd been assaulted and brought here.

He tried drawing himself up to a sitting position, but immediately felt a strong hand try to keep him down.

"You should take it slow, Gabe," his father said, his voice thick with emotion. He persisted, and Callie positioned the pillows at his back, propping him up.

Before he could even ask any questions, Callie spoke, "Ben called your father, and he picked you up off the street. He went down to the police station to answer questions with Tom McLaughlin, who saw your attackers leave the Cafe at the same time. Ben called me at the Starek's, told me what happened."

Tom McLaughlin, he thought, struck by the familiarity of that name. He scrunched up his face when he remembered he'd heard it on the lips of Merrick and shook his head when Callie offered him a glass of water. The image of an average size, middle-aged miner with reddish-blond hair and hooded blue eyes came to mind. He remembered the man's impassive expression at the Company Store the afternoon Merrick refused to give him the bar behind the counter. How the man had shifted uncomfortably in his boots, but said nothing to challenge the store clerk. He'd let that go, but not this. Gabe was in too much pain, however, to consider a quiet miner's mercurial nature or possible change of heart. At least someone had witnessed his attackers and reported who they were to the authorities.

Edward started in, the lines in his forehead prevalent. "I asked Ben what brought this on. I thought it might be the fallout with Merrick and that petition circling around town to see you go, but he thinks they were roughing you up for seeing Callie."

Gabe winced, wishing his father wouldn't recount specifics in front of her, when she was already on the brink of tears.

"Who would do this?" she asked. "Who would be so put out that they . . . ?"

Gabe laughed, though defiant tears stood in his eyes. "A lot of people, Callie. A lot of people would be so incensed that you wouldn't even believe . . ."

Edward moved forward, capped a protective hand on her shoulder and said, "There's an old miner named Trip Evers and another man, Paul Dightman being held at the Ellensburg Jail, at least for a while, and then we press charges."

Callie backhanded tears as soon as they started. A few drops splashed between her fingers and landed on Gabe's blanket. He saw a vein pulse in her forehead and couldn't bring himself to tell her that she wouldn't have to suffer the indignity of Paul's retaliation for long—he and she would go their separate ways.

"Don't cry," Gabe said softly, reaching up to take her hand in his before closing his eyes again, the light too much to bear.

Edward spoke close to her ear. "This isn't your fault."

"No," Callie said, her voice level, "but it's especially not his."

Gabe heard his father sigh deeply.

"Some people aren't ready to see the world any differently, but their hatred hurts them. Limits them. Keeps them small."

Gabe tried not to shrug off his father's words. Did those people ever really suffer for their preconceived notions? Or were they forever self-protected by generational beliefs that it had always been this way? He had no desire to entertain their presumptions based on the color of his skin. Those presumptions allowed them to categorize and minimize him before they even knew his name. All he'd ever wanted was to be treated as any other man.

✧ ✧ ✧

Word spread quickly through town about what Trip Evers and his accomplice, Paul Dightman had done. Some stopped Gabe when he was recovered and out again to tell him they were sorry that man and his sidekick had ever laid hands on him. They'd never think twice about signing that wretched petition, they told him. It was foolish for Merrick to think he could remove Burke's main man, they told him. They didn't know that Ben had discovered it on the ground beside Gabe and torn it up, scattered the shreds to the wind.

Most maintained their silence when they saw him, but gave him curious, if not sympathetic expressions. He knew he was quite a sight. His right eye was swollen for more than a week, his lips looked like a bee had stung them. There was only so much idleness he could take, though, and after the better part of a week at the house helping his father take orders, he had to get back to town. Even if it meant that more people would talk. Meanwhile his father utilized the aftermath to press charges against the men.

As soon as he was released from the jail, Paul made his disdain for Burke Enterprises known. An unsigned pamphlet circulated about Burke and his company. It claimed that ever since Burke had taken over management of the Company Store, trust in the mining company had eroded. Burke was clearly a man who had his own interests in mind. Had anyone seen that enviable home he lived in on the outskirts of Roslyn? And did everyone know that he had an unsavory past he wanted to keep hidden? It was one that involved a romantic liaison with a colored woman. That's right, it said—the young black man Burke employed was his own son.

It didn't take long before even more townspeople were speaking in hushed tones. Gabe hated the intensity of their stares, but he couldn't let them intimidate him out of the job he needed to get done. It seemed to him his father managed the public scrutiny and the ridicule of his eldest son with more difficulty. He told Gabe he'd make arrangements for him to lodge in Seattle for a longer time. How ironic that Burke had brought his family there to enjoy obscurity, and now he was sending his son away to escape close scrutiny.

He'd yet to tell Callie that he was leaving—likely she already knew they were done and over, he hadn't answered her calls in the last few days. He knew that any protests about his new arrangements were futile, but before he packed his bags for the west side of the mountains, he dropped by his father's office for a conversation he knew was long overdue.

"Why are we letting them win?" Gabe asked, heat beating in his eyes. "Now the entire town knows who I am. I thought you said that didn't bother you."

Edward looked up from his appointment book.

"It doesn't. I should have told people you were my son over the last ten years." He rose to his feet. "I'm sorry that I let people draw their own conclusions and that you had to watch yourself more than . . ." He turned away. When he turned back, he said, "I'd have done so many things differently, Gabe."

"Would you ?" Gabe asked, feeling the edge in those words, but refusing to give way to his father's melancholy. "Tell me, what would you have done different? Announced that you had a black son from the get-go so vendors would have looked elsewhere? Insisted that your wife treat me with an ounce of respect? Told Julia and Jamie they could call me "brother"? What would you have done differently, Edward? I'd like to know."

Gabe saw that his father's jaw was rigid, but he was so used to restraint and it wasn't serving him anymore.

"And I also want to know, Edward, why you were compelled to move here . . . to refurbish my late grandfather's boarding house, knowing it would draw interest?"

"I've told you this, Gabe," his father said, ruffling his graying hair. "I've been drawn to the Upper County since my late father brought me here. It's a mostly quiet, beautiful place to live. . . ."

"Until it's not," Gabe said, finishing that thought for him. "You've been drawn to this place since you met my mother. And you've come to idolize it as you've idolized her."

Edward rolled up his sleeves before he looked back at his son. He shook his head. "You're right about most things that you say. I can see my faults laid bare. I can see where I've failed you. I'd tell you I was sorry if it would help. But you're not right about her. I always loved your mother. Maybe we could have made a different choice. I could have been stronger . . . but I wasn't." He settled back in his seat, and though Gabe's heart wrestled with seeing his father for once look so lost and small, he didn't have any consolation. He wasn't the one to give it.

"I don't . . . I don't know how much longer I'll work for your company," he said quietly, wishing there wasn't a twinge of guilt attached to his words. Before he'd only felt an indignant burn rise in his chest, but these words—that he'd so long kept to himself—pained him. "I do admire everything you've managed from your father and built on your own, but I don't think I'm meant to follow in your footsteps. There are other things I'd like to do."

Edward sank further into his chair. He folded his hands over his desk and surprised his son by offering a tightly held smile. "Tell me, Gabe, what is it that you'd like to do? I've long admired your independent streak and wouldn't ever make you feel that you had to stay. You'd still remain a shareholder in Burke Enterprises, you know. You have as much stock as Jamie and Julia."

Gabe bit down on his lip before raising his chin to his father. "I'd like to go into real estate to help more black families purchase homes and start their own businesses," he said. "There are still a lot of implied rules about where we can be, and it's something that can change. And I know to get started in that, I'll need to work on a lot of cars, wait tables . . ."

"Or continue working at the docks for our company until you're able to do that full time," Edward said, rising to his feet and nodding his head, hopeful. He drew closer to Gabe and settled a hand on his shoulder. Gabe surprised himself by not flinching or moving away. Just moments ago, he'd recounted all the burdens he'd been compelled to carry. "I'm sorry for the ways in which I've failed you. I know I can do better." Pain flickered in his father's pupils. Gabe regretted the approach he'd taken moments before, but there wasn't enough in his father's words that warranted apology. Long-held emotion threatened to overtake him. The most he could offer was a firm nod and a promise that he'd call soon as he made it to the west side.

Chapter 44

1913

BEFORE HER SON was five years old, Lily knew Gabe could see that he was a curiosity to certain people. He noticed the extended stares of performers in the back rooms on nights he'd been brought by to give her a good luck kiss or a warm dinner plate. He took note when a passerby in Seattle looked from his mother to him and back again to her.

She didn't take kindly to a fellow singer's observation. *He's the best of both worlds. More beautiful than most.* What was meant as a compliment, Lily took as a misplaced observation. Francine, with her artificially bronzed skin and blond plaited hair, had no notion that her remarks did nothing to lift Gabe's station in life. What had belonging to both black and white done for him so far in this life? Most often Lily steered her eyes ahead and pretended she hadn't heard the hitch in anyone's throats as she passed with her lighter-skinned child in her arms. She would never allow her beautiful boy to become their circus spectacle. But it wasn't so easy to teach her son to avoid the inquiry of strangers. His skin tone and hers were different, but her Gabe was a black boy. The attention people gave him only frustrated Lily since culture at large still regarded him as inferior. If there were a trade-off for their considerable pauses and blatant stares, she might abide it better. But he would be forever categorized by color.

"Mama," he finally said one afternoon, when she held his sticky fingers in between her own. She'd treated him to an ice cream cone in the Central District and found herself delighting in him, even as some of the dessert never made it to his lips. "Why am I not as dark as you? Why don't I look just like you? Grandma . . . I heard her say something to Mrs. Johnson—'That white father better keep paying, or even better, show up for a visit.'"

Lily momentarily dropped her hold of his hand, her lips pursed. Why couldn't her mother be more cautious with her words? How many times had she told Georgina that while Eddy had proposed to her, she was the one who deemed their union couldn't be? She'd seen the purple mottled bruising above Eddy's eye more than once and knew his place in his father's company might be lost if he were to marry her. How many vendors would they lose once word escaped that Eddy was wed to a colored woman?

Perhaps she'd wanted to press him further, insist beyond his tears, that he'd risk it all to be her husband, but he'd at one point relented and said that he would always provide for her and their child. And she'd decided to swallow down harsh tears instead of pummeling his chest, pressing him with questions—*Why won't you fight for me . . . for us? You think this is difficult for you? This baby and me. This is difficult for us. . . .*

But even those years ago, when she'd told her mother she was pregnant with a white businessman's baby, she'd refused to speak harshly of Edward Burke. They'd fallen for each other quickly, she said. In Roslyn of all places. Perhaps traveling to the place her father died was more heartrending than she'd imagined, and she'd needed a reprieve—even if it wasn't something that could endure. He entered her life at the perfect moment, when she wanted adoration, a listening ear, someone to stroke the back of her arm and tell her she was extraordinary.

Her mother's eyes had been hot at the recounting of their love, and Georgina's distrust of the young businessman could not have etched itself into her slanted eyebrows any more.

"White men have always been drawn to us, Liliana. I could have told you this years ago. But they don't see us to the front door." There was no appeasing Georgina since Lily had shaken her head at Eddy's somewhat reluctant proposal. He hadn't gotten down on his knees to right the wrong.

The careless words of Bella and her mother made Lily grit her teeth even now, as she bent to her son's level on the Seattle sidewalk. She had made the decision that Edward wouldn't spend time with Gabe until he was older—say eight, nine, or ten. What were they doing, speaking of visits as if to sweep aside her determination? She hadn't seen the sense in it after her boy, at no more than two years, had been made to wait at length with her on the docks, drawing the unsavory attention of Edward's father. She could still hear his words as he brushed by her. *This really isn't the place for women and children.* He knew exactly who she was. She saw alarm in those russet eyes of his and a lingering observance of the young boy clutched in her arms. Gabe's grandfather had averted his attention before she could make any declaration about their rights.

She lingered now with five-year-old Gabe, even as the Seattle rain dashed her new apple-red dress. She owed him truths that those most interested in knowing about him did not. "Gabriel, you aren't as dark as me because your father is the business-man we met by the docks a few years ago. His name is Edward Burke, and he's white. . . . I don't know if you remember him since you were so young that afternoon we went to see him." Even in the broken-down telling, she knew that her little boy wouldn't likely understand, not knowing yet the facts of life and how he was comprised of both his mother and his father.

"He wanted us to go to a restaurant since it was windy and just started raining, but you said we better not," Gabe said, fully surprising her. "You told me we'd been waiting a long time and that it was probably best for us to go back home."

She wrinkled her nose. "I started having doubts about our visiting him, you see. Not because we wouldn't have had a nice enough meal, but because I didn't want to find out where we could or couldn't dine. Sometimes that's too much work, know-ing which places are alright for us." She cleared her throat, wishing there were words to make this easier. That was only the partial truth. Several years hadn't been enough time to numb her to Eddy's charms. He'd shown up that early evening with rain-splattered trousers, shaking his head in apology for keeping her waiting. There was a softness to his eyes that held her, despite her greatest efforts to forget.

She might have had the tenacity to try a few establishments, knowing that her feminine charms made it harder for folk to refuse her. But she hadn't the energy after seeing the clouds cross the senior Mr. Burke's eyes. He knew of Gabriel's existence—Ed had gone to his father and insisted a trust be written up in the boy's name, or he would quit the company.

"Wouldn't he know where to take us?" Gabe asked, his wisdom far surpassing his meager years. "If he's the one who wanted to see us, wouldn't he know where we could go?"

Lily kissed the top of his head and took his fingers up in her own. "He named a few places, son, but I wasn't sure as he was that they served colored folk, too. There are considerations your father will never have to make." She turned to him. "That's a decision I made for us that particular afternoon. Your father . . . he's one of the busiest men I know and very successful. But you'd be underfoot when he has all those orders coming in. If, when you're older, you want to spend more time with your father, you can go back to that dock and I won't stop you." She smiled in spite of her sadness. "Not that I could if I tried."

Chapter 45

1933

CALLIE FELT LIKE winter had stolen over her by the time Gabe finally returned her call and asked her to meet at the meadow behind the Church of Christ. It had been more than a week since he'd been attacked, and while he'd been the one to console her after she saw what they'd done to him, he'd quickly retreated from her. Not only had he gone silent on her, Mrs. Burke had formally let her go. Callie remained with the Stareks, not prepared to show defeat to her parents yet.

By the time she arrived at Church of Christ, she didn't care if Mrs. Jacobson saw them again. She tried to brace herself, still any imminent tears, and show him a firm resolve. She wondered if he'd notice that she'd lost weight underneath her black wool coat.

As soon as she spied him getting out of his truck and walking toward her, Callie felt her heart jolt. He gave her a brief nod, but today there were no smiles. They walked to the meadow in the near silence until he could finally turn to her, away from the threat of others. "Callie, I'm sorry I haven't returned your calls."

"Are you?" she asked, proud of herself for refusing to melt.

He nodded, his jaw more solemn than usual and his eyes glazing over her with a palpable distance. Their boots sunk in the until now untouched snow. "My father says he needs my help over in Seattle more now," Gabe said, playing with the brim of the newsboy cap that rested in his hands. "And to be honest with you, I don't know how long I'll stay, working for his company."

Callie felt her nose start to run and swept a mitten over it. She'd braced herself for this, so why did it still hurt so much? Is this your back-door, merciful way of breaking up with me? Her heart fought against this moment, though she'd known it was coming. "It's best this way," he added. "My stepmother made it clear that I couldn't continue to see you and still have you work there—"

"She let me go," Callie said, breaking up any speech he may have prepared. When he couldn't find any words, she continued. "It was right after you were attacked. I showed up at the door, and she stepped out on the porch to tell me that someone had shot all the windows out and left a bigoted note for your father to find."

Gabe swallowed. "Did she call it bigoted? Because as much as she didn't appreciate her windows being shot out, I hardly suspect she was troubled with the message."

Callie nodded, wiping her nose again. "She did. I told her that the same thing happened to my family just before Christmas, but that I wasn't willing to let it stop us. I wouldn't let them win," Callie said defiantly, even though she knew men like Trip and Paul already had. She could feel she was losing him. She lowered her eyes to her snow-covered boots.

"You went through all that trouble and told my father you loved me," Callie said in a voice she didn't recognize.

He nodded slowly, and the distance he'd attempted to forge between them fled. His pupils flickered.

"Oh Callie, I do. That's never changed. I'm sorry . . . I'm sorry that I have to leave like this . . ."

She shook her head at him. "Don't be sorry. If you love me like you say you do, don't leave me standing here, telling me you're not going to keep seeing me."

"There's another love your father described," Gabe said, moving toward her and, allowing his fingers to trace back her hair from her forehead. "Loving you enough to let you have a different life, Callie, a better one."

She shook her head. "That's not what I want, Gabe."

"Then what do you want?" he asked, taking a step back and righting his hat over his head. "To be ridiculed and turned away from more places than you can count? To hear people call you a n—lover? Don't look at me as if you're shocked to hear that, Callie. That's the exact word Trip used before he knocked me to the ground." When Callie stepped closer, she could see there were tears standing in his eyes. "I want something different for you, Callie. I want you to have the best, the happiest, the . . ."

She moved closer to him and walked into his arms, placed her head on his chest, close enough to listen to his heartbeat. He sighed against her hair. "You're not . . . you're not making this any easier, Callie. Not for yourself and not for me." He pulled her back, held her at the elbows and said, "I'll talk with Burke about getting your position back. Margaret is being unreasonable, and you don't deserve . . ."

She shook her head. "He agreed to let me go, though I could tell he didn't favor her decision. He wrote me a check, and that was most generous of him." She coughed into her hands, wished the wind wouldn't make her eyes water. "I can't force an arrangement that she doesn't want, though it saddens me to lose my time with the children. It saddens me more to . . ." She couldn't finish her thought, and Gabe placed his hand on the small of her back, leading her from the meadow.

"I know," he said. "I know, Callie. I'm sorry I have to leave." He turned toward her and drew his hand to her cheek. "I'm still so glad I met you. I wouldn't change that, though it might be selfish of me. Will you forgive me for that?"

"How could I not?" she said, summoning a smile. It might be the last thing she gave him.

Chapter 46

THE WEEKS PASSED slowly, and Callie could hardly contain her sorrow. How difficult it was for her to manage the mundane without letting lethargy steal in like unwelcome dust. One glance at her reflection, and she could see that she was only a ghost of her former self. She tried pinching her cheeks, willing some of her color back, but it didn't help.

Bess needed a hand and took pity on her, granting her a small allowance for her efforts, in addition to room and board. Together they more than filled the hours mending garments. Though the Stareks were sympathetic listeners, there was only so much she could say about the abrupt end to her romance with Gabe Ward. Folding and unfolding her hands, she insisted it was for the best. And no, she wasn't ready to return to her parents' house. The source of their argument was no longer a concern, but she couldn't abide how they'd handled it. She said hello to them at the end of service at Mt. Pisgah on Sundays and kindly refused her father's invitation to move back in. Despite this, he continued to repeat it.

"Callie," her father said, resting his hand on her forearm one Sunday. "Why don't you come home? Your mother and I—we've heard that you're no longer working for the Burkes." He swallowed.

He'd finally taken a razor to his face. She could see a drop of blood he'd tried to stunt and could smell the scent of his soap. "Even if you were still there, we'd like to have you back with us. I s'pose I could have handled a few things differently. . . ."

She knew that those words cost him, and yet she had no plans to live under his roof again. Her decision wasn't wrought in anger. She hadn't felt her home was with her parents since Paul called off their engagement, but she hadn't another place to rest her head. And now she did, if only for a little while.

"Thank you," she said softly, "but my arrangement with the Stareks is best since I'm working so much for Bess. I'm still able to send some of my earnings—"

He shook his head abruptly. "That won't be necessary." He dropped his hand from her arm but didn't move. "Are you sure you're doing alright? You've lost your color, and you're thin. Thinner than is good for you."

She nodded, moved that he'd noticed anything about her appearance when his focus during the past year had been so myopic. Perhaps the thick white fog that had covered his days this past year was starting to dissipate. If that could happen for him, she trusted it would be no different for her. "I'll be fine," she said, willing reassurance into her voice. "Bess is trying to fatten me up and so is Nick, any opportunity he gets."

Walking away from the position at the Burkes and saying goodbye to Gabe left her with a void. Her interests dulled. More than once Bess pointed out her prominent collarbone, so she raised a fork to her mouth. She couldn't taste a thing. Sunrise and sunset failed to move her, even the more striking displays of sun and moon. The first tug of spring with its early blooms and strawberry-scented air hardly registered. Sometimes she felt like she was on the outside of her life, looking in, wondering about the purpose of it.

She didn't seek Lucy out, hardly expecting understanding from the friend who had warned her about her choices. But they crossed paths on Pennsylvania Avenue one early March evening. Lucy rushed over to her. "Callie, come with me," she said, motioning her toward the Roslyn Cafe.

Callie wasn't hungry, but knew better than to turn down her friend's offer if she didn't want to give her significant cause for worry. Once seated across from each other and sipping on chamomile tea, Lucy reached out and took Callie's hand in her own. "Cal, you're not alright, are you? You don't look well."

"Thank you," Callie said, her voice wan. She raised a hand to her unwashed hair and looked down. She'd worn the same navy-colored dress a few days in a row. "I'm having a hard time bouncing back, is all. But I'll get there."

"You're still not back at your parents' house?" Lucy asked, her blonde hair gleaming against the fading light of the front windows.

Callie shook her head. "My position is gone, and Gabe is gone . . . but it doesn't change how I feel about him. You don't have to know someone long to love them. I still—"

Lucy tightened her hold on Callie's hand and leveled with her, so that her hazel eyes fixed intently on her face.

"Please tell me. You're not pregnant, are you?"

Callie slowly lowered her water glass to the table and looked at her, amazed. "No. That's impossible, Lucy. Don't you think you'd be the first one I'd come too should I ever find myself . . ."

Lucy's color deepened, though she didn't easily embarrass. "I hoped so, but I thought I'd ask. With you not going home and looking so washed out, I thought it might be a possibility. Even a slight one."

Callie pursed her lips. "It's not. But if I ever found myself facing something difficult, you're the first one I'd come to. And I hope you know that works both ways." She was kind enough not to mention that the odds were in her friend's favor since she knew Lucy and her fiancé hadn't waited.

"We'll get married this summer," Lucy said quietly, tracing a watermark on the table. When she looked back up, the intensity in her eyes returned. "I'm worried about you. Look, you're the best friend I have, and I hate to see you hurt. I hate what people have already done to you and to him. Is there anyone you could go to that would help . . .?"

"I've prayed a lot more lately" Callie said, taking a sip of the tea, though she hardly craved it. "And though I don't always know what God would have me do, I know He understands my heart more than anyone. More than the Stareks. Even you."

Lucy nodded at that. "I'll add my prayers to yours, then." She motioned toward the young waitress and requested two pieces of chocolate cake warmed with a scoop of ice cream. It was the last indulgence Callie would have ordered for herself—she hadn't even eaten dinner—but she couldn't refuse her best friend's kindness. "Slow down and let yourself enjoy it as you wait for answers. Your life isn't going to stay so gray and drab, Callie. You have to trust that things will get better. That God won't leave you. You're a heck of a lot stronger than you think."

I will get better. Callie repeated this later that night, alone in the Starek's guest room with her back against the oak headboard, her eyes trained on the rose-colored wallpaper. She pulled her knees up to her chest and wrapped her arms around herself. *This sadness won't have the last word.* She'd start by nourishing herself more. She promptly got up, tiptoed to the kitchen and rummaged around for a midnight snack. There was no need for her collarbone to jut out in a sad plea, not when she wasn't destitute.

✧ ✧ ✧

She was walking back to the seamstress' house on an unusually warm spring evening when the tall, redheaded worker for Burke Enterprises bounded down the steep stairs outside the Brick. In the weeks since Gabe had left, her heart hadn't mended, but she'd started training her mind not to spiral into unhappiness. There was no use in replaying their stolen kiss, the warmth of his gaze, his hands encircling her waist. So when thoughts crept in, she began to pray for him instead, turning him over to the One who loved him even more.

Callie narrowed her eyes as Ben approached her. She hadn't the slightest notion what he'd have to say. She no longer had any ties to the Burke family, and there was no unfinished business between the two of them that came to mind.

"Miss Callie," he started in, nearly out of breath. "Forgive me if I startled you. I saw you out the window, and I knew I had to speak with you soon as I saw you again. I've been thinking of tracking you down for the last few days, but when you were right there before me, I knew—"

She straightened the belt of her much worn green dress while she waited for him to proceed. She was glad that she'd taken efforts that day with a brush and that she hadn't left her face without a touch of makeup. Callie knew she shouldn't care, but she didn't want Ben reporting back to Gabe that she'd stopped looking after herself once he'd gone.

"I was out at the docks recently working on an order with Gabe," Ben said, twisting his hat in his hand. "And perhaps this isn't my place at all . . . but he hasn't gotten over you. He's thrown himself into his work and he gets a lot done, but he's heartsick. . . . and I wanted to know if you felt the same."

She inwardly questioned God. Why was Ben approaching her, asking her questions that picked at a scab still so fresh? Hadn't she done the right thing, turning him over in her prayer when thoughts of him invaded her mind?

"I took him out for a drink the other night, and he's not the same. Gabe, he's always been calculated, a deep thinker, smart as heck. Laughter doesn't always come easily to him, but now it's like pulling at a stubborn root, trying to get him to smile." Ben shook his head, and a curl of red fell over his eye.

"Why are you telling me this?" Callie asked, harsher than she intended. She wrung out her hands despite her greatest efforts to remain composed. "It's only that . . . I'm not sure it helps, knowing that he's sad about me. Perhaps you've mistaken his melancholy for me when it's a rift with his father that's caused this tension."

Ben shook his head. "Forgive me if I've overstepped myself, but I know that his sadness is not for his father, it's for you. He told me he's been in love with you since the afternoon you spoke at the Company Store."

She hadn't known this, couldn't have known it. She felt lost, all the steadiness she'd fought for in the weeks since he'd gone slipping away. "Why tell me this, Ben?" she asked, feeling the water well in her eyes too easily. "We're no longer together, and there's nothing I can do to change that except try . . . try my best to move on."

Ben rolled his tobacco to the other cheek. "Do you want to move on from him?"

Callie shook her head, her tears still holding at least. "What does it matter what I want? The rule-book's been written for us, and I'm doing the best I can to move for—"

Facing her, Ben reached for her shoulders and fixed his steady green eyes on hers. "I'm not asking you these questions to be cruel. Do you think you could trust me?"

She didn't know what compelled her to nod, but there was understanding in his kind eyes. There was something about his spirit which spoke of his own pain and understanding.

"What if I told you, Callie, there could be another way for you and Gabe?"

She raised her chin up to boldly meet his eyes. "I'd tell you to leave well enough alone even if you have the best intentions. Gabe's made his decision even if he struggles like I do to accept it."

But Ben was already shaking his head. "The decision is tearing you both apart. Look. His love for you hasn't changed at all, and if you feel the same, this is something worth fighting for. I think . . . I think I could help you."

Chapter 47

THERE WAS SOMEONE Callie felt compelled to see. But even so, she shook as she raised her knuckles to the door of the small blue house on the corner of Washington Avenue. It was beyond the dinner hour, and smoke spiraled from the chimney. Funny how you could grow up knowing people in the community and yet hardly remember what the interior of their home looked like. It had been years since she'd set foot inside. Her exchanges with the Jacobsons happened mostly on front porches.

The odds were in her favor that Mr. Jacobson would be home. The trouble would be getting past his wife at the door. But it was Sam who answered her knock. He'd replaced his mining wear for a blue shirt and denim, and still a sheen of dust clung to him. He smiled graciously and welcomed her in, directing her to a place on the sofa in the sitting room. "Callie Rushton. It's good to see you. What brings you here?"

She could hear clanging about in the kitchen and prayed that she'd get in a word before Mrs. Jacobson entered the room. She glanced around and took in the vibrant decor: several table-side lamps, framed portraits of family from ages past, silk flowers in reds and oranges. Even in her worry Callie paused before meeting the eyes of her father's oldest friend. "Thank you for inviting me in, Mr. Jacobson," she said. "I don't know why I felt so led to come here tonight, but I thought maybe you could help me." She took a deep breath.

There was no reproach in his gaze, only patience and under-standing as he waited for her to continue.

"As you know, Gabe and I were seeing each other . . . even though so many didn't approve, but he had to leave town be-cause of us. And other reasons. . . ." She waited to gauge his reaction, but saw his expression was unchanged. "I haven't been myself since he left, and I hear from Gabe's friend, Ben, that he misses me too. . . . So much so, that Ben's encouraging me to go to him."

She kneaded her hands and hoped that her coming here wasn't the most foolish thing she'd ever done. What was to stop the preacher from confiding in her father or trying to put a blunt end to her plans?

"Ben is helping me with the arrangements, and I . . . I don't know what will happen. I just don't think I can live with myself if I don't tell him how much I love him." When she glanced back up, Mrs. Jacobson was standing beneath the door frame. The expression she wore was more contemplative than she'd expected. There was no ready smile, but she didn't scold her either. She met Mrs. Jacobson's eyes and saw unexpected kind-ness written there.

"Oh Lord in heaven," she said softly. "There's no stopping you two, is there?" She shook her head, but went to her hus-band, who held his hand out to her and urged her to take a seat on the sofa beside him. "There's nothing like young love, is there, Sam?" And then to Callie, "You know your folks won't approve, don't you?"

Callie nodded. "I'm not wanting to dishonor them." She felt herself warm. "I'll return quickly if Gabe doesn't want me to—"

"And if he does want you to stay?" Mrs. Jacobson asked, rais-ing a hand to adjust her gold earring. She hurried on. "Have you considered what happens then? Look, Gabe is easy on the eyes, and there's a kindness about him, but the novelty wears off, and marriage is hard as it is . . ."

She glanced over at Sam, who gave her momentary side eye before chuckling in agreement.

"I don't think we're talking marriage yet, Tessa," the preacher told her, patting her hand.

Mrs. Jacobson wouldn't be swayed. "I'm sure they know this state has no ban on intermarrying." She looked directly at Callie. "I'm not saying you can find just any preacher or that it's an encouraged practice, but it's not impossible. I'm not saying I agree . . . since it's so seldom done, but . . ."

Callie's warmth rose up her neck. "Oh, I'm not thinking that Gabe—"

"If that young man isn't ready for exactly that, then you come home, Callie," Mrs. Jacobson said, firm. "It's not fair to him, and it's not good for your heart."

Mr. Jacobson said nothing to his wife's urging, but sought Callie's attention once more. "When you first sat down, you said you wanted my help, Callie. I intend to call Gabe in a few days' time to offer guidance. I've been worried about him since I heard about the attack and didn't have the chance to talk with him. . . . But how would you like me to help you?"

Callie's mouth was dry. "In all honesty, I don't know what help I need. . . . I don't feel I can have this conversation with my folks, so I came to you, hoping that you might understand and . . . pray for us." She looked up meekly and reached into the recesses in her purse for a folded piece of paper. "I also wrote my parents a letter, and knowing my father, he'll come here to confide in you. . . ." Though she'd long since sealed the letter, the words played a refrain in her mind even now:

Please know that I'm forever grateful to be your daughter.
I understand that your concern for me is rooted in love,
and even so, I must see where this road with Gabe leads.

Mrs. Jacobson, who saw where this was going, shook her head. "Your daddy hasn't sought Sam out in months, Callie. You best not leave an important letter with us, or it might stay in our hands as seasons come and go. No, you go on and put that letter under a rock on the front porch. You make sure it don't blow away."

Callie nodded and closed her eyes. "It's my fault my father hasn't been to see you," she said. "He hasn't said as much, but I know it is." She expected Mrs. Jacobson to say more, but it was Sam's soothing voice that filled the room.

"I've missed him, and I won't say that it doesn't hurt me any, but I know Bill. I hope that his heart will soften, and that we'll mend anything that's strained." He let his voice drift. "But what I'm focused on right now is you. Tessa and I . . . we will pray for you now. Yes, we will, won't we, wife?"

She nodded and withheld her reservations. "They're gonna need every ounce of our prayers, Lord knows." She adjusted her earring once more and surprised Callie by reaching out her hand and taking it up in her own.

✧ ✧ ✧

As the train neared Seattle, Callie wondered if it was all a mistake. She'd told herself before packing her bags that even if Gabe changed his mind about her, she had to give love with him one more chance. Even so, she could feel a drop of sweat fall between her shoulder blades, could hear her erratic breathing as she tried to brace herself for Gabe's reaction.

When she stole a glance over at Ben Livingston, she thought she could see his own misgivings. He mulled over his chew, giving rapt attention to the rain-splashed windshield. He hadn't turned to speak to her in some time. She inhaled, shaken by his own sacrifices. Here was a man desperately in need of his position, putting his own best interests aside to help reunite two people who might not even end up together. The sound of her exhalation seemed to catch his attention and he looked over at her as they pulled into the station.

"He won't turn you away." Ben pressed her hand. "Even if . . . even if . . . you both decide not to see each other anymore, he wouldn't be so cold. Gabe . . . he can be elusive about his own needs, but he won't shut you out."

She wasn't so sure. She had never set foot in the city before and was taken with the height of the buildings and the number of umbrellas nodding down the slanted streets. The rain fell like steady tears, and she drew a hand to her hair, wishing she'd thought to wear a hat. The water dashed upon her cheeks, but she didn't have the time for vanity. Her one attempt to smooth out the travel wrinkles from her well-worn green dress showed her it was futile.

She soon found she hadn't the capacity at that moment to commit anything to memory—not the name of a cafe on the corner or the church across the street—not when she didn't know how Gabe would receive her. Her doubts felt like pot-holes staggered across the road. She had to steel her eyes ahead, follow the direction Ben pointed out for her, down the stairs to reach the modest apartment where Gabe lodged.

When they ended up at No. 4, Ben gently moved in front of her. "Step back for a minute. Let me tell him you're here."

She stepped back and tried to hide behind a heavy post, her unspoken prayer that Gabe would receive her warmly. If she was grateful for anything, it was that she'd had the foresight to leave her suitcase in the back of the car. How presumptuous it would have been to arrive with it in hand. The thought of it made her tremble. She hung back, feeling ever the fool as they waited for Gabe to open the door.

He answered the second knock. "Ben! I wasn't expecting— what are you doing here?" he asked. "Had I known you'd be back so soon, I'd have cleaned up the place, cooked you a meal." Gabe clapped a hand on his friend's shoulder.

His voice tugged on her heart, but as of yet, she hadn't raised her eyes to look on him.

Ben rocked back in his work boots.

"Gabe—" he said, his voice thin, "my friend . . . I hope you won't mind my making the effort, but I've brought someone with me today."

His words were met with silence, but Callie could no longer remain partially hidden behind the post, even in the early darkness. She stepped forward, saw the man she loved standing before her. He wore a rolled-up work shirt and khaki pants.

He was barefoot and hadn't taken a razor to his face in at least a few days.

Gabe looked questioningly at Ben, and then his eyes landed on hers.

"Callie . . ." Her resistance gave whenever he spoke her name, the ache almost too much to bear. "What did you travel all this way for . . . ?" He looked to Ben and laughed, incredulous. "I know I spoke about missing her the other night, but how much whiskey did we tip back?"

Ben shifted the tobacco to his other cheek. "Whiskey? Gabe, we've been talking to the preacher—"

So here it was, his answer. She tried to shelter herself from his rejection, but felt tears burn in her throat.

"There's been a misunderstanding. I didn't mean to interrupt your dinner, Gabe. You have a good evening, alright? Ben, please walk me back to the car." She felt a swell of fury toward Ben for helping encourage this predicament, but knew she'd have to whittle it down. He'd been sorely mistaken, but he hadn't meant to hurt her. She turned her back, not trusting herself to keep from crying.

Gabe edged past Ben and reached for Callie, but she was already retreating from him.

"Callie, stop!"

Though he was much faster, she wore shoes. She could bolt toward Ben's car, though she had no keys to start it and didn't know how to drive it. She could run into a corner cafe and order up something to warm her trembling hands. But she slowed herself down and let him grasp her shoulders. He spun her around. She could hear his heart beating fast.

"I'm sorry. I wasn't expecting you, and I tripped over my words."

"No, I think you meant them," Callie said. "It's true, Ben told me that you missed me and encouraged me to come, and I did so against my better judgment. I wish I'd known that you only spoke so freely of me under the haze of a drunken stupor. Now that I know—"

"But you don't know, Callie," he said, amber sparks in his eyes imploring her. "I spoke of you then, but so many other times too. Times when I hadn't a thing to drink." He swallowed deep. "I love you and . . . I thought the purest form of that was giving you up . . . so you wouldn't have to have your windows broken out or hear people laugh at us. I still think it's better for you to live without that ridicule. But since we've been apart, I've struggled. It feels dishonest somehow, as if I'm carrying on without half my heart."

"And what about what's best for you?" she asked, letting the water stream down her face. "What would you do if I said I was willing to accept that difficulty above the unbearable choice of leaving you?"

He looked at her for a moment. "I'd tell you that you might live to regret this . . . but that I'm not interested in refusing what we both want."

She lifted her head slightly, tears still merging with the softly falling rain. "And what it is that we both want?"

"To be together." He took her hand in his and raised it to his lips. He got down on one knee, paying no heed to the rain's interference. "Callie, I love you. I realize this might come a bit sudden, but since you've been away I told myself I wouldn't be foolish enough to let you walk out of my sight twice. I told myself that should you ever come back, you were meant to stay. . . . If that's what you want, too."

She nodded up at him, her heart full.

"Will you be my wife?"

Chapter 48

WHEN THEY WALKED back toward the apartment, hand-in-hand, Ben smiled in spite of the cold he undoubtedly felt. "That's what I was hoping for. Now let me go get her bag—"

Gabe shot his friend a discreet expression to let him know that was out of the question. "I will find somewhere for her to stay until we're married. It wouldn't be—" He cleared his throat, and Callie laughed uncomfortably.

"We can get a marriage license quickly. I have a preacher in mind."

She glanced over at him. "You already found a preacher for us?"

Gabe pressed her hand and nodded assent. "The first few said no, but I found someone who told me he'd be honored."

Gabe motioned for Ben to step inside. Even though he was soaked, Ben gestured to Callie to cross the threshold first.

"I would have cleaned if I'd known you were coming," Gabe said gently, two steps behind her.

She shrugged his worries away and said that it didn't matter. She felt curious to see his apartment, envision where second-hand furniture could go, contemplate where she could hang the pictures she'd find. But as she walked in, she saw it was already furnished with lamps and side tables and a sofa. A red geranium plant sat near the kitchen window.

Gabe grew sheepish about the things he'd left out on the

counters—half-filled coffee mugs, papers, plates, an empty bottle of whiskey. "I hoped you'd come, but I didn't know if you would," he said by way of explanation.

She stopped drinking in her surroundings long enough to turn to him and throw her arms around his neck. She murmured against his collar. "It's perfect."

✧ ✧ ✧

If ever there was a time Gabe wished he could pick up the phone and call his mother it was now. If she were alive, he knew the exchange wouldn't be seamless. But she'd support him in the end, and her love would surround him and Callie.

He thought of the times where she'd captured his face in her palms and spoken promise over him while he was growing up. "You'll make your granddaddy proud," she said, unable to shake the notion that David was watching over them, no matter the years he'd been gone. "He came to Washington intent on finding a better life, and those dreams will be realized through you."

Gabe remembered turning to her, a curious expression on his face. "Mama," he'd said, never outgrowing that term of endearment for her. "They're realized in you, too."

Her eyes had misted. "Oh, I don't know about that," she'd said.

He'd nodded, holding to what he'd said. Willed back his emotion. "You've made a name for yourself in Seattle. . . . Do you know how many people come out to hear you sing? From all different walks of life?" It wouldn't have happened for her without a bold, undaunted spirit. "You're a household name."

He looked to the place on the wall where he'd finally framed her image and promised himself that he'd never let her likeness be contained in a drawer again. For so long Margaret hadn't wanted his mother's name spoken of at all, and to avoid her ridicule, he had stopped mentioning her. He kept Lily to himself, both his favorite picture of her and the letters from her father that she carried with her until the end. He wasn't interested in doing that anymore, and he wouldn't let either of their names go silent on his lips. One day his children would know where they came from, what tenacity flowed through their veins. The world would be theirs for the taking, too.

✧ ✧ ✧

They were only made to wait for a few days before they could marry, but those hours stretched long like the sand trickling through an hourglass for Callie. She couldn't fully dismiss all thoughts of those against them. The night they were to wed at Mt. Zion, Gabe directed her to their future bedroom and set her suitcase on the bed. "You don't even have to change, Cal. You're already beautiful."

Callie laughed. The navy dress she wore was rain-soaked and wrinkled, her hair had come loose from its curls, and she knew the nearest mirror—if there was one—would tell her there were improvements to be made. When the door closed behind her she suddenly felt overwhelmed. Never before had she been so torn asunder by feelings of sorrow and bliss. It had been a long several days. She'd spent long hours researching music schools she might attend and seamstress positions she might apply for, but her mind kept returning to her parents and what they must be thinking right now. How grieved by her choices they must be. Here she was—she hadn't even told her best friend that she was leaving town for fear Lucy would try to prevent her from doing so. Guilt pricked her like a needle.

Shoving her emotions aside, she studied what Gabe had already done with the place. The bedroom, she saw, was recently painted a soft, sky blue. There was a dresser, two side tables, and a bed, which she sank down on. *Think only of this*, she told herself. Drawing her knees beneath her, she willed back tears. *Please help them understand.* It was an unusual prayer for the happiest day of her life.

Remembering that there wasn't much time to spare, she opened her suitcase and removed the simple, yet beautiful dress Mrs. Starek had placed in her arms before she left. It had never been claimed after the seamstress shop closed, and

Callie wondered why, as its ethereal blue fell over her like water. Without time to properly curl her hair again, she pinned it back, pinched her cheeks, and reapplied the soft red lipstick Lucy had accidentally left at the house. When she came back here tonight she would be Mrs. Gabriel Ward. She'd had a small inkling that this might happen, but now that it was unfolding even better than she'd imagined, she could hardly believe it.

✧ ✧ ✧

Candles lit the quaint little church where Gabe and Callie exchanged their marriage vows before Preacher Davison and Ben Livingston. Instead of backhanding tears, Callie glowed at Gabe as she vowed to be with him through richer and poorer until death do them part. She glanced down to see him place a small gold band on her left hand.

"It was my grandmother's," he told her.

Within minutes of their arrival at the church, the preacher proclaimed them man and wife, his kind eyes blessing them as they made their way into an oft-abrasive world. What God had joined, let no man pull asunder. They proudly signed their marriage certificate, both filled with gratitude for the right to do so.

Callie turned heads left and right as Gabe escorted her back to his truck, her dress taking well to her shape, a natural glow illuminating her already becoming features.

"That's a pretty girl you got there," a tall, distinguished man with a mustache told Gabe, admiring her. She beamed at the compliment and wondered—if only for a moment—if she should announce they were newly married. She spun the gold ring on her finger, unused to its weight, and decided that was symbol enough.

The man looked over his shoulder, and with a flourish of his hand, said, "You're welcome to my music hall. We'd love to see a good-looking couple like you take to the dance floor. You can dance, can't you?"

Gabe graciously told the man, "She can sing too, but we'll take you up on that another time. We have other plans for tonight." He then looked over his shoulder at his new wife, unable to resist a playful wink.

Callie restrained a laugh before she gripped Gabe's hand and let him help her in the passenger side of the truck. Less than five minutes later they were home. Ben had wisely bowed out for the evening, and Callie could barely believe it. She moved down the stairs ahead of Gabe, and he caught her arm, causing her to turn around. "What is it?" she asked, pausing when she caught the blend of desire and love in his eyes.

Gabe kissed her at the top of her hair and said, "Would you like a glass of wine before we head to—"

She shook her head. "No, you bootlegger. Perhaps another night." She laughed at him. "I won't be long," she said, making it to the bedroom before he could get there.

Callie unpinned her hair, let it fall to her shoulders in dark waves. She let her wedding gown fall to the floor. In its place she wore a simple rose-colored slip. There was nothing particularly memorable about it, or so she thought. She threw open the door and watched as Gabe quickly set aside a water glass, the contents all but untouched. She laughed at how close it came to slipping from his fingers. He stepped into the room, and she walked into his arms. He drew her closer to his chest and held her back only to assess her beauty. He let his hands graze over her silken form.

"Where did you get this?" he whispered, appreciating the scarcity of the fabric.

His eyes danced as he sank to the edge of the bed and pulled her between his knees. Although she'd thought she was beyond nervousness, there was a momentary startle in her throat, and Gabe took it for a spark of hesitation. His fingers touched the ends of her hair and stopped there.

"We don't have to move so—"

She smiled up at him and said, "I just can't believe we're finally married. I'm so happy." She placed her hands on the back of his shoulders, and he drew her closer. His kisses fell on her, and she closed her eyes as she rested back on the pillow. He rose over her.

✧ ✧ ✧

Callie awoke spinning her ring, undeniable proof that marrying Gabe Ward wasn't merely a figment of her imagination. Impossible though it seemed, she'd slept more soundly that night in Gabe's arms than she had for the many months preceding it. What was done was done, and there was nothing that would make her wish she could go back, not even the relief or preference of her loved ones. She smiled to herself as she saw the gold of his wedding band catch with the morning sunlight streaming through their bedroom window.

Chapter 49

LIFE IN SEATTLE kept them so busy that their thoughts didn't stray to Roslyn for quite some time. It wasn't until the end of that August—when the sun cast its generous warmth on their shoulders—that Gabe pressed his lips to the back of Callie's hand and whispered, "Would you like to go back home? Just for a visit?"

Her automatic assent was strangled by thoughts of what might go wrong. More vandalism when people heard they were married. Another attack on Gabe by a bigot lurking in the shadows. Hard stares. Unspoken exclusion. Stated opposition. They'd need to prepare themselves for all of it.

As if reading her thoughts, Gabe drew Callie back in his arms and capped his hands on the small swell around her middle. "My father will let us stay with them."

"But Margaret . . ." Callie started in, thinking of the brewing ire in the woman's eyes when she'd seen Callie to the door for the last time. *You didn't put my children first. You only thought of yourself.*

Gabe shook his head sharply. "If she so much as treats you with a shred of disrespect, tell me. You no longer work for her, Callie. You're my wife."

"Alright then," Callie said, turning her neck to look at her husband. "Let's go. I'd like to see Julia and Jamie. I felt terrible, having to leave them so quickly. I hope they forgive me."

She dug her fingernails into her palms, unwilling to speak

of Will—the brother who'd disowned her for the choice she'd made to marry the man she loved. While she'd spoken with her parents within a week of their quiet wedding, Will had let his heart grow callous toward her. He'd let her know—in written form—that she'd brought shame to the Rushton name and that he would no longer correspond with her. In his distinctive slant, he'd written that while their parents might come around to acceptance, he believed they were only doing so because she'd forced their hands. He wouldn't be pushed to accept an unnatural union and would mourn the sister he'd lost. Will's response bruised her heart, but she couldn't go against her belief that God had brought her and Gabe together. Not for him or anyone.

Several days after they'd given word they were returning to Roslyn for a visit, Gabe's aunt Annie opened the door wide and smiled up at them. She reached for their suitcases, but Gabe stepped forward and said, "No, I'll take care of it." At this, she stopped to size up her nephew. "It's not the same here without you."

Her chocolate eyes shone, even as she turned next to Callie. "The children can't wait to see you. And truth be told, I could use the break. . . ."

"You mean you don't have a new tutor . . .?"

Annie shook her head so swiftly, a dark tendril escaped her makeshift bun. "No. I don't think they wanted to take their chances after you . . . knowing they wouldn't find someone better."

True to her assumptions, Jamie and Julia, hearing they had company, burst from their upstairs bedrooms and bounded down the stairs. Jamie raced first into his older brother's arms.

"Why have you taken so long?" he asked.

Julia stopped before Callie. She was more of a summertime child than Callie could have expected. Freckles exposed the sun's kiss on her cheeks. Her hair ribbon threatened to slide off.

"You came back, Miss Callie!" she said, reaching for Callie's hand. "Would you take us on more adventures?" She stole a glance at her aunt across the room. "Annie takes us outdoors, but it's mostly to feed the horse or clean out the stall. With you, we went everywhere. I know I didn't always want to go, but sometimes I do."

✧ ✧ ✧

Gabe waited until the second night they were in Roslyn to ask Callie if she would join him on an adventure of their own. He'd seen lilies flourishing about Roslyn and he wanted a few to lay on his grandfather's grave. They made their way up the hill together the following morning. As they came into the clearing where the three men were buried, Gabe let go of Callie's hand and moved a few paces before her. Solemnity washed over him, and his eyes fell to the earthen floor.

I will at least give you a marker, Gabe thought, tightening his hold on the green stems of the orange lilies. Callie caught him at the elbow and nodded toward a few bundles of multicolored wildflowers already laid down across all three graves.

"Think they're from Ruthie?" he asked, feeling a well of water at the back of his eyes.

At Callie's slow nod, he knelt down to add his own gift to his grandfather's modest grave. He rested above the uneven ground and refused to look away. Instead of coming back to his feet, he lifted some of the warm earth in his hands, let it sift and sort between his fingers.

"Roslyn won't forget you." he promised. *We won't forget you or the men who came with you to make a better life. The women and children who followed you here.*

He rose back to his feet, wiping his eyes with the back of his hands.

Callie rested a hand between his shoulder blades. "Are you alright?" she asked softly.

He nodded. "I wish he was still here sometimes," he said. "That he'd had the chance to raise my mother and one day meet me."

The sheer indignity of the memorial had kept him from

coming there often, but David Ward couldn't be diminished in life or death. His name carried on no matter where his body rested. Gabe turned toward Callie and drew a strand of hair away from her eyes, his only prayer that he would learn with however many years he was given, how to leave such a mark.

Author's Note

The Emblem is a work of fiction that takes its inspiration from actual events that have been on my mind and heart for a long time. The book you hold was first drafted more than ten years ago. I tinkered with the premise of the story in my imagination for even longer. Growing up, I remember watching the musical *Show Boat* for the first time, and the dilemma of love across color lines posed itself to me. Even after my mom explained the foolishness of that mindset—that people couldn't be together in times past due to differences in skin color—I began to ponder those man-made restraints, the injustice and inequality of it. I wrote a story about such a love against the odds as a teenager called *A Fading Smile*. It took years and further research to realize the impossibility of such a love during the time in which I set it (the Civil War). But that didn't mean the story was done. It would simply have to wait.

Around the time that my nephew, who is of mixed heritage, was born eleven years ago, my desire to write this novel returned. Through reading, I discovered that interracial marriage was extremely limited in the 1930s, and Washington was the only state on the West Coast to permit it. While it couldn't have been easy, and there were attempts to stop it, such a union wasn't impossible. Even ninety years ago Washington was deemed a more "progressive" state than so many others. It was a place where residents weren't restricted by a one-drop rule like so many others.

Some years ago I sat down with Roslyn historian, Nick Henderson, to mull over story ideas and I learned from him the legacy of Roslyn's Black Pioneers. Their collective presence in Washington state began in 1888-1889, when more than 300 African American workers came by train to work the mines. They weren't told they'd be strikebreakers until Pinkerton guards boarded the trains in Montana. Many Black miners were handed rifles and told to protect themselves, lest bloodshed arise. Because of the angered striking miners, the Black miners were made to dislodge in Ronald, WA, near the No. 3 mine.

While certain historical sources are quick to note the eventual partnerships and near equality between white and Black men alike, other documentation, such as the book, *Coal Town in the Cascades*, reminds us that it wasn't a seamless transition. Not by a long-shot. While Black workers eventually gained their footing (after more than 200 white workers left the region), they often experienced overt and covert discrimination. There were business establishments African American people knew not to frequent since their presence wasn't welcome. (In the book, Gabe visits places under the protection of Burke Enterprises, but wouldn't likely have been permitted service on his own).

In the first few years of the Black miners' arrival, the Roslyn Cemetery didn't even allow a place for their dead to be buried. And while there aren't many written sources, members of the Craven family, the last remaining descendants of Black miners still in Roslyn, will tell you the nuances of growing up in Roslyn, WA—the joys, the trials, the injustices, and their ancestors' legacy. The Cravens acknowledged the unmarked graves, but told me that their loved ones reside in Mt. Olivet Cemetery, where their father Samuel and later brothers Nathaniel, Wes and Will Craven have worked as gravediggers.

Before his passing in the spring of 2019, Dr. Raymond Hall, Professor of African and Black Studies at Central Washington University, was working closely with Roslyn historian Nick Henderson on further research regarding the gravesites, reportedly located behind Vukonich's store in Ronald. He hoped to fund a grant for ground radar penetration so a memorial could be placed at the exact site, but passed away before this project was brought to completion. Even if this particular aspiration didn't come to fruition, Dr. Hall's work uplifted and centered Roslyn's Black pioneers in ways still felt by the region.

Every August the Cravens and their cousins, the Harts, gather for the Roslyn Black Pioneer Picnic. At this event, open to family and friends, the elders recount their heritage and disclose sources that live on in libraries ("Through Open Eyes: Ninety-Five Years of Roslyn's Black History", orchestrated by Mrs. Ethel Craven along with numerous newspaper clippings). They will tell you of their family's presence here—one that is a testament to hard work, perseverance, and faith. Sit down long enough and you'll walk away knowing that their grandmother, Harriet Jackson (Taylor) Williams, arrived in Roslyn at the age of seventeen with her young son in tow, eager to escape an abusive marriage. She would go on to homestead thousands of acres, marry her second husband, David Williams, and be the pioneer whose image adorns cakes and T-shirts at family get-togethers. She would give birth to Ethel Florence Williams, who would one day marry Samuel Lawrence Craven, and together they would have thirteen children. They are willing to tell you of their mother's heart for others and their father's courage in the mines. They speak of how they themselves made a life throughout Washington State, becoming teachers (Harriet Joyce Hawkins), Lead Secretaries at Boeing (Ethel Craven-Sweet), Counselor (Kanashibushan Craven), and the first Black Mayor of Washington (Will Craven) among other callings. They will also tell you of injustices: slights at the Company Store and teachers who let prejudice determine who was treated fairly in the classroom. The Cravens speak to the past and current need to further the work of justice and equality.

The actual history of the Black miners who first came to Washington state is more powerful and resounding than a work of fiction could ever be, but my hope in writing a novel is to draw readers in and have them empathize with my characters as they are confronted with hardship, heartbreak, and racism. While it is understood that I have limits of insight as a white writer, it's my prayer that this story inspires readers to know more of Washington's state history and those who bettered us. Please note that while certain establishments were fixtures in the 1930s (The Brick and the Company Store among them), some establishments are renamed for storytelling purposes.

My writing friend, Marissa Harrison (*Rain City Lights*), told me—"African American history is American history." Those words encouraged me through latter drafts and major revisions. As a writer, I aspire to share stories that matter—stories that aren't always the first to be told, but are every bit as important.

For more on the research behind *The Emblem*, please visit the blog on my author page: www.alisaweis.com

Further Reading

BROWN, AUSTIN CHANNING: *I'm Still Here: Black Dignity in a World Made for Whiteness*, Convergent Books, 2018.

BULLOCK, DAVID: *Coal Wars: Unions, Strikes, and Violence in Depression Era Central WA*, Washington State University Press, 2018.

ELLENSBURG PUBLIC LIBRARY: *"Through Open Eyes: Ninety-Five Years of Roslyn's Black History."*

GOPO, PATRICE: *All the Colors We Will See*, Thomas Nelson, 2018.

LITCHFIELD, SUE: *Roslyn Through Time*, America Through Time, 2018.

MEREDITH, CARA: *The Color of Life: A Journey Toward Love and Racial Justice*, Zondervan, 2019.

OPERATION UPLIFT: *Spawn of Coal Dust: History of Roslyn 1886-1955*, Community Development Program, Roslyn, WA, 1955.

SHIDELER, JOHN: *Coal Town in the Cascades: A Centennial History of Roslyn and Cle Elum*, Futurepast, 2006.

STEVENSON, BRYAN: *Just Mercy: A Story of Justice and Redemption*, Spiegel and Grau, 2014.

TAYLOR, QUINTARD: *The Forging of a Black Community: Seattle's Central District from 1870 through the Civil Rights Era*, University of Washington Press, 1994.

TRIMBLE, JAYMI: *Roslyn: Images of America*, Arcadia Publishing, 2008.

WALLENSTEIN, PETER: *Race, Sex, and the Freedom to Marry: Loving vs. Virginia*, University Press of Kansas, 2014.

WILKERSON, ISABEL: *The Warmth of Other Suns: The Epic Story of America's Great Migration*, Random House, 2010.

WILLIAMS, GREGORY HOWARD: *Life on the Color Line: The True Story of a White Boy Who Discovered He Was Black*, Plume Books, 1996.

Acknowledgements

Those who know me well know that *The Emblem* has been on my heart for a long time. Thank you to everyone who has made this dream become an actual book.

Thank you to the readers of *The Emblem* in its various stages, including: Megan Aldridge, Joni Bennett, E. Hank Buchmann, Phyllis Charmaine Chaney, Larry Fowler, Marissa Harrison, C.R. Hedgcock, Keyna Houston, Charlene Kauzlarich, Makenzi Koyen, Shelly Koyen, Sue Litchfield, Susan McBryde, Rachel Ng, Charity Rattray, John Schrupp, Rebekah Ueland, and Donna Vild.

Thanks to Jennifer Moorman, for your early edits on this novel. I'm grateful to work alongside one such as gifted with words, who points me to wonder and magic.

Thank you to Elli Seifert for your tireless edits, proofing, and beautiful typesetting. It's such a blessing and relief to work with an analytical artist, and I'd be honored to work with you again..

Where could I be without a writer friend like Marissa Harrison, who lent an ear and critical feedback at every stage of the process? Thank you for your insight that made the final draft better.

I'm grateful to Nancy Archer for your talents on our second cover together. Thank you for your willingness to stay up late some nights, going back and forth with me on ideas and bringing out beauty.

Thank you to Jonathan Reed for posing with a variety of lilies for the cover. I appreciate your words of encouragement: they helped me in the latter stages of this novel.

Thank you, Misty Gates, for going down to the Port Orchard

waterfront to take author pictures of me free of charge and for hosting me at my first book club meeting. Your kindness means a lot.

I'm grateful to my former newspaper editors, Joanna Markell and Joel Martin, for helping me gain confidence back in the day with stories you allowed me to write.

I'd like to thank my writing groups: Inkblots and Kitsap Writers Forum for reminding me I'm not alone in this often isolating endeavor. And thank you to the Ridge Book Club for being the first to support me.

E. Hank Buchmann (Hank), I count myself as blessed to have an ongoing correspondence with a writing mentor and author such as yourself. How inspiring it is to see the book-shelves of places like Barnes & Noble and Masons in Moses Lake fill with your work.

Thank you to Douglas Bond for more than twenty years of writing mentorship. Your belief in me carried me a long way, and it still does. You have that impact because you were/are the teacher that made the difference.

Thank you to Donna McCaskill for becoming a mentor to me in my early 20's and instilling belief in me both professionally and personally. Your positive guidance is with me still.

Nick Henderson, thank you for so patiently answering my questions on all things Roslyn related. How I love sitting down with you at Pioneer Coffee to hear you reminisce about the past of Roslyn.

Thanks to Sue Litchfield, for so kindly pointing out critical plot elements that needed revision, aspects of the story I never would have known without a historian's knowledge.

Sarah Thompson, I'm ever grateful that you stopped at my book table several summers ago at the Roslyn Farmer's Market and encouraged me to attend the Roslyn Black Pioneer Picnic, where you graciously introduced me to members of the family.

Thanks to Jim Fossett of the Northern Kittitas County Tribune for so enthusiastically running my research articles and for being a tremendous support.

To the Craven family: my thanks to Beulah Grimm for being the first Craven to welcome me at the Roslyn Black Pioneer Picnic and for sharing so much of your family history with me through continued correspondence. And to Harriet Joyce Hawkins, Ethel Craven-Sweet, Kanashibushan Craven, and Will Craven. I'm honored and grateful for your willingness to be interviewed on the Roslyn Black Pioneers. Your family history is one that inspires and will continue to do so because the level of courage and perseverance doesn't happen in every genealogy. Thank you so much.

Heartfelt appreciation to my beautiful friends, Maribeth Dreher, Monica Jauvert, and Rachel Hass for always being there.

Thank you to Steve and Kim Triller (Dad and Mom) for your support that is now thirty-nine years and counting and for reminding me of God's care for me in good times and trials.

Thank you to my sister, Kaeley Triller-Harms, for expert plot direction and to her family, Daniel, Tristan, and Evie for keeping the fun alive.

Thank you to my siblings Meagan Triller, Christie Triller, and Heath Triller for your continued guidance and belief. You're a creative lot, and I'm glad we can bounce ideas off each other.

I'm grateful to my in-laws, Doug and Susie Weis, longtime Roslyn residents, for lending me books off your shelf for research, and encouraging me.

And finally, thank you, Justin, for loving me even when this writing gig seemed never ending (because sometimes it is). To Trenton and Josie for listening to Mom run over her plot synopsis too many times to count and for being my greatest gifts in this world. Thank you to God for giving me a love of words.

About the Author

Since she was a little girl, Alisa Weis has filled countless pages with words as an outlet for her imagination. She found plenty of inspiration simply from growing up in the scenic Pacific Northwest and being the oldest of five kids. Her love of stories led her to pursue a BA in English Literature and Writing from Whitworth University and a Master in Secondary Education (English) from the University of Phoenix. Alisa enjoys working in her local school district, running, frequenting coffeehouses, and spending time with her husband, Justin, and their two wonderful children, Trenton and Josie.

Learn more about Alisa at her website: www.alisaweis.com